The King of Schnorrers

The King of Schnorrers

Israel Zangwill

MINT EDITIONS

The King of Schnorrers was first published in 1894.

This edition published by Mint Editions 2021.

ISBN 9781513282749 | E-ISBN 9781513287768

Published by Mint Editions®

 MINT
EDITIONS

minteditionbooks.com

Publishing Director: Jennifer Newens
Design & Production: Rachel Lopez Metzger
Project Manager: Micaela Clark
Typesetting: Westchester Publishing Services

The King of Schnorrers

Israel Zangwill

MINT EDITIONS

The King of Schnorrers was first published in 1894.

This edition published by Mint Editions 2021.

ISBN 9781513282749 | E-ISBN 9781513287768

Published by Mint Editions®

 MINT
EDITIONS

minteditionbooks.com

Publishing Director: Jennifer Newens
Design & Production: Rachel Lopez Metzger
Project Manager: Micaela Clark
Typesetting: Westchester Publishing Services

Contents

THE KING OF SCHNORRERS

I

Showing How the Wicked Philanthropist was Turned Into a Fish-Porter

In the days when Lord George Gordon became a Jew, and was suspected of insanity; when, out of respect for the prophecies, England denied her Jews every civic right except that of paying taxes; when the *Gentleman's Magazine* had ill words for the infidel alien; when Jewish marriages were invalid and bequests for Hebrew colleges void; when a prophet prophesying Primrose Day would have been set in the stocks, though Pitt inclined his private ear to Benjamin Goldsmid's views on the foreign loans—in those days, when Tevele Schiff was Rabbi in Israel, and Dr. de Falk, the Master of the Tetragrammaton, saint and Cabbalistic conjuror, flourished in Wellclose Square, and the composer of "The Death of Nelson" was a choir-boy in the Great Synagogue; Joseph Grobstock, pillar of the same, emerged one afternoon into the spring sunshine at the fag-end of the departing stream of worshippers. In his hand was a large canvas bag, and in his eye a twinkle.

There had been a special service of prayer and thanksgiving for the happy restoration of his Majesty's health, and the cantor had interceded tunefully with Providence on behalf of Royal George and "our most amiable Queen, Charlotte." The congregation was large and fashionable—far more so than when only a heavenly sovereign was concerned—and so the courtyard was thronged with a string of *Schnorrers* (beggars), awaiting the exit of the audience, much as the vestibule of the opera-house is lined by footmen.

They were a motley crew, with tangled beards and long hair that fell in curls, if not the curls of the period; but the gaberdines of the German Ghettoes had been in most cases exchanged for the knee-breeches and many-buttoned jacket of the Londoner. When the clothes one has brought from the Continent wear out, one must needs adopt the attire of one's superiors, or be reduced to buying. Many bore staves, and had their loins girded up with coloured handkerchiefs, as though ready at any moment to return from the Captivity. Their woebegone air was achieved almost entirely by not washing—it owed little to nature, to adventitious aids in the shape of deformities. The merest sprinkling boasted of physical afflictions, and none exposed sores like the lazars of Italy or contortions like the cripples of Constantinople. Such crude methods are eschewed in the fine art of *schnorring*. A green shade might denote weakness of sight, but the stone-blind man bore no braggart placard—his infirmity was an old established concern well known to the public, and conferring upon the proprietor a definite status in the community. He was no anonymous atom, such as drifts blindly through Christendom, vagrant and apologetic. Rarest of all sights in this pageantry of Jewish pauperdom was the hollow trouser-leg or the empty sleeve, or the wooden limb fulfilling either and pushing out a proclamatory peg.

When the pack of *Schnorrers* caught sight of Joseph Grobstock, they fell upon him full-cry, blessing him. He, nothing surprised, brushed pompously through the benedictions, though the twinkle in his eye became a roguish gleam. Outside the iron gates, where the throng was thickest, and where some elegant chariots that had brought worshippers from distant Hackney were preparing to start, he came to a standstill, surrounded by clamouring *Schnorrers*, and dipped his hand slowly and ceremoniously into the bag. There was a moment of breathless expectation among the beggars, and Joseph Grobstock had a moment of exquisite consciousness of importance, as he stood there swelling in the sunshine. There was no middle class to speak of in the eighteenth-century Jewry; the world was divided into rich and poor, and the rich were very, very rich, and the poor very, very poor, so that everyone knew his station. Joseph Grobstock was satisfied with that in which it had pleased God to place him. He was a jovial, heavy-jowled creature, whose clean-shaven chin was doubling, and he was habited like a person of the first respectability in a beautiful blue body-coat with a row of big yellow buttons. The frilled shirt front, high collar of the very newest fashion, and copious white neckerchief showed off the massive fleshiness of the red throat. His hat was of the Quaker pattern, and his head did not fail of the periwig and the pigtail, the latter being heretical in name only.

What Joseph Grobstock drew from the bag was a small white-paper packet, and his sense of humour led him to place it in the hand furthest from his nose; for it was a broad humour, not a subtle. It enabled him to extract pleasure from seeing a fellow-mortal's hat rollick in the wind, but did little to alleviate the chase for his own. His jokes clapped you on the back, they did not tickle delicately.

Such was the man who now became the complacent cynosure of all eyes, even of those that had no appeal in them, as soon as the principle of his eleemosynary operations had broken on the crowd. The first *Schnorrer*, feverishly tearing open his package, had found a florin, and, as by electricity, all except the blind beggar were aware that Joseph Grobstock was distributing florins. The distributor partook of the general consciousness, and his lips twitched. Silently he dipped again into the bag, and, selecting the hand nearest, put a second white package into it. A wave of joy brightened the grimy face, to change instantly to one of horror.

"You have made a mistake—you have given me a penny!" cried the beggar.

"Keep it for your honesty," replied Joseph Grobstock imperturbably, and affected not to enjoy the laughter of the rest. The third mendicant ceased laughing when he discovered that fold on fold of paper sheltered a tiny sixpence. It was now obvious that the great man was distributing prize-packets, and the excitement of the piebald crowd grew momently. Grobstock went on dipping, lynx-eyed against second applications. One of the few pieces of gold in the lucky-bag fell to the solitary lame man, who danced in his joy on his sound leg, while the poor blind man pocketed his halfpenny, unconscious of ill-fortune, and merely wondering why the coin came swathed in paper.

By this time Grobstock could control his face no longer, and the last episodes of the lottery were played to the accompaniment of a broad grin. Keen and complex was his enjoyment. There was not only the general surprise at this novel feat of alms; there were the special surprises of detail written on face after face, as it flashed or fell or frowned in congruity with the contents of the envelope, and for undercurrent a delicious hubbub of interjections and benedictions, a stretching and withdrawing of palms, and a swift shifting of figures, that made the scene a farrago of excitements. So that the broad grin was one of gratification as well as of amusement, and part of the gratification sprang from a real kindliness of heart—for Grobstock was an easy-going man with whom the world had gone easy. The *Schnorrers* were exhausted before the packets, but the philanthropist was in no anxiety to be rid of the remnant. Closing the mouth of the considerably lightened bag and clutching it tightly by the throat, and recomposing his face to gravity, he moved slowly down the street like a stately treasure-ship flecked by the sunlight. His way led towards Goodman's Fields, where his mansion was situate, and he knew that the fine weather would bring out *Schnorrers* enough. And, indeed, he had not gone many paces before he met a figure he did not remember having seen before.

Leaning against a post at the head of the narrow passage which led to Bevis Marks was a tall, black-bearded, turbaned personage, a first glance at whom showed him of the true tribe. Mechanically Joseph Grobstock's hand went to the lucky-bag, and he drew out a neatly-folded packet and tendered it to the stranger.

The stranger received the gift graciously, and opened it gravely, the philanthropist loitering awkwardly to mark the issue. Suddenly the dark face became a thunder-cloud, the eyes flashed lightning.

"An evil spirit in your ancestors' bones!" hissed the stranger, from between his flashing teeth. "Did you come here to insult me?"

"Pardon, a thousand pardons!" stammered the magnate, wholly taken aback. "I fancied you were a—a—a—poor man."

"And, therefore, you came to insult me!"

"No, no, I thought to help you," murmured Grobstock, turning from red to scarlet. Was it possible he had foisted his charity upon an undeserving millionaire? No! Through all the clouds of his own confusion and the recipient's anger, the figure of a *Schnorrer* loomed too plain for mistake. None but a *Schnorrer* would wear a home-made turban, issue of a black cap crossed with a white kerchief; none but a *Schnorrer* would unbutton the first nine buttons of his waistcoat, or, if this relaxation were due to the warmth of the weather, counteract it by wearing an over-garment, especially one as heavy as a blanket, with buttons the size of compasses and flaps reaching nearly to his shoe-buckles, even though its length were only congruous with that of his undercoat, which already reached the bottoms of his knee-breeches. Finally, who but a *Schnorrer* would wear this overcoat cloak-wise, with dangling sleeves, full of armless suggestion from a side view? Quite apart from the shabbiness of the snuff-coloured fabric, it was amply evident that the wearer did not dress by rule or measure. Yet the disproportions of his attire did but enhance the picturesqueness of a personality that would be striking even in a bath, though it was not likely to be seen there. The beard was jet black, sweeping and unkempt, and ran up his cheeks to meet the raven hair, so that the vivid face was framed in black; it was a long, tapering face with sanguine lips gleaming at the heart of a black bush; the eyes were large and lambent, set in deep sockets under black arching eyebrows; the nose was long and Coptic; the brow low

ISRAEL ZANGWILL

but broad, with straggling wisps of hair protruding from beneath the turban. His right hand grasped a plain ashen staff.

Worthy Joseph Grobstock found the figure of the mendicant only too impressive; he shrank uneasily before the indignant eyes.

"I meant to help you," he repeated.

"And this is how one helps a brother in Israel?" said the *Schnorrer*, throwing the paper contemptuously into the philanthropist's face. It struck him on the bridge of the nose, but impinged so mildly that he felt at once what was the matter. The packet was empty—the *Schnorrer* had drawn a blank; the only one the good-natured man had put into the bag.

("IT STRUCK HIM ON THE BRIDGE OF THE NOSE.")

The *Schnorrer's* audacity sobered Joseph Grobstock completely; it might have angered him to chastise the fellow, but it did not. His better nature prevailed; he began to feel shamefaced, fumbled sheepishly in his pocket for a crown; then hesitated, as fearing this peace-offering would not altogether suffice with so rare a spirit, and that he owed the stranger more than silver—an apology to wit. He proceeded honestly to pay it, but with a maladroit manner, as one unaccustomed to the currency.

"You are an impertinent rascal," he said, "but I daresay you feel hurt. Let me assure you I did not know there was nothing in the packet. I did not, indeed."

"Then your steward has robbed me!" exclaimed the *Schnorrer* excitedly. "You let him make up the packets, and he has stolen my money—the thief, the transgressor, thrice-cursed who robs the poor."

"You don't understand," interrupted the magnate meekly. "I made up the packets myself."

"Then, why do you say you did not know what was in them? Go, you mock my misery!"

"Nay, hear me out!" urged Grobstock desperately. "In some I placed gold, in the greater number silver, in a few copper, in one alone—nothing. That is the one you have drawn. It is your misfortune."

"*My* misfortune!" echoed the *Schnorrer* scornfully. "It is *your* misfortune—I did not even draw it. The Holy One, blessed be He, has punished you for your heartless jesting with the poor—making a sport for yourself of their misfortunes, even as the Philistines sported with Samson. The good deed you might have put to your account by a gratuity to me, God has taken from you. He has declared you unworthy of achieving righteousness through me. Go your way, murderer!"

"Murderer!" repeated the philanthropist, bewildered by this harsh view of his action.

"Yes, murderer! Stands it not in the Talmud that he who shames another is as one who spills his blood? And have you not put me to shame—if anyone had witnessed your almsgiving, would he not have laughed in my beard?"

The pillar of the Synagogue felt as if his paunch were shrinking.

"But the others—" he murmured deprecatingly. "I have not shed their blood—have I not given freely of my hard-earned gold?"

"For your own diversion," retorted the *Schnorrer* implacably. "But what says the Midrash? There is a wheel rolling in the world—not he who is rich to-day is rich to-morrow, but this one He brings up, and this one He brings down, as is said in the seventy-fifth Psalm. Therefore, lift not up your horn on high, nor speak with a stiff neck."

He towered above the unhappy capitalist, like an ancient prophet denouncing a swollen monarch. The poor man put his hand involuntarily to his high collar as if to explain away his apparent arrogance, but in reality because he was not breathing easily under the *Schnorrer's* attack.

"You are an uncharitable man," he panted hotly, driven to a line of defence he had not anticipated. "I did it not from wantonness, but from faith in Heaven. I know well that God sits turning a wheel—therefore I did not presume to turn it myself. Did I not let Providence select who should have the silver and who the gold, who the copper and who the emptiness? Besides, God alone knows who really needs my assistance—I have made Him my almoner; I have cast my burden on the Lord."

"Epicurean!" shrieked the *Schnorrer*. "Blasphemer! Is it thus you would palter with the sacred texts? Do you forget what the next verse says: 'Bloodthirsty and deceitful men shall not live out half their days'? Shame on you—you a *Gabbai* (treasurer) of the Great Synagogue. You see I know you, Joseph Grobstock. Has not the beadle of your Synagogue boasted to me that you have given him a guinea for brushing your spatterdashes? Would you think of offering *him* a packet? Nay, it is the poor that are trodden on—they whose merits are in excess of those of beadles. But the Lord will find others to take up his loans—for he who hath pity on the poor lendeth to the Lord. You are no true son of Israel."

The *Schnorrer's* tirade was long enough to allow Grobstock to recover his dignity and his breath.

"If you really knew me, you would know that the Lord is considerably in my debt," he rejoined quietly. "When next you would discuss me, speak with the Psalms-men, not the beadle. Never have I neglected the needy. Even now, though you have been insolent and uncharitable, I am ready to befriend you if you are in want."

"If I am in want!" repeated the *Schnorrer* scornfully. "Is there anything I do not want?"

"You are married?"

"You correct me—wife and children are the only things I do *not* lack."

"No pauper does," quoth Grobstock, with a twinkle of restored humour.

"No," assented the *Schnorrer* sternly. "The poor man has the fear of Heaven. He obeys the Law and the Commandments. He marries while he is young—and his spouse is not cursed with barrenness. It is the rich man who transgresses the Judgment, who delays to come under the Canopy."

"Ah! well, here is a guinea—in the name of my wife," broke in Grobstock laughingly. "Or stay—since you do not brush spatterdashes—here is another."

"In the name of my wife," rejoined the *Schnorrer* with dignity, "I thank you."

"Thank me in your own name," said Grobstock. "I mean tell it me."

"I am Manasseh Bueno Barzillai Azevedo da Costa," he answered simply.

"A Sephardi!" exclaimed the philanthropist.

"Is it not written on my face, even as it is written on yours that you are a Tedesco? It is the first time that I have taken gold from one of your lineage."

"Oh, indeed!" murmured Grobstock, beginning to feel small again.

"Yes—are we not far richer than your community? What need have I to take the good deeds away from my own people—they have too few opportunities for beneficence as it is, being so many of them wealthy; brokers and West India merchants, and—"

"But I, too, am a financier, and an East India Director," Grobstock reminded him.

"Maybe; but your community is yet young and struggling—your rich men are as the good men in Sodom for multitude. You are the immigrants of yesterday—refugees from the Ghettoes of Russia and Poland and Germany. But we, as you are aware, have been established here for generations; in the Peninsula our ancestors graced the courts of kings, and controlled the purse-strings of princes; in Holland we held the empery of trade. Ours have been the poets and scholars in Israel. You cannot expect that we should recognise your rabble, which prejudices us in the eyes of England. We made the name of Jew honourable; you degrade it. You are as the mixed multitude which came up with our forefathers out of Egypt."

"Nonsense!" said Grobstock sharply. "All Israel are brethren."

"Esau was the brother of Israel," answered Manasseh sententiously. "But you will excuse me if I go a-marketing, it is such a pleasure to handle gold." There was a note of wistful pathos in the latter remark which took off the edge of the former, and touched Joseph with compunction for bandying words with a hungry man whose loved ones were probably starving patiently at home.

"Certainly, haste away," he said kindly.

"I shall see you again," said Manasseh, with a valedictory wave of his hand, and digging his staff into the cobblestones he journeyed forwards without bestowing a single backward glance upon his benefactor.

Grobstock's road took him to Petticoat Lane in the wake of Manasseh. He had no intention of following him, but did not see why he should change his route for fear of the *Schnorrer*, more especially as Manasseh did not look back. By this time he had become conscious again of the bag he carried, but he had no heart to proceed with the fun. He felt conscience stricken, and had recourse to his pockets instead in his progress through the narrow jostling market-street, where he scarcely ever bought anything personally save fish and good deeds. He was a connoisseur in both. To-day he picked up many a good deed cheap, paying pennies for articles he did not take away—shoe-latchets and cane-strings, barley-sugar and butter-cakes. Suddenly, through a chink in an opaque mass of human beings, he caught sight of a small attractive salmon on a fishmonger's slab. His eye glittered, his chops watered. He elbowed his way to the vendor, whose eye caught a corresponding gleam, and whose finger went to his hat in respectful greeting.

"Good afternoon, Jonathan," said Grobstock jovially, "I'll take that salmon there—how much?"

"Pardon me," said a voice in the crowd, "I am just bargaining for it."

Grobstock started. It was the voice of Manasseh.

"Stop that nonsense, da Costa," responded the fishmonger. "You know you won't give me my price. It is the only one I have left," he added, half for the benefit of Grobstock. "I couldn't let it go under a couple of guineas."

"Here's your money," cried Manasseh with passionate contempt, and sent two golden coins spinning musically upon the slab.

In the crowd sensation, in Grobstock's breast astonishment, indignation, and bitterness. He was struck momentarily dumb. His face purpled. The scales of the salmon shone like a celestial vision that was fading from him by his own stupidity.

"I'll take that salmon, Jonathan," he repeated, spluttering. "Three guineas."

"Pardon me," repeated Manasseh, "it is too late. This is not an auction." He seized the fish by the tail.

Grobstock turned upon him, goaded to the point of apoplexy. "You!" he cried. "You—you—rogue! How dare you buy salmon!"

("You Rogue! How Dare You Buy Salmon!")

"Rogue yourself!" retorted Manasseh. "Would you have me steal salmon?"

"You have stolen my money, knave, rascal!"

"Murderer! Shedder of blood! Did you not give me the money as a free-will offering, for the good of your wife's soul? I call on you before all these witnesses to confess yourself a slanderer!"

"Slanderer, indeed! I repeat, you are a knave and a jackanapes. You—a pauper—a beggar—with a wife and children. How can you have the face to go and spend two guineas—two whole guineas—all you have in the world—on a mere luxury like salmon?"

Manasseh elevated his arched eyebrows.

"If I do not buy salmon when I have two guineas," he answered quietly, "when shall I buy salmon? As you say, it is a luxury; very dear. It is only on rare occasions like this that my means run to it." There was a dignified pathos about the rebuke that mollified the magnate. He felt that there was reason in the beggar's point of view—though it was a point to which he would never himself have risen, unaided. But righteous anger still simmered in him; he felt vaguely that there was something to be said in reply, though he also felt that even if he knew what it was, it would have to be said in a lower key to correspond with

Manasseh's transition from the high pitch of the opening passages. Not finding the requisite repartee he was silent.

"In the name of my wife," went on Manasseh, swinging the salmon by the tail, "I ask you to clear my good name which you have bespattered in the presence of my very tradesmen. Again I call upon you to confess before these witnesses that you gave me the money yourself in charity. Come! Do you deny it?"

"No, I don't deny it," murmured Grobstock, unable to understand why he appeared to himself like a whipped cur, or how what should have been a boast had been transformed into an apology to a beggar.

"In the name of my wife, I thank you," said Manasseh. "She loves salmon, and fries with unction. And now, since you have no further use for that bag of yours, I will relieve you of its burden by taking my salmon home in it." He took the canvas bag from the limp grasp of the astonished Tedesco, and dropped the fish in. The head protruded, surveying the scene with a cold, glassy, ironical eye.

"Good afternoon all," said the *Schnorrer* courteously.

"One moment," called out the philanthropist, when he found his tongue. "The bag is not empty—there are a number of packets still left in it."

"So much the better!" said Manasseh soothingly. "You will be saved from the temptation to continue shedding the blood of the poor, and I shall be saved from spending *all* your bounty upon salmon—an extravagance you were right to deplore."

"But—but!" began Grobstock.

"No—no 'buts,'" protested Manasseh, waving his bag deprecatingly. "You were right. You admitted you were wrong before; shall I be less magnanimous now? In the presence of all these witnesses I acknowledge the justice of your rebuke. I ought not to have wasted two guineas on one fish. It was not worth it. Come over here, and I will tell you something." He walked out of earshot of the by-standers, turning down a side alley opposite the stall, and beckoned with his salmon bag. The East India Director had no course but to obey. He would probably have followed him in any case, to have it out with him, but now he had a humiliating sense of being at the *Schnorrer's* beck and call.

"Well, what more have you to say?" he demanded gruffly.

"I wish to save you money in future," said the beggar in low, confidential tones. "That Jonathan is a son of the separation! The salmon is not worth two guineas—no, on my soul! If you had not come up I should have got it for twenty-five shillings. Jonathan stuck on the price when he thought you would buy. I trust you will not let me be the loser by your arrival, and that if I should find less than seventeen shillings in the bag you will make it up to me."

The bewildered financier felt his grievance disappearing as by sleight of hand.

Manasseh added winningly: "I know you are a gentleman, capable of behaving as finely as any Sephardi."

This handsome compliment completed the *Schnorrer's* victory, which was sealed by his saying, "And so I should not like you to have it on your soul that you had done a poor man out of a few shillings."

Grobstock could only remark meekly: "You will find more than seventeen shillings in the bag."

"Ah, why were you born a Tedesco!" cried Manasseh ecstatically. "Do you know what I have a mind to do? To come and be your Sabbath-guest! Yes, I will take supper with you next Friday, and we will welcome the Bride—the holy Sabbath—together! Never before have I sat at the table of a Tedesco—but you—you are a man after my own heart. Your soul is a son of Spain. Next Friday at six—do not forget."

"But—but I do not have Sabbath-guests," faltered Grobstock.

"Not have Sabbath-guests! No, no, I will not believe you are of the sons of Belial, whose table is spread only for the rich, who do not proclaim your equality with the poor even once a week. It is your fine nature that would hide its benefactions. Do not I, Manasseh Bueno Barzillai Azevedo da Costa, have at my Sabbath-table every week Yankelé ben Yitzchok—a Pole? And if I have a Tedesco at my table, why should I draw the line there? Why should I not permit you, a Tedesco, to return the hospitality to me, a Sephardi? At six, then! I know your house well—it is an elegant building that does credit to your taste—do not be uneasy—I shall not fail to be punctual. *A Dios!*"

This time he waved his stick fraternally, and stalked down a turning. For an instant Grobstock stood glued to the spot, crushed by a sense of the inevitable. Then a horrible thought occurred to him.

Easy-going man as he was, he might put up with the visitation of Manasseh. But then he had a wife, and, what was worse, a livery servant. How could he expect a livery servant to tolerate such a guest? He might fly from the town on Friday evening, but that would necessitate troublesome explanations. And Manasseh would come again the next Friday. That was certain. Manasseh would be like grim death—his coming, though it might be postponed, was inevitable. Oh, it was too terrible. At all costs he must revoke the invitation(?). Placed between Scylla and Charybdis, between Manasseh and his manservant, he felt he could sooner face the former.

"Da Costa!" he called in agony. "Da Costa!"

The *Schnorrer* turned, and then Grobstock found he was mistaken in imagining he preferred to face da Costa.

"You called me?" enquired the beggar.

"Ye—e—s," faltered the East India Director, and stood paralysed.

"What can I do for you?" said Manasseh graciously.

"Would you mind—very much—if I—if I asked you—"

"Not to come," was in his throat, but stuck there.

"If you asked me—" said Manasseh encouragingly.

"To accept some of my clothes," flashed Grobstock, with a sudden inspiration. After all, Manasseh was a fine figure of a man. If he could get him to doff those musty garments of his he might almost pass him off as a prince of the blood, foreign by his beard—at any rate he could be certain of making him acceptable to the livery servant. He breathed freely again at this happy solution of the situation.

"Your cast-off clothes?" asked Manasseh. Grobstock was not sure whether the tone was supercilious or eager. He hastened to explain. "No, not quite that. Second-hand things I am still wearing. My old clothes were already given away at Passover to Simeon the Psalms-man. These are comparatively new."

"Then I would beg you to excuse me," said Manasseh, with a stately wave of the bag.

"Oh, but why not?" murmured Grobstock, his blood running cold again.

"I cannot," said Manasseh, shaking his head.

"But they will just about fit you," pleaded the philanthropist.

"That makes it all the more absurd for you to give them to Simeon the Psalms-man," said Manasseh sternly. "Still, since he is your clothes-receiver, I could not think of interfering with his office. It is not etiquette. I am surprised you should ask me if I should mind. Of course I should mind—I should mind very much."

"But he is not my clothes-receiver," protested Grobstock. "Last Passover was the first time I gave them to him, because my cousin, Hyam Rosenstein, who used to have them, has died."

"But surely he considers himself your cousin's heir," said Manasseh. "He expects all your old clothes henceforth."

"No. I gave him no such promise."

Manasseh hesitated.

"Well, in that case—"

"In that case," repeated Grobstock breathlessly.

"On condition that I am to have the appointment permanently, of course."

"Of course," echoed Grobstock eagerly.

"Because you see," Manasseh condescended to explain, "it hurts one's reputation to lose a client."

"Yes, yes, naturally," said Grobstock soothingly. "I quite understand." Then, feeling himself slipping into future embarrassments, he added timidly, "Of course they will not always be so good as the first lot, because—"

"Say no more," Manasseh interrupted reassuringly, "I will come at once and fetch them."

"No. I will send them," cried Grobstock, horrified afresh.

"I could not dream of permitting it. What! Shall I put you to all that trouble which should rightly be mine? I will go at once—the matter shall be settled without delay, I promise you; as it is written, 'I made haste and delayed not!' Follow me!" Grobstock suppressed a groan. Here had all his manoeuvring landed him in a worse plight than ever. He would have to present Manasseh to the livery servant without even that clean face which might not unreasonably have been expected for the Sabbath. Despite the text quoted by the erudite *Schnorrer*, he strove to put off the evil hour.

"Had you not better take the salmon home to your wife first?" said he.

"My duty is to enable you to complete your good deed at once. My wife is unaware of the salmon. She is in no suspense."

Even as the *Schnorrer* spake it flashed upon Grobstock that Manasseh was more presentable with the salmon than without it—in fact, that the salmon was the salvation of the situation. When Grobstock bought fish he often hired a man to carry home the spoil. Manasseh would have all the air of such a loafer. Who would suspect that the fish and even the bag belonged to the porter, though purchased with the gentleman's money? Grobstock silently thanked Providence for the ingenious way in which it had contrived to save his self-respect. As a mere fish-carrier Manasseh would attract no second glance from the household; once safely in, it would be comparatively easy to smuggle him out, and when he did come on Friday night it would be in the metamorphosing glories of a body-coat, with his unspeakable undergarment turned into a shirt and his turban knocked into a cocked hat.

They emerged into Aldgate, and then turned down Leman Street, a fashionable quarter, and so into Great Prescott Street. At the critical street corner Grobstock's composure began to desert him: he took out his handsomely ornamented snuff-box and administered to himself a mighty pinch. It did him good, and he walked on and was well nigh arrived at his own door when Manasseh suddenly caught him by a coat button.

"Stand still a second," he cried imperatively.

"What is it?" murmured Grobstock, in alarm.

"You have spilt snuff all down your coat front," Manasseh replied severely. "Hold the bag a moment while I brush it off."

Joseph obeyed, and Manasseh scrupulously removed every particle with such patience that Grobstock's was exhausted.

"Thank you," he said at last, as politely as he could. "That will do."

"No, it will not do," replied Manasseh. "I cannot have my coat spoiled. By the time it comes to me it will be a mass of stains if I don't look after it."

"Oh, is that why you took so much trouble?" said Grobstock, with an uneasy laugh.

"Why else? Do you take me for a beadle, a brusher of gaiters?" enquired Manasseh haughtily. "There now! that is the cleanest I can get it. You would escape these droppings if you held your snuff-box so—" Manasseh gently took the snuff-box and began to explain, walking on a few paces.

"Ah, we are at home!" he cried, breaking off the object-lesson suddenly. He pushed open the gate, ran up the steps of the mansion and knocked thunderously, then snuffed himself magnificently from the bejewelled snuff-box.

Behind came Joseph Grobstock, slouching limply, and carrying Manasseh da Costa's fish.

II

Showing How the King Reigned

When he realised that he had been turned into a fish-porter, the financier hastened up the steps so as to be at the *Schnorrer's* side when the door opened.

The livery-servant was visibly taken aback by the spectacle of their juxtaposition.

"This salmon to the cook!" cried Grobstock desperately, handing him the bag.

Da Costa looked thunders, and was about to speak, but Grobstock's eye sought his in frantic appeal. "Wait a minute; I will settle with you," he cried, congratulating himself on a phrase that would carry another meaning to Wilkinson's ears. He drew a breath of relief when the flunkey disappeared, and left them standing in the spacious hall with its statues and plants.

"Is this the way you steal my salmon, after all?" demanded da Costa hotly.

"Hush, hush! I didn't mean to steal it! I will pay you for it!"

"I refuse to sell! You coveted it from the first—you have broken the Tenth Commandment, even as these stone figures violate the Second. Your invitation to me to accompany you here at once was a mere trick. Now I understand why you were so eager."

"No, no, da Costa. Seeing that you placed the fish in my hands, I had no option but to give it to Wilkinson, because—because—" Grobstock would have had some difficulty in explaining, but Manasseh saved him the pain.

"You had to give *my* fish to Wilkinson!" he interrupted. "Sir, I thought you were a fine man, a man of honour. I admit that I placed my fish in your hands. But because I had no hesitation in allowing you to carry it, this is how you repay my confidence!"

In the whirl of his thoughts Grobstock grasped at the word "repay" as a swimmer in a whirlpool grasps at a straw.

"I will repay your money!" he cried. "Here are your two guineas. You will get another salmon, and more cheaply. As you pointed out, you could have got this for twenty-five shillings."

"Two guineas!" exclaimed Manasseh contemptuously. "Why you offered Jonathan, the fishmonger, three!"

Grobstock was astounded, but it was beneath him to bargain. And he remembered that, after all, he *would* enjoy the salmon.

"Well, here are three guineas," he said pacifically, offering them.

"Three guineas!" echoed Manasseh, spurning them. "And what of my profit?"

"Profit!" gasped Grobstock.

"Since you have made me a middle-man, since you have forced me into the fish trade, I must have my profits like anybody else."

"Here is a crown extra!"

"And my compensation?"

"What do you mean?" enquired Grobstock, exasperated. "Compensation for what?"

"For what? For two things at the very least," Manasseh said unswervingly. "In the first place," and as he began his logically divided reply his tone assumed the sing-song sacred to Talmudical dialectics, "compensation for not eating the salmon myself. For it is not as if I offered it you—I merely entrusted it to you, and it is ordained in Exodus that if a man shall deliver unto his neighbour an ass, or an ox, or a sheep, or any beast to keep, then for every matter of trespass, whether it be for ox, for ass, for sheep, for raiment, or for any manner of lost thing, the man shall receive double, and therefore you should pay me six guineas. And secondly—"

"Not another farthing!" spluttered Grobstock, red as a turkey-cock.

"Very well," said the *Schnorrer* imperturbably, and, lifting up his voice, he called "Wilkinson!"

"Hush!" commanded Grobstock. "What are you doing?"

"I will tell Wilkinson to bring back my property."

"Wilkinson will not obey you."

"Not obey *me*! A servant! Why he is not even black! All the Sephardim I visit have black pages—much grander than Wilkinson— and they tremble at my nod. At Baron D'Aguilar's mansion in Broad Street Buildings there is a retinue of twenty-four servants, and they—"

"And what is your second claim?"

"Compensation for being degraded to fishmongering. I am not of those who sell things in the streets. I am a son of the Law, a student of the Talmud."

"If a crown piece will satisfy each of these claims—"

"I am not a blood-sucker—as it is said in the Talmud, Tractate Passover, 'God loves the man who gives not way to wrath nor stickles for his rights'—that makes altogether three guineas and three crowns."

"Yes. Here they are."

Wilkinson reappeared. "You called me, sir?" he said.

"No, I called you," said Manasseh, "I wished to give you a crown."

And he handed him one of the three. Wilkinson took it, stupefied, and retired.

"Did I not get rid of him cleverly?" said Manasseh. "You see how he obeys me!"

"Ye-es."

"I shall not ask you for more than the bare crown I gave him to save your honour."

"To save my honour!"

"Would you have had me tell him the real reason I called him was that his master was a thief? No, sir, I was careful not to shed your blood in public, though you had no such care for mine."

"Here is the crown!" said Grobstock savagely. "Nay, here are three!" He turned out his breeches-pockets to exhibit their absolute nudity.

"No, no," said Manasseh mildly, "I shall take but two. You had best keep the other—you may want a little silver." He pressed it into the magnate's hand.

"You should not be so prodigal in future," he added, in kindly reproach. "It is bad to be left with nothing in one's pocket—I know the feeling, and can sympathise with you." Grobstock stood speechless, clasping the crown of charity.

Standing thus at the hall door, he had the air of Wilkinson, surprised by a too generous vail.

Da Costa cut short the crisis by offering his host a pinch from the jewel-crusted snuff-box. Grobstock greedily took the whole box, the beggar resigning it to him without protest. In his gratitude for this unexpected favour, Grobstock pocketed the silver insult without further ado, and led the way towards the second-hand clothes. He walked gingerly, so as not to awaken his wife, who was a great amateur of the siesta, and might issue suddenly from her apartment like a spider, but Manasseh stolidly thumped on the stairs with his staff. Happily the carpet was thick.

The clothes hung in a mahogany wardrobe with a plateglass front in Grobstock's elegantly appointed bedchamber.

Grobstock rummaged among them while Manasseh, parting the white Persian curtains lined with pale pink, gazed out of the window towards the Tenterground that stretched in the rear of the mansion. Leaning on his staff, he watched the couples promenading among the sunlit parterres and amid the shrubberies, in the cool freshness of declining day. Here and there the vivid face of a dark-eyed beauty gleamed like a passion-flower. Manasseh surveyed the scene with bland benevolence; at peace with God and man.

He did not deign to bestow a glance upon the garments till Grobstock observed: "There! I think that's all I can spare." Then he turned leisurely and regarded—with the same benign aspect—the litter Grobstock had spread upon the bed—a medley of articles in excellent condition, gorgeous neckerchiefs piled in three-cornered hats, and buckled shoes trampling on white waistcoats. But his eye had scarcely rested on them a quarter of a minute when a sudden flash came into it, and a spasm crossed his face.

"Excuse me!" he cried, and hastened towards the door.

"What's the matter?" exclaimed Grobstock, in astonished apprehension. Was his gift to be flouted thus?

"I'll be back in a moment," said Manasseh, and hurried down the stairs.

Relieved on one point, Grobstock was still full of vague alarms. He ran out on the landing. "What do you want?" he called down as loudly as he dared.

"My money!" said Manasseh.

Imagining that the *Schnorrer* had left the proceeds of the sale of the salmon in the hall, Joseph Grobstock returned to his room, and occupied himself half-mechanically in sorting the garments he had thrown higgledy-piggledy upon the bed. In so doing he espied amid the heap a pair of pantaloons entirely new and unworn which he had carelessly thrown in. It was while replacing this in the wardrobe that he heard sounds of objurgation. The cook's voice—Hibernian and high-pitched—travelled unmistakably to his ears, and brought fresh trepidation to his heart. He repaired to the landing again, and craned his neck over the balustrade. Happily the sounds were evanescent; in another minute Manasseh's head reappeared, mounting. When his left hand came in sight, Grobstock perceived it was grasping the lucky-bag with which a certain philanthropist had started out so joyously that afternoon. The unlucky-bag he felt inclined to dub it now.

"I have recovered it!" observed the *Schnorrer* cheerfully. "As it is written, 'And David recovered all that the Amalekites had taken.' You see in the excitement of the moment I did not notice that you had stolen my packets of silver as well as my salmon. Luckily your cook had not yet removed the fish from the bag—I chid her all the same for neglecting to put it into water, and she opened her mouth not in wisdom. If she had not been a heathen I should have suspected her of trickery, for I knew nothing of the amount of money in the bag, saving your assurance that it did not fall below seventeen shillings, and it would have been easy for her to replace the fish. Therefore, in the words of David, will I give thanks unto Thee, O Lord, among the heathen."

The mental vision of the irruption of Manasseh into the kitchen was not pleasant to Grobstock. However, he only murmured: "How came you to think of it so suddenly?"

"Looking at your clothes reminded me. I was wondering if you had left anything in the pockets."

The donor started—he knew himself a careless rascal—and made as if he would overhaul his garments. The glitter in Manasseh's eye petrified him.

"Do you—do you—mind my looking?" he stammered apologetically.

"Am I a dog?" quoted the *Schnorrer* with dignity. "Am I a thief that you should go over my pockets? If, when I get home," he conceded, commencing to draw distinctions with his thumb, "I should find anything in my pockets that is of no value to anybody but you, do you fear I will not return it? If, on the other hand, I find anything that is of value to me, do you fear I will not keep it?"

"No, but—but—" Grobstock broke down, scarcely grasping the argumentation despite his own clarity of financial insight; he only felt vaguely that the *Schnorrer* was—professionally enough—begging the question.

"But what?" enquired Manasseh. "Surely you need not me to teach you your duty. You cannot be ignorant of the Law of Moses on the point."

"The Law of Moses says nothing on the point!"

"Indeed! What says Deuteronomy? 'When thou reapest thine harvest in thy field, and hast forgot a sheaf in the field, thou shalt not go again to fetch it: it shall be for the stranger, for the fatherless, and for the widow.' Is it not further forbidden to go over the boughs of thy olive-tree again, or to gather the fallen fruit of thy vineyard? You will admit that Moses would have added a prohibition against searching minutely the pockets of cast-off garments, were it not that for forty years our ancestors had to wander in the wilderness in the same clothes, which miraculously waxed with their growth. No, I feel sure you will respect the spirit of the law, for when I went down into your kitchen and examined the door-post to see if you had nailed up a *mezuzah* upon it, knowing that many Jews only flaunt *mezuzahs* on door-posts visible to visitors, it rejoiced me to find one below stairs."

Grobstock's magnanimity responded to the appeal. It would be indeed petty to scrutinise his pockets, or to feel the linings for odd coins. After all he had Manasseh's promise to restore papers and everything of no value.

"Well, well," he said pleasantly, consoled by the thought his troubles had now come to an end—for that day at least—"take them away as they are."

"It is all very well to say take them away," replied Manasseh, with a touch of resentment, "but what am I to take them in?"

"Oh—ah—yes! There must be a sack somewhere—"

"And do you think I would carry them away in a sack? Would you have me look like an old clo' man? I must have a box. I see several in the box-room."

"Very well," said Grobstock resignedly. "If there's an empty one you may have it."

Manasseh laid his stick on the dressing-table and carefully examined the boxes, some of which were carelessly open, while every lock had a key sticking in it. They had travelled far and wide with Grobstock, who invariably combined pleasure with business.

"There is none quite empty," announced the *Schnorrer*, "but in this one there are only a few trifles—a pair of galligaskins and such like—so that if you make me a present of them the box *will* be empty, so far as you are concerned."

"All right," said Grobstock, and actually laughed. The nearer the departure of the *Schnorrer*, the higher his spirits rose.

Manasseh dragged the box towards the bed, and then for the first time since his return from the under-regions, surveyed the medley of garments upon it.

The light-hearted philanthropist, watching his face, saw it instantly change to darkness, like a tropical landscape. His own face grew white. The *Schnorrer* uttered an inarticulate cry, and turned a strange, questioning glance upon his patron.

"What is it now?" faltered Grobstock.

"I miss a pair of pantaloons!"

Grobstock grew whiter. "Nonsense! nonsense!" he muttered.

"I—miss—a—pair—of—pantaloons!" reiterated the *Schnorrer* deliberately.

"Oh, no—you have all I can spare there," said Grobstock uneasily. The *Schnorrer* hastily turned over the heap.

Then his eye flashed fire; he banged his fist on the dressing-table to accompany each *staccato* syllable.

"I—miss—a—pair—of—pan—ta—loons!" he shrieked.

The weak and ductile donor had a bad quarter of a minute.

"Perhaps," he stammered at last, "you—m—mean—the new pair I found had got accidentally mixed up with them."

"Of course I mean the new pair! And so you took them away! Just because I wasn't looking. I left the room, thinking I had to do with a man of honour. If you had taken an old pair I shouldn't have minded so much; but to rob a poor man of his brand-new breeches!"

"I must have them," cried Grobstock irascibly. "I have to go to a reception to-morrow, and they are the only pair I shall have to wear. You see I—"

"Oh, very well," interrupted the *Schnorrer*, in low, indifferent tones.

After that there was a dead silence. The *Schnorrer* majestically folded some silk stockings and laid them in the box. Upon them he packed other garments in stern, sorrowful *hauteur*. Grobstock's soul began to tingle with pricks of compunction. Da Costa completed his task, but could not shut the overcrowded box. Grobstock silently seated his weighty person upon the lid. Manasseh neither resented nor welcomed him. When he had turned the key he mutely tilted the sitter off the box and shouldered it with consummate ease. Then he took his staff and strode from the room. Grobstock would have followed him, but the *Schnorrer* waved him back.

"On Friday, then," the conscience-stricken magnate said feebly.

Manasseh did not reply; he slammed the door instead, shutting in the master of the house.

Grobstock fell back on the bed exhausted, looking not unlike the tumbled litter of clothes he replaced. In a minute or two he raised himself and went to the window, and stood watching the sun set behind the trees of the Tenterground. "At any rate I've done with him," he said, and hummed a tune. The sudden bursting open of the door froze it upon his lips. He was almost relieved to find the intruder was only his wife.

"What have you done with Wilkinson?" she cried vehemently. She was a pale, puffy-faced, portly matron, with a permanent air of remembering the exact figure of her dowry.

"With Wilkinson, my dear? Nothing."

"Well, he isn't in the house. I want him, but cook says you've sent him out."

"I? Oh, no," he returned, with dawning uneasiness, looking away from her sceptical gaze.

Suddenly his pupils dilated. A picture from without had painted itself on his retina. It was a picture of Wilkinson—Wilkinson the austere, Wilkinson the unbending—treading the Tenterground gravel, curved beneath a box! Before him strode the *Schnorrer*.

Never during all his tenure of service in Goodman's Fields had Wilkinson carried anything on his shoulders but his livery. Grobstock would have as soon dreamt of his wife consenting to wear cotton. He rubbed his eyes, but the image persisted.

He clutched at the window curtains to steady himself.

"My Persian curtains!" cried his wife. "What is the matter with you?"

"He must be the Baal Shem himself!" gasped Grobstock unheeding.

"What is it? What are you looking at?"

"N—nothing."

Mrs. Grobstock incredulously approached the window and stared through the panes. She saw Wilkinson in the gardens, but did not recognise him in his new attitude. She concluded that her husband's agitation must have some connection with a beautiful brunette who was tasting the cool of the evening in a sedan chair, and it was with a touch of asperity that she said: "Cook complains of being insulted by a saucy fellow who brought home your fish."

"Oh!" said poor Grobstock. Was he never to be done with the man?

"How came you to send him to her?"

His anger against Manasseh resurged under his wife's peevishness.

"My dear," he cried, "I did not send him anywhere—except to the devil."

"Joseph! You might keep such language for the ears of creatures in sedan chairs."

And Mrs. Grobstock flounced out of the room with a rustle of angry satin.

When Wilkinson reappeared, limp and tired, with his pompousness exuded in perspiration, he sought his master with a message, which he delivered ere the flood of interrogation could burst from Grobstock's lips.

"Mr. da Costa presents his compliments, and says that he has decided on reconsideration not to break his promise to be with you on Friday evening."

"Oh, indeed!" said Grobstock grimly. "And, pray, how came you to carry his box?"

"You told me to, sir!"

"*I* told you!"

"I mean he told me you told me to," said Wilkinson wonderingly. "Didn't you?"

Grobstock hesitated. Since Manasseh *would* be his guest, was it not imprudent to give him away to the livery-servant? Besides, he felt a secret pleasure in Wilkinson's humiliation—but for the *Schnorrer* he would never have known that Wilkinson's gold lace concealed a pliable personality. The proverb "Like master like man" did not occur to Grobstock at this juncture.

"I only meant you to carry it to a coach," he murmured.

"He said it was not worth while—the distance was so short."

"Ah! Did you see his house?" enquired Grobstock curiously.

"Yes; a very fine house in Aldgate, with a handsome portico and two stone lions."

Grobstock strove hard not to look surprised.

"I handed the box to the footman."

Grobstock strove harder.

Wilkinson ended with a weak smile: "Would you believe, sir, I thought at first he brought home your fish! He dresses so peculiarly. He must be an original."

"Yes, yes; an eccentric like Baron D'Aguilar, whom he visits," said Grobstock eagerly. He wondered, indeed, whether he was not speaking the truth. Could he have been the victim of a practical joke, a prank? Did not a natural aristocracy ooze from every pore of his mysterious visitor? Was not every tone, every gesture, that of a man born to rule? "You must remember, too," he added, "that he is a Spaniard."

"Ah, I see," said Wilkinson in profound accents.

"I daresay he dresses like everybody else, though, when he dines or sups out," Grobstock added lightly. "I only brought him in by accident. But go to your mistress! She wants you."

"Yes, sir. Oh, by the way, I forgot to tell you he hopes you will save him a slice of his salmon."

"Go to your mistress!"

"You did not tell me a Spanish nobleman was coming to us on Friday," said his spouse later in the evening.

"No," he admitted curtly.

"But is he?"

"No—at least, not a nobleman."

"What then? I have to learn about my guests from my servants."

"Apparently."

"Oh! and you think that's right!"

"To gossip with your servants? Certainly not."

"If my husband will not tell me anything—if he has only eyes for sedan chairs."

Joseph thought it best to kiss Mrs. Grobstock.

"A fellow-Director, I suppose?" she urged, more mildly.

"A fellow-Israelite. He has promised to come at six."

Manasseh was punctual to the second. Wilkinson ushered him in. The hostess had robed herself in her best to do honour to a situation which her husband awaited with what hope he could. She looked radiant in a gown of blue silk; her hair was done in a tuft and round her neck was an "esclavage," consisting of festoons of gold chains. The Sabbath table was equally festive with its ponderous silver candelabra, coffee-urn, and consecration cup, its flower-vases, and fruit-salvers. The dining-room itself was a handsome apartment; its buffets glittered with Venetian glass and Dresden porcelain, and here and there gilt pedestals supported globes of gold and silver fish.

At the first glance at his guest Grobstock's blood ran cold.

Manasseh had not turned a hair, nor changed a single garment. At the next glance Grobstock's blood boiled. A second figure loomed in Manasseh's wake—a short *Schnorrer*, even dingier than da Costa, and with none of his dignity, a clumsy, stooping *Schnorrer*, with a cajoling grin on his mud-coloured, hairy face. Neither removed his headgear.

Mrs. Grobstock remained glued to her chair in astonishment.

"Peace be unto you," said the King of *Schnorrers*, "I have brought with me my friend Yankelé ben Yitzchok of whom I told you."

Yankelé nodded, grinning harder than ever.

"You never told me he was coming," Grobstock rejoined, with an apoplectic air.

"Did I not tell you that he always supped with me on Friday evenings?" Manasseh reminded him quietly. "It is so good of him to accompany me even here—he will make the necessary third at grace."

The host took a frantic surreptitious glance at his wife. It was evident that her brain was in a whirl, the evidence of her senses conflicting with vague doubts of the possibilities of Spanish grandeeism and with a lingering belief in her husband's sanity.

Grobstock resolved to snatch the benefit of her doubts. "My dear," said he, "this is Mr. da Costa."

"Manasseh Bueno Barzillai Azevedo da Costa," said the *Schnorrer*.

The dame seemed a whit startled and impressed. She bowed, but words of welcome were still congealed in her throat.

"And this is Yankelé ben Yitzchok," added Manasseh. "A poor friend of mine. I do not doubt, Mrs. Grobstock, that as a pious woman, the daughter of Moses Bernberg (his memory for a blessing), you prefer grace with three."

"Any friend of yours is welcome!" She found her lips murmuring the conventional phrase without being able to check their output.

"I never doubted that either," said Manasseh gracefully. "Is not the hospitality of Moses Bernberg's beautiful daughter a proverb?"

Moses Bernberg's daughter could not deny this; her salon was the rendezvous of rich bagmen, brokers and bankers, tempered by occasional young bloods and old bucks not of the Jewish faith (nor any other). But she had never before encountered a personage so magnificently shabby, nor extended her proverbial hospitality to a Polish *Schnorrer* uncompromisingly musty. Joseph did not dare meet her eye.

"Sit down there, Yankelé," he said hurriedly, in ghastly genial accents, and he indicated a chair at the farthest possible point from the hostess. He placed Manasseh next to his Polish parasite, and seated himself as a buffer between his guests and his wife. He was burning with inward indignation at the futile rifling of his wardrobe, but he dared not say anything in the hearing of his spouse.

"It is a beautiful custom, this of the Sabbath guest, is it not, Mrs. Grobstock?" remarked Manasseh as he took his seat. "I never neglect it—even when I go out to the Sabbath-meal as to-night."

The late Miss Bernberg was suddenly reminded of auld lang syne: her father (who according to a wag of the period had divided his time between the Law and the profits) having been a depositary of ancient tradition. Perhaps these obsolescent customs, unsuited to prosperous times, had lingered longer among the Spanish grandees. She seized an early opportunity, when the Sephardic *Schnorrer* was taking his coffee from Wilkinson, of putting the question to her husband, who fell in weakly with her illusions. He knew there was no danger of Manasseh's beggarly status leaking out; no expressions of gratitude were likely to fall from that gentleman's lips. He even hinted that da Costa dressed so fustily to keep his poor friend in countenance. Nevertheless, Mrs. Grobstock, while not without admiration for the Quixotism, was not without resentment for being dragged into it. She felt that such charity should begin and end at home.

"I see you did save me a slice of salmon," said Manasseh, manipulating his fish.

"What salmon was that?" asked the hostess, pricking up her ears.

"One I had from Mr. da Costa on Wednesday," said the host.

"Oh, that! It was delicious. I am sure it was very kind of you, Mr. da Costa, to make us such a nice present," said the hostess, her resentment diminishing. "We had company last night, and everybody praised it till none was left. This is another, but I hope it is to your liking," she finished anxiously.

"Yes, it's very fair, very fair, indeed. I don't know when I've tasted better, except at the house of the President of the *Deputados*. But Yankelé here is a connoisseur in fish, not easy to please. What say you, Yankelé?"

Yankelé munched a muffled approval.

"Help yourself to more bread and butter, Yankelé," said Manasseh. "Make yourself at home—remember you're my guest." Silently he added: "The other fork!"

Grobstock's irritation found vent in a complaint that the salad wanted vinegar.

"How can you say so? It's perfect," said Mrs. Grobstock. "Salad is cook's speciality."

Manasseh tasted it critically. "On salads you must come to me," he said. "It does not want vinegar," was his verdict; "but a little more oil would certainly improve it. Oh, there is no one dresses salad like Hyman!"

Hyman's fame as the *Kosher chef* who superintended the big dinners at the London Tavern had reached Mrs. Grobstock's ears, and she was proportionately impressed.

"They say his pastry is so good," she observed, to be in the running.

"Yes," said Manasseh, "in kneading and puffing he stands alone."

"Our cook's tarts are quite as nice," said Grobstock roughly.

"We shall see," Manasseh replied guardedly. "Though, as for almond-cakes, Hyman himself makes none better than I get from my cousin, Barzillai of Fenchurch Street."

"Your cousin!" exclaimed Grobstock, "the West Indian merchant!"

"The same—formerly of Barbadoes. Still, your cook knows how to make coffee, though I can tell you do not get it direct from the plantation like the wardens of my Synagogue."

Grobstock was once again piqued with curiosity as to the *Schnorrer's* identity.

"You accuse me of having stone figures in my house," he said boldly, "but what about the lions in front of yours?"

"I have no lions," said Manasseh.

"Wilkinson told me so. Didn't you, Wilkinson?"

"Wilkinson is a slanderer. That was the house of Nathaniel Furtado."

Grobstock began to choke with chagrin. He perceived at once that the *Schnorrer* had merely had the clothes conveyed direct to the house of a wealthy private dealer.

"Take care!" exclaimed the *Schnorrer* anxiously, "you are spluttering sauce all over that waistcoat, without any consideration for me."

Joseph suppressed himself with an effort. Open discussion would betray matters to his wife, and he was now too deeply enmeshed in falsehoods by default. But he managed to whisper angrily, "Why did you tell Wilkinson I ordered him to carry your box?"

"To save your credit in his eyes. How was he to know we had quarrelled? He would have thought you discourteous to your guest."

"That's all very fine. But why did you sell my clothes?"

"You did not expect me to wear them? No, I know my station, thank God."

"What is that you are saying, Mr. da Costa?" asked the hostess.

"Oh, we are talking of Dan Mendoza," replied Grobstock glibly; "wondering if he'll beat Dick Humphreys at Doncaster."

"Oh, Joseph, didn't you have enough of Dan Mendoza at supper last night?" protested his wife.

"It is not a subject *I* ever talk about," said the *Schnorrer*, fixing his host with a reproachful glance.

Grobstock desperately touched his foot under the table, knowing he was selling his soul to the King of *Schnorrers*, but too flaccid to face the moment.

"No, da Costa doesn't usually," he admitted. "Only Dan Mendoza being a Portuguese I happened to ask if he was ever seen in the Synagogue."

"If I had my way," growled da Costa, "he should be excommunicated—a bruiser, a defacer of God's image!"

"By gad, no!" cried Grobstock, stirred up. "If you had seen him lick the Badger in thirty-five minutes on a twenty-four foot stage—"

"Joseph! Joseph! Remember it is the Sabbath!" cried Mrs. Grobstock.

"I would willingly exchange our Dan Mendoza for your David Levi," said da Costa severely.

David Levi was the literary ornament of the Ghetto; a shoe-maker and hat-dresser who cultivated Hebrew philology and the Muses, and broke a lance in defence of his creed with Dr. Priestley, the discoverer of Oxygen, and Tom Paine, the discoverer of Reason.

"Pshaw! David Levi! The mad hatter!" cried Grobstock. "He makes nothing at all out of his books."

"You should subscribe for more copies," retorted Manasseh.

"I would if you wrote them," rejoined Grobstock, with a grimace.

"I got six copies of his *Lingua Sacra*," Manasseh declared with dignity, "and a dozen of his translation of the Pentateuch."

"You can afford it!" snarled Grobstock, with grim humour. "I have to earn my money."

"It is very good of Mr. da Costa, all the same," interposed the hostess. "How many men, born to great possessions, remain quite indifferent to learning!"

"True, most true," said da Costa. "Men-of-the-Earth, most of them."

After supper he trolled the Hebrew grace hilariously, assisted by Yankelé, and ere he left he said to the hostess, "May the Lord bless you with children!"

"Thank you," she answered, much moved.

"You see I should be so pleased to marry your daughter if you had one."

"You are very complimentary," she murmured, but her husband's exclamation drowned hers, "You marry my daughter!"

"Who else moves among better circles—would be more easily able to find her a suitable match?"

"Oh, in *that* sense," said Grobstock, mollified in one direction, irritated in another.

"In what other sense? You do not think I, a Sephardi, would marry her myself!"

"My daughter does not need your assistance," replied Grobstock shortly.

"Not yet," admitted Manasseh, rising to go; "but when the time comes, where will you find a better marriage broker? I have had a finger in the marriage of greater men's daughters. You see, when I recommend a maiden or a young man it is from no surface knowledge. I have seen them in the intimacy of their homes—above all I am able to say whether they are of a good, charitable disposition. Good Sabbath!"

"Good Sabbath," murmured the host and hostess in farewell. Mrs. Grobstock thought he need not be above shaking hands, for all his grand acquaintances.

"This way, Yankelé," said Manasseh, showing him to the door. "I am so glad you were able to come—you must come again."

III

Showing How his Majesty Went to the Theatre and was Wooed

As Manasseh the Great, first beggar in Europe, sauntered across Goodman's Fields, attended by his Polish parasite, both serenely digesting the supper provided by the Treasurer of the Great Synagogue, Joseph Grobstock, a martial music clove suddenly the quiet evening air, and set the *Schnorrers'* pulses bounding. From the Tenterground emerged a squad of recruits, picturesque in white fatigue dress, against which the mounted officers showed gallant in blue surtouts and scarlet-striped trousers.

"Ah!" said da Costa, with swelling breast. "There go my soldiers!"

"Your soldiers!" exclaimed Yankelé in astonishment.

"Yes—do you not see they are returning to the India House in Leadenhall Street?"

"And vat of dat?" said Yankelé, shrugging his shoulders and spreading out his palms.

"What of that? Surely you have not forgotten that the clodpate at whose house I have just entertained you is a Director of the East India Company, whose soldiers these are?"

"Oh," said Yankelé, his mystified face relaxing in a smile. The smile fled before the stern look in the Spaniard's eyes; he hastened to conceal his amusement. Yankelé was by nature a droll, and it cost him a good deal to take his patron as seriously as that potentate took himself. Perhaps if Manasseh Bueno Barzillai Azevedo da Costa had had more humour he would have had less momentum. Your man of action is blind in one eye. Cæsar would not have come and conquered if he had really seen.

Wounded by that temporary twinkle in his client's eye, the patron moved on silently, in step with the military air.

"It is a beautiful night," observed Yankelé in contrition. The words had hardly passed his lips before he became conscious that he had spoken the truth. The moon was peeping from behind a white cloud, and the air was soft, and broken shadows of foliage lay across the path, and the music was a song of love and bravery. Somehow, Yankelé began to think of da Costa's lovely daughter. Her face floated in the moonlight.

ISRAEL ZANGWILL

Manasseh shrugged his shoulders, unappeased.

"When one has supped well, it is always a beautiful night," he said testily. It was as if the cloud had overspread the moon, and a thick veil had fallen over the face of da Costa's lovely daughter. But Yankelé recovered himself quickly.

"Ah, yes," he said, "you have indeed made it a beaudiful night for me."

The King of *Schnorrers* waved his staff deprecatingly.

"It is alvays a beaudiful night ven I am mid *you*," added Yankelé, undaunted.

"It is strange," replied Manasseh musingly, "that I should have admitted to my hearth and Grobstock's table one who is, after all, but a half-brother in Israel."

"But Grobstock is also a Tedesco," protested Yankelé.

"That is also what I wonder at," rejoined da Costa. "I cannot make out how I have come to be so familiar with him."

"You see!" ventured the Tedesco timidly. "P'raps ven Grobstock had really had a girl you might even have come to marry her."

"Guard your tongue! A Sephardi cannot marry a Tedesco! It would be a degradation."

"Yes—but de oder vay round. A Tedesco *can* marry a Sephardi, not so? Dat is a rise. If Grobstock's daughter had married you, she vould have married above her," he ended, with an ingenuous air.

"True," admitted Manasseh. "But then, as Grobstock's daughter does not exist, and my wife does—!"

"Ah, but if you vas me," said Yankelé, "vould you rader marry a Tedesco or a Sephardi?"

"A Sephardi, of course. But—"

"I vill be guided by you," interrupted the Pole hastily. "You be de visest man I have ever known."

"But—" Manasseh repeated.

"Do not deny it. You be! Instantly vill I seek out a Sephardi maiden and ved her. P'raps you crown your counsel by choosing von for me. Vat?"

Manasseh was visibly mollified.

"How do I know your taste?" he asked hesitatingly.

"Oh, any Spanish girl would be a prize," replied Yankelé. "Even ven she had a face like a Passover cake. But still I prefer a Pentecost blossom."

"What kind of beauty do you like best?"

"Your daughter's style," plumply answered the Pole.

"But there are not many like that," said da Costa unsuspiciously.

"No—she is like de Rose of Sharon. But den dere are not many handsome faders."

Manasseh bethought himself. "There is Gabriel, the corpse-watcher's daughter. People consider his figure and deportment good."

"Pooh! Offal! She's ugly enough to keep de Messiah from coming. Vy, she's like cut out of de fader's face! Besides, consider his occupation! You vould not advise dat I marry into such a low family! Be you not my benefactor?"

"Well, but I cannot think of any good-looking girl that would be suitable."

Yankelé looked at him with a roguish, insinuating smile. "Say not dat! Have you not told Grobstock you be de first of marriage-brokers?"

But Manasseh shook his head.

"No, you be quite right," said Yankelé humbly; "I could not get a really beaudiful girl unless I married your Deborah herself."

"No, I am afraid not," said Manasseh sympathetically.

Yankelé took the plunge.

"Ah, vy can I not hope to call you fader-in-law?"

Manasseh's face was contorted by a spasm of astonishment and indignation. He came to a standstill.

"Dat must be a fine piece," said Yankelé quickly, indicating a flamboyant picture of a fearsome phantom hovering over a sombre moat.

They had arrived at Leman Street, and had stopped before Goodman's Fields Theatre. Manasseh's brow cleared.

"It is *The Castle Spectre*," he said graciously. "Would you like to see it?"

"But it is half over—"

"Oh, no," said da Costa, scanning the play bill. "There was a farce by O'Keefe to start with. The night is yet young. The drama will be just beginning."

"But it is de Sabbath—ve must not pay."

Manasseh's brow clouded again in wrathful righteous surprise. "Did you think I was going to pay?" he gasped.

"N-n-no," stammered the Pole, abashed. "But you haven't got no orders?"

"Orders? Me? Will you do me the pleasure of accepting a seat in my box?"

"In your box?"

"Yes, there is plenty of room. Come this way," said Manasseh. "I haven't been to the play myself for over a year. I am too busy always. It will be an agreeable change."

Yankelé hung back, bewildered.

"Through this door," said Manasseh encouragingly. "Come—you shall lead the way."

"But dey vill not admit me!"

"Will not admit you! When I give you a seat in my box! Are you mad? Now you shall just go in without me—I insist upon it. I will show you Manasseh Bueno Barzillai Azevedo da Costa is a man whose word is the Law of Moses; true as the Talmud. Walk straight through the portico, and, if the attendant endeavours to stop you, simply tell him Mr. da Costa has given you a seat in his box."

Not daring to exhibit scepticism—nay, almost confident in the powers of his extraordinary protector, Yankelé put his foot on the threshold of the lobby.

"But you be coming, too?" he said, turning back.

"Oh, yes, I don't intend to miss the performance. Have no fear."

Yankelé walked boldly ahead, and brushed by the door-keeper of the little theatre without appearing conscious of him; indeed, the official was almost impressed into letting the *Schnorrer* pass unquestioned as one who had gone out between the acts. But the visitor was too dingy for anything but the stage-door—he had the air of those nondescript beings who hang mysteriously about the hinder recesses of playhouses. Recovering himself just in time, the functionary (a meek little Cockney) hailed the intruder with a backward-drawing "Hi!"

"Vat you vant?" said Yankelé, turning his head.

"Vhere's your ticket?"

"Don't vant no ticket."

"Don't you? I does," rejoined the little man, who was a humorist.

"Mr. da Costa has given me a seat in his box."

"Oh, indeed! You'd swear to that in the box?"

"By my head. He gave it me."

"A seat in his box?"

"Yes."

"Mr. da Costa, you vos a-sayin', I think?"

"The same."

"Ah! this vay, then!"

And the humorist pointed to the street.

Yankelé did not budge.

"This vay, my lud!" cried the little humorist peremptorily.

"I tells you I'm going into Mr. da Costa's box!"

"And I tells you you're a-goin' into the gutter." And the official seized him by the scruff of the neck and began pushing him forwards with his knee.

"Now then! what's this?"

A stern, angry voice broke like a thunderclap upon the humorist's ears. He released his hold of the *Schnorrer* and looked up, to behold a strange, shabby, stalwart figure towering over him in censorious majesty.

"Why are you hustling this poor man?" demanded Manasseh.

"He wanted to sneak in," the little Cockney replied, half apologetically, half resentfully. "Expect 'e 'ails from Saffron 'Ill, and 'as 'is eye on the vipes. Told me some gammon—a cock-and-bull story about having a seat in a box."

"In Mr. da Costa's box, I suppose?" said Manasseh, ominously calm, with a menacing glitter in his eye.

"Ye-es," said the humorist, astonished and vaguely alarmed. Then the storm burst.

"You impertinent scoundrel! You jackanapes! You low, beggarly rapscallion! And so you refused to show my guest into my box!"

"Are you Mr. da Costa?" faltered the humorist.

"Yes, *I* am Mr. da Costa, but *you* won't much longer be door-keeper, if this is the way you treat people who come to see your pieces. Because, forsooth, the man looks poor, you think you can bully him safely—forgive me, Yankelé, I am so sorry I did not manage to come here before you, and spare you this insulting treatment! And as for you, my fine fellow, let me tell you that you make a great mistake in judging from appearances. There are some good friends of mine who could buy up your theatre and you and your miserable little soul at a moment's notice, and to look at them you would think they were cadgers. One of these days—hark you!—you will kick out a person of quality, and be kicked out yourself."

"I—I'm very sorry, sir."

"Don't say that to me. It is my guest you owe an apology to. Yes— and, by Heaven! you shall pay it, though he is no plutocrat, but only what he appears. Surely, because I wish to give a treat to a poor man who has, perhaps, never been to the play in his life, I am not bound to send him to the gallery—I can give him a corner in my box if I choose. There is no rule against that, I presume?"

"No, sir, I can't say as there is," said the humorist humbly. "But you will allow, sir, it's rayther unusual."

"Unusual! Of course, it's unusual. Kindness and consideration for the poor are always unusual. The poor are trodden upon at every opportunity, treated like dogs, not men. If I had invited a drunken fop, you'd have met him hat in hand (no, no, you needn't take it off to me now; it's too late). But a sober, poor man—by gad! I shall report your incivility to the management, and you'll be lucky if I don't thrash you with this stick into the bargain."

"But 'ow vos I to know, sir?"

"Don't speak to me, I tell you. If you have anything to urge in extenuation of your disgraceful behaviour, address your remarks to my guest."

"You'll overlook it this time, sir," said the little humorist, turning to Yankelé.

"Next time, p'raps, you believe me ven I say I have a seat in Mr. da Costa's box," replied Yankelé, in gentle reproach.

"Well, if *you're* satisfied, Yankelé," said Manasseh, with a touch of scorn, "I have no more to say. Go along, my man, show us to our box."

The official bowed and led them into the corridor. Suddenly he turned back.

"What box is it, please?" he said timidly.

"Blockhead!" cried Manasseh. "Which box should it be? The empty one, of course."

"But, sir, there are two boxes empty," urged the poor humorist deprecatingly, "the stage-box and the one by the gallery."

"Dolt! Do I look the sort of person who is content with a box on the ceiling? Go back to your post, sir—I'll find the box myself—Heaven send you wisdom—go back, some one might sneak in while you are away, and it would just serve you right."

The little man slunk back half dazed, glad to escape from this overwhelming personality, and in a few seconds Manasseh stalked into the empty box, followed by Yankelé, whose mouth was a grin and whose eye a twinkle. As the Spaniard took his seat there was a slight outburst of clapping and stamping from a house impatient for the end of the *entr'acte*.

Manasseh craned his head over the box to see the house, which in turn craned to see him, glad of any diversion, and some people, imagining the applause had reference to the new-comer, whose head appeared to be that of a foreigner of distinction, joined in it. The contagion spread, and in a minute Manasseh was the cynosure of all eyes and the unmistakable recipient of an "ovation." He bowed twice or thrice in unruffled dignity.

There were some who recognised him, but they joined in the reception with wondering amusement. Not a few, indeed, of the audience were Jews, for Goodman's Fields was the Ghetto Theatre, and the Sabbath was not a sufficient deterrent to a lax generation. The audiences—mainly German and Poles—came to the little unfashionable playhouse as one happy family. Distinctions of rank were trivial, and gallery held converse with circle, and pit collogued with box. Supper parties were held on the benches.

In a box that gave on the pit a portly Jewess sat stiffly, arrayed in the very pink of fashion, in a spangled robe of India muslin, with a diamond necklace and crescent, her head crowned by terraces of curls and flowers.

"Betsy!" called up a jovial feminine voice from the pit, when the applause had subsided.

"Betsy" did not move, but her cheeks grew hot and red. She had got on in the world, and did not care to recognise her old crony.

"Betsy!" iterated the well-meaning woman. "By your life and mine, you must taste a piece of my fried fish." And she held up a slice of cold plaice, beautifully browned.

Betsy drew back, striving unsuccessfully to look unconscious. To her relief the curtain rose, and *The Castle Spectre* walked. Yankelé, who had scarcely seen anything but private theatricals, representing the discomfiture of the wicked Haman and the triumph of Queen Esther (a *rôle* he had once played himself, in his mother's old clothes), was delighted with the thrills and terrors of the ghostly melodrama. It was not till the conclusion of the second act that the emotion the beautiful but injured heroine cost him welled over again into matrimonial speech.

"Ve vind up de night glorious," he said.

"I am glad you like it. It is certainly an enjoyable performance," Manasseh answered with stately satisfaction.

"Your daughter, Deborah," Yankelé ventured timidly, "do she ever go to de play?"

"No, I do not take my womankind about. Their duty lies at home. As it is written, I call my wife not 'wife' but 'home.'"

"But dink how dey vould enjoy deirselves!"

"We are not sent here to enjoy ourselves."

"True—most true," said Yankelé, pulling a smug face. "Ve be sent here to obey de Law of Moses. But do not remind me I be a sinner in Israel."

"How so?"

"I am twenty-five—yet I have no vife."

"I daresay you had plenty in Poland."

"By my soul, not. Only von, and her I gave *gett* (divorce) for barrenness. You can write to de Rabbi of my town."

"Why should I write? It's not my affair."

"But I vant it to be your affair."

Manasseh glared. "Do you begin that again?" he murmured.

"It is not so much dat I desire your daughter for a vife as you for a fader-in-law."

"It cannot be!" said Manasseh more gently.

"Oh dat I had been born a Sephardi!" said Yankelé with a hopeless groan.

"It is too late now," said da Costa soothingly.

"Dey say it's never too late to mend," moaned the Pole. "Is dere no vay for me to be converted to Spanish Judaism? I could easily pronounce Hebrew in your superior vay."

"Our Judaism differs in no essential respect from yours—it is a question of blood. You cannot change your blood. As it is said, 'And the blood is the life.'"

"I know, I know dat I aspire too high. Oh, vy did you become my friend, vy did you make me believe you cared for me—so dat I tink of you day and night—and now, ven I ask you to be my fader-in-law, you say it cannot be. It is like a knife in de heart! Tink how proud and happy I should be to call you my fader-in-law. All my life vould be devoted to you—my von thought to be vordy of such a man."

"You are not the first I have been compelled to refuse," said Manasseh, with emotion.

"Vat helps me dat dere be other *Schlemihls* (unlucky persons)?" quoted Yankelé, with a sob. "How can I live midout you for a fader-in-law?"

"I am sorry for you—more sorry than I have ever been."

"Den you do care for me! I vill not give up hope. I vill not take no for no answer. Vat is dis blood dat it should divide Jew from Jew, dat it should prevent me becoming de son-in-law of de only man I have ever loved? Say not so. Let me ask you again—in a month or a year—even twelve months vould I vait, ven you vould only promise not to pledge yourself to anoder man."

"But if I became your father-in-law—mind, I only say if—not only would I not keep you, but you would have to keep my Deborah."

"And supposing?"

"But you are not able to keep a wife!"

"Not able? Who told you dat?" cried Yankelé indignantly.

"You yourself! Why, when I first befriended you, you told me you were blood-poor."

"Dat I told you as a *Schnorrer*. But now I speak to you as a suitor."

"True," admitted Manasseh, instantly appreciating the distinction.

"And as a suitor I tell you I can *schnorr* enough to keep two vives."

"But do you tell this to da Costa the father or da Costa the marriage-broker?"

"Hush!" from all parts of the house as the curtain went up and the house settled down. But Yankelé was no longer in *rapport* with the play; the spectre had ceased to thrill and the heroine to touch. His mind was busy with feverish calculations of income, scraping together every penny he could raise by hook or crook. He even drew out a crumpled piece of paper and a pencil, but thrust them back into his pocket when he saw Manasseh's eye.

"I forgot," he murmured apologetically. "Being at de play made me forget it was de Sabbath." And he pursued his calculations mentally; this being naturally less work.

When the play was over the two beggars walked out into the cool night air.

"I find," Yankelé began eagerly in the vestibule, "I make at least von hundred and fifty pounds"—he paused to acknowledge the farewell salutation of the little door-keeper at his elbow—"a hundred and fifty a year."

"Indeed!" said Manasseh, in respectful astonishment.

"Yes! I have reckoned it all up. Ten are de sources of charity—"

"As it is written," interrupted Manasseh with unction, "'With ten sayings was the world created; there were ten generations from Noah to Abraham; with ten trials our father Abraham was tried; ten miracles were wrought for our fathers in Egypt and ten at the Red Sea; and ten things were created on the eve of the Sabbath in the twilight!' And now it shall be added, 'Ten good deeds the poor man affords the rich man.' Proceed, Yankelé."

"First comes my allowance from de Synagogue—eight pounds. Vonce a veek I call and receive half-a-crown."

"Is that all? Our Synagogue allows three-and-six."

"Ah!" sighed the Pole wistfully. "Did I not say you be a superior race?"

"But that only makes six pound ten!"

"I know—de oder tirty shillings I allow for Passover cakes and groceries. Den for Synagogue-knocking I get ten guin—"

"Stop! stop!" cried Manasseh, with a sudden scruple. "Ought I to listen to financial details on the Sabbath?"

"Certainly, ven dey be connected vid my marriage—vich is a Commandment. It is de Law ve really discuss."

"You are right. Go on, then. But remember, even if you can prove you can *schnorr* enough to keep a wife, I do not bind myself to consent."

"You be already a fader to me—vy vill you not be a fader-in-law? Anyhow, you vill find me a fader-in-law," he added hastily, seeing the blackness gathering again on da Costa's brow.

"Nay, nay, we must not talk of business on the Sabbath," said Manasseh evasively. "Proceed with your statement of income."

"Ten guineas for Synagogue-knocking. I have twenty clients who—"

"Stop a minute! I cannot pass that item."

"Vy not? It is true."

"Maybe! But Synagogue-knocking is distinctly *work*!"

"Vork?"

"Well, if going round early in the morning to knock at the doors of twenty pious persons, and rouse them for morning service, isn't work, then the Christian bell-ringer is a beggar. No, no! Profits from this source I cannot regard as legitimate."

"But most *Schnorrers* be Synagogue-knockers!"

"Most *Schnorrers* are Congregation-men or Psalms-men," retorted the Spaniard witheringly. "But I call it debasing. What! To assist at the services for a fee! To worship one's Maker for hire! Under such conditions to pray is to work." His breast swelled with majesty and scorn.

"I cannot call it vork," protested the *Schnorrer*. "Vy at dat rate you vould make out dat de minister vorks? or de preacher? Vy, I reckon fourteen pounds a year to my services as Congregation-man."

"Fourteen pounds! As much as that?"

"Yes, you see dere's my private customers as vell as de Synagogue. Ven dere is mourning in a house dey cannot alvays get together ten friends for de services, so I make von. How can you call that vork? It is friendship. And the more dey pay me de more friendship I feel," asserted Yankelé with a twinkle. "Den de Synagogue allows me a little extra for announcing de dead."

In those primitive times, when a Jewish newspaper was undreamt of, the day's obituary was published by a peripatetic *Schnorrer*, who went about the Ghetto rattling a pyx—a copper money-box with a handle and a lid closed by a padlock. On hearing this death-rattle, anyone who felt curious would ask the *Schnorrer*:

"Who's dead to-day?"

"So-and-so ben So-and-so—funeral on such a day—mourning service at such an hour," the *Schnorrer* would reply, and the enquirer would piously put something into the "byx," as it was called. The collection was handed over to the Holy Society—in other words, the Burial Society.

"P'raps you call that vork?" concluded Yankelé, in timid challenge.

"Of course I do. What do you call it?"

"Valking exercise. It keeps me healty. Vonce von of my customers (from whom I *schnorred* half-a-crown a veek) said he was tired of my coming and getting it every Friday. He vanted to compound mid me for six pound a year, but I vouldn't."

"But it was a very fair offer. He only deducted ten shillings for the interest on his money."

"Dat I didn't mind. But I vanted a pound more for his depriving me of my valking exercise, and dat he vouldn't pay, so he still goes on giving me de half-crown a veek. Some of dese charitable persons are terribly mean. But vat I vant to say is dat I carry de byx mostly in the streets vere my customers lay, and it gives me more standing as a *Schnorrer*."

"No, no, that is a delusion. What! Are you weak-minded enough to believe that? All the philanthropists say so, of course, but surely you know that *schnorring* and work should never be mixed. A man cannot do two things properly. He must choose his profession, and stick to it. A friend of mine once succumbed to the advice of the philanthropists instead of asking mine. He had one of the best provincial rounds in the kingdom, but in every town he weakly listened to the lectures of the president of the congregation inculcating work, and at last he actually invested the savings of years in jewellery, and went round trying to peddle it. The presidents all bought something to encourage him (though they beat down the price so that there was no profit in it), and they all expressed their pleasure at his working for his living, and showing a manly independence. 'But I *schnorr* also,' he reminded them, holding out his hand when they had finished. It was in vain. No one gave him a farthing. He had blundered beyond redemption. At one blow he had destroyed one of the most profitable connections a *Schnorrer* ever had, and without even getting anything for the goodwill. So if you will be guided by me, Yankelé, you will do nothing to assist the philanthropists to keep you. It destroys their satisfaction. A *Schnorrer* cannot be too careful. And once you begin to work, where are you to draw the line?"

"But you be a marriage-broker yourself," said Yankelé imprudently.

"That!" thundered Manasseh angrily, "That is not work! That is pleasure!"

"Vy look! Dere is Hennery Simons," cried Yankelé, hoping to divert his attention. But he only made matters worse.

Henry Simons was a character variously known as the Tumbling Jew, Harry the Dancer, and the Juggling Jew. He was afterwards to become famous as the hero of a slander case which deluged England with pamphlets for and against, but for the present he had merely outraged the feelings of his fellow *Schnorrers* by budding out in a direction so rare as to suggest preliminary baptism. He stood now playing antic and sleight-of-hand tricks—surrounded by a crowd—a curious figure crowned by a velvet skull-cap from which wisps of hair protruded, with a scarlet handkerchief thrust through his girdle. His face was an olive oval, bordered by ragged tufts of beard and stamped with melancholy.

"You see the results of working," cried Manasseh. "It brings temptation to work on Sabbath. That Epicurean there is profaning the Holy Day. Come away! A *Schnorrer* is far more certain of The-World-To-Come. No, decidedly, I will not give my daughter to a worker, or to a *Schnorrer* who makes illegitimate profits."

"But I *make* de profits all de same," persisted Yankelé.

"You make them to-day—but to-morrow? There is no certainty about them. Work of whatever kind is by its very nature unreliable. At any moment trade may be slack. People may become less pious, and you lose your Synagogue-knocking. Or more pious—and they won't want congregation-men."

"But new Synagogues spring up," urged Yankelé.

"New Synagogues are full of enthusiasm," retorted Manasseh. "The members are their own congregation-men."

Yankelé had his roguish twinkle. "At first," he admitted, "but de *Schnorrer* vaits his time."

Manasseh shook his head. "*Schnorring* is the only occupation that is regular all the year round," he said. "Everything else may fail—the greatest commercial houses may totter to the ground; as it is written, 'He humbleth the proud.' But the *Schnorrer* is always secure. Whoever falls, there are always enough left to look after *him*. If you were a father, Yankelé, you would understand my feelings. How can a man allow his daughter's future happiness to repose on a basis so uncertain as work? No, no. What do you make by your district visiting? Everything turns on that."

"Twenty-five shilling a veek!"

"Really?"

"Law of Moses! In sixpences, shillings, and half-crowns. Vy in Houndsditch alone, I have two streets all except a few houses."

"But are they safe? Population shifts. Good streets go down."

"Dat twenty-five shillings is as safe as Mocatta's business. I have it all written down at home—you can inspect de books if you choose."

"No, no," said Manasseh, with a grand wave of his stick. "If I did not believe you, I should not entertain your proposal for a moment. It rejoices me exceedingly to find you have devoted so much attention to this branch. I always held strongly that the rich should be visited in their own homes, and I grieve to see this personal touch, this contact with the very people to whom you give the good deeds, being replaced by lifeless circulars. One owes it to one's position in life to afford the wealthy classes the opportunity of charity warm from the heart; they should not be neglected and driven in their turn to write cheques in cold blood, losing all that human sympathy which comes from personal intercourse—as it is written, 'Charity delivers from death.' But do you think charity that is given publicly through a secretary and advertised in annual reports has so great a redeeming power as that slipped privately into the hands of the poor man, who makes a point of keeping secret from every donor what he has received from the others?"

"I am glad you don't call collecting de money vork," said Yankelé, with a touch of sarcasm which was lost on da Costa.

"No, so long as the donor can't show any 'value received' in return. And there's more friendship in *such* a call, Yankelé, than in going to a house of mourning to pray for a fee."

"Oh," said Yankelé, wincing. "Den p'raps you strike out all my Year-Time item!"

"Year-Time! What's that?"

"Don't you know?" said the Pole, astonished. "Ven a man has Year-Time, he feels charitable for de day."

"Do you mean when he commemorates the anniversary of the death of one of his family? We Sephardim call that 'making years'! But are there enough Year-Times, as you call them, in your Synagogue?"

"Dere might be more—I only make about fifteen pounds. Our colony is, as you say, too new. De Globe Road Cemetery is as empty as a Synagogue on veek-days. De faders have left *deir* faders on de Continent, and kept many Year-Times out of de country. But in a few years many faders and moders must die off here, and every parent leaves two or tree sons to have Year-Times, and every child two or tree broders and a fader. Den every day more German Jews come here—vich means more and more to die. I tink indeed it vould be fair to double this item."

"No, no; stick to facts. It is an iniquity to speculate in the misfortunes of our fellow-creatures."

"Somebody must die dat I may live," retorted Yankelé roguishly; "de vorld is so created. Did you not quote, 'Charity delivers from death'? If people lived for ever, *Schnorrers* could not live at all."

"Hush! The world could not exist without *Schnorrers*. As it is written, 'And Repentance and *Prayer* and CHARITY avert the evil decree.' Charity is put last—it is the climax—the greatest thing on earth. And the *Schnorrer* is the greatest man on earth; for it stands in the Talmud, 'He who causes is greater than he who does.' Therefore, the *Schnorrer* who causes charity is even greater than he who gives it."

"Talk of de devil," said Yankelé, who had much difficulty in keeping his countenance when Manasseh became magnificent and dithyrambic. "Vy, dere is Greenbaum, whose fader vas buried yesterday. Let us cross over by accident and vish him long life."

"Greenbaum dead! Was that the Greenbaum on 'Change, who was such a rascal with the wenches?"

"De same," said Yankelé. Then approaching the son, he cried, "Good Sabbath, Mr. Greenbaum; I vish you long life. Vat a blow for de community!"

"It comforts me to hear you say so," said the son, with a sob in his voice.

"Ah, yes!" said Yankelé chokingly. "Your fader vas a great and good man—just my size."

"I've already given them away to Baruch the glazier," replied the mourner.

"But he has his glaziering," remonstrated Yankelé. "I have noting but de clothes I stand in, and dey don't fit me half so vell as your fader's vould have done."

"Baruch has been very unfortunate," replied Greenbaum defensively. "He had a misfortune in the winter, and he has never got straight yet. A child of his died, and, unhappily, just when the snowballing was at its height, so that he lost seven days by the mourning." And he moved away.

"Did I not say work was uncertain?" cried Manasseh.

"Not all," maintained the *Schnorrer*. "What of de six guineas I make by carrying round de Palm-branch on Tabernacles to be shaken by de voomans who cannot attend Synagogue, and by blowing de trumpet for de same voomans on New Year, so dat dey may break deir fasts?"

"The amount is too small to deserve discussion. Pass on."

"Dere is a smaller amount—just half dat—I get from de presents to de poor at de Feast of Lots, and from de Bridegrooms of de Beginning and de Bridegrooms of de Law at de Rejoicing of de Law, and dere is about four pounds ten a year from de sale of clothes given to me. Den I have a lot o' meals given me—dis, I have reckoned, is as good as seven pounds. And, lastly, I cannot count de odds and ends under ten guineas. You know dere are alvays legacies, gifts, distributions—all unexpected. You never know who'll break out next."

"Yes, I think it's not too high a percentage of your income to expect from unexpected sources," admitted Manasseh. "I have myself lingered about 'Change Alley or Sampson's Coffee House just when the jobbers have pulled off a special coup, and they have paid me quite a high percentage on their profits."

"And I," boasted Yankelé, stung to noble emulation, "have made two sov'rans in von minute out of Gideon de bullion-broker. He likes to give *Schnorrers* sov'rans, as if in mistake for shillings, to see vat dey'll do. De fools hurry off, or move slowly avay, as if not noticing, or put it quickly in de pocket. But dose who have visdom tell him he's made a mistake, and he gives dem anoder sov'ran. Honesty is de best policy with Gideon. Den dere is Rabbi de Falk, de Baal Shem—de great Cabbalist. Ven—"

"But," interrupted Manasseh impatiently, "you haven't made out your hundred and fifty a year."

Yankelé's face fell. "Not if you cut out so many items."

"No, but even all inclusive it only comes to a hundred and forty-three pounds nineteen shillings."

"Nonsense!" said Yankelé, staggered. "How can you know so exact?"

"Do you think I cannot do simple addition?" responded Manasseh sternly. "Are not these your ten items?"

	£	s.	d.
1. Synagogue Pension, with Passover extras	8	0	0
2. Synagogue-knocking	10	10	0
3. District Visiting	65	0	0
4. As Congregation-man and Pyx-bearer	14	0	0
5. Year-Times	15	0	0
6. Palm-branch and Trumpet Fees	6	6	0
7. Purim-presents, &c.	3	3	0
8. Sale of Clothes	4	10	0
9. Equivalent of Free Meals	7	0	0
10. Miscellanea, the unexpected	10	10	0
Total	£143	19	0

"A child could sum it up," concluded Manasseh severely. Yankelé was subdued to genuine respect and consternation by da Costa's marvellous memory and arithmetical genius. But he rallied immediately. "Of course, I also reckoned on a dowry mid my bride, if only a hundred pounds."

"Well, invested in Consols, that would not bring you four pounds more," replied Manasseh instantly.

"The rest vill be made up in extra free meals," Yankelé answered no less quickly. "For ven I take your daughter off your hands you vill be able to afford to invite me more often to your table dan you do now."

"Not at all," retorted Manasseh, "for now that I know how well off you are I shall no longer feel I am doing a charity."

"Oh, yes, you vill," said Yankelé insinuatingly. "You are too much a man of honour to know as a private philantropist vat I have told de marriage-broker, de fader-in-law and de fellow *Schnorrer*. Besides, I vould have de free meals from you as de son-in-law, not de *Schnorrer*."

"In that relation I should also have free meals from you," rejoined Manasseh.

"I never dared to tink you vould do me de honour. But even so I can never give you such good meals as you give me. So dere is still a balance in my favour."

"That is true," said da Costa thoughtfully. "But you have still about a guinea to make up."

Yankelé was driven into a corner at last. But he flashed back, without perceptible pause, "You do not allow for vat I save by my piety. I fast twenty times a year, and surely dat is at least anoder guinea per annum."

"But you will have children," retorted da Costa.

Yankelé shrugged his shoulders.

"Dat is de affair of de Holy One, blessed be He. Ven He sends dem He vill provide for dem. You must not forget, too, dat mid *your* daughter de dowry vould be noting so small as a hundred pounds."

"My daughter will have a dowry befitting her station, certainly," said Manasseh, with his grandest manner; "but then I had looked forward to her marrying a king of *Schnorrers*."

"Vell, but ven I marry her I shall be."

"How so?"

"I shall have *schnorred* your daughter—the most precious thing in the world! And *schnorred* her from a king of *Schnorrers*, too!! And I shall have *schnorred* your services as marriage-broker into de bargain!!!"

IV

Showing how the Royal Wedding was Arranged

M anasseh Bueno Barzillai Azevedo da Costa was so impressed by his would-be son-in-law's last argument that he perpended it in silence for a full minute. When he replied, his tone showed even more respect than had been infused into it by the statement of the aspirant's income. Manasseh was not of those to whom money is a fetish; he regarded it merely as something to be had for the asking. It was intellect for which he reserved his admiration. That was strictly not transferable.

"It is true," he said, "that if I yielded to your importunities and gave you my daughter, you would thereby have approved yourself a king of *Schnorrers*, of a rank suitable to my daughter's, but an analysis of your argument will show that you are begging the question."

"Vat more proof do you vant of my begging powers?" demanded Yankelé, spreading out his palms and shrugging his shoulders.

"Much greater proof," replied Manasseh. "I ought to have some instance of your powers. The only time I have seen you try to *schnorr* you failed."

"Me! ven?" exclaimed Yankelé indignantly.

"Why, this very night. When you asked young Weinstein for his dead father's clothes!"

"But he had already given them away!" protested the Pole.

"What of that? If anyone had given away *my* clothes, I should have demanded compensation. You must really be above rebuffs of that kind, Yankelé, if you are to be my son-in-law. No, no, I remember the dictum of the Sages: 'To give your daughter to an uncultured man is like throwing her bound to a lion.'"

"But you have also seen me *schnorr* mid success," remonstrated the suitor.

"Never!" protested Manasseh vehemently.

"Often!"

"From whom?"

"From you!" said Yankelé boldly.

"From *me!*" sneered Manasseh, accentuating the pronoun with infinite contempt. "What does that prove? I am a generous man. The test is to *schnorr* from a miser."

"I *vill schnorr* from a miser!" announced Yankelé desperately.

"You will!"

"Yes. Choose your miser."

"No, I leave it to you," said da Costa politely.

"Vell, Sam Lazarus, de butcher shop!"

"No, not Sam Lazarus, he once gave a *Schnorrer* I know elevenpence."

"Elevenpence?" incredulously murmured Yankelé.

"Yes, it was the only way he could pass a shilling. It wasn't bad, only cracked, but he could get no one to take it except a *Schnorrer*. He made the man give him a penny change though. 'Tis true the man afterwards laid out the shilling at Lazarus's shop. Still a really great miser would have added that cracked shilling to his hoard rather than the perfect penny."

"No," argued Yankelé, "dere vould be no difference, since he does not spend."

"True," said da Costa reflectively, "but by that same token a miser is not the most difficult person to tackle."

"How do you make dat out?"

"Is it not obvious? Already we see Lazarus giving away elevenpence. A miser who spends nothing on himself may, in exceptional cases, be induced to give away something. It is the man who indulges himself in every luxury and gives away nothing who is the hardest to *schnorr* from. He has a *use* for his money—himself! If you diminish his store you hurt him in the tenderest part—you rob him of creature comforts. To *schnorr* from such a one I should regard as a higher and nobler thing than to *schnorr* from a mere miser."

"Vell, name your man."

"No—I couldn't think of taking it out of your hands," said Manasseh again with his stately bow. "Whomever you select I will abide by. If I could not rely on your honour, would I dream of you as a son-in-law?"

"Den I vill go to Mendel Jacobs, of Mary Axe."

"Mendel Jacobs—oh, no! Why, he's married! A married man cannot be entirely devoted to himself."

"Vy not? Is not a vife a creature comfort? P'raps also she comes cheaper dan a housekeeper."

"We will not argue it. I will not have Mendel Jacobs."

"Simon Kelutski, de vine-merchant."

"He! He is quite generous with his snuff-box. I have myself been offered a pinch. Of course I did not accept it."

Yankelé selected several other names, but Manasseh barred them all, and at last had an inspiration of his own.

"Isn't there a Rabbi in your community whose stinginess is proverbial? Let me see, what's his name?"

"A Rabbi!" murmured Yankelé disingenuously, while his heart began to palpitate with alarm.

"Yes, isn't there—Rabbi Bloater!"

Yankelé shook his head. Ruin stared him in the face—his fondest hopes were crumbling.

"I know it's some fishy name—Rabbi Haddock—no it isn't. It's Rabbi Remorse something."

Yankelé saw it was all over with him.

"P'raps you mean Rabbi Remorse Red-herring," he said feebly, for his voice failed him.

"Ah, yes! Rabbi Remorse Red-herring," said Manasseh. "From all I hear—for I have never seen the man—a king of guzzlers and topers, and the meanest of mankind. Now if you could dine with *him* you might indeed be called a king of *Schnorrers*."

Yankelé was pale and trembling. "But *he* is married!" he urged, with a happy thought.

"Dine with him to-morrow," said Manasseh inexorably. "He fares extra royally on the Sabbath. Obtain admission to his table, and you shall be admitted into my family."

"But you do not know the man—it is impossible!" cried Yankelé.

"That is the excuse of the bad *Schnorrer*. You have heard my ultimatum. No dinner, no wife. No wife—no dowry!"

"Vat vould dis dowry be?" asked Yankelé, by way of diversion.

"Oh, unique—quite unique. First of all there would be all the money she gets from the Synagogue. Our Synagogue gives considerable dowries to portionless girls. There are large bequests for the purpose."

Yankelé's eyes glittered.

"Ah, vat gentlemen you Spaniards be!"

"Then I daresay I should hand over to my son-in-law all my Jerusalem land."

"Have you property in de Holy Land?" said Yankelé.

"First class, with an unquestionable title. And, of course, I would give you some province or other in this country."

"What!" gasped Yankelé.

"Could I do less?" said Manasseh blandly. "My own flesh and blood, remember! Ah, here is my door. It is too late to ask you in. Good Sabbath! Don't forget your appointment to dine with Rabbi Remorse Red-herring to-morrow."

"Good Sabbath!" faltered Yankelé, and crawled home heavy-hearted to Dinah's Buildings, Tripe Yard, Whitechapel, where the memory of him lingers even unto this day.

Rabbi Remorse Red-herring was an unofficial preacher who officiated at mourning services in private houses, having a gift of well-turned eulogy. He was a big, burly man with overlapping stomach and a red beard, and his spiritual consolations drew tears. His clients knew him to be vastly self-indulgent in private life, and abstemious in the matter of benevolence; but they did not confound the *rôles*. As a mourning preacher he gave every satisfaction: he was regular and punctual, and did not keep the congregation waiting, and he had had considerable experience in showing that there was yet balm in Gilead.

He had about five ways of showing it—the variants depending upon the circumstances. If, as not infrequently happened, the person deceased was a stranger to him, he would enquire in the passage: "Was it man or woman? Boy or girl? Married or single? Any children? Young 'uns or old 'uns?"

When these questions had been answered, he was ready. He knew exactly which of his five consolatory addresses to deliver—they were all sufficiently vague and general to cover considerable variety of circumstance, and even when he misheard the replies in the passage, and dilated on the grief of a departed widower's relict, the results were not fatal throughout. The few impossible passages might be explained by the mishearing of the audience. Sometimes—very rarely—he would venture on a supplementary sentence or two fitting the specific occasion, but very cautiously, for a man with a reputation for extempore addresses cannot be too wary of speaking on the spur of the moment.

Off obituary lines he was a failure; at any rate, his one attempt to preach from an English Synagogue pulpit resulted in a nickname. His theme was Remorse, which he explained with much care to the congregation.

"For instance," said the preacher, "the other day I was walking over

London Bridge, when I saw a fishwife standing with a basket of red-herrings. I says, 'How much?' She says, 'Two for three-halfpence.' I says, 'Oh, that's frightfully dear! I can easily get three for twopence.' But she wouldn't part with them at that price, so I went on, thinking I'd meet another woman with a similar lot over the water. They were lovely fat herrings, and my chaps watered in anticipation of the treat of eating them. But when I got to the other end of the bridge there was no other fishwife to be seen. So I resolved to turn back to the first fishwife, for, after all, I reflected, the herrings were really very cheap, and I had only complained in the way of business. But when I got back the woman was just sold out. I could have torn my hair with vexation. Now, that's what I call Remorse."

After that the Rabbi was what the congregation called Remorse; also Red-herring.

The Rabbi's fondness for concrete exemplification of abstract ideas was not, however, to be stifled, and there was one illustration of Charity which found a place in all the five sermons of consolation.

"If you have a pair of old breeches, send them to the Rabbi."

Rabbi Remorse Red-herring was, however, as is the way of preachers, himself aught but a concrete exemplification of the virtues he inculcated. He lived generously—through other people's generosity—but no one could boast of having received a farthing from him over and above what was due to them; while *Schnorrers* (who deemed considerable sums due to them) regarded him in the light of a defalcating bankrupt. He, for his part, had a countervailing grudge against the world, fancying the work he did for it but feebly remunerated. "I get so little," ran his bitter plaint, "that I couldn't live, *if it were not for the fasts*." And, indeed, the fasts of the religion were worth much more to him than to Yankelé; his meals were so profuse that his savings from this source were quite a little revenue. As Yankelé had pointed out, he was married. And his wife had given him a child, but it died at the age of seven, bequeathing to him the only poignant sorrow of his life. He was too jealous to call in a rival consolation preacher during those dark days, and none of his own five sermons seemed to fit the case. It was some months before he took his meals regularly.

At no time had anyone else taken meals in his house, except by law entitled. Though she had only two to cook for, his wife habitually provided for three, counting her husband no mere unit. Herself she reckoned as a half.

It was with intelligible perturbation, therefore, that Yankelé, dressed in some other man's best, approached the house of Rabbi Remorse Red-herring about a quarter of an hour before the Sabbath mid-day meal, intent on sharing it with him.

"No dinner, no marriage!" was da Costa's stern ukase.

What wonder if the inaccessible meal took upon itself the grandiosity of a wedding feast! Deborah da Costa's lovely face tantalised him like a mirage.

The Sabbath day was bleak, but chiller was his heart. The Rabbi had apartments in Steward Street, Spitalfields, an elegant suite on the ground-floor, for he stinted himself in nothing but charity. At the entrance was a porch—a pointed Gothic arch of wood supported by two pillars. As Yankelé mounted the three wooden steps, breathing as painfully as if they were three hundred, and wondering if he would ever get merely as far as the other side of the door, he was assailed by the temptation to go and dine peacefully at home, and represent to da Costa that he had feasted with the Rabbi. Manasseh would never know, Manasseh had taken no steps to ascertain if he satisfied the test or not. Such carelessness, he told himself in righteous indignation, deserved fitting punishment. But, on the other hand, he recalled Manasseh's trust in him; Manasseh believed him a man of honour, and the patron's elevation of soul awoke an answering chivalry in the parasite.

He decided to make the attempt at least, for there would be plenty of time to say he had succeeded, after he had failed.

Vibrating with tremors of nobility as well as of apprehension, Yankelé lifted the knocker. He had no programme, trusting to chance and mother-wit.

Mrs. Remorse Red-herring half opened the door.

"I vish to see de Rabbi," he said, putting one foot within.

"He is engaged," said the wife—a tiny thin creature who had been plump and pretty. "He is very busy talking with a gentleman."

"Oh, but I can vait."

"But the Rabbi will be having his dinner soon."

"I can vait till after dinner," said Yankelé obligingly.

"Oh, but the Rabbi sits long at table."

"I don't mind," said Yankelé with undiminished placidity, "de longer de better."

The poor woman looked perplexed. "I'll tell my husband," she said at last.

Yankelé had an anxious moment in the passage.

"The Rabbi wishes to know what you want," she said when she returned.

"I vant to get married," said Yankelé with an inspiration of veracity.

"But my husband doesn't marry people."

"Vy not?"

"He only brings consolation into households," she explained ingenuously.

"Vell, I won't get married midout him," Yankelé murmured lugubriously.

The little woman went back in bewilderment to her bosom's lord. Forthwith out came Rabbi Remorse Red-herring, curiosity and cupidity in his eyes. He wore the skull-cap of sanctity, but looked the gourmand in spite of it.

"Good Sabbath, sir! What is this about your getting married?"

"It's a long story," said Yankelé, "and as your good vife told me your dinner is just ready, I mustn't keep you now."

"No, there are still a few minutes before dinner. What is it?"

Yankelé shook his head. "I couldn't tink of keeping you in dis draughty passage."

"I don't mind. I don't feel any draught."

"Dat's just vere de danger lays. You don't notice, and one day you find yourself laid up mid rheumatism, and you vill have Remorse," said Yankelé with a twinkle. "Your life is precious—if *you* die, who vill console de community?"

It was an ambiguous remark, but the Rabbi understood it in its most flattering sense, and his little eyes beamed. "I would ask you inside," he said, "but I have a visitor."

"No matter," said Yankelé, "vat I have to say to you, Rabbi, is not private. A stranger may hear it."

Still undecided, the Rabbi muttered, "You want me to marry you?"

"I have come to get married," replied Yankelé.

"But I have never been called upon to marry people."

"It's never too late to mend, dey say."

"Strange—strange," murmured the Rabbi reflectively.

"Vat is strange?"

"That you should come to me just to-day. But why did you not go to Rabbi Sandman?"

"Rabbi Sandman!" replied Yankelé with contempt. "Vere vould be de good of going to him?"

"But why not?"

"Every *Schnorrer* goes to him," said Yankelé frankly.

"Hum!" mused the Rabbi. "Perhaps there *is* an opening for a more select marrier. Come in, then, I can give you five minutes if you really don't mind talking before a stranger."

He threw open the door, and led the way into the sitting-room.

Yankelé followed, exultant; the outworks were already carried, and his heart beat high with hope. But at his first glance within, he reeled and almost fell.

Standing with his back to the fire and dominating the room was Manasseh Bueno Barzillai Azevedo da Costa!

"Ah, Yankelé, good Sabbath!" said da Costa affably.

"G-g-ood Sabbath!" stammered Yankelé.

"Why, you know each other!" cried the Rabbi.

"Oh, yes," said Manasseh, "an acquaintance of yours, too, apparently."

"No, he is just come to see me about something," replied the Rabbi.

"I thought you did not know the Rabbi, Mr. da Costa?" Yankelé could not help saying.

"I didn't. I only had the pleasure of making his acquaintance half an hour ago. I met him in the street as he was coming home from morning service, and he was kind enough to invite me to dinner."

Yankelé gasped; despite his secret amusement at Manasseh's airs, there were moments when the easy magnificence of the man overwhelmed him, extorted his reluctant admiration. How in Heaven's name had the Spaniard conquered at a blow!

Looking down at the table, he now observed that it was already laid for dinner—and for three! He should have been that third. Was it fair of Manasseh to handicap him thus? Naturally, there would be infinitely less chance of a fourth being invited than a third—to say nothing of the dearth of provisions. "But, surely, you don't intend to stay to dinner!" he complained in dismay.

"I have given my word," said Manasseh, "and I shouldn't care to disappoint the Rabbi."

"Oh, it's no disappointment, no disappointment," remarked Rabbi Remorse Red-herring cordially, "I could just as well come round and see you after dinner."

"After dinner I never see people," said Manasseh majestically; "I sleep."

The Rabbi dared not make further protest: he turned to Yankelé and asked, "Well, now, what's this about your marriage?"

"I can't tell you before Mr. da Costa," replied Yankelé, to gain time.

"Why not? You said anybody might hear."

"Noting of the sort. I said a stranger might hear. But Mr. da Costa isn't a stranger. He knows too much about de matter."

"What shall we do, then?" murmured the Rabbi.

"I can vait till after dinner," said Yankelé, with good-natured carelessness. "*I* don't sleep—"

Before the Rabbi could reply, the wife brought in a baked dish, and set it on the table. Her husband glowered at her, but she, regular as clockwork, and as unthinking, produced the black bottle of *schnapps*. It was her husband's business to get rid of Yankelé; her business was to bring on the dinner. If she had delayed, he would have raged equally. She was not only wife, but maid-of-all-work.

Seeing the advanced state of the preparations, Manasseh da Costa took his seat at the table; obeying her husband's significant glance, Mrs. Red-herring took up her position at the foot. The Rabbi himself sat down at the head, behind the dish. He always served, being the only person he could rely upon to gauge his capacities. Yankelé was left standing. The odour of the meat and potatoes impregnated the atmosphere with wistful poetry.

Suddenly the Rabbi looked up and perceived Yankelé. "Will you do as we do?" he said in seductive accents.

The *Schnorrer's* heart gave one wild, mad throb of joy. He laid his hand on the only other chair.

"I don't mind if I do," he said, with responsive amiability.

"Then go home and have *your* dinner," said the Rabbi.

Yankelé's wild heart-beat was exchanged for a stagnation as of death. A shiver ran down his spine. He darted an agonised appealing glance at Manasseh, who sniggered inscrutably.

"Oh, I don't tink I ought to go avay and leave you midout a tird man for grace," he said, in tones of prophetic rebuke. "Since I *be* here, it vould be a sin not to stay."

The Rabbi, having a certain connection with religion, was cornered; he was not able to repudiate such an opportunity of that more pious form of grace which needs the presence of three males.

"Oh, I should be very glad for you to stay," said the Rabbi, "but, unfortunately, we have only three meat-plates."

"Oh, de dish vill do for me."

"Very well, then!" said the Rabbi.

And Yankelé, with the old mad heart-beat, took the fourth chair, darting a triumphant glance at the still sniggering Manasseh.

The hostess rose, misunderstanding her husband's optical signals, and fished out a knife and fork from the recesses of a chiffonier. The host first heaped his own plate high with artistically coloured potatoes and stiff meat—less from discourtesy than from life-long habit—then divided the remainder in unequal portions between Manasseh and the little woman, in rough correspondence with their sizes. Finally, he handed Yankelé the empty dish.

"You see there is nothing left," he said simply. "We didn't even expect one visitor."

"First come, first served," observed Manasseh, with his sphinx-like expression, as he fell-to.

Yankelé sat frozen, staring blankly at the dish, his brain as empty. He had lost.

Such a dinner was a hollow mockery—like the dish. He could not expect Manasseh to accept it, quibbled he ever so cunningly. He sat for a minute or two as in a dream, the music of knife and fork ringing mockingly in his ears, his hungry palate moistened by the delicious savour. Then he shook off his stupor, and all his being was desperately astrain, questing for an idea. Manasseh discoursed with his host on neo-Hebrew literature.

"We thought of starting a journal at Grodno," said the Rabbi, "only the funds—"

"Be you den a native of Grodno?" interrupted Yankelé.

"Yes, I was born there," mumbled the Rabbi, "but I left there twenty years ago." His mouth was full, and he did not cease to ply the cutlery.

"Ah!" said Yankelé enthusiastically, "den you must be de famous preacher everybody speaks of. I do not remember you myself, for I vas a boy, but dey say ve haven't got no such preachers nowaday."

"In Grodno my husband kept a brandy shop," put in the hostess.

There was a bad quarter of a minute of silence. To Yankelé's relief, the Rabbi ended it by observing, "Yes, but doubtless the gentleman (you will excuse me calling you that, sir, I don't know your real name) alluded to my fame as a boy-Maggid. At the age of five I preached to audiences of many hundreds, and my manipulation of texts, my demonstrations that they did not mean what they said, drew tears even

ISRAEL ZANGWILL

from octogenarians familiar with the Torah from their earliest infancy. It was said there never was such a wonder-child since Ben Sira."

"But why did you give it up?" enquired Manasseh.

"It gave me up," said the Rabbi, putting down his knife and fork to expound an ancient grievance. "A boy-Maggid cannot last more than a few years. Up to nine I was still a draw, but every year the wonder grew less, and, when I was thirteen, my Bar-Mitzvah (confirmation) sermon occasioned no more sensation than those of the many other lads whose sermons I had written for them. I struggled along as boyishly as I could for some time after that, but it was in a losing cause. My age won on me daily. As it is said, 'I have been young, and now I am old.' In vain I composed the most eloquent addresses to be heard in Grodno. In vain I gave a course on the emotions, with explanations and instances from daily life—the fickle public preferred younger attractions. So at last I gave it up and sold *vodki*."

"Vat a pity! Vat a pity!" exclaimed Yankelé, "after vinning fame in de Torah!"

"But what is a man to do? He is not always a boy," replied the Rabbi. "Yes, I kept a brandy shop. That's what I call Degradation. But there is always balm in Gilead. I lost so much money over it that I had to emigrate to England, where, finding nothing else to do, I became a preacher again." He poured himself out a glass of *schnapps*, ignoring the water.

"I heard nothing of de *vodki* shop," said Yankelé; "it vas svallowed up in your earlier fame."

The Rabbi drained the glass of *schnapps*, smacked his lips, and resumed his knife and fork. Manasseh reached for the unoffered bottle, and helped himself liberally. The Rabbi unostentatiously withdrew it beyond his easy reach, looking at Yankelé the while.

"How long have you been in England?" he asked the Pole.

"Not long," said Yankelé.

"Ha! Does Gabriel the cantor still suffer from neuralgia?"

Yankelé looked sad. "No—he is dead," he said.

"Dear me! Well, he was tottering when I knew him. His blowing of the ram's horn got wheezier every year. And how is his young brother, Samuel?"

"He is dead!" said Yankelé.

"What, he too! Tut, tut! He was so robust. Has Mendelssohn, the stonemason, got many more girls?"

"He is dead!" said Yankelé.

"Nonsense!" gasped the Rabbi, dropping his knife and fork. "Why, I heard from him only a few months ago."

"He is dead!" said Yankelé.

"Good gracious me! Mendelssohn dead!" After a moment of emotion he resumed his meal. "But his sons and daughters are all doing well, I hope. The eldest, Solomon, was a most pious youth, and his third girl, Neshamah, promised to be a rare beauty."

"They are dead!" said Yankelé.

This time the Rabbi turned pale as a corpse himself. He laid down his knife and fork automatically.

"D—dead," he breathed in an awestruck whisper. "All?"

"Everyone. De same cholera took all de family."

The Rabbi covered his face with his hands. "Then poor Solomon's wife is a widow. I hope he left her enough to live upon."

"No, but it doesn't matter," said Yankelé.

"It matters a great deal," cried the Rabbi.

"She is dead," said Yankelé.

"Rebecca Schwartz dead!" screamed the Rabbi, for he had once loved the maiden himself, and, not having married her, had still a tenderness for her.

"Rebecca Schwartz," repeated Yankelé inexorably.

"Was it the cholera?" faltered the Rabbi.

"No, she vas heart-broke."

Rabbi Remorse Red-herring silently pushed his plate away, and leaned his elbows upon the table and his face upon his palms, and his chin upon the bottle of *schnapps* in mournful meditation.

"You are not eating, Rabbi," said Yankelé insinuatingly.

"I have lost my appetite," said the Rabbi.

"Vat a pity to let food get cold and spoil! You'd better eat it."

The Rabbi shook his head querulously.

"Den I vill eat it," cried Yankelé indignantly. "Good hot food like dat!"

"As you like," said the Rabbi wearily. And Yankelé began to eat at lightning speed, pausing only to wink at the inscrutable Manasseh; and to cast yearning glances at the inaccessible *schnapps* that supported the Rabbi's chin.

Presently the Rabbi looked up: "You're quite sure all these people are dead?" he asked with a dawning suspicion.

"May my blood be poured out like this *schnapps*," protested Yankelé, dislodging the bottle, and vehemently pouring the spirit into a tumbler, "if dey be not."

The Rabbi relapsed into his moody attitude, and retained it till his wife brought in a big willow-pattern china dish of stewed prunes and pippins. She produced four plates for these, and so Yankelé finished his meal in the unquestionable status of a first-class guest. The Rabbi was by this time sufficiently recovered to toy with two platefuls in a melancholy silence which he did not break till his mouth opened involuntarily to intone the grace.

When grace was over he turned to Manasseh and said, "And what was this way you were suggesting to me of getting a profitable Sephardic connection?"

"I did, indeed, wonder why you did not extend your practice as consolation preacher among the Spanish Jews," replied Manasseh gravely. "But after what we have just heard of the death-rate of Jews in Grodno, I should seriously advise you to go back there."

"No, they cannot forget that I was once a boy," replied the Rabbi with equal gravity. "I prefer the Spanish Jews. They are all well-to-do. They may not die so often as the Russians, but they die better, so to speak. You will give me introductions, you will speak of me to your illustrious friends, I understand."

"You understand!" repeated Manasseh in dignified astonishment. "You do not understand. I shall do no such thing."

"But you yourself suggested it!" cried the Rabbi excitedly.

"I? Nothing of the kind. I had heard of you and your ministrations to mourners, and meeting you in the street this afternoon for the first time, it struck me to enquire why you did not carry your consolations into the bosom of my community where so much more money is to be made. I said I wondered you had not done so from the first. And you—invited me to dinner. I still wonder. That is all, my good man." He rose to go.

The haughty rebuke silenced the Rabbi, though his heart was hot with a vague sense of injury.

"Do you come my way, Yankelé?" said Manasseh carelessly.

The Rabbi turned hastily to his second guest.

"When do you want me to marry you?" he asked.

"You have married me," replied Yankelé.

"I?" gasped the Rabbi. It was the last straw.

"Yes," reiterated Yankelé. "Hasn't he, Mr. da Costa?"

His heart went pit-a-pat as he put the question.

"Certainly," said Manasseh without hesitation.

Yankelé's face was made glorious summer. Only two of the quartette knew the secret of his radiance.

"There, Rabbi," he cried exultantly. "Good Sabbath!"

"Good Sabbath!" added Manasseh.

"Good Sabbath," dazedly murmured the Rabbi.

"Good Sabbath," added his wife.

"Congratulate me!" cried Yankelé when they got outside.

"On what?" asked Manasseh.

"On being your future son-in-law, of course."

"Oh, on *that*? Certainly, I congratulate you most heartily." The two *Schnorrers* shook hands. "I thought you were asking for compliments on your manoeuvring."

"Vy, doesn't it deserve dem?"

"No," said Manasseh magisterially.

"No?" queried Yankelé, his heart sinking again. "Vy not?"

"Why did you kill so many people?"

"Somebody must die dat I may live."

"You said that before," said Manasseh severely. "A good *Schnorrer* would not have slaughtered so many for his dinner. It is a waste of good material. And then you told lies!"

"How do you know they are not dead?" pleaded Yankelé.

The King shook his head reprovingly. "A first-class *Schnorrer* never lies," he laid it down.

"I might have made truth go as far as a lie—if you hadn't come to dinner yourself."

"What is that you say? Why, I came to encourage you by showing you how easy your task was."

"On de contrary, you made it much harder for me. Dere vas no dinner left."

"But against that you must reckon that since the Rabbi had already invited one person, he couldn't be so hard to tackle as I had fancied."

"Oh, but you must not judge from yourself," protested Yankelé. "You be not a *Schnorrer*—you be a miracle."

"But I should like a miracle for my son-in-law also," grumbled the King.

"And if you had to *schnorr* a son-in-law, you vould get a miracle," said Yankelé soothingly. "As he has to *schnorr* you, *he* gets the miracle."

"True," observed Manasseh musingly, "and I think you might therefore be very well content without the dowry."

"So I might," admitted Yankelé, "only *you* vould not be content to break your promise. I suppose I shall have some of de dowry on de marriage morning."

"On that morning you shall get my daughter—without fail. Surely that will be enough for one day!"

"Vell, ven do I get de money your daughter gets from de Synagogue?"

"When she gets it from the Synagogue, of course."

"How much vill it be?"

"It may be a hundred and fifty pounds," said Manasseh pompously. Yankelé's eyes sparkled.

"And it may be less," added Manasseh as an after-thought.

"How much less?" enquired Yankelé anxiously.

"A hundred and fifty pounds," repeated Manasseh pompously.

"D'you mean to say I may get noting?"

"Certainly, if she gets nothing. What I promised you was the money she gets from the Synagogue. Should she be fortunate enough in the *sorteo*—"

"De *sorteo*! Vat is dat?"

"The dowry I told you of. It is accorded by lot. My daughter has as good a chance as any other maiden. By winning her you stand to win a hundred and fifty pounds. It is a handsome amount. There are not many fathers who would do as much for their daughters," concluded Manasseh with conscious magnanimity.

"But about de Jerusalem estate!" said Yankelé, shifting his standpoint. "I don't vant to go and live dere. De Messiah is not yet come."

"No, you will hardly be able to live on it," admitted Manasseh.

"You do not object to my selling it, den?"

"Oh, no! If you are so sordid, if you have no true Jewish sentiment!"

"Ven can I come into possession?"

"On the wedding day if you like."

"One may as vell get it over," said Yankelé, suppressing a desire to rub his hands in glee. "As de Talmud says, 'One peppercorn to-day is better dan a basketful of pumpkins to-morrow.'"

"All right! I will bring it to the Synagogue."

"Bring it to de Synagogue!" repeated Yankelé in amaze. "Oh, you mean de deed of transfer."

"The deed of transfer! Do you think I waste my substance on solicitors? No, I will bring the property itself."

"But how can you do dat?"

"Where is the difficulty?" demanded Manasseh with withering contempt. "Surely a child could carry a casket of Jerusalem earth to Synagogue!"

"A casket of earth! Is your property in Jerusalem only a casket of earth?"

"What then? You didn't expect it would be a casket of diamonds?" retorted Manasseh, with gathering wrath. "To a true Jew a casket of Jerusalem earth is worth all the diamonds in the world."

"But your Jerusalem property is a fraud!" gasped Yankelé.

"Oh, no, you may be easy on that point. It's quite genuine. I know there is a good deal of spurious Palestine earth in circulation, and that many a dead man who has clods of it thrown into his tomb is nevertheless buried in unholy soil. But this casket I was careful to obtain from a Rabbi of extreme sanctity. It was the only thing he had worth *schnorring*."

"I don't suppose I shall get more dan a crown for it," said Yankelé, with irrepressible indignation.

"That's what I say," returned Manasseh; "and never did I think a son-in-law of mine would meditate selling my holy soil for a paltry five shillings! I will not withdraw my promise, but I am disappointed in you—bitterly disappointed. Had I known this earth was not to cover your bones, it should have gone down to the grave with me, as enjoined in my last will and testament, by the side of which it stands in my safe."

"Very vell, I von't sell it," said Yankelé sulkily.

"You relieve my soul. As the *Mishnah* says, 'He who marries a wife for money begets froward children.'"

"And vat about de province in England?" asked Yankelé, in low, despondent tones. He had never believed in *that*, but now, behind all his despair and incredulity, was a vague hope that something might yet be saved from the crash.

"Oh, you shall choose your own," replied Manasseh graciously. "We will get a large map of London, and I will mark off in red pencil the domain in which I *schnorr*. You will then choose any district in this— say, two main streets and a dozen byways and alleys—which shall be marked off in blue pencil, and whatever province of my kingdom you pick, I undertake not to *schnorr* in, from your wedding-day onwards. I need not tell you how valuable such a province already is; under careful administration, such as you would be able to give it, the revenue from it might be doubled, trebled. I do not think your tribute to me need be more than ten per cent."

Yankelé walked along mesmerised, reduced to somnambulism by his magnificently masterful patron.

"Oh, here we are!" said Manasseh, stopping short. "Won't you come in and see the bride, and wish her joy?"

A flash of joy came into Yankelé's own face, dissipating his glooms. After all there was always da Costa's beautiful daughter—a solid, substantial satisfaction. He was glad she was not an item of the dowry.

The unconscious bride opened the door.

"Ah, ha, Yankelé!" said Manasseh, his paternal heart aglow at the sight of her loveliness. "You will be not only a king, but a rich king. As it is written, 'Who is rich? He who hath a beautiful wife.'"

SHOWING HOW THE KING DISSOLVED
THE MAHAMAD

Manasseh da Costa (thus docked of his nominal plenitude in the solemn writ) had been summoned before the Mahamad, the intended union of his daughter with a Polish Jew having excited the liveliest horror and displeasure in the breasts of the Elders of the Synagogue. Such a Jew did not pronounce Hebrew as they did!

The Mahamad was a Council of Five, no less dread than the more notorious Council of Ten. Like the Venetian Tribunal, which has unjustly monopolised the attention of history, it was of annual election, and it was elected by a larger body of Elders, just as the Council of Ten was chosen by the aristocracy. "The gentlemen of the Mahamad," as they were styled, administered the affairs of the Spanish-Portuguese community, and their oligarchy would undoubtedly be a byword for all that is arbitrary and inquisitorial but for the widespread ignorance of its existence. To itself the Mahamad was the centre of creation. On one occasion it refused to bow even to the authority of the Lord Mayor of London. A Sephardic Jew lived and moved and had his being "by permission of the Mahamad." Without its consent he could have no legitimate place in the scheme of things. Minus "the permission of the Mahamad" he could not marry; with it he could be divorced readily. He might, indeed, die without the sanction of the Council of Five, but this was the only great act of his life which was free from its surveillance, and he could certainly not be buried save "by permission of the Mahamad." The Haham himself, the Sage or Chief Rabbi of the congregation, could not unite his flock in holy wedlock without the "permission of the Mahamad." And this authority was not merely negative and passive, it was likewise positive and active. To be a Yahid—a recognised congregant—one had to submit one's neck to a yoke more galling even than that of the Torah, to say nothing of the payment of Finta, or poll-tax. Woe to him who refused to be Warden of the Captives—he who ransomed the chained hostages of the Moorish Corsairs, or the war prisoners held in durance by the Turks—or to be President of the Congregation, or Parnass of the Holy Land, or Bridegroom of the Law, or any of the numerous dignitaries of a complex constitution. Fines, frequent and heavy—for the benefit of the poor-box—awaited him "by permission of the Mahamad." Unhappy the wight who misconducted himself in Synagogue "by offending the president, or grossly insulting any other person," as the ordinance deliciously ran. Penalties, stringent and harrying, visited these and other offences—deprivation of the "good deeds," of swathing the Holy Scroll, or opening the Ark; ignominious relegation to seats behind the reading-desk, withdrawal of the franchise, prohibition against shaving for a term of weeks! And if, accepting office, the Yahid failed in the punctual and regular discharge of his duties, he was mulcted and chastised none the less. A fine of forty pounds drove from the Synagogue Isaac Disraeli, collector of *Curiosities of Literature*, and made possible that curiosity of politics, the career of Lord Beaconsfield. The fathers of the Synagogue, who drew up their constitution in pure Castilian in the days when Pepys noted the indecorum in their little Synagogue in King Street, meant their statutes to cement, not thus to disintegrate, the community. 'Twas a tactless tyranny, this of the Mahamad, an inelastic administration of a cast-iron codex wrought "in good King Charles's golden days," when the colony of Dutch-Spanish exiles was as a camp in enemies' country, in need of military *régime*; and it co-operated with the attractions of an unhampered "Christian" career in driving many a brilliant family beyond the gates of the Ghetto, and into the pages of Debrett. Athens is always a dangerous rival to Sparta.

But the Mahamad itself moved strictly in the grooves of prescription. That legalistic instinct of the Hebrew, which had evolved the most gigantic and minute code of conduct in the world, had beguiled these latter-day Jews into super-adding to it a local legislation that grew into two hundred pages of Portuguese—an intertangled network of *Ascamot* or regulations, providing for every contingency of Synagogue politics, from the quarrels of members for the best seats down to the dimensions of their graves in the *Carreira*, from the distribution of "good deeds" among the rich to the distribution of Passover Cakes among the poor. If the wheels and pulleys of the communal life moved "by permission of the Mahamad," the Mahamad moved by permission of the *Ascamot*.

The Solemn Council was met—"in complete Mahamad." Even the Chief of the Elders was present, by virtue of his privilege, making a sixth; not to count the Chancellor or Secretary, who sat flutteringly fingering the Portuguese Minute Book on the right of the President. He was a little man, an odd medley of pomp and bluster, with a snuff-smeared upper lip, and a nose that had dipped in the wine when it was red. He had a grandiose sense of his own importance, but it was a pride that had its roots in humility, for he felt himself great because he was the servant of greatness. He lived "by permission of the Mahamad." As an official he was theoretically inaccessible. If you approached him on a matter he would put out his palms deprecatingly and pant, "I must consult the Mahamad." It was said of him that he had once been asked the time, and that he had automatically panted, "I must consult the Mahamad." This consultation was the merest form; in practice the Secretary had more influence than the Chief Rabbi, who was not allowed to recommend an applicant for charity, for the quaint reason that the respect entertained for him might unduly prejudice the Council in favour of his candidate. As no gentleman of the Mahamad could possibly master the statutes in his year of office, especially as only a rare member understood the Portuguese in which they had been ultimately couched, the Secretary was invariably referred to, for he was permanent, full of saws and precedents, and so he interpreted the law with impartial inaccuracy—"by permission of the Mahamad." In his heart of hearts he believed that the sun rose and the rain fell—"by permission of the Mahamad."

The Council Chamber was of goodly proportions, and was decorated by gold lettered panels, inscribed with the names of pious donors, thick as saints in a graveyard, overflowing even into the lobby. The flower and chivalry of the Spanish Jewry had sat round that Council-table, grandees who had plumed and ruffled it with the bloods of their day, clanking their swords with the best, punctilious withal and ceremonious, with the stately Castilian courtesy still preserved by the men who were met this afternoon, to whom their memory was as faint as the fading records of the panels. These descendants of theirs had still elaborate salutations and circumlocutions, and austere dignities of debate. "God-fearing men of capacity and respectability," as the *Ascama* demanded, they were also men of money, and it gave them a port and a repose. His Britannic Majesty graced the throne no better than the President of the Mahamad, seated at the head of the long table in his alcoved arm-chair, with the Chief of the Elders on his left, and the Chancellor on his right, and his Councillors all about him. The westering sun sent a pencil of golden light through the Norman windows as if anxious to record the names of those present in gilt letters—"by permission of the Mahamad."

"Let da Costa enter," said the President, when the agenda demanded the great *Schnorrer's* presence.

The Chancellor fluttered to his feet, fussily threw open the door, and beckoned vacancy with his finger till he discovered Manasseh was not in the lobby. The beadle came hurrying up instead.

"Where is da Costa?" panted the Chancellor. "Call da Costa."

"Da Costa!" sonorously intoned the beadle with the long-drawn accent of court ushers.

The corridor rang hollow, empty of Manasseh. "Why, he was here a moment ago," cried the bewildered beadle. He ran down the passage, and found him sure enough at the end of it where it abutted on the street. The King of *Schnorrers* was in dignified converse with a person of consideration.

"Da Costa!" the beadle cried again, but his tone was less awesome and more tetchy. The beggar did not turn his head.

"Mr. da Costa," said the beadle, now arrived too near the imposing figure to venture on familiarities with it. This time the beggar gave indications of restored hearing. "Yes, my man," he said, turning and advancing a few paces to meet the envoy. "Don't go, Grobstock," he called over his shoulder.

"Didn't you hear me calling?" grumbled the beadle.

"I heard you calling da Costa, but I naturally imagined it was one of your drinking companions," replied Manasseh severely.

"The Mahamad is waiting for you," faltered the beadle.

"Tell *the gentlemen* of the Mahamad," said Manasseh, with reproving emphasis, "that I shall do myself the pleasure of being with them presently. Nay, pray don't hurry away, my dear Grobstock," he went on, resuming his place at the German magnate's side—"and so your wife is taking the waters at Tunbridge Wells. In faith, 'tis an excellent regimen for the vapours. I am thinking of sending my wife to Buxton— the warden of our hospital has his country-seat there."

"But you are wanted," murmured Grobstock, who was anxious to escape. He had caught the *Schnorrer's* eye as its owner sunned himself in the archway, and it held him.

"'Tis only a meeting of the Mahamad I have to attend," he said indifferently. "Rather a nuisance—but duty is duty."

Grobstock's red face became a setting for two expanded eyes.

"I thought the Mahamad was your chief Council," he exclaimed.

"Yes, there are only five of us," said Manasseh lightly, and, while Grobstock gaped incredulous, the Chancellor himself shambled up in pale consternation.

"You are keeping the gentlemen of the Mahamad waiting," he panted imperiously.

"Ah, you are right, Grobstock," said Manasseh with a sigh of resignation. "They cannot get on without me. Well, you will excuse me, I know. I am glad to have seen you again—we shall finish our chat at your house some evening, shall we? I have agreeable recollections of your hospitality."

"My wife will be away all this month," Grobstock repeated feebly.

"Ha! ha! ha!" laughed Manasseh roguishly. "Thank you for the reminder. I shall not fail to aid you in taking advantage of her absence. Perhaps mine will be away, too—at Buxton. Two bachelors, ha! ha! ha!" and, proffering his hand, he shook Grobstock's in gracious farewell. Then he sauntered leisurely in the wake of the feverishly impatient Chancellor, his staff tapping the stones in measured tardiness.

"Good afternoon, gentlemen," he observed affably as he entered the Council Chamber.

"You have kept us waiting," sharply rejoined the President of the Mahamad, ruffled out of his regal suavity. He was a puffy, swarthy personage, elegantly attired, and he leaned forward on his velvet throne, tattooing on the table with bediamonded fingers.

"Not so long as you have kept *me* waiting," said Manasseh with quiet resentment. "If I had known you expected me to cool my heels in the corridor I should not have come, and, had not my friend the Treasurer of the Great Synagogue opportunely turned up to chat with me, I should not have stayed."

"You are impertinent, sir," growled the President.

"I think, sir, it is you who owe me an apology," maintained Manasseh unflinchingly, "and, knowing the courtesy and high breeding which has always distinguished your noble family, I can only explain your present tone by your being unaware I have a grievance. No doubt it is your Chancellor who cited me to appear at too early an hour."

The President, cooled by the quiet dignity of the beggar, turned a questioning glance upon the outraged Chancellor, who was crimson and quivering with confusion and indignation.

"It is usual t-t-to summon persons before the c-c-commencement of the meeting," he stammered hotly. "We cannot tell how long the prior business will take."

"Then I would respectfully submit to the Chief of the Elders," said Manasseh, "that at the next meeting of his august body he move a resolution that persons cited to appear before the Mahamad shall take precedence of all other business."

The Chief of the Elders looked helplessly at the President of the Mahamad, who was equally at sea. "However, I will not press that point now," added Manasseh, "nor will I draw the attention of the committee to the careless, perfunctory manner in which the document summoning me was drawn up, so that, had I been a stickler for accuracy, I need not have answered to the name of Manasseh da Costa."

"But that *is* your name," protested the Chancellor.

"If you will examine the Charity List," said Manasseh magnificently, "you will see that my name is Manasseh Bueno Barzillai Azevedo da Costa. But you are keeping the gentlemen of the Mahamad waiting." And with a magnanimous air of dismissing the past, he seated himself on the nearest empty chair at the foot of the table, leaned his elbows on the table, and his face on his hands, and gazed across at the President immediately opposite. The Councillors were so taken aback by his unexpected bearing that this additional audacity was scarcely noted. But the Chancellor, wounded in his inmost instincts, exclaimed irately, "Stand up, sir. These chairs are for the gentlemen of the Mahamad."

"And being gentlemen," added Manasseh crushingly, "they know better than to keep an old man on his legs any longer."

"If you were a gentleman," retorted the Chancellor, "you would take that thing off your head."

"If you were not a Man-of-the-Earth," rejoined the beggar, "you would know that it is not a mark of disrespect for the Mahamad, but of respect for the Law, which is higher than the Mahamad. The rich man can afford to neglect our holy religion, but the poor man has only the Law. It is his sole luxury."

The pathetic tremor in his voice stirred a confused sense of wrong-doing and injustice in the Councillors' breasts. The President felt vaguely that the edge of his coming impressive rebuke had been turned, if, indeed, he did not sit rebuked instead. Irritated, he turned on the Chancellor, and bade him hold his peace.

"He means well," said Manasseh deprecatingly. "He cannot be expected to have the fine instincts of the gentlemen of the Mahamad.

May I ask you, sir," he concluded, "to proceed with the business for which you have summoned me? I have several appointments to keep with clients."

The President's bediamonded fingers recommenced their ill-tempered tattoo; he was fuming inwardly with a sense of baffled wrath, of righteous indignation made unrighteous. "Is it true, sir," he burst forth at last in the most terrible accents he could command in the circumstances, "that you meditate giving your daughter in marriage to a Polish Jew?"

"No," replied Manasseh curtly.

"No?" articulated the President, while a murmur of astonishment went round the table at this unexpected collapse of the whole case.

"Why, your daughter admitted it to my wife," said the Councillor on Manasseh's right.

Manasseh turned to him, expostulant, tilting his chair and body towards him. "My daughter is going to marry a Polish Jew," he explained with argumentative forefinger, "but I do not meditate giving her to him."

"Oh, then, you will refuse your consent," said the Councillor, hitching his chair back so as to escape the beggar's progressive propinquity. "By no means," quoth Manasseh in surprised accents, as he drew his chair nearer again, "I have already consented. I do not *meditate* consenting. That word argues an inconclusive attitude."

"None of your quibbles, sirrah," cried the President, while a scarlet flush mantled on his dark countenance. "Do you not know that the union you contemplate is disgraceful and degrading to you, to your daughter, and to the community which has done so much for you? What! A Sephardi marry a Tedesco! Shameful."

"And do you think I do not feel the shame as deeply as you?" enquired Manasseh, with infinite pathos. "Do you think, gentlemen, that I have not suffered from this passion of a Tedesco for my daughter? I came here expecting your sympathy, and do you offer me reproach? Perhaps you think, sir"—here he turned again to his right-hand neighbour, who, in his anxiety to evade his pertinacious proximity, had half-wheeled his chair round, offering only his back to the argumentative forefinger—"perhaps you think, because I have consented, that I cannot condole with you, that I am not at one with you in lamenting this blot on our common 'scutcheon; perhaps you think"—here he adroitly twisted his chair into argumentative position on the other side of the Councillor, rounding him like a cape—"that, because you have no sympathy with my tribulation, I have no sympathy with yours. But, if I have consented, it is only because it was the best I could do for my daughter. In my heart of hearts I have repudiated her, so that she may practically be considered an orphan, and, as such, a fit person to receive the marriage dowry bequeathed by Rodriguez Real, peace be upon him."

"This is no laughing matter, sir," thundered the President, stung into forgetfulness of his dignity by thinking too much of it.

"No, indeed," said Manasseh sympathetically, wheeling to the right so as to confront the President, who went on stormily, "Are you aware, sir, of the penalties you risk by persisting in your course?"

"I risk no penalties," replied the beggar.

"Indeed! Then do you think anyone may trample with impunity upon our ancient *Ascamot*?"

"Our ancient *Ascamot*!" repeated Manasseh in surprise. "What have they to say against a Sephardi marrying a Tedesco?"

The audacity of the question rendered the Council breathless. Manasseh had to answer it himself.

"They have nothing to say. There is no such *Ascama*." There was a moment of awful silence. It was as though he had disavowed the Decalogue.

"Do you question the first principle of our constitution?" said the President at last, in low, ominous tones. "Do you deny that your daughter is a traitress? Do you—?"

"Ask your Chancellor," calmly interrupted Manasseh. "He is a Man-of-the-Earth, but he should know your statutes, and he will tell you that my daughter's conduct is nowhere forbidden."

"Silence, sir," cried the President testily. "Mr. Chancellor, read the *Ascama*."

The Chancellor wriggled on his chair, his face flushing and paling by turns; all eyes were bent upon him in anxious suspense. He hemmed and ha'd and coughed, and took snuff, and blew his nose elaborately.

"There is n-n-no express *Ascama*," he stuttered at last. Manasseh sat still, in unpretentious triumph.

The Councillor who was now become his right-hand neighbour was the first to break the dazed silence, and it was his first intervention.

"Of course, it was never actually put into writing," he said in stern reproof. "It has never been legislated against, because it has never been conceived possible. These things are an instinct with every right-minded Sephardi. Have we ever legislated against marrying Christians?"

Manasseh veered round half a point of the compass, and fixed the new opponent with his argumentative forefinger. "Certainly we have," he replied unexpectedly. "In Section XX, Paragraph II." He quoted the *Ascama* by heart, rolling out the sonorous Portuguese like a solemn indictment. "If our legislators had intended to prohibit intermarriage with the German community, they would have prohibited it."

"There is the Traditional Law as well as the Written," said the Chancellor, recovering himself. "It is so in our holy religion, it is so in our constitution."

"Yes, there are precedents assuredly," cried the President eagerly.

"There is the case of one of our Treasurers in the time of George II.," said the little Chancellor, blossoming under the sunshine of the President's encouragement, and naming the ancestor of a Duchess of to-day. "He wanted to marry a beautiful German Jewess."

"And was interdicted," said the President.

"Hem!" coughed the Chancellor. "He—he was only permitted to marry her under humiliating conditions. The Elders forbade the attendance of the members of the House of Judgment, or of the Cantors; no celebration was to take place in the *Snoga*; no offerings were to be made for the bridegroom's health, nor was he even to receive the bridegroom's call to the reading of the Law."

"But the Elders will not impose any such conditions on my son-in-law," said Manasseh, skirting round another chair so as to bring his forefinger to play upon the Chief of the Elders, on whose left he had now arrived in his argumentative advances. "In the first place he is not one of us. His desire to join us is a compliment. If anyone has offended your traditions, it is my daughter. But then she is not a male, like the Treasurer cited; she is not an active agent, she has not gone out of her way to choose a Tedesco—she has been chosen. Your masculine precedents cannot touch her."

"Ay, but we can touch you," said the contemporary Treasurer, guffawing grimly. He sat opposite Manasseh, and next to the Chancellor.

"Is it fines you are thinking of?" said Manasseh with a scornful glance across the table. "Very well, fine me—if you can afford it. You know that I am a student, a son of the Law, who has no resources but what you allow him. If you care to pay this fine it is your affair. There is always room in the poor-box. I am always glad to hear of fines. You had better make up your mind to the inevitable, gentlemen. Have I not had to do it? There is no *Ascama* to prevent my son-in-law having all the usual privileges—in fact, it was to ask that he might receive the bridegroom's call to the Law on the Sabbath before his marriage that I really came. By Section III, Paragraph I, you are empowered to admit any person about to marry the daughter of a Yahid." Again the sonorous Portuguese rang out, thrilling the Councillors with all that quintessential awfulness of ancient statutes in a tongue not understood. It was not till a quarter of a century later that the *Ascamot* were translated into English, and from that moment their authority was doomed.

The Chancellor was the first to recover from the quotation. Daily contact with these archaic sanctities had dulled his awe, and the President's impotent irritation spurred him to action.

"But you are *not* a Yahid," he said quietly. "By Paragraph V. of the same section, any one whose name appears on the Charity List ceases to be a Yahid."

"And a vastly proper law," said Manasseh with irony. "Everybody may vote but the *Schnorrer*." And, ignoring the Chancellor's point at great length, he remarked confidentially to the Chief of the Elders, at whose elbow he was still encamped, "It is curious how few of your Elders perceive that those who take the charity are the pillars of the Synagogue. What keeps your community together? Fines. What ensures respect for your constitution? Fines. What makes every man do his duty? Fines. What rules this very Mahamad? Fines. And it is the poor who provide an outlet for all these moneys. Egad, do you think your members would for a moment tolerate your penalties, if they did not know the money was laid out in 'good deeds'? Charity is the salt of riches, says the Talmud, and, indeed, it is the salt that preserves your community."

"Have done, sir, have done!" shouted the President, losing all regard for those grave amenities of the ancient Council Chamber which Manasseh did his best to maintain. "Do you forget to whom you are talking?"

"I am talking to the Chief of the Elders," said Manasseh in a wounded tone, "but if you would like me to address myself to you—" and wheeling round the Chief of the Elders, he landed his chair next to the President's.

"Silence, fellow!" thundered the President, shrinking spasmodically from his confidential contact. "You have no right to a voice at all; as the Chancellor has reminded us, you are not even a Yahid, a congregant."

"Then the laws do not apply to me," retorted the beggar quietly. "It is only the Yahid who is privileged to do this, who is prohibited from doing that. No *Ascama* mentions the *Schnorrer*, or gives you any authority over him."

"On the contrary," said the Chancellor, seeing the President disconcerted again, "he is bound to attend the weekday services. But this man hardly ever does, sir." "I *never* do," corrected Manasseh, with touching sadness. "That is another of the privileges I have to forego in order to take your charity; I cannot risk appearing to my Maker in the light of a mercenary."

"And what prevents you taking your turn in the graveyard watches?" sneered the Chancellor.

The antagonists were now close together, one on either side of the President of the Mahamad, who was wedged between the two bobbing, quarrelling figures, his complexion altering momently for the blacker, and his fingers working nervously.

"What prevents me?" replied Manasseh. "My age. It would be a sin against heaven to spend a night in the cemetery. If the body-snatchers did come they might find a corpse to their hand in the watch-tower. But I do my duty—I always pay a substitute."

"No doubt," said the Treasurer. "I remember your asking me for the money to keep an old man out of the cemetery. Now I see what you meant."

"Yes," began two others, "and I—"

"Order, gentlemen, order," interrupted the President desperately, for the afternoon was flitting, the sun was setting, and the shadows of twilight were falling. "You must not argue with the man. Hark you, my fine fellow, we refuse to sanction this marriage; it shall not be performed by our ministers, nor can we dream of admitting your son-in-law as a Yahid."

"Then admit him on your Charity List," said Manasseh.

"We are more likely to strike *you* off! And, by gad!" cried the President, tattooing on the table with his whole fist, "if you don't stop this scandal instanter, we will send you howling."

"Is it excommunication you threaten?" said Manasseh, rising to his feet. There was a menacing glitter in his eye.

"This scandal must be stopped," repeated the President, agitatedly rising in involuntary imitation.

"Any member of the Mahamad could stop it in a twinkling," said Manasseh sullenly. "You yourself, if you only chose."

"If I only chose?" echoed the President enquiringly.

"If you only chose my daughter. Are you not a bachelor? I am convinced she could not say nay to anyone present—excepting the Chancellor. Only no one is really willing to save the community from this scandal, and so my daughter must marry as best she can. And yet, it is a handsome creature who would not disgrace even a house in Hackney."

Manasseh spoke so seriously that the President fumed the more. "Let her marry this Pole," he ranted, "and you shall be cut off from us in life and death. Alive, you shall worship without our walls, and dead you shall be buried 'behind the boards.'"

"For the poor man—excommunication," said Manasseh in ominous soliloquy. "For the rich man—permission to marry the Tedesco of his choice."

"Leave the room, fellow," vociferated the President. "You have heard our ultimatum!"

But Manasseh did not quail.

"And you shall hear mine," he said, with a quietness that was the more impressive for the President's fury. "Do not forget, Mr. President, that you and I owe allegiance to the same brotherhood. Do not forget that the power which made you can unmake you at the next election; do not forget that if I have no vote I have vast influence; that there is not a Yahid whom I do not visit weekly; that there is not a *Schnorrer* who would not follow me in my exile. Do not forget that there is another community to turn to—yes! that very Ashkenazic community you contemn—with the Treasurer of which I talked but just now; a community that waxes daily in wealth and greatness while you sleep in your sloth." His tall form dominated the chamber, his head seemed to touch the ceiling. The Councillors sat dazed as amid a lightning-storm.

"Jackanapes! Blasphemer! Shameless renegade!" cried the President, choking with wrath. And being already on his legs, he dashed to the bell and tugged at it madly, blanching the Chancellor's face with the perception of a lost opportunity.

"I shall not leave this chamber till I choose," said Manasseh, dropping stolidly into the nearest chair and folding his arms.

At once a cry of horror and consternation rose from every throat, every man leapt threateningly to his feet, and Manasseh realised that he was throned on the alcoved arm-chair!

But he neither blenched nor budged.

"Nay, keep your seats, gentlemen," he said quietly.

The President, turning at the stir, caught sight of the *Schnorrer*, staggered and clutched at the mantel. The Councillors stood spellbound for an instant, while the Chancellor's eyes roved wildly round the walls, as if expecting the gold names to start from their panels. The beadle rushed in, terrified by the strenuous tintinnabulation, looked instinctively towards the throne for orders, then underwent petrifaction on the threshold, and stared speechless at Manasseh, what time the President, gasping like a landed cod, vainly strove to utter the order for the beggar's expulsion.

"Don't stare at me, Gomez," Manasseh cried imperiously. "Can't you see the President wants a glass of water?"

The beadle darted a glance at the President, and, perceiving his condition, rushed out again to get the water.

This was the last straw. To see his authority usurped as well as his seat maddened the poor President. For some seconds he strove to mouth an oath, embracing his supine Councillors as well as this beggar on horseback, but he produced only an inarticulate raucous cry, and reeled sideways. Manasseh sprang from his chair and caught the falling form in his arms. For one terrible moment he stood supporting it in a tense silence, broken only by the incoherent murmurs of the unconscious lips; then crying angrily, "Bestir yourselves, gentlemen, don't you see the President is ill?" he dragged his burden towards the table, and, aided by the panic-stricken Councillors, laid it flat thereupon, and threw open the ruffled shirt. He swept the Minute Book to the floor with an almost malicious movement, to make room for the President.

The beadle returned with the glass of water, which he well-nigh dropped.

"Run for a physician," Manasseh commanded, and throwing away the water carelessly, in the Chancellor's direction, he asked if anyone had any brandy. There was no response.

"Come, come, Mr. Chancellor," he said, "bring out your phial." And the abashed functionary obeyed.

"Has any of you his equipage without?" Manasseh demanded next of the Mahamad.

They had not, so Manasseh despatched the Chief of the Elders in quest of a sedan chair. Then there was nothing left but to await the physician.

"You see, gentlemen, how insecure is earthly power," said the *Schnorrer* solemnly, while the President breathed stertorously, deaf to his impressive moralising. "It is swallowed up in an instant, as Lisbon was engulfed. Cursed are they who despise the poor. How is the saying of our sages verified—'The house that opens not to the poor opens to the physician.'" His eyes shone with unearthly radiance in the gathering gloom.

The cowed assembly wavered before his words, like reeds before the wind, or conscience-stricken kings before fearless prophets.

When the physician came he pronounced that the President had had a slight stroke of apoplexy, involving a temporary paralysis of the right foot. The patient, by this time restored to consciousness, was conveyed home in the sedan chair, and the Mahamad dissolved in confusion. Manasseh was the last to leave the Council Chamber. As he stalked into the corridor he turned the key in the door behind him with a vindictive twist. Then, plunging his hand into his breeches-pocket, he gave the beadle a crown, remarking genially, "You must have your usual perquisite, I suppose."

The beadle was moved to his depths. He had a burst of irresistible honesty. "The President gives me only half-a-crown," he murmured.

"Yes, but he may not be able to attend the next meeting," said Manasseh. "And I may be away, too."

VI

Showing How the King Enriched the Synagogue

The Synagogue of the Gates of Heaven was crowded—members, orphan boys, *Schnorrers*, all were met in celebration of the Sabbath. But the President of the Mahamad was missing. He was still inconvenienced by the effects of his stroke, and deemed it most prudent to pray at home. The Council of Five had not met since Manasseh had dissolved it, and so the matter of his daughter's marriage was left hanging, as indeed was not seldom the posture of matters discussed by Sephardic bodies. The authorities thus passive, Manasseh found scant difficulty in imposing his will upon the minor officers, less ready than himself with constitutional precedent. His daughter was to be married under the Sephardic canopy, and no jot of synagogual honour was to be bated the bridegroom. On this Sabbath—the last before the wedding—Yankelé was to be called to the Reading of the Law like a true-born Portuguese. He made his first appearance in the Synagogue of his bride's fathers with a feeling of solemn respect, not exactly due to Manasseh's grandiose references to the ancient temple. He had walked the courtyard with levity, half prepared, from previous experience of his intended father-in-law, to find the glories insubstantial. Their unexpected actuality awed him, and he was glad he was dressed in his best. His beaver hat, green trousers, and brown coat equalled him with the massive pillars, the gleaming candelabra, and the stately roof. Da Costa, for his part, had made no change in his attire; he dignified his shabby vestments, stuffing them with royal manhood, and wearing his snuff-coloured over-garment like a purple robe. There was, in sooth, an official air about his habiliment, and to the worshippers it was as impressively familiar as the black stole and white bands of the Cantor. It seemed only natural that he should be called to the Reading first, quite apart from the fact that he was a *Cohen*, of the family of Aaron, the High Priest, a descent that, perhaps, lent something to the loftiness of his carriage.

When the Minister intoned vigorously, "The good name, Manasseh, the son of Judah, the Priest, the man, shall arise to read in the Law,"

ISRAEL ZANGWILL

every eye was turned with a new interest on the prospective father-in-law. Manasseh arose composedly, and, hitching his sliding prayer-shawl over his left shoulder, stalked to the reading platform, where he chanted the blessings with imposing flourishes, and stood at the Minister's right hand while his section of the Law was read from the sacred scroll. There was many a man of figure in the congregation, but none who became the platform better. It was beautiful to see him pay his respects to the scroll; it reminded one of the meeting of two sovereigns. The great moment, however, was when, the section being concluded, the Master Reader announced Manasseh's donations to the Synagogue. The financial statement was incorporated in a long Benediction, like a coin wrapped up in folds of paper. This was always a great moment, even when inconsiderable personalities were concerned, each man's generosity being the subject of speculation before and comment after. Manasseh, it was felt, would, although a mere *Schnorrer*, rise to the height of the occasion, and offer as much as seven and sixpence. The shrewder sort suspected he would split it up into two or three separate offerings, to give an air of inexhaustible largess.

The shrewder sort were right and wrong, as is their habit.

The Master Reader began his quaint formula, "May He who blessed our Fathers," pausing at the point where the Hebrew is blank for the amount. He span out the prefatory "Who vows"—the last note prolonging itself, like the vibration of a tuning-fork, at a literal pitch of suspense. It was a sensational halt, due to his forgetting the amounts or demanding corroboration at the eleventh hour, and the stingy often recklessly amended their contributions, panic-struck under the pressure of imminent publicity.

"Who vows—" The congregation hung upon his lips. With his usual gesture of interrogation, he inclined his ear towards Manasseh's mouth, his face wearing an unusual look of perplexity; and those nearest the platform were aware of a little colloquy between the *Schnorrer* and the Master Reader, the latter bewildered and agitated, the former stately. The delay had discomposed the Master as much as it had whetted the curiosity of the congregation. He repeated:

"Who vows—*cinco livras*"—he went on glibly without a pause—"for charity—for the life of Yankov ben Yitzchok, his son-in-law, &c., &c." But few of the worshippers heard any more than the *cinco livras* (five pounds). A thrill ran through the building. Men pricked up their ears, incredulous, whispering one another. One man deliberately moved from his place towards the box in which sat the Chief of the Elders, the presiding dignitary in the absence of the President of the Mahamad.

"I didn't catch—how much was that?" he asked.

"Five pounds," said the Chief of the Elders shortly. He suspected an irreverent irony in the Beggar's contribution.

The Benediction came to an end, but ere the hearers had time to realise the fact, the Master Reader had started on another. "May He who blessed our fathers!" he began, in the strange traditional recitative. The wave of curiosity mounted again, higher than before.

"Who vows—"

The wave hung an instant, poised and motionless.

"*Cinco livras!*"

The wave broke in a low murmur, amid which the Master imperturbably proceeded, "For oil—for the life of his daughter Deborah, &c." When he reached the end there was a poignant silence.

Was it to be *da capo* again?

"May He who blessed our fathers!"

The wave of curiosity surged once more, rising and subsiding with this ebb and flow of financial Benediction.

"Who vows—*cinco livras*—for the wax candles."

This time the thrill, the whisper, the flutter, swelled into a positive buzz. The gaze of the entire congregation was focussed upon the Beggar, who stood impassive in the blaze of glory. Even the orphan boys, packed in their pew, paused in their inattention to the Service, and craned their necks towards the platform. The veriest magnates did not thus play piety with five pound points. In the ladies' gallery the excitement was intense. The occupants gazed eagerly through the grille. One woman—a buxom dame of forty summers, richly clad and jewelled—had risen, and was tiptoeing frantically over the woodwork, her feather waving like a signal of distress. It was Manasseh's wife. The waste of money maddened her, each donation hit her like a poisoned arrow; in vain she strove to catch her spouse's eye. The air seemed full of gowns and toques and farthingales flaming away under her very nose, without her being able to move hand or foot in rescue; whole wardrobes perished at each Benediction. It was with the utmost difficulty she restrained herself from shouting down to her prodigal lord. At her side the radiant Deborah vainly tried to pacify her by assurances that Manasseh never intended to pay up.

"Who vows—" The Benediction had begun for a fourth time.

"*Cinco livras* for the Holy Land." And the sensation grew. "For the life of this holy congregation, &c."

The Master Reader's voice droned on impassively, interminably.

The fourth Benediction was drawing to its close, when the beadle was seen to mount the platform and whisper in his ear. Only Manasseh overheard the message.

"The Chief of the Elders says you must stop. This is mere mockery. The man is a *Schnorrer*, an impudent beggar."

The beadle descended the steps, and after a moment of inaudible discussion with da Costa, the Master Reader lifted up his voice afresh.

The Chief of the Elders frowned and clenched his praying-shawl angrily. It was a fifth Benediction! But the Reader's sing-song went on, for Manasseh's wrath was nearer than the magnate's.

"Who vows—*cinco livras*—for the Captives—for the life of the Chief of the Elders!"

The Chief bit his lip furiously at this delicate revenge; galled almost to frenzy by the aggravating foreboding that the congregation would construe his message as a solicitation of the polite attention. For it was of the amenities of the Synagogue for rich people to present these Benedictions to one another. And so the endless stream of donatives flowed on, provoking the hearers to fever pitch. The very orphan boys forgot that this prolongation of the service was retarding their breakfasts indefinitely. Every warden, dignitary and official, from the President of the Mahamad down to the very Keeper of the Bath, was honoured by name in a special Benediction, the chief of Manasseh's weekly patrons were repaid almost in kind on this unique and festive occasion. Most of the congregation kept count of the sum total, which was mounting, mounting . . .

Suddenly there was a confusion in the ladies' gallery, cries, a babble of tongues. The beadle hastened upstairs to impose his authority. The rumour circulated that Mrs. da Costa had fainted and been carried out. It reached Manasseh's ears, but he did not move. He stood at his post, unfaltering, donating, blessing.

"Who vows—*cinco livras*—for the life of his wife, Sarah!" And a faint sardonic smile flitted across the Beggar's face.

The oldest worshipper wondered if the record would be broken. Manasseh's benefactions were approaching thrillingly near the highest total hitherto reached by any one man upon any one occasion. Every brain was troubled by surmises. The Chief of the Elders, fuming impotently, was not alone in apprehending a blasphemous mockery; but the bulk imagined that the *Schnorrer* had come into property or had always been a man of substance, and was now taking this means of restoring to the Synagogue the funds he had drawn from it. And the fountain of Benevolence played on.

The record figure was reached and left in the rear. When at length the poor Master Reader, sick unto death of the oft-repeated formula (which might just as well have covered all the contributions the first time, though Manasseh had commanded each new Benediction as if by an after-thought), was allowed to summon the Levite who succeeded Manasseh, the Synagogue had been enriched by a hundred pounds. The last Benediction had been coupled with the name of the poorest *Schnorrer* present—an assertion and glorification of Manasseh's own order that put the coping-stone on this sensational memorial of the Royal Wedding. It was, indeed, a kingly munificence, a sovereign graciousness. Nay, before the Service was over, Manasseh even begged the Chief of the Elders to permit a special *Rogation* to be said for a sick person. The Chief, meanly snatching at this opportunity of reprisals, refused, till, learning that Manasseh alluded to the ailing President of the Mahamad, he collapsed ingloriously.

But the real hero of the day was Yankelé, who shone chiefly by reflected light, but yet shone even more brilliantly than the Spaniard, for to him was added the double lustre of the bridegroom and the stranger, and he was the cause and centre of the sensation.

His eyes twinkled continuously throughout.

The next day, Manasseh fared forth to collect the hundred pounds!

The day being Sunday, he looked to find most of his clients at home. He took Grobstock first as being nearest, but the worthy speculator and East India Director espied him from an upper window, and escaped by a back-door into Goodman's Fields—a prudent measure, seeing that the incredulous Manasseh ransacked the house in quest of him. Manasseh's manner was always a search-warrant.

The King consoled himself by paying his next visit to a personage who could not possibly evade him—none other than the sick President of the Mahamad. He lived in Devonshire Square, in solitary splendour. Him Manasseh bearded in his library, where the convalescent was sorting his collection of prints. The visitor had had himself announced as a gentleman on synagogual matters, and the public-spirited President had not refused himself to the business. But when he caught sight of

Manasseh, his puffy features were distorted, he breathed painfully, and put his hand to his hip.

"You!" he gasped.

"Have a care, my dear sir! Have a care!" said Manasseh anxiously, as he seated himself. "You are still weak. To come to the point—for I would not care to distract too much a man indispensable to the community, who has already felt the hand of the Almighty for his treatment of the poor—"

He saw that his words were having effect, for these prosperous pillars of the Synagogue were mightily superstitious under affliction, and he proceeded in gentler tones. "To come to the point, it is my duty to inform you (for I am the only man who is certain of it) that while you have been away our Synagogue has made a bad debt!"

"A bad debt!" An angry light leapt into the President's eyes. There had been an ancient practice of lending out the funds to members, and the President had always set his face against the survival of the policy. "It would not have been made had I been there!" he cried.

"No, indeed," admitted Manasseh. "You would have stopped it in its early stages. The Chief of the Elders tried, but failed."

"The dolt!" cried the President. "A man without a backbone. How much is it?"

"A hundred pounds!"

"A hundred pounds!" echoed the President, seriously concerned at this blot upon his year of office. "And who is the debtor?"

"I am."

"You! You have borrowed a hundred pounds, you—you jackanapes!"

"Silence, sir! How dare you? I should leave this apartment at once, were it not that I cannot go without your apology. Never in my life have I borrowed a hundred pounds—nay, never have I borrowed one farthing. I am no borrower. If you are a gentleman, you will apologise!"

"I am sorry if I misunderstood," murmured the poor President, "but how, then, do you owe the money?"

"How, then?" repeated Manasseh impatiently. "Cannot you understand that I have donated it to the Synagogue?"

The President stared at him open-mouthed.

"I vowed it yesterday in celebration of my daughter's marriage."

The President let a sigh of relief pass through his open mouth. He was even amused a little.

"Oh, is that all? It was like your deuced effrontery; but still, the Synagogue doesn't lose anything. There's no harm done."

"What is that you say?" enquired Manasseh sternly. "Do you mean to say I am not to pay this money?"

"How can you?"

"How can I? I come to you and others like you to pay it for me."

"Nonsense! Nonsense!" said the President, beginning to lose his temper again. "We'll let it pass. There's no harm done."

"And this is the President of the Mahamad!" soliloquised the *Schnorrer* in bitter astonishment. "This is the chief of our ancient, godly Council! What, sir! Do you hold words spoken solemnly in Synagogue of no account? Would you have me break my solemn vow? Do you wish to bring the Synagogue institutions into contempt? Do you—a man already once stricken by Heaven—invite its chastisement again?"

The President had grown pale—his brain was reeling.

"Nay, ask its forgiveness, sir," went on the King implacably; "and make good this debt of mine in token of your remorse, as it is written, 'And repentance, and prayer, and *charity* avert the evil decree.'"

"Not a penny!" cried the President, with a last gleam of lucidity, and strode furiously towards the bell-pull. Then he stood still in sudden recollection of a similar scene in the Council Chamber.

"You need not trouble to ring for a stroke," said Manasseh grimly. "Then the Synagogue is to be profaned, then even the Benediction which I in all loyalty and forgiveness caused to be said for the recovery of the President of the Mahamad is to be null, a mockery in the sight of the Holy One, blessed be He!"

The President tottered into his reading-chair.

"How much did you vow on my behalf?"

"Five pounds."

The President precipitately drew out a pocket-book and extracted a crisp Bank of England note.

"Give it to the Chancellor," he breathed, exhausted.

"I am punished," quoth Manasseh plaintively as he placed it in his bosom. "I should have vowed ten for you." And he bowed himself out.

In like manner did he collect other contributions that day from Sephardic celebrities, pointing out that now a foreign Jew—Yankelé to wit—had been admitted to their communion, it behoved them to show themselves at their best. What a bad effect it would have on Yankelé if a Sephardi was seen to vow with impunity! First impressions were everything, and they could not be too careful. It would not do for Yankelé to circulate contumelious reports of them among his kin. Those who remonstrated with him over his extravagance he reminded that he had only one daughter, and he drew their attention to the favourable influence his example had had on the Saturday receipts. Not a man of those who came after him in the Reading had ventured to offer half-crowns. He had fixed the standard in gold for that day at least, and who knew what noble emulation he had fired for the future?

Every man who yielded to Manasseh's eloquence was a step to reach the next, for Manasseh made a list of donors, and paraded it reproachfully before those who had yet to give. Withal, the most obstinate resistance met him in some quarters. One man—a certain Rodriques, inhabiting a mansion in Finsbury Circus—was positively rude.

"If I came in a carriage, you'd soon pull out your ten-pound note for the Synagogue," sneered Manasseh, his blood boiling.

"Certainly I would," admitted Rodriques laughing. And Manasseh shook off the dust of his threshold in disdain.

By reason of such rebuffs, his collection for the day only reached about thirty pounds, inclusive of the value of some depreciated Portuguese bonds which he good-naturedly accepted as though at par.

Disgusted with the meanness of mankind, da Costa's genius devised more drastic measures. Having carefully locked up the proceeds of Sunday's operations, and, indeed, nearly all his loose cash, in his safe, for, to avoid being put to expense, he rarely carried money on his person, unless he gathered it *en route*, he took his way to Bishopsgate Within, to catch the stage for Clapton. The day was bright, and he hummed a festive Synagogue tune as he plodded leisurely with his stick along the bustling, narrow pavements, bordered by costers' barrows at one edge, and by jagged houses, overhung by grotesque signboards, at the other, and thronged by cits in worsted hose.

But when he arrived at the inn he found the coach had started. Nothing concerned, he ordered a post-chaise in a supercilious manner, criticising the horses, and drove to Clapton in style, drawn by a pair of spanking steeds, to the music of the postillion's horn. Very soon they drew out of the blocked roads, with their lumbering procession of carts, coaches, and chairs, and into open country, green with the fresh verdure of the spring. The chaise stopped at "The Red Cottage," a pretty villa, whose façade was covered with Virginian creeper that blushed in the autumn. Manasseh was surprised at the taste with which the lawn was laid out in the Italian style, with grottoes and marble figures. The householder, hearing the windings of the horn, conceived himself visited by a person of quality, and sent a message that he was in the hands of his hairdresser, but would be down in less than half an hour. This was of a piece with Manasseh's information concerning the man—a certain Belasco, emulous of the great fops, an amateur of satin waistcoats and novel shoestrings, and even said to affect a spying-glass when he showed at Vauxhall. Manasseh had never seen him, not having troubled to go so far afield, but from the handsome appurtenances of the hall and the staircase he augured the best. The apartments were even more to his liking; they were oak panelled, and crammed with the most expensive objects of art and luxury. The walls of the drawing-room were frescoed, and from the ceiling depended a brilliant lustre, with seven spouts for illumination.

Having sufficiently examined the furniture, Manasseh grew weary of waiting, and betook himself to Belasco's bedchamber.

"You will excuse me, Mr. Belasco," he said, as he entered through the half open door, "but my business is urgent."

The young dandy, who was seated before a mirror, did not look up, but replied, "Have a care, sir, you well nigh startled my hairdresser."

"Far be it from me to willingly discompose an artist," replied Manasseh drily, "though from the elegance of the design, I venture to think my interruption will not make a hair's-breadth of difference. But I come on a matter which the son of Benjamin Belasco will hardly deny is more pressing than his toilette."

"Nay, nay, sir, what can be more momentous?"

"The Synagogue!" said Manasseh austerely.

"Pah! What are you talking of, sir?" and he looked up cautiously for the first time at the picturesque figure. "What does the Synagogue want of me? I pay my *finta* and every bill the rascals send me. Monstrous fine sums, too, egad—"

"But you never go there!"

"No, indeed, a man of fashion cannot be everywhere. Routs and rigotti play the deuce with one's time."

"What a pity!" mused Manasseh ironically. "One misses you there. 'Tis no edifying spectacle—a slovenly rabble with none to set the standard of taste."

The pale-faced beau's eyes lit up with a gleam of interest.

"Ah, the clods!" he said. "You should yourself be a buck of the eccentric school by your dress. But I stick to the old tradition of elegance."

"You had better stick to the old tradition of piety," quoth Manasseh. "Your father was a saint, you are a sinner in Israel. Return to the Synagogue, and herald your return by contributing to its finances. It has made a bad debt, and I am collecting money to reimburse it."

The young exquisite yawned. "I know not who you may be," he said at length, "but you are evidently not one of us. As for the Synagogue I am willing to reform its dress, but dem'd if I will give a shilling more to its finances. Let your slovenly rabble of tradesmen pay the piper—I cannot afford it!"

"*You* cannot afford it!"

"No—you see I have such extravagant tastes."

"But I give you the opportunity for extravagance," expostulated Manasseh. "What greater luxury is there than that of doing good?"

"Confound it, sir, I must ask you to go," said Beau Belasco coldly. "Do you not perceive that you are disconcerting my hairdresser?"

"I could not abide a moment longer under this profane, if tasteful, roof," said Manasseh, backing sternly towards the door. "But I would make one last appeal to you, for the sake of the repose of your father's soul, to forsake your evil ways."

"Be hanged to you for a meddler," retorted the young blood. "My money supports men of genius and taste—it shall not be frittered away on a pack of fusty shopkeepers."

The *Schnorrer* drew himself up to his full height, his eyes darted fire. "Farewell, then!" he hissed in terrible tones. "*You will make the third at Grace!*"

He vanished—the dandy started up full of vague alarm, forgetting even his hair in the mysterious menace of that terrifying sibilation.

"What do you mean?" he cried.

"I mean," said Manasseh, reappearing at the door, "that since the world was created, only two men have taken their clothes with them to the world to come. One was Korah, who was swallowed down, the other was Elijah, who was borne aloft. It is patent in which direction the third will go."

The sleeping chord of superstition vibrated under Manasseh's dexterous touch.

"Rejoice, O young man, in your strength," went on the Beggar, "but a day will come when only the corpse-watchers will perform your toilette. In plain white they will dress you, and the devil shall never know what a dandy you were."

"But who are you, that I should give you money for the Synagogue?" asked the Beau sullenly. "Where are your credentials?"

"Was it to insult me that you called me back? Do I look a knave? Nay, put up your purse. I'll have none of your filthy gold. Let me go."

Gradually Manasseh was won round to accepting ten sovereigns.

"For your father's sake," he said, pocketing them. "The only thing I will take for your sake is the cost of my conveyance. I had to post hither, and the Synagogue must not be the loser."

Beau Belasco gladly added the extra money, and reseated himself before the mirror, with agreeable sensations in his neglected conscience. "You see," he observed, half apologetically, for Manasseh still lingered, "one cannot do everything. To be a prince of dandies, one needs all one's time." He waved his hand comprehensively around the walls which were lined with wardrobes. "My buckskin breeches were the result of nine separate measurings. Do you note how they fit?"

"They scarcely do justice to your eminent reputation," replied Manasseh candidly.

Beau Belasco's face became whiter than even at the thought of earthquakes and devils. "They fit me to bursting!" he breathed.

"But are they in the pink of fashion?" queried Manasseh. "And assuredly the nankeen pantaloons yonder I recollect to have seen worn last year."

"My tailor said they were of a special cut—'tis a shape I am introducing, baggy—to go with frilled shirts."

Manasseh shook his head sceptically, whereupon the Beau besought him to go through his wardrobe, and set aside anything that lacked originality or extreme fashionableness. After considerable reluctance Manasseh consented, and set aside a few cravats, shirts, periwigs, and suits from the immense collection.

"Aha! That is all you can find," said the Beau gleefully.

"Yes, that is all," said Manasseh sadly. "All I can find that does any justice to your fame. These speak the man of polish and invention; the rest are but tawdry frippery. Anybody might wear them."

"Anybody!" gasped the poor Beau, stricken to the soul.

"Yes, I might wear them myself."

"Thank you! Thank you! You are an honest man. I love true criticism, when the critic has nothing to gain. I am delighted you called. These rags shall go to my valet."

"Nay, why waste them on the heathen?" asked Manasseh, struck with a sudden thought. "Let me dispose of them for the benefit of the Synagogue."

"If it would not be troubling you too much!"

"Is there anything I would not do for Heaven?" said Manasseh with a patronising air. He threw open the door of the adjoining piece suddenly, disclosing the scowling valet on his knees. "Take these down, my man," he said quietly, and the valet was only too glad to hide his confusion at being caught eavesdropping by hastening down to the drive with an armful of satin waistcoats.

("The Scowling Valet on His Knees.")

Manasseh, getting together the remainder, shook his head despairingly. "I shall never get these into the post-chaise," he said. "You will have to lend me your carriage."

"Can't you come back for them?" said the Beau feebly.

"Why waste the Synagogue's money on hired vehicles? No, if you will crown your kindness by sending the footman along with me to help me unpack them, you shall have your equipage back in an hour or two."

So the carriage and pair were brought out, and Manasseh, pressing into his service the coachman, the valet, and the footman, superintended the packing of the bulk of Beau Belasco's wardrobe into the two vehicles. Then he took his seat in the carriage, the coachman and the gorgeous powdered footman got into their places, and with a joyous fanfaronade on the horn, the procession set off, Manasseh bowing graciously to the master of "The Red House," who was waving his beruffled hand from a window embowered in greenery. After a pleasant drive, the vehicles halted at the house, guarded by stone lions, in which dwelt Nathaniel Furtado, the wealthy private dealer, who willingly gave fifteen pounds for the buck's belaced and embroidered vestments, besides being inveigled into a donation of a guinea towards the Synagogue's bad debt. Manasseh thereupon dismissed the chaise with a handsome gratuity, and drove in state in the now-empty carriage, attended by the powdered footman, to Finsbury Circus, to the mansion of Rodriques. "I have come for my ten pounds," he said, and reminded him of his promise (?). Rodriques laughed, and swore, and laughed again, and swore that the carriage was hired, to be paid for out of the ten pounds.

"Hired?" echoed Manasseh resentfully. "Do you not recognise the arms of my friend, Beau Belasco?" And he presently drove off with the note, for Rodriques had a roguish eye. And then, parting with the chariot, the King took his way on foot to Fenchurch Street, to the house of his cousin Barzillai, the ex-planter of Barbadoes, and now a West Indian merchant.

Barzillai, fearing humiliation before his clerks, always carried his relative off to the neighbouring Franco's Head Tavern, and humoured him with costly liquors.

"But you had no right to donate money you did not possess; it was dishonest," he cried with irrepressible ire.

"Hoity toity!" said Manasseh, setting down his glass so vehemently that the stem shivered. "And were you not called to the Law after me? And did you not donate money?"

"Certainly! But I *had* the money."

"What! *With* you?"

"No, no, certainly not. I do not carry money on the Sabbath."

"Exactly. Neither do I."

"But the money was at my bankers'."

"And so it was at mine. *You* are my bankers, you and others like you. You draw on your bankers—I draw on mine." And his cousin being thus confuted, Manasseh had not much further difficulty in wheedling two pounds ten out of him.

"And now," said he, "I really think you ought to do something to lessen the Synagogue's loss."

"But I have just given!" quoth Barzillai in bewilderment.

"*That* you gave to me as your cousin, to enable your relative to discharge his obligations. I put it strictly on a personal footing. But now I am pleading on behalf of the Synagogue, which stands to lose heavily. You are a Sephardi as well as my cousin. It is a distinction not unlike the one I have so often to explain to you. You owe me charity, not only as a cousin, but as a *Schnorrer* likewise." And, having wrested another guinea from the obfuscated merchant, he repaired to Grobstock's business office in search of the defaulter.

But the wily Grobstock, forewarned by Manasseh's promise to visit him, and further frightened by his Sunday morning call, had denied himself to the *Schnorrer* or anyone remotely resembling him, and it was not till the afternoon that Manasseh ran him to earth at Sampson's coffee-house in Exchange Alley, where the brokers foregathered, and 'prentices and students swaggered in to abuse the Ministers, and all kinds of men from bloods to barristers loitered to pick up hints to easy riches. Manasseh detected his quarry in the furthermost box, his face hidden behind a broadsheet.

"Why do you always come to me?" muttered the East India Director helplessly.

"Eh?" said Manasseh, mistrustful of his own ears. "I beg your pardon."

"If your own community cannot support you," said Grobstock, more loudly, and with all the boldness of an animal driven to bay, "why not go to Abraham Goldsmid, or his brother Ben, or to Van Oven, or Oppenheim—they're all more prosperous than I."

"Sir!" said Manasseh wrathfully. "You are a skilful—nay, a famous, financier. You know what stocks to buy, what stocks to sell, when to follow a rise, and when a fall. When the Premier advertises the loans, a thousand speculators look to you for guidance. What would you say if *I* presumed to interfere in your financial affairs—if I told you to issue these shares or to call in those? You would tell me to mind my own business; and you would be perfectly right. Now *Schnorring* is *my* business. Trust me, I know best whom to come to. You stick to stocks and leave *Schnorring* alone. You are the King of Financiers, but I am the King of *Schnorrers*."

Grobstock's resentment at the rejoinder was mitigated by the compliment to his financial insight. To be put on the same level with the Beggar was indeed unexpected.

"Will you have a cup of coffee?" he said.

"I ought scarcely to drink with you after your reception of me," replied Manasseh unappeased. "It is not even as if I came to *schnorr* for myself; it is to the finances of our house of worship that I wished to give you an opportunity of contributing."

"Aha! your vaunted community hard up?" queried Joseph, with a complacent twinkle.

"Sir! We are the richest congregation in the world. We want nothing from anybody," indignantly protested Manasseh, as he absent-mindedly took the cup of coffee which Grobstock had ordered for him. "The difficulty merely is that, in honour of my daughter's wedding, I have donated a hundred pounds to the Synagogue which I have not yet managed to collect, although I have already devoted a day-and-a-half of my valuable time to the purpose."

"But why do you come to me?"

"What! Do you ask me that again?"

"I—I—mean," stammered Grobstock—"why should I contribute to a Portuguese Synagogue?"

Manasseh clucked his tongue in despair of such stupidity. "It is just you who should contribute more than any Portuguese."

"I?" Grobstock wondered if he was awake.

"Yes, you. Was not the money spent in honour of the marriage of a German Jew? It was a splendid vindication of your community."

"This is too much!" cried Grobstock, outraged and choking.

"Too much to mark the admission to our fold of the first of your sect! I am disappointed in you, deeply disappointed. I thought you would have applauded my generous behaviour."

"I don't care what you thought!" gasped Grobstock. He was genuinely exasperated at the ridiculousness of the demand, but he was also pleased to find himself preserving so staunch a front against the insidious *Schnorrer*. If he could only keep firm now, he told himself, he might emancipate himself for ever. Yes, he would be strong, and Manasseh should never dare address him again. "I won't pay a stiver," he roared.

"If you make a scene I will withdraw," said Manasseh quietly. "Already there are ears and eyes turned upon you. From your language people will be thinking me a dun and you a bankrupt."

"They can go to the devil!" thundered Grobstock, "and you too!"

"Blasphemer! You counsel me to ask the devil to contribute to the Synagogue! I will not bandy words with you. You refuse, then, to contribute to this fund?"

"I do, I see no reason."

"Not even the five pounds I vowed on behalf of Yankelé himself—one of your own people?"

"What! I pay in honour of Yankelé—a dirty *Schnorrer*!"

"Is this the way you speak of your guests?" said Manasseh, in pained astonishment. "Do you forget that Yankelé has broken bread at your table? Perhaps this is how you talk of me when my back is turned. But, beware! Remember the saying of our sages, 'You and I cannot live in the world,' said God to the haughty man. Come, now! No more paltering or taking refuge in abuse. You refuse me this beggarly five pounds?"

"Most decidedly."

"Very well, then!"

Manasseh called the attendant.

"What are you about to do?" cried Grobstock apprehensively.

"You shall see," said Manasseh resolutely, and when the attendant came, he pressed the price of his cup of coffee into his hand.

Grobstock flushed in silent humiliation. Manasseh rose.

Grobstock's fatal strain of weakness gave him a twinge of compunction at the eleventh hour.

"You see for yourself how unreasonable your request was," he murmured.

"Do not strive to justify yourself, I am done with you," said Manasseh. "I am done with you as a philanthropist. For the future you may besnuff and bespatter your coat as much as you please, for all the trouble I shall ever take. As a financier, I still respect you, and may yet come to you, but as a philanthropist, never."

"Anything I can do—" muttered Grobstock vaguely.

"Let me see!" said Manasseh, looking down upon him thoughtfully. "Ah, yes, an idea! I have collected over sixty pounds. If you would invest this for me—"

"Certainly, certainly," interrupted Grobstock, with conciliatory eagerness.

"Good! With your unrivalled knowledge of the markets, you could easily bring it up to the necessary sum in a day or two. Perhaps even there is some grand *coup* on the *tapis*, something to be bulled or beared in which you have a hand."

Grobstock nodded his head vaguely. He had already remembered that the proceeding was considerably below his dignity; he was not a stockbroker, never had he done anything of the kind for anyone.

"But suppose I lose it all?" he asked, trying to draw back.

"Impossible," said the *Schnorrer* serenely. "Do you forget it is a Synagogue fund? Do you think the Almighty will suffer His money to be lost?"

"Then why not speculate yourself?" said Grobstock craftily.

"The Almighty's honour must be guarded. What! Shall He be less well served than an earthly monarch? Do you think I do not know your financial relations with the Court? The service of the Almighty demands the best men. I was the best man to collect the money—you are the best to invest it. To-morrow morning it shall be in your hands."

"No, don't trouble," said Grobstock feebly. "I don't need the actual money to deal with."

"I thank you for your trust in me," replied Manasseh with emotion. "Now you speak like yourself again. I withdraw what I said to you. I *will* come to you again—to the philanthropist no less than financier. And—and I am sorry I paid for my coffee." His voice quivered.

Grobstock was touched. He took out a sixpence and repaid his guest with interest. Manasseh slipped the coin into his pocket, and shortly afterwards, with some final admonitions to his stock-jobber, took his leave.

Being in for the job, Grobstock resolved to make the best of it. His latent vanity impelled him to astonish the Beggar. It happened that he *was* on the point of a magnificent manoeuvre, and alongside his own triton Manasseh's minnow might just as well swim. He made the sixty odd pounds into six hundred.

A few days after the Royal Wedding, the glories of which are still a tradition among the degenerate *Schnorrers* of to-day, Manasseh struck the Chancellor breathless by handing him a bag containing five score of sovereigns. Thus did he honourably fulfil his obligation to the Synagogue, and with more celerity than many a Warden. Nay, more! Justly considering the results of the speculation should accrue to the Synagogue, whose money had been risked, he, with Quixotic scrupulousness, handed over the balance of five hundred pounds to the Mahamad, stipulating only that it should be used to purchase a life-annuity (styled the Da Costa Fund) for a poor and deserving member of the congregation, in whose selection he, as donor, should have the ruling voice. The Council of Five eagerly agreed to his conditions, and a special junta was summoned for the election. The donor's choice fell upon Manasseh Bueno Barzillai Azevedo da Costa, thenceforward universally recognised, and hereby handed down to tradition, as the King of *Schnorrers*.

THE SEMI-SENTIMENTAL DRAGON

There was nothing about the outside of the Dragon to indicate so large a percentage of sentiment. It was a mere every-day Dragon, with the usual squamous hide, glittering like silver armour, a commonplace crested head with a forked tongue, a tail like a barbed arrow, a pair of fan-shaped wings, and four indifferently ferocious claws, one per foot. How it came to be so susceptible you shall hear, and then, perhaps, you will be less surprised at its unprecedented and undragonlike behaviour.

Once upon a time, as the good old chronicler, Richard Johnson, relateth, Egypt was oppressed by a Dragon who made a plaguy to-do unless given a virgin daily for dinner. For twenty-four years the menu was practicable; then the supply gave out. There was absolutely no virgin left in the realm save Sabra, the king's daughter. As 365×24 only $= 8760$, I suspect that the girls were anxious to dodge the Dragon by marrying in haste. The government of the day seems to have been quite unworthy of confidence and utterly unable to grapple with the situation, and poor Ptolemy was reduced to parting with the Princess, though even so destruction was only staved off for a day, as virgins would be altogether "off" on the morrow. So short-sighted was the Egyptian policy that this does not appear to have occurred to anybody. At the last moment an English tourist from Coventry, known as George (and afterwards sainted by an outgoing administration sent to his native borough by the country), resolved to tackle the monster. The chivalrous Englishman came to grief in the encounter, but by rolling under an orange tree he was safe from the Dragon so long as he chose to stay there, and so in the end had no difficulty in despatching the creature; which suggests that the soothsayers and the magicians would have been much better occupied in planting orange trees than in sacrificing virgins. Thus far the story, which is improbable enough to be an allegory.

Now many centuries after these events did not happen, a certain worthy citizen, an illiterate fellow, but none the worse for that, made them into a pantomime—to wit, *St. George and the Dragon; or, Harlequin Tom Thumb*. And the same was duly played at a provincial theatre, with a lightly clad chorus of Egyptian lasses, in glaring contradiction of the dearth of such in the fable, and a Sabra who sang to them a topical song about the County Council.

Curiously enough, in private life, Sabra, although her name was Miss on the posters, was really a Miss. She was quite as young and pretty as she looked, too, and only rouged herself for the sake of stage perspective. I don't mean to say she was as beautiful as the Egyptian princess, who was as straight as a cedar and wore her auburn hair in wanton ringlets, but she was a sprightly little body with sparkling eyes and a complexion that would have been a good advertisement to any soap on earth. But better than Sabra's skin was Sabra's heart, which though as yet untouched by man was full of love and tenderness, and did not faint under the burden of supporting her mother and the household. For instead of having a king for a sire, Sabra had a drunken scene-shifter for a father. Everybody about the theatre liked Sabra, from the actor-manager (who played St. George) to the stage door-keeper (who played St. Peter). Even her under-study did not wish her ill.

Needless, therefore, to say it was Sabra who made the Dragon semi-sentimental. Not in the "book," of course, where his desire to eat her remained purely literal. Real Dragons keep themselves aloof from sentiment, but a stage Dragon is only human. Such a one may be entirely the slave of sentiment, and it was perhaps to the credit of our Dragon that only half of him was in the bonds. The other half—and that the better half—was saturnine and teetotal, and answered to the name of Davie Brigg.

Davie was the head man on the Dragon. He played the anterior parts, waggled the head and flapped the wings and sent gruesome grunts and penny squibs through the "firebreathing" jaws. He was a dour middle-aged, but stagestruck, Scot, very proud of his rapid rise in the profession, for he had begun as a dramatist.

The rear of the Dragon was simply known as Jimmy.

Jimmy was a wreck. His past was a mystery. His face was a brief record of baleful experiences, and he had the aspirates of a gentleman. He had gone on the stage to be out of the snow and the rain. Not knowing this, the actor-manager paid him ninepence a night. His wages just kept him in beer-money. The original Sabra tamed two lions, but perhaps it was a greater feat to tame this half of a Dragon.

Jimmy's tenderness for Sabra began at rehearsal, when he saw a good deal of her, and felicitated himself on the fact that they were on in the same scenes. After a while, however, he perceived this to be a doleful drawback, for whereas at rehearsal he could jump out of his skin and breathe himself and feast his eyes on Sabra when the Dragon was disengaged, on the stage he was forced to remain cramped in darkness while Ptolemy was clowning or St. George executing a step dance. Sabra was invisible, except for an odd moment or so between the scenes when he caught sight of her gliding to her dressing-room like a streak of discreet sunshine. Still he had his compensations; her dulcet notes reached his darkness (mellowed by the painted canvas and the tin scales sewn over it), as the chant of the unseen cuckoo reaches the woodland wanderer. Sometimes, when she sang that song about the County Council, he forgot to wag his tail.

Thus was Love blind, while Indifference in the person of Davie Brigg looked its full through the mask that stood for the monster's head. After a bit Jimmy conceived a mad envy of his superior's privileges; he longed to see Sabra through the Dragon's mouth. He was so weary of the little strip of stage under the Dragon's belly, which, even if he peered through the breathing-holes in the patch of paint-disguised gauze let into its paunch, was the most he could see. One night he asked Davie to change places with him. Davie's look of surprise and consternation was beautiful to see.

"Do I hear aricht?" he asked.

"Just for a night," said Jimmy, abashed.

"But d'ye no ken this is a speakin' part?"

("'But D'ye No Ken This a Speakin' Part?'")

"I did—not—know—that," faltered Jimmy.

"Where's your ears, mon?" inquired Davie sternly. "Dinna ye hear me growlin' and grizzlin' and squealin' and skirlin'?"

"Y—e—s," said Jimmy. "But I thought you did it at random."

"Thocht I did it at random!" cried Davie, holding up his hands in horror. "And mebbe also ye thocht onybody could do't!"

Jimmy's shamed silence gave consent also to this unflinching interpretation of his thought.

"Ah weel!" said Davie, with melancholy resignation, "this is the artist's reward for his sweat and labour. Why, mon, let me tell ye, ilka note is not ainly timed but modulatit to the dramatic eenterest o' the moment, and that I hae practised the squeak hours at a time wi' a bagpiper. Tak' my place, indeed! Are ye fou again, or hae ye tint your senses?"

"But you could do the words all the same. I only want to see for once."

"And how d'ye think the words should sound, coming from the creature's belly? And what should ye see! You should nae ken where to go, I warrant. Come, I'll spier ye. Where d'ye come in for the fight with St. George—is it R 2 E or L U E?"

"L U E," replied Jimmy feebly.

"Ye donnered auld runt!" cried Davie triumphantly. "'Tis neither one nor t'other. 'Tis R C. Why, ye're capable of deein' up stage instead of down! Ye'd spoil my great scene. And ye are to remember I wad bear the wyte for 't, for naebody but our two sel's should ken the truth. Nay, nay, my mon. I hae my responsibeelities to the management. Ye're all verra weel in a subordinate position, but dinna ye aspire to more than beseems your abeelities. I am richt glad ye spoke me. Eh, but it would be an awfu' thing if I was taken bad and naebody to play the part. I'll warn the manager to put on an under-study betimes."

"Oh, but let *me* be the under-study, then," pleaded Jimmy.

Davie sniffed scornfully.

"'Tis a braw thing, ambeetion," he said, "but there's a proverb about it ye ken, mebbe."

"But I'll notice everything you do, and exactly how you do it!"

Davie relented a little.

"Ah, weel," he said cautiously, "I'll bide a wee before speaking to the manager."

But Davie remained doggedly robust, and so Jimmy still walked in darkness. He often argued the matter out with his superior, maintaining that they ought to toss for the position—head or tail. Failing to convince Davie, he offered him fourpence a night for the accommodation, but Davie saw in this extravagance evidence of a determined design to supplant him. In despair Jimmy watched for a chance of slipping into the wire framework before Davie, but the conscientious artist was always at his post first. They held dialogues on the subject, while with pantomimic license the chorus of Egyptian lasses was dancing round the Dragon as if it were a maypole. Their angry messages to each other vibrated along the wires of their prison-house, rending the Dragon with intestinal war. Weave your cloud-wrought Utopias, O social reformer, but wherever men inhabit, there jealousy and disunion shall creep in, and this gaudy canvas tent with its tin roofing was a hotbed of envy, hatred, and all uncharitableness. Yet Love was there, too—a stranger, purer passion than the battered Jimmy had ever known; for it had the unselfishness of a love that can never be more than a dream, that the beloved can never even know of. Perhaps, if Jimmy had met Sabra before he left off being a gentleman—!

The silent, hopeless longing, the chivalrous devotion yearning dumbly within him, did not stop his beer; he drank more to drown his thoughts. Every night he entered into his part gladly, knowing himself elevated in the zoological scale, not degraded, by an assumption that made him only half a beast. It was kind of Providence to hide him wholly away from her vision, so that her bright eyes might not be sullied by the sight of his foulness. None of the grinning audience suspected the tragedy of the hind legs of the Dragon, as blindly following their leader, they went "galumphing" about the stage. The innocent children marvelled at the monster, in wide-eyed excitement, unsuspecting even its humanity, much less its double nature; only Davie knew that in that Dragon there were the ruins of a man and the makings of a great actor!

"Why are ye sae anxious to stand in my shoon?" he would ask, when the hind legs became too obstreperous.

"I don't want to be in your shoes; I only want to see the stage for once."

But Davie would shake his head incredulously, making the Dragon's mask wobble at the wrong cues. At last, once when Sabra was singing, poor Jimmy, driven to extremities, confessed the truth, and had the mortification of feeling the wires vibrate with the Scotchman's silent laughter. He blushed unseen.

But it transpired that Davie's amusement was not so much scornful as sceptical. He still suspected the tail of a sinister intention to wag the Dragon.

"Nae, nae," he said, "ye shallna get me to swallow that. Ye're an unco puir creature, but ye're no sa daft as to want the moon. She's a bonnie lassie, and I willna be surprised if she catches a coronet in the end, when she makes a name in Lunnon; for the swells here, though I see a wheen foolish faces nicht after nicht in the stalls, are but a puir lot. Eh, but it's a gey grand tocher is a pretty face. In the meanwhiles, like a canny girl, she's settin' her cap at the chief."

"Hold your tongue!" hissed the hind legs. "She's as pure as an angel."

"Hoot-toot!" answered the head. "Dinna leebel the angels. It's no an angel that lets her manager give her sly squeezes and saft kisses that are nae in the stage directions."

"Then she can't know he's a married man," said the hind legs hoarsely.

"Dinna fash yoursel'—she kens that full weel and a thocht or two more. Dod! Ye should just see how she and St. George carry on after my death scene, when he's supposit to ha' rescued her and they fall a-cuddlin'."

"You're a liar!" said the hind legs.

Davie roared and breathed burning squibs and capered about, and Jimmy had to prance after him in involuntary pursuit. He felt choking in his stuffy hot black rollicking dungeon. The thought of this bloated sexagenarian faked up as a *jeune premier*, pawing that sweet little girl, sickened him.

"Dom'd leear yersel!" resumed Davie, coming to a standstill. "I maun believe my own eyes, what they tell me nicht after nicht."

"Then let me see for myself, and I'll believe you."

"Ye dinna catch me like that," said Davie, chuckling.

After that poor Jimmy's anxiety to see the stage became feverish. He even meditated malingering and going in front of the house, but could only have got a distant view, and at the risk of losing his place in an overcrowded profession. His opportunity came at length, but not till the pantomime was half run out and the actor-manager sought to galvanise it by a "second edition," which in sum meant a new lot of the variety entertainers who came on and played copophones before Ptolemy, did card-tricks in the desert, and exhibited trained poodles to the palm-trees. But Davie, determined to rise to the occasion, thought out a fresh conception of his part, involving three new grunts, and was so busy rehearsing them at home that he forgot the flight of the hours and arrived at the theatre only in time to take second place in the Dragon that was just waiting, half-manned, at the wing. He was so flustered that he did not even think of protesting for the first few minutes. When he did protest, Jimmy said, "What are you jawing about? This is a second edition, isn't it?" and caracoled around, dragging the unhappy Davie in his train.

"I'll tell the chief," groaned the hind legs.

"All right, let him know you were late," answered the head cheerfully.

"Eh, but it's pit-mirk, here. I canna see onything."

"You see I'm no liar. Shall I send a squib your way?"

"Nay, nay, nae larking. Mind the business or you'll ruin my reputation."

"Mind my business, I'll mind yours," replied Jimmy joyously, for the lovely Sabra was smiling right in his eyes. A Dragon divided against itself cannot stand, so Davie had to wait till the beast came off. To his horror Jimmy refused to budge from his shell. He begged for just one "keek" at the stage, but Jimmy replied: "You don't catch me like that." Davie said little more, but he matured a crafty plan, and in the next scene he whispered:—

"Jimmy!"

"Shut up, Davie; I'm busy."

ISRAEL ZANGWILL

"I've got a pin, and if ye shallna promise to restore me my richts after the next exit, ye shall feel the taste of it."

"You'll just stay where you are," came back the peremptory reply.

Deep went the pin in Jimmy's rear, and the Dragon gave such a howl that Davie's blood ran cold. Too late he remembered that it was not the Dragon's cue, and that he was making havoc of his own professional reputation. Through the canvas he felt the stern gaze of the actor-manager. He thought of pricking Jimmy only at the howling cues, but then the howl thus produced was so superior to his own, that if Jimmy chose to claim it, he might be at once engaged to replace him in the part. What a dilemma!

Poor Davie! As if it was not enough to be cut off from all the brilliant spectacle, pent in pitchy gloom and robbed of all his "fat" and his painfully rehearsed "second edition" touches. He felt like one of those fallen archangels of the footlights who live to bear Ophelia's bier on boards where they once played Hamlet.

Far different emotions were felt at the Dragon's head, where Jimmy's joy faded gradually away, replaced by a passion of indignation, as with love-sharpened eyes he ascertained for himself the true relations of the actor-manager with his "principal girl." He saw from his coign of vantage the poor modest little thing shrinking before the cowardly advances of her employer, who took every possible advantage of the stage potentialities, in ways the audience could not discriminate from the acting. Alas! what could the gentle little bread-winner do? But Jimmy's blood was boiling. Davie's great scene arrived: the battle royal between St. George and the Dragon. Sabra, bewitchingly radiant in white Arabian silk, stood under the orange-tree where the pendent fruit was labelled three a penny. Here St. George, in knightly armour clad, retired between the rounds, to be sponged by the fair Sabra, from whose lips he took the opportunity of drinking encouragement. When the umpire cried "Time!" Jimmy uttered inarticulate cries of real rage and malediction, vomiting his squibs straight at the champion's eyes with intent to do him grievous bodily injury. But squibs have their own ways of jumping, and the actor-manager's face was protected by his glittering burgonet.

At last Jimmy and Davie were duly despatched by St. George's trusty sword, Ascalon, which passed right between them and stuck out on the other side amid the frantic applause of the house. The Dragon reeled cumbrously sideways and bit the dust, of which there was plenty. Then Sabra rushed forward from under the orange-tree and encircled her hero's hauberk with a stage embrace, while St. George, lifting up his visor, rained kiss after kiss on Sabra's scarlet face, and the "gods" went hoarse with joy.

"Oh, sir!" Jimmy heard the still small voice of the bread-winner protest feebly again and again amid the thunder, as she tried to withdraw herself from her employer's grasp. This was the last straw. Anger and the foul air of his prison wrought up Jimmy to asphyxiation point. What wonder if the Dragon lost his head completely?

Davie will never forget the horror of that moment when he felt himself dragged upwards as by an irresistible tornado, and knew himself for a ruined actor. Mechanically he essayed to cling to the ground, but in vain. The dead Dragon was on its feet in a moment; in another, Jimmy had thrown off the mask, showing a shock of hair and a blotched crimson face, spotted with great beads of perspiration. Unconscious of this culminating outrage, Davie made desperate prods with his pin, but Jimmy was equally unconscious of the pricks. The thunder died abruptly. A dead silence fell upon the whole house—you could have heard Davie's pin drop. St. George, in amazed consternation, released his hold of Sabra and cowered back before the wild glare of the bloodshot eyes. "How dare you?" rang out in hoarse screaming accents from the protruding head, and with one terrific blow of its right fore-leg the hybrid monster felled Sabra's insulter to the ground.

The astonished St. George lay on his back, staring up vacantly at the flies.

"I'll teach you how to behave to a lady!" roared the Dragon.

Then Davie tugged him frantically backwards, but Jimmy cavorted obstinately in the centre of the stage, which the actor-manager had taken even in his fall, so that the Dragon's hind legs trampled blindly on Davie's prostrate chief, amid the hysterical convulsions of the house.

NEXT MORNING THE LOCAL PAPERS were loud in their praises of the "Second Edition" of *St. George and the Dragon*, especially of the "genuinely burlesque and topsy-turvy episode in which the Dragon rises from the dead to read St. George a lesson in chivalry; a really side-splitting conception, made funnier by the grotesque revelation of the constituents of the Dragon, just before it retires for the night."

The actor-manager had no option but to adopt this reading, so had to be hoofed and publicly reprimanded every evening during the rest of the season, glad enough to get off so cheaply.

Of course, Jimmy was dismissed, but St. George was painfully polite to Sabra ever after, not knowing but what Jimmy was in the gallery with a brickbat, and perhaps not unimpressed by the lesson in chivalry he was receiving every evening.

Perhaps you think the Dragon deserved to marry Sabra, but that would be really too topsy-turvy, and the sentimental beast himself was quite satisfied to have rescued her from St. George.

But the person who profited most by Jimmy's sacrifice was Davie, who stepped into a real speaking part, emerged from the obscurity of his surroundings, burst his swaddling clothes, and made his appearance on the stage—a thing he could scarcely be said to have done in the Dragon's womb.

And so the world wags.

AN HONEST LOG-ROLLER

Louis Maunders was writing an anonymous novel, and a large circle of friends and acquaintances expected it to make a big hit. Louis Maunders was so modest that he distrusted his own opinion, and was glad to find his friends sharing it in this matter. It strengthened him. He carried the manuscript unostentatiously about in a long brief bag, while the book was writing, and worked at it during all his spare moments. Even in omnibuses he was to be seen scribbling hard with a stylus, and neglecting to attend to the conductor. The plot of the story was sad and heartrending, for Louis was only twenty-one. Louis refused to give those roseate pictures of life which the conventional novelist turns out to please the public. He objected to "happy endings." In real life, he said, no story ends happily; for the end of everybody's story is Death. In this book he said some bitter things about Life which it would have winced to hear, had it been alive. As for Death, he doubted whether it was worth dying. Towards Nature he took a tone of haughty superiority, and expressed himself disrespectfully on the subject of Fate. He mocked at it through the lips of his hero, and altogether seemed qualifying for the liver complaint, which is the Prometheus myth done into modern English. He taught that the only Peace for man lies in snapping the fingers at Fortune, taking her buffets and her favours with equal contempt, and generally teaching her to know her place. The soul of the Philosopher, he said, would stand grinning cynically though the planetary system were sold off by auction. These lessons were taught with great tragic power in Maunders' novel, and he was looking forward to the time when it should be in print, and on all the carpets of conversation. He was extremely gratified to find his friends thinking so well of its prospects, for it was pleasing to him to discover that he had chosen his circle so well, and had such intelligent friends. It did not seem to him at all unlikely that he would make his fortune with this novel; and he hurried on with it, till the masterpiece needed only a few final touches and a few last insults to Fate. Then he left the bag in a hansom cab. When he remembered his forgetfulness, he was distracted. He raved like a maniac—and like a maniac did not even write his ravings down for after use. He applied at Scotland Yard, but the superintendent said that drivers brought there only articles of value. He sent paragraphs to the papers, asking even of the *Echo* where his lost novel was. But the *Echo* answered not. Several spiteful papers insinuated that he was a liar, and a high-class comic paper went out of its way to make a joke, and to call his book "The Mystery of a

Hansom Cab." The annoying part of the business was that after getting all this gratuitous advertisement, in itself enough to sell two editions, the book still refused to come up for publication. Maunders was too heart-broken to write another. For months he went about, a changed being. He had put the whole of himself into that book, and it was lost. He mourned for the departed manuscript, and generously extolled its virtues. For years he remained faithful to its memory; and its pages were made less dry with his tears. But the most intemperate grief wears itself out at last; and after a few years of melancholy, Maunders rallied and became a critic.

As a critic he set in with great severity, and by carefully refraining from doing anything himself, gained a great reputation far and wide. In due course he joined the staff of the *Acadæum*, where his signed contributions came to be looked for with profound respect by the public and with fear and trembling by authors. For Maunders' criticism was so very superior, even for the *Acadæum*, of which the trade motto was "Stop here for Criticism—superior to anything in the literary market." Maunders flayed and excoriated Marsyas till the world accepted him as Apollo.

What Maunders was most down upon was novel-writing. Not having to follow them himself, he had high ideals of art; and woe to the unfortunate author who thought he had literary and artistic instinct when he had only pen and paper. Maunders was especially severe upon the novels of young authors, with their affected style and jejune ideas. Perhaps the most brilliant criticism he ever wrote was a merciless dissection of a book of this sort, reeking with the insincerity and crudity of youth, full of accumulated ignorance of life, and brazening it out by flashy cynicism.

A week after this notice appeared, his oldest and dearest friend called upon him and asked him for an explanation.

"What do you mean?" said Maunders.

"When I read your slashing notice of 'A Fingersnap for Fate,' I at once got the book."

"What! After I had disembowelled it; after I had shown it was a stale sausage stuffed with old and putrid ideas?"

"Well, to tell the truth," said his friend, a little crestfallen at having to confess, "I always get the books you pitch into. So do lots of people. We are only plain, ordinary, homespun people, you know; so we feel sure that whatever you praise will be too superior for us, while what you condemn will suit us to a *t*. That is why the great public studies and respects your criticisms. You are our literary pastor and monitor. Your condemnation is our guide-post, and your praise is our *Index Expurgatorius*. But for you we should be lost in the wilderness of new books."

"And this is all the result of my years of laborious criticism," fumed the *Acadæum* critic. "Proceed, sir."

"Well, what I came to say was, that if my memory does not play me a trick after all these years, 'A Fingersnap for Fate' is your long-lost novel."

"What!" shrieked the great critic; "my long-lost child! Impossible."

"Yes," persisted his oldest and dearest friend. "I recognised it by the strawberry mark in Cap. II., where the hero compares the younger generation to fresh strawberries smothered in stale cream. I remember your reading it to me!"

"Heavens! The whole thing comes back to me," cried the critic. "Now I know why I damned it so unmercifully for plagiarism! All the while I was reading it, there was a strange, haunting sense of familiarity."

"But, surely you will expose the thief!"

"How can I? It would mean confessing that I wrote the book myself. That I slated it savagely, is nothing. That will pass as a good joke, if not a piece of rare modesty. But confess myself the author of such a wretched failure!"

"Excuse me," said his friend. "It is not a failure. It is a very popular success. It is selling like wildfire. Excuse the inaccurate simile; but you know what I mean. Your notice has sent the sale up tremendously. Ever since your notice appeared, the printing presses have been going day and night and are utterly unable to cope with the demand. Oh, you must not let a rogue make a fortune out of you like this. That would be too sinful."

So the great critic sought out the thief. And they divided the profits. And then the thief, who was a fool as well as a rogue, wrote another book—all out of his own head this time. And the critic slated it. And they divided the profits.

A TRAGI-COMEDY OF CREEDS

Not much before midnight in a midland town—a thriving commercial town, whose dingy back streets swarmed with poverty and piety—a man in a soft felt hat and a white tie was hurrying home over a bridge that spanned a dark crowded river. He had missed the tram, and did not care to be seen out late, but he could not afford a cab. Suddenly he felt a tug at his long black coat-tail. Vaguely alarmed and definitely annoyed, he turned round quickly. A breathless, roughly-clad, rugged-featured man loosed his hold of the skirt.

"'Scuse me, sir—I've been running," gasped the stranger, placing his horny hand on his breast and panting.

"What is it? What do you want?" said the gentleman impatiently.

"My wife's dying," jerked the man.

"I'm very sorry," murmured the gentleman incredulously, expecting some conventional street-plea.

"Awful sudden attack—this last of hers—only came on an hour ago."

"I'm not a doctor."

"No, sir, I know. I don't want a doctor. He's there and only gives her ten minutes to live. Come with me at once, please."

"Come with you? Why, what good can I do?"

"You're a clergyman!"

"A clergyman!" repeated the other.

"Yes—aren't you?"

The wearer of the white tie looked embarrassed.

"Ye-es," he stammered. "In a—in a way. But I'm not the sort of clergyman your wife will be wanting."

"No?" said the man, puzzled and pained. Then with a sudden dread in his voice: "You're not a Catholic clergyman?"

"No," was the unhesitating reply.

"Oh, then it's all right!" cried the man, relieved. "Come with me, sir, for God's sake. Don't let us waste time." His face was lit up with anxious appeal.

But still the clergyman hesitated.

"You're making a mistake," he murmured. "I am not a Christian clergyman." He turned to resume his walk.

"Not a Christian clergyman!" exclaimed the man, as who should say "not a black negro!"

"No—I am a Jewish minister."

"That don't matter," broke in the man, almost before he could finish the sentence. "As long as you're not a Catholic. Oh, don't go away now, sir!" His voice broke piteously. "Don't go away after I've been chasing you for five minutes—I saw your rig-out—I beg pardon, your coat and hat—in the distance just as I came out of the house. Walk back with me, anyhow," he pleaded, seeing the Jew's hesitation, "Oh! for pity's sake, walk back with me at once and we can discuss it as we go along. I know I should never get hold of another parson in time at this hour of the night."

The man's accents were so poignant, his anxiety was so apparently sincere, that the minister's humanity could scarcely resist the solicitation to walk back at least. He would still have time to decide whether to enter the house or not—whether the case were genuine or a mere trap concealing robbery or worse. The man took a short cut through evil-looking slums that did not increase the minister's confidence. He wondered what his flock would think if they saw their pastor in such company. He was a young unmarried minister, and the reputation of such in provincial Jewish congregations, overflowing with religion and tittle-tattle, is as a pretty unprotected orphan girl's.

"Why don't you go to your own clergyman?" he asked.

"I've got none," said the man half-apologetically. "I don't believe in nothing myself. But you know what women are!"

The minister sniffed, but did not deny the weakness of the sex.

"Betsy goes to some place or other every Sunday almost; sometimes she's there and back from a service before I'm up, and so long as the breakfast's ready I don't mind. I don't ask her no questions, and in return she don't bother about my soul—leastways, not for these ten years, ever since she's had kids to convert. We get along all right, the missus and me and the kids. Oh, but it's all come to an end now," he concluded, with a sob.

"Yes, but my good fellow," protested the minister, "I told you you were making a mistake. You know nothing about religion; but what your wife wants is some one to talk to her of Jesus, or to give her the Sacrament, or the Confession, or something, for I confess I'm not very clear about the forms of Christianity; and I haven't got any wafers or things of that sort. No, I couldn't do it, even if I had a mind to. It would ruin my position if it were known. But apart from that, I really can't do it. I wouldn't know what to say, and I couldn't bring my tongue to say it if I did."

"Oh, but you believe in *something*?" persisted the man piteously.

"H'm! Yes, I can't deny that," said the minister; "but it's not the same something that your wife believes in."

"You believe in a God, don't you?"

The minister felt a bit chagrined at being catechised in the elements of his religion.

"Of course!" he said fretfully.

"There! I knew it," cried the man in triumph. "None of us do in our shop; but, of course, clergymen are different. But if you believe in a God, that's enough, ain't it? You're both religious folk."

"No, it isn't enough—at least, not for your wife."

"Oh, well, you needn't let out, sir, need you? So long as you talk of God and keep clear of the Pope. I've heard her going on about a Scarlet Woman to the kids. (God bless their little hearts! I wonder what they'll do without her!) She'll never know, sir, and she'll die happy. I've done my duty. She whispered I wasn't to bring a Roman Catholic, poor thing. I fancy I heard her say once they're even worse than Jews. Oh, I don't mean that, sir. You're sure you're not a Roman Catholic?" he concluded anxiously.

"Quite sure."

"Well, sir, you'll keep the rest dark, won't you? There's no call to let out you don't believe the same other things as her."

"I shall tell no lie," said the minister firmly. "You have called me in to give consolation to your dying wife, and I shall do my duty as best I can. Is this the house?"

"Yes, sir—right at the top."

The minister conquered a last impulse of mistrust, and looked round cautiously to be sure he was unobserved. Charity was not a strong point with his flock, and certainly his proceedings were suspicious. Even if they learnt the truth, he was not at all sure they would not consider his praying with a dying Christian akin to blasphemy. On the whole he must be credited with some courage in mounting that black, ill-smelling, interminable staircase. He found himself in a gloomy garret at last, lighted by an oil-lamp. A haggard woman lay with shut eyes on an iron bed, her chilling hands clasping the hands of the "converted" kids, a boy of ten and a girl of seven, who stood blubbering in their night-attire. The doctor leaned against the head of the bed, the ungainly shadows of the group sprawling across the blank wall. He had done all he could—without hope of payment—to ease the poor woman's last moments. He was a big-brained, large-hearted Irishman, a Roman Catholic, who thought science and religion might be the best of friends. The husband looked at him in frantic interrogation.

"You are not too late," replied the doctor.

"Thank God!" said the atheist. "Betsy, old girl, here is the clergyman."

The cloud seemed to pass off the blind face, and a wave of wan sunlight to traverse it; slowly the eyes opened, the hands withdrew themselves from the children's grasp, and the palms met for prayer.

"Christ Jesus—" began the lips mechanically.

The minister was hot with confusion and a-quiver with emotion. He knew not what to say, as automatically he drew out a Hebrew prayer-book from his pocket and began reading the Deathbed Confession in the English version that appeared on the alternate pages.

"I acknowledge unto Thee, O Lord, my God, and the God of my fathers, that both my cure and my death are in Thy hands . . ." As he read, the dying lips moved, mumbling the words after him. How often had those white lips prayed that the stiff-necked Jews might find grace and be saved from damnation; how often had those poor, rough hands put pennies into conversionist collecting-boxes after toiling hard to scrape them together; so that only she might suffer by their diversion from the household treasury.

The prayer went on, the mournful monotone thrilling through the hot, dim, oil-reeking attic, and awing the weeping children into silence. The atheist stood by reverently, torn by conflicting emotions; glad the poor foolish creature had her wish, and on thorns lest she should live long enough to discover the deception. There was no room in his overcharged heart for personal grief just then. "Make known to me the path of life; in Thy presence is fulness of joy; at Thy right hand are pleasures for evermore." An ecstatic look overspread the plain, careworn face, she stretched out her arms as if to embrace some unseen vision.

"Yes, I am coming . . . Jesus," she murmured. Then her hands dropped heavily upon her breast; the face grew rigid, the eyes closed. Involuntarily the minister seized the hand nearest him. He felt it respond faintly to his clasp in unconsciousness of the pagan pollution of his touch. He read on, "Thou who art the Father of the fatherless and the Judge of the widow, protect my beloved kindred with whose soul my own is knit."

The lips still echoed him almost imperceptibly, the departing spirit lulled into peace by the prayer of the unbeliever. "Into Thy hand I commend my spirit. Thou hast redeemed me, O Lord God of truth. Amen and Amen."

And in that last Amen, with a final gleam of blessedness flitting across her sightless face, the poor Christian toiler breathed out her life of pain, holding the Jew's hand. There was a moment of solemn silence, the three men becoming as the little children in the presence of the eternal mystery.

IT LEAKED OUT, AS EVERYTHING did in that gossipy town, and among that gossipy Jewish congregation. To the minister's relief, his flock took it better than he expected.

"What a blessed privilege for that heathen female!" was all their comment.

THE MEMORY CLEARING HOUSE

W hen I moved into better quarters on the strength of the success of my first novel, I little dreamt that I was about to be the innocent instrument of a new epoch in telepathy. My poor Geraldine—but I must be calm; it would be madness to let them suspect I am insane. No, these last words must be final. I cannot afford to have them discredited. I cannot afford any luxuries now.

Would to Heaven I had never written that first novel! Then I might still have been a poor, unhappy, struggling, realistic novelist; I might still have been residing at 109, Little Turncot Street, Chapelby Road, St. Pancras. But I do not blame Providence. I knew the book was conventional even before it succeeded. My only consolation is that Geraldine was part-author of my misfortunes, if not of my novel. She it was who urged me to abandon my high ideals, to marry her, and live happily ever afterwards. She said if I wrote only one bad book it would be enough to establish my reputation; that I could then command my own terms for the good ones. I fell in with her proposal, the banns were published, and we were bound together. I wrote a rose-tinted romance, which no circulating library could be without, instead of the veracious picture of life I longed to paint; and I moved from 109, Little Turncot Street, Chapelby Road, St. Pancras, to 22, Albert Flats, Victoria Square, Westminster.

A few days after we had sent out the cards, I met my friend O'Donovan, late member for Blackthorn. He was an Irishman by birth and profession, but the recent General Election had thrown him out of work. The promise of his boyhood and of his successful career at Trinity College was great, but in later years he began to manifest grave symptoms of genius. I have heard whispers that it was in the family, though he kept it from his wife. Possibly I ought not to have sent him a card and have taken the opportunity of dropping his acquaintance. But Geraldine argued that he was not dangerous, and that we ought to be kind to him just after he had come out of Parliament.

O'Donovan was in a rage.

"I never thought it of you!" he said angrily, when I asked him how he was. He had a good Irish accent, but he only used it when addressing his constituents.

"Never thought what?" I enquired in amazement.

"That you would treat your friends so shabbily."

"Wh-what, didn't you g-get a card?" I stammered. "I'm sure the wife—"

"Don't be a fool!" he interrupted. "Of course I got a card. That's what I complain of."

I stared at him blankly. The social experiences resulting from my marriage had convinced me that it was impossible to avoid giving offence. I had no reason to be surprised, but I was.

"What right have you to move and put all your friends to trouble?" he enquired savagely.

"I have put myself to trouble," I said, "but I fail to see how I have taxed *your* friendship."

"No, of course not," he growled. "I didn't expect you to see. You're just as inconsiderate as everybody else. Don't you think I had enough trouble to commit to memory '109, Little Turncot Street, Chapelby Road, St. Pancras,' without being unexpectedly set to study '21, Victoria Flats—?'"

"22, Albert Flats," I interrupted mildly.

"There you are!" he snarled. "You see already how it harasses my poor brain. I shall never remember it."

"Oh yes, you will," I said deprecatingly. "It is much easier than the old address. Listen here! '22, Albert Flats, Victoria Square, Westminster.' 22—a symmetrical number, the first double even number; the first is two, the second is two, too, and the whole is two, two, too—quite æsthetical, you know. Then all the rest is royal—Albert, Albert the Good, see. Victoria—the Queen. Westminster—Westminster Palace. And the other words—geometrical terms, Flat, Square. Why, there never was such an easy address since the days of Adam before he moved out of Eden," I concluded enthusiastically.

"It's easy enough for you, no doubt," he said, unappeased. "But do you think you're the only acquaintance who's not contented with his street and number? Bless my soul, with a large circle like mine, I find myself charged with a new schoolboy task twice a month. I shall have to migrate to a village where people have more stability of character. Heavens! Why have snails been privileged with a domiciliary constancy denied to human beings?"

"But you ought to be grateful," I urged feebly. "Think of 22, Albert Flats, Victoria Square, Westminster, and then think of what I might have moved to. If I have given you an imposition, at least admit it is a light one."

"It isn't so much the new address I complain of, it's the old. Just imagine what a weary grind it has been to master—'109, Little Turncot Street, Chapelby Road, St. Pancras.' For the last eighteen months I have been grappling with it, and now, just as I am letter perfect and postcard secure, behold all my labour destroyed, all my pains made ridiculous. It's the waste that vexes me. Here is a piece of information, slowly and laboriously acquired, yet absolutely useless. Nay, worse than useless; a positive hindrance. For I am just as slow at forgetting as at picking up. Whenever I want to think of your address, up it will spring, '109, Little Turncot Street, Chapelby Road, St. Pancras.' It cannot be scotched—it must lie there blocking up my brains, a heavy, uncouth mass, always ready to spring at the wrong moment; a possession of no value to anyone but the owner, and not the least use to *him*."

He paused, brooding on the thought in moody silence. Suddenly his face changed.

"But isn't it of value to anybody *but* the owner?" he exclaimed excitedly. "Are there not persons in the world who would jump at the chance of acquiring it? Don't stare at me as if I was a comet. Look here! Suppose some one had come to me eighteen months ago and said, 'Patrick, old man, I have a memory I don't want. It's 109, Little Turncot Street, Chapelby Road, St. Pancras! You're welcome to it, if it's any use to you.' Don't you think I would have fallen on that man's—or woman's—neck, and watered it with my tears? Just think what a saving of brain-force it would have been to me—how many petty vexations it would have spared me! See here, then! Is your last place let?"

"Yes," I said. "A Mr. Marrow has it now."

"Ha!" he said, with satisfaction. "Now there must be lots of Mr. Marrow's friends in the same predicament as I was—people whose brains are softening in the effort to accommodate '109, Little Turncot Street, Chapelby Road, St. Pancras.' Psychical science has made such great strides in this age that with a little ingenuity it should surely not be impossible to transfer the memory of it from my brain to theirs."

"But," I gasped, "even if it was possible, why should you give away what you don't want? That would be charity."

"You do not suspect me of that?" he cried reproachfully. "No, my ideas are not so primitive. For don't you see that there is a memory *I* want—'33, Royal Flats—'"

"22, Albert Flats," I murmured shame-facedly.

"22, Albert Flats," he repeated witheringly. "You see how badly I want it. Well, what I propose is to exchange my memory of '109, Little Turncot Street, Chapelby Road, St. Pancras'" (he always rolled it slowly on his tongue with morbid self-torture and almost intolerable reproachfulness), "for the memory of '22, Albert Square.'"

"But you forget," I said, though I lacked the courage to correct him again, "that the people who want '109, Little Turncot Street,' are not the people who possess '22, Albert Flats.'"

"Precisely; the principle of direct exchange is not feasible. What is wanted, therefore, is a Memory Clearing House. If I can only discover the process of thought-transference, I will establish one, so as to bring the right parties into communication. Everybody who has old memories to dispose of will send me in particulars. At the end of each week I will publish a catalogue of the memories in the market, and circulate it among my subscribers, who will pay, say, a guinea a year. When the subscriber reads his catalogue and lights upon any memory he would like to have, he will send me a postcard, and I will then bring him into communication with the proprietor, taking, of course, a commission upon the transaction. Doubtless, in time, there will be a supplementary catalogue devoted to 'Wants,' which may induce people to scour their brains for half-forgotten reminiscences, or persuade them to give up memories they would never have parted with otherwise. Well, my boy, what do you think of it?"

"It opens up endless perspectives," I said, half-dazed.

"It will be the greatest invention ever known!" he cried, inflaming himself more and more. "It will change human life, it will make a new epoch, it will effect a greater economy of human force than all the machines under the sun. Think of the saving of nerve-tissue, think of the prevention of brain-irritation. Why, we shall all live longer through it—centenarians will become as cheap as American millionaires."

Live longer through it! Alas, the mockery of the recollection! He left me, his face working wildly. For days the vision of it interrupted my own work. At last, I could bear the suspense no more and went to his house. I found him in ecstasies and his wife in tears. She was beginning to suspect the family skeleton.

"*Eureka!*" he was shouting. "*Eureka!*"

"What is the matter?" sobbed the poor woman. "Why don't you speak English? He has been going on like this for the last five minutes," she added, turning pitifully to me.

("'What is the Matter?'")

"*Eureka!*" shouted O'Donovan. "I must say it. No new invention is complete without it."

ISRAEL ZANGWILL

"Bah! I didn't think you were so conventional," I said contemptuously. "I suppose you have found out how to make the memory-transferring machine?"

"I have," he cried exultantly. "I shall christen it the noemagraph, or thought-writer. The impression is received on a sensitised plate which acts as a medium between the two minds. The brow of the purchaser is pressed against the plate, through which a current of electricity is then passed."

He rambled on about volts and dynamic psychometry and other hard words, which, though they break no bones, should be strictly confined in private dictionaries.

"I am awfully glad you came in," he said, resuming his mother tongue at last—"because if you won't charge me anything I will try the first experiment on you."

I consented reluctantly, and in two minutes he rushed about the room triumphantly shouting, "22, Albert Flats, Victoria Square, Westminster," till he was hoarse. But for his enthusiasm I should have suspected he had crammed up my address on the sly.

He started the Clearing House forthwith. It began humbly as an attic in the Strand. The first number of the catalogue was naturally meagre. He was good enough to put me on the free list, and I watched with interest the development of the enterprise. He had canvassed his acquaintances for subscribers, and begged everybody he met to send him particulars of their cast-off memories. When he could afford to advertise a little, his *clientèle* increased. There is always a public for anything *bizarre*, and a percentage of the population would send thirteen stamps for the Philosopher's Stone, post free. Of course, the rest of the population smiled at him for an ingenious quack.

The "Memories on Sale" catalogue grew thicker and thicker. The edition issued to the subscribers contained merely the items, but O'Donovan's copy comprised also the names and addresses of the vendors, and now and again he allowed me to have a peep at it in strict confidence. The inventor himself had not foreseen the extraordinary uses to which his noemagraph would be put, nor the extraordinary developments of his business. Here are some specimens culled at random from No. 13 of the Clearing House catalogue when O'Donovan still limited himself to facilitating the sale of superfluous memories:—

1. 25, Portsdown Avenue, Maida. Vale.
3. 13502, 17208 (banknote numbers).

12. History of England (a few Saxon kings missing), as successful in a recent examination by the College of Preceptors. Adapted to the requirements of candidates for the Oxford and Cambridge Local and the London Matriculation.

17. Paley's Evidences, together with a job lot of dogmatic theology (second-hand), a valuable collection by a clergyman recently ordained, who has no further use for them.

26. A dozen whist wrinkles, as used by a retiring speculator. Excessively cheap.

29. Mathematical formulæ (complete sets; all the latest novelties and improvements, including those for the higher plane curves, and a selection of the most useful logarithms), the property of a dying Senior Wrangler. Applications must be immediate, and no payment need be made to the heirs till the will has been proved.

35. Arguments in favour of Home Rule (warranted sound); proprietor, distinguished Gladstonian M.P., has made up his mind to part with them at a sacrifice. Eminently suitable for bye-elections. Principals only.

58. Witty wedding speech, as delivered amid great applause by a bridegroom. Also an assortment of toasts, jocose and serious, in good condition. Reduction on taking a quantity.

Politicians, clergymen, and ex-examinees soon became the chief customers. Graduates in arts and science hastened to discumber their memories of the useless load of learning which had outstayed its function of getting them on in the world. Thus not only did they make some extra money, but memories which would otherwise have rapidly faded were turned over to new minds to play a similarly beneficent part in aiding the careers of the owners. The fine image of Lucretius was realised, and the torch of learning was handed on from generation to generation. Had O'Donovan's business been as widely known as it deserved, the curse of cram would have gone to roost for ever, and a finer physical race of Englishmen would have been produced. In the hands of honest students the invention might have produced intellectual giants, for each scholar could have started where his predecessor left off, and added more to his wealth of lore, the moderns standing upon the shoulders of the ancients in a more literal sense than Bacon dreamed. The memory of Macaulay, which all Englishmen rightly reverence, might have been possessed by his schoolboy. As it was, omniscient idiots abounded, left colossally wise by their fathers, whose painfully acquired memories they inherited without the intelligence to utilise them.

O'Donovan's Parliamentary connection was a large one, doubtless merely because of his former position and his consequent contact with political circles. Promises to constituents were always at a discount, the supply being immensely in excess of the demand; indeed, promises generally were a drug in the market.

Instead of issuing the projected supplemental catalogue of "Memories Wanted," O'Donovan by this time saw his way to buying them up on spec. He was not satisfied with his commission. He had learnt by experience the kinds that went best, such as exam. answers, but he resolved to have all sorts and be remembered as the Whiteley of Memory. Thus the Clearing House very soon developed into a storehouse. O'Donovan's advertisement ran thus:—

WANTED! Wanted! Wanted! Memories! Memories! Best Prices in the Trade. Happy, Sad, Bitter, Sweet (as Used by Minor Poets). High Prices for Absolutely Pure Memories. Memories, Historical, Scientific, Pious, &c. Good Memories! Special Terms to Liars. Precious Memories (Exeter Hall-marked). New Memories for Old! Lost Memories Recovered while you wait. Old Memories Turned equal to New.

O'Donovan soon sported his brougham. Any day you went into the store (which now occupied the whole of the premises in the Strand) you could see endless traffic going on. I often loved to watch it. People who were tired of themselves came here to get a complete new outfit of memories, and thus change their identities. Plaintiffs, defendants, and witnesses came to be fitted with memories that would stand the test of the oath, and they often brought solicitors with them to advise them in selecting from the stock. Counsel's opinion on these points was regarded as especially valuable. Statements that would wash and stand rough pulling about were much sought after. Gentlemen and ladies writing reminiscences and autobiographies were to be met with at all hours, and nothing was more pathetic than to see the humble artisan investing his hard-earned "tanner" in recollections of a seaside holiday.

In the buying-up department trade was equally brisk, and people who were hard-up were often forced to part with their tenderest recollections. Memories of dead loves went at five shillings a dozen, and all those moments which people had vowed never to forget were sold at starvation prices. The memories "indelibly engraven" on hearts were invariably faded and only sold as damaged. The salvage from the most ardent fires of affection rarely paid the porterage. As a rule, the dearest memories were the cheapest. Of the memory of favours there was always a glut, and often heaps of diseased memories had to be swept away at the instigation of the sanitary inspector. Memories of wrongs done, being rarely parted with except when their owners were at their last gasp, fetched fancy prices. Mourners' memories ruled especially lively. In the Memory Exchange, too, there was always a crowd, the temptation to barter worn-out memories for new proving irresistible.

One day O'Donovan came to me, crying "*Eureka!*" once more.

"Shut up!" I said, annoyed by the idiotic Hellenicism.

"Shut up! Why, I shall open ten more shops. I have discovered the art of duplicating, triplicating, polyplicating memories. I used only to be able to get one impression out of the sensitised plate, now I can get any number."

"Be careful!" I said. "This may ruin you."

"How so?" he asked scornfully.

"Why, just see—suppose you supply two candidates for a science degree with the same chemical reminiscences, you lay them under a suspicion of copying; two after-dinner speakers may find themselves recollecting the same joke; several autobiographers may remember their making the same remark to Gladstone. Unless your customers can be certain they have the exclusive right in other people's memories, they will fall away."

"Perhaps you are right," he said. "I must '*Eureka*' something else." His Greek was as defective as if he had had a classical education.

What he found was "The Hire System." Some people who might otherwise have been good customers objected to losing their memories entirely. They were willing to part with them for a period. For instance, when a man came up to town or took a run to Paris, he did not mind dispensing with some of his domestic recollections, just for a change. People who knew better than to forget themselves entirely profited by the opportunity of acquiring the funds for a holiday, merely by leaving some of their memories behind them. There were always others ready to hire for a season the discarded bits of personality, and thus remorse was done away with, and double lives became a luxury within the reach of the multitude. To the very poor, O'Donovan's new development proved an invaluable auxiliary to the pawn-shop. On Monday mornings, the pavement outside was congested with wretched-looking women anxious to pawn again the precious memories they had taken out with Saturday's wages. Under this hire system it became possible to pledge the memories of the absent *for* wine instead of in it. But the most gratifying result was its enabling pious relatives to redeem the memories of the dead, on payment of the legal interest. It was great fun to watch O'Donovan strutting about the rooms of his newest branch, swelling with pride like a combination cock and John Bull.

The experiences he gained here afforded him the material for a final development, but, to be strictly chronological, I ought first to mention the newspaper into which the catalogue evolved. It was called *In Memoriam*, and was published at a penny, and gave a prize of a thousand pounds to any reader who lost his memory on the railway, and who applied for the reward in person. *In Memoriam* dealt with everything relating to memory, though, dishonestly enough, the articles were all original. So were the advertisements, which were required to have reference to the objects of the Clearing House—*e.g.*,

A PHILANTHROPIC GENTLEMAN of good *address*, who has travelled a great deal, wishes to offer his *addresses* to impecunious *young ladies* (orphans preferred). Only those genuinely desirous of changing their residences, and with weak memories, need apply.

And now for the final and fatal "*Eureka.*" The anxiety of some persons to hire out their memories for a period led O'Donovan to see that it was absurd for him to pay for the use of them. The owners were only too glad to dodge remorse. He hit on the sublime idea that they ought to pay *him*. The result was the following advertisement in *In Memoriam* and its contemporaries:—

AMNESIA AGENCY! O'Donovan's Anodyne. Cheap Forgetfulness—Complete or Partial. Easy Amnesia—Temporary or Permanent. Haunting Memories Laid! Consciences Cleared. Cares carefully Removed without Gas or Pain. The London address of Lethe is 1001, Strand. Don't forget it.

Quite a new class of customers rushed to avail themselves of the new pathological institution. What attracted them was having to pay. Hitherto they wouldn't have gone if you paid *them*, as O'Donovan used to do. Widows and widowers presented themselves in shoals for treatment, with the result that marriages took place even within the year of mourning—a thing which obviously could not be done under any other system. I wonder whether Geraldine—but let me finish now!

How well I remember that bright summer's morning when, wooed without by the liberal sunshine, and disgusted with the progress I was making with my new study in realistic fiction, I threw down my pen, strolled down the Strand, and turned into the Clearing House. I passed through the selling department, catching a babel of cries from the counter-jumpers—"Two gross anecdotes? Yes, sir; this way, sir. Half-dozen proposals; it'll be cheaper if you take a dozen, miss. Can I do anything more for you, mum? Just let me show you a sample of our innocent recollections. The Duchess of Bayswater has just taken some. Anything in the musical line this morning, signor? We have some lovely new recollections just in from impecunious composers. Won't you take a score? Good morning, Mr. Clement Archer. We have the very thing for you—a memory of Macready playing Wolsey, quite clear and in excellent preservation; the only one in the market. Oh, no, mum; we have already allowed for these memories being slightly soiled. Jones, this lady complains the memories we sent her were short."

O'Donovan was not to be seen. I passed through the Buying Department, where the employees were beating down the prices of "kind remembrances," and through the Hire Department, where the clerks were turning up their noses at the old memories that had been pledged so often, into the Amnesia Agency. There I found the great organiser peering curiously at a sensitised plate.

"Oh," he said, "is that you? Here's a curiosity."

"What is it?" I asked.

"The memory of a murder. The patient paid well to have it off his mind, but I am afraid I shall miss the usual second profit, for who will buy it again?"

"I will!" I cried, with a sudden inspiration. "Oh! what a fool I have been. I should have been your best customer. I ought to have bought up all sorts of memories, and written the most veracious novel the world has seen. I haven't got a murder in my new book, but I'll work one in at once. '*Eureka!*'"

"Stash that!" he said revengefully. "You can have the memory with pleasure. I couldn't think of charging an old friend like you, whose moving from an address, which I've sold, to 22, Albert Flats, Victoria Square, Westminster, made my fortune."

That was how I came to write the only true murder ever written. It appears that the seller, a poor labourer, had murdered a friend in Epping Forest, just to rob him of half-a-crown, and calmly hid him under some tangled brushwood. A few months afterwards, having unexpectedly come into a fortune, he thought it well to break entirely with his past, and so had the memory extracted at the Agency. This, of course, I did not mention, but I described the murder and the subsequent feelings of the assassin, and launched the book on the world with a feeling of exultant expectation.

Alas! it was damned universally for its tameness and the improbability of its murder scenes. The critics, to a man, claimed to be authorities on the sensations of murderers, and the reading public, aghast, said I was flying in the face of Dickens. They said the man would have taken daily excursions to the corpse, and have been forced to invest in a season ticket to Epping Forest; they said he would have started if his own shadow crossed his path, not calmly have gone on drinking beer like an innocent babe at its mother's breast. I determined to have the laugh of them. Stung to madness, I wrote to the papers asserting the truth of my murder, and giving the exact date and the place of burial. The next day a detective found the body, and I was arrested. I asked the police to send for O'Donovan, and gave them the address of the Amnesia Agency, but O'Donovan denied the existence of such an institution, and said he got his living as secretary of the Shamrock Society.

I raved and cursed him then—now it occurs to me that he had perhaps submitted himself (and everybody else) to amnesiastic treatment. The jury recommended me to mercy on the ground that to commit a murder for the artistic purpose of describing the sensations bordered on insanity; but even this false plea has not saved my life.

It may. A petition has been circulated by Mudie's, and even at the eighth hour my reprieve may come. Yet, if the third volume of my life be closed to-morrow, I pray that these, my last words, may be published in an *édition de luxe*, and such of the profits as the publisher can spare be given to Geraldine.

If I am reprieved, I will never buy another murderer's memory, not for all the artistic ideals in the world, I'll be hanged if I do.

MATED BY A WAITER

I

BLACK AND WHITE

Jones! I mention him here because he is the first and last word of the story. It is the story of what might be called a game of chess between me and him; for I never made a move, but he made a counter-move. You must remember though that he played, so to speak, blindfold, while I started the game, not with the view of mating him, but merely for the fun of playing.

There was to be a Review of the Fleet, and the inhabitants of Ryde rejoiced, as befitted sons of the sea. Although many of them would be reduced to living in their cellars, like their own black-beetles, so that they might harbour the patriotic immigrant, they sacrificed themselves ungrudgingly. No, it was not the natives who grumbled.

My friends, Jack Woolwich and Merton Towers, being in the Civil Service, naturally desired to pay a compliment to the less civil department of State, and picked their month's holiday so as to include the Review. They took care to let the Review come out at the posterior extremity of the holiday, so as to find them quite well and in the enjoyment of excellent quarters at economical rates. They selected a comfortable but unfashionable hotel, at moderate but uninclusive terms, and joyously stretched their free limbs unswaddled by red-tape. Soon London became a forgotten nightmare.

They wrote to me irregularly, tantalising me unwittingly with glimpses of buoyant wave and sunny pasture. It fretted me to be immured in the stone-prison of the metropolis, and my friends' letters did but sprinkle sea-salt on my wounds; for I was working up a medical practice in the northern district, and my absence might prove fatal—not so much, perhaps, to my patients as to my prospects. I was beginning to be recognised as a specialist in throats and eyes, and I invariably sent my clients' ears to my old hospital chum, Robins, which increased the respect of the neighbourhood for my professional powers. Your general practitioner is a suspiciously omniscient person, and it is far sager to know less and to charge more.

"My dear Ted," wrote the Woolwich Infant (of course we could not escape calling Jack Woolwich thus), "I do wish we had you here. Such larks! We've got the most comical cuss of a waiter you ever saw. I feel sure he would appeal irresistibly to your sense of humour. He seems to boss the whole establishment. His name is Jones; and when you have known him a day you feel that he is the only Jones—the only Jones possible. He is a middle-aged man, with a slight stoop and a cat-like crawl. His face is large and flabby, ornamented with mutton-chop whiskers, streaked as with the silver of half a century of tips. He is always at your elbow—a mercenary Mephistopheles—suggesting drives or sails, and recommending certain yachts, boats, and carriages with insinuative irresistibleness. He has the tenacity of an army of able-bodied leeches, and if you do not take his advice he spoils your day. You may shake him off by fleeing into the interior of the Isle, or plunging into the sea; but you cannot be always trotting about or bathing; and at mealtimes he waits upon those who have disregarded his recommendations. He has a hopelessly corruptive effect on the soul, and I, who have always prided myself on my immaculate moral get-up, was driven to desperate lying within twenty-four hours of my arrival. I told him how much I had enjoyed the carriage-drive he had counselled, or the sail he had sanctioned by his approval; and, in return, he regaled me with titbits at our *table d'hôte* dinner. But the next day he followed me about with large, reproachful eyes, in grieved silence. I saw that he knew all; and I dragged myself along with my tail between my legs, miserably asking myself how I could regain his respect.

"Wherever I turned I saw nothing but those dilated orbs of rebuke. I took refuge in my bedroom, but he glided in to give me a bad French halfpenny the chambermaid had picked up under my bed; and the implied contrast to be read in those eyes, between the honesty of the establishment and my own, was more than I could bear. I flew into a passion—the last resource of detected guilt—and irrelevantly told him I would choose my own amusements, and that I had not come down to increase his commissions.

"Ted, till my dying day I shall not forget the dumb martyrdom of those eyes! When he was sufficiently recovered to speak, he swore, in a voice broken by emotion, that he would scorn taking commissions from the quarters I imagined. Ashamed of my unjust suspicions, I apologised, and went out that afternoon alone for a trip in the *Mayblossom*, and was violently sick. Merton funked it because the weather was rough, and had a lucky escape; but he had to meet Jones in the evening.

"Merton's theory is, that Jones doesn't get commissions, for the simple reason that the wagonettes and broughams and bath-chairs and boats and yachts he recommends all belong to him, and that the nominal proprietors are men of straw, stuffed by the only Jones. This theory is, I must admit, borne out by the evidence of O'Rafferty, a jolly old Irishman, whose wife died here early in the year, and who has been making holiday ever since. He says that Jones had a week off in March when there was hardly anybody in the hotel, and he was to be seen driving a wagonette between Ryde and Cowes daily. And, indeed, there is something curiously provincial and plebeian about Jones's mind which suggests a man who has risen from the cab-ranks.

"His ideas of tips are delightfully democratic, and you cannot insult him even with twopence. He handles a bottle of cheap claret as reverently as a Russian the image of his saint, and he has never got over his awe of champagne. To drink Monopole at dinner is to mount a pedestal of dignity, and I completely recovered his esteem by drowning the memories of that awful marine experience in a pint of 'dry.' When he draws the champagne cork he has a sacerdotal air, and he pours out the foaming liquid with the obsequiousness of an archbishop placing on his sovereign's head the crown he may never hope to do more than touch. But perhaps the best proof of the humbleness of his origin is his veneration for the aristocracy. An average waiter is, from the nature of his occupation, liable to be brought into contact with the bluest of blood, and to have his undiminished reverence for it tempered with a good-natured perception of mortal foibles. But Jones's attitude is one of awestruck unquestioning worship. He speaks of a lord with bated breath, and he dare not, even in conversation, ascend to a duke.

"It would seem that this is not one of the hotels which the aristocrat's fancy turns to thoughts of; for apparently only one lord has ever stayed here, judging by the frequency with which Jones whispers his name. Though some of us seem to have a beastly lot of money, and to do all the year round what Merton and I can only indulge in for a month, we are a rather plebeian company I fear, and it is simply overwhelming the way Jones rams Lord Porchester down our throats.

"'When his lordship stayed here he partic'larly admired the view from that there window.' 'His lordship wouldn't drink anything but Pommery Green-oh; he used to swallow it by tumblersful, as you or I might rum-and-water, sir.' 'Ah, sir! Lord Porchester hired the *Mayblossom* all to himself, and often said: "By Jove! she's like a sea-gull. She almost comes near my own little beauty. I think I shall have to buy her, by gad I shall! and let them race each other.'"

"And the fellow is such an inveterate gossip that everybody here knows everybody else's business. The proprietor is a quiet, gentlemanly fellow, and is the only person in the place who keeps his presence of mind in the presence of Jones, and is not in mental subjugation to the flabby, florid, crawling boss of the rest of the show.

"You may laugh, but I warrant you wouldn't be here a day before Jones would get the upper hand of you. On the outside, of course, he is as fixedly deferential as if every moment were to be your last, and the cab were waiting to take you to the Station; but inwardly, you feel he is wound about you like a boa-constrictor. I do so long to see him swathing you in his coils! Won't you come down, and give your patients a chance?"

"My dear Jack," I wrote back to the Infant, "I am so sorry that you are having bad weather. You don't say so, but when a man covers six sheets of writing-paper I know what it means. I must say you have given me an itching to try my strength with the only Jones; but, alas! this is a musical neighbourhood, and there is a run on sore throats, so I must be content to enjoy my Jones by deputy. Is there any other attraction about the shanty?"

Merton Towers took up the running:

"Barring ourselves and Jones," he wrote, "and perhaps O'Rafferty, there isn't a decent human being in the hotel. The ladies are either old and ugly, or devoted to their husbands. The only ones worth talking to are in the honeymoon stage. But Jones is worth a hundred petticoats: he is tremendous fun. We've got a splendid spree on now. I think the Infant told you that Jones has not enjoyed that actual contact with the 'hupper suckles' which his simple snobbish soul so thoroughly deserves; and that, in spite of the eternal Lord Porchester, his acquaintance is less with the *beau monde* than with the Bow and Bromley *monde*. Since the Infant and I discovered this we have been putting on the grand air. Unfortunately, it was too late to claim titles; but we have managed to convey the impression that, although commoners and plain misters, we have yet had the privilege of rubbing against the purple. We have casually and carelessly dropped hints of aristocratic acquaintances, and Jones has bowed down and picked them up reverently.

"The other day, when he brought us our Chartreuse after dinner, the Infant said: 'Ah! I suppose you haven't got Damtidam in stock?' The only Jones stared awestruck. 'Of course not! How can it possibly have penetrated to these parts yet?' I struck in with supercilious reproach. 'Damtidam! What is that, sir?' faltered Jones. 'What! you don't mean to say you haven't even heard of it?' cried the Infant in amaze. Jones looked miserable and apologetic. 'It's the latest liqueur,' I explained graciously. 'Awfully expensive; made by a new brotherhood of Anchorites in Dalmatia, who have secluded themselves from the world in order to concoct it. They only serve the aristocracy; but, of course, now and then a millionaire manages to get hold of a bottle. Lord Everett made me a present of some a couple of months ago, but I use it very, very sparingly, and I daresay the flask's at least half-full. I have it in my portmanteau.' 'How does it taste, sir?' enquired Jones, in a hushed, solemn whisper. 'Damtidam is not the sort of thing that would please the uncultured palate,' I replied haughtily. 'It's what they call an acquired taste, ain't it, sir?' he asked wistfully. 'Would you like to have a drop?' I said affably. 'Oh, Towers!' cried the Infant, 'what would Lord Everett say?' 'Well, but how is Lord Everett to know?' I responded. 'Jones will never let on.' 'His lordship shall never hear a word from my lips,' Jones protested gratefully. 'But you won't like it at first. To really enjoy Damtidam, you'll have to have several goes at it. Have you got a little phial?' Jones ran and fetched the phial, and I fished out of my portmanteau the bottle of dyspepsia mixture you gave us and filled Jones's phial. I watched him glide into the garden and put the phial to his lips with a heavenly expression, through which some suggestions of purgatory subsequently flitted. That was yesterday.

"'Well, Jones, how do you like Damtidam?' I enquired genially this morning. 'Very 'igh-class, very 'igh-class in its taste, thank you, sir,' he replied. 'It's 'ardly for the likes o' me, I'm afraid; but as you've been good enough to give me some, I'll make so bold as to enjoy it. I 'ad a second sip at it this morning, and I liked it a deal better than yesterday. It requires time to get the taste, sir; but, depend upon it, I'll do my best to acquire it.' 'I wish you success!' I cried. 'Once you get used to it, it's simply delicious. Why, I'd never travel without a bottle of it. I often take it in the middle of the night. You finish that phial, Jones; never mind the cost. I'm writing to Lord Everett to-day, and I'll drop him a broad hint that I should like another.'

"Eureka! As I write this a glorious idea has occurred to me. I *am* writing to you to-day, and you *are* the giver of the Damtidam, *alias* dyspepsia mixture. Oh, if you could only come down and pose as Lord Everett! What larks we should have! Do, old boy; it'll be the greatest spree we've ever had. Don't say 'no.' You want a change, you know you do; or you'll be on the sick-list yourself soon. Come, if only for a week! Surely you can find a chum to take your practice. How about Robins? He can't be all ears. I daresay he's equal to looking after your throats and eyes for a week. The Infant joins with me, and says that if you don't come he'll kill off Jones, and deprive you for ever of the pleasure of knowing him.

I remain,
Yours till Jones's death,
MERTON TOWERS

"P.S.—When you come, bring a dozen of Damtidam."

The prospect of becoming Lord Everett flattered and tickled me, and was a daily temptation to me in my dreary drudgery. To the appeal of the pictured visions of woods and waters was added the alluring figure of Jones, standing a little bent amid the smiling landscape, acquiring a taste for Damtidam; his pasty face kneaded ecstatically, his hand on the pit of his stomach. At last I could stand it no longer, I went to see Robins, and I wrote to my friends:

"Jones wins! Expect me about ten days before the Review, so that we can return to town together.

"When I first asked Robins to take my eyes, he was inclined to dash them; but the moment I let him into the plot against Jones, he agreed to do all my work on condition of being informed of the progress of the campaign.

"I shan't tell anyone I'm leaving town, and Robins will forward my letters in an envelope addressed to Lord Everett.

"P.S.—I am bottling a special brand of Damtidam."

II

A Difficult Opening

The proudest moment of Jones's life was probably when he assisted me to alight from the carriage I had ordered at the station. I wore a light duster, a straw hat, and goloshes (among other things), together with the air of having come over in the same steamboat as the Conqueror. I may as well mention here that I am tall, almost as tall as the Woolwich Infant, who frequently stands six foot two on my pet corn (Towers, by the way, is a short squat man, whose delusion that he is handsome can be read plainly upon his face). My features, like my habits, are regular. By complexion I belong to the fair sex; but there is a masculine vigour about my physique and my language which redeems me from effeminateness. I do not mention my tawny moustache, because that is not an exclusively male trait in these days of women's rights.

"Good morning, my lord!" said Jones, his obeisance so low and his voice so loud that I had to give the driver half-a-crown.

I nodded almost imperceptibly, knowing that the surest way to impress Jones with my breeding was to display no trace of it. I strolled languidly into the hall, deferentially followed by the Infant and Merton Towers, leaving Jones distracted between the desire to handle my luggage and to show me my room.

"Hexcuse me, my lord," said Jones, fluttered. "Jane, run for the master."

"Excuse *me*, my lord," said the Infant; "I'll run up and wash for lunch. See you in a moment. Come along, Merton. It's so beastly high-up. When are you going to get a lift, Jones?"

"In a moment, sir; in a moment!" replied Jones automatically.

He seemed half-dazed.

The quiet, gentlemanly young proprietor, who appeared to have been disturbed in his studies, for he held a volume of Dickens in his hand, conducted me to a gorgeously furnished bedroom on the first floor facing the sea.

"It's the best we can do for your lordship," he said apologetically; "but with the Review so near—"

I waved my hand impatiently, wishing he could have done worse for me. In town I had been too busy to realise the situation in detail; but now it began to dawn upon me that it was going to be an expensive joke. Besides, I was separated from my friends, who were corridors away and flights higher, and convivial meetings at midnight would mean disagreeable stockinged wanderings for somebody—a mere shadow of a trifle, no doubt, but little things like that worry more than they look. I was afraid to ask the price of this swell bedroom, and I began to comprehend the meaning of *noblesse oblige*.

"The sitting-room adjoins," said the hotel-keeper, suddenly opening a door and ushering me into a magnificent chamber, with a lofty ceiling and a dado. The furniture was plush-covered and suggestive of footmen. "I presume you will not be taking your meals in public?"

"H'm! H'm!" I muttered, tugging at my moustache. Then, struck by a bright idea, I said: "What do Mr. Woolwich and Mr. Towers do?"

"They join the *table d'hôte*, your lordship," said the proprietor. "They didn't require a sitting-room they said, as they should be almost entirely in the open air."

"Oh! well, I could hardly leave my friends," I said reflectively; "I suppose I shall have to join them at the *table d'hôte*."

"I daresay they would like to have your lordship with them," said the proprietor, with a faint, flattering smile.

I smiled internally at my cunning in getting out of the sitting-room.

"It's an awful bore," I yawned; "but I'm afraid they'd be annoyed if I ate up here alone, so—"

"You'll invite them up here for all meals? Yes, my lord," said Jones at my elbow.

He had sidled up with his cat-like crawl. Through the open door of communication I saw he had deposited my boxes in the gorgeous bedroom. There was a moment of tense silence, in which I struggled desperately for a response. The brazen shudder of a gong vibrated through the house.

"Is that lunch?" I asked in relief, making a step towards the door.

"Yes, my lord," said Jones; "but not your lordship's lunch. It will be laid here immediately, my lord. I will go at once and convey your invitation to your lordship's friends."

He hastened from the room, leaving me dumbfounded. I did not enjoy Jones as much as I had anticipated. In a moment a pretty parlour-maid arrived to lay the cloth. I became conscious that I was hungry and thirsty and travel-stained, and I determined to let things slide till after lunch, when I could easily set them right. The sunshine was flooding the room, and the sea was a dance of diamonds. The sight of the prandial preparations softened me. I retired to my beautiful bedroom and plunged my face into a basin of water.

There was a knock at the door.

"Come in!" I spluttered.

"Your hot water, my lord!" It was Jones.

"I've got into enough already," I thought. "Don't want it," I growled peremptorily; "I always wash in cold."

I would have my way in small things, I resolved, if I could not have it in great.

"Certainly, your lordship; this is only for shaving."

My cheeks grew hot beneath the fingers washing them. I remembered that I had overslept myself that morning, and neglected shaving lest I should miss my train. There were but a few microscopic hairs, yet I felt at once I had not the face to meet Jones at lunch.

"Thank you!" I said savagely.

When I had wiped my eyes I found he was still in the room, bent in meek adoration.

"What in the devil do you want now?" I thundered.

His eyes lit up with rapture. It was as though I had made oath I was a nobleman and removed his last doubt.

"Pommery Green-oh or Hideseek, my lord?"

I cursed silently. I am of an easy-going disposition, and in my most penurious student days, had to spend twenty-five per cent more on my modest lunch whenever the waiter said: "Stout or bitter, sir?" But the present alternative was far more terrible. I was on the point of saying I was a teetotaller, when I remembered that would shut off my nocturnal whisky-and-water, and condemn me to goody-goody beverages at meals. I remembered, too, that Jones intended the champagne as much for my friends as myself, and that lords are proverbially disassociated from temperance. Oh! it was horrible that this oleaginous snob should rob a poor man of his beer! Perhaps I could escape with claret. In my agitation I commenced lathering my chin and returned no answer at all. The voice of Jones came at last, charged with deeper respect, but inevitable as the knell of doom.

"Did you say Pommery Green-oh! my lord?"

"No!" I yelled defiantly.

"Thank you, my lord. Lord Porchester was very partial to our Hideseek—when he was here. We have an excellent year."

"I wish you had twelve months," I thought furiously. Then when the door closed upon him, I ground my razor savagely and muttered: "All right! I'll take it out of you in Damtidam."

I heard the bustle of my friends arriving to lunch, and I shaved myself hastily. Then slipping on my coat and dabbing a bit of sticking-plaster on my chin, I threw open the door violently; for I was not going to let those two fellows off an exhibition of slang. They should have thought out the plot more fully; have hired me a moderate bedroom in advance, and not have let me in for the luxuries of Lucullus. It was a cowardly desertion, their leaving me at the critical moment, and they should learn what I thought of it.

"You ruffians!" I began; but the words died on my lips. Jones was waiting at table.

It ought to have been a delicious lunch: broiled chickens and apple-tart; the cool breeze coming through the open window, the sea and the champagne sparkling. But I, who was hungriest, enjoyed it least; Jones, who ate nothing, enjoyed it most. The Infant and Merton Towers simply overflowed with high spirits, keeping up a running fire of aristocratic allusions, which galled me beyond endurance.

"By the way, how is the dowager-duchess?" wound up the Infant.

"D— the dowager-duchess!" I roared, losing the remains of my temper.

Jones grew radiant, and the Infant winked irritating approval of my natural touches. Such contempt for duchesses could only be bred of familiarity. At last I could contain myself no longer; I must either explode or have a fit. I sent Jones for cigarettes.

Directly the door closed those two men turned upon me.

"I say, old fellow," exclaimed Towers reproachfully, "isn't this just going it a little too far?"

"What in creation made you take these howling apartments?" asked the Infant. "Review time, too! They've been saving up these rooms, foreseeing there would be some tip-top swells crowded out of the fashionable hotels. Why, there's a cosy little crib next to ours I made sure you'd have."

"Well, I call this cool!" I gasped.

"So it is," said the Infant; "I admit that. It's the coolest room in the house. It'll be real jolly up here; and if you can stand the racket I'm sure I'm not the chap to grumble."

"You must have been doing beastly well, old man," Towers put in enviously; "to feed us like critics on chicken and champagne. I suppose they'll be opening new cemeteries down your way presently."

"Look here, my fine fellows," I said ferociously, "don't you forget that there's plenty of room still in Ryde Churchyard."

"Hallo, Ted!" cried the Infant, looking up with ingenuous surprise, "I thought you came down here on a holiday?"

"Stash that!" I said. "It's you who've got me into this hole, and you know it."

"Hole!" cried Towers, looking round the room in amaze. "He calls this a hole! Hang it all, my boy, are you a millionaire? I call this good enough for a lord."

"Yes; but as I'm neither," I said grimly, "I should like you to understand that I'm not going to pay for this spread."

"What!" gasped the Infant. "Invite a man to lunch, and expect him to square the bill?"

"I never invited you!" I said indignantly.

"Who then?" said Towers sternly.

"Jones!" I answered.

"Yes, my lord! Sorry to have kept your lordship waiting; but I think you will find these cigarettes to your liking. I haven't been at this box since Lord Porchester was here, and it got mislaid."

"Take them away!" I roared. "They're Egyptians!"

"Yes, my lord!" said Jones, in delight.

He glided proudly from the room.

"'Jones invited us?'" pursued the Infant. "What rot! As if Jones would dare do anything you hadn't told him. *We* are his slaves. But you? Why, he hangs on your words!"

"D— him! I should like to see him hanging on something higher!" I cried.

"Yes, your language *is* low," admitted the Infant. "But, seriously, what's all the row about? I thought this champagne lunch was a bit of realism, just to start off with."

I explained briefly how Jones had coiled himself around me, even as they had described. The dado echoed their ribald laughter.

"Oh, well," said the Infant, "it's only right you should give a lunch the day you come into a peerage. It's really too much to expect us to pay scot, when there was a beautiful lunch of cold beef and pickles waiting for us in the dining-room, and included in our terms per week. We aren't going to pay for two lunches."

"I don't mind the lunch," I said, smiling, my sense of humour returning now that I had poured forth my grievance. "I'd gladly give

ISRAEL ZANGWILL

you chaps a lunch any day, and I'm pleased you enjoyed it so much. But, for the rest, I'm going to run this joke by syndicate, or not at all. I only came down with a tenner."

"A pound a day!" said Towers, "that ought to be enough."

"Why, there's a pound gone bang over this lunch already!" I retorted.

"And then there's the apartments," put in the Infant roguishly. "I wonder what they'll tot up to?"

"Jones alone knows," I groaned.

He came in—a veritable devil—while his name was on my lips, with a new box of cigarettes.

"Clear away!" I said briefly.

He cleared away, and we breathed freely. We leaned back in the plush-covered easy-chairs, sending rings of fragrant smoke towards the blue horizon, and I felt more able to face the situation calmly.

"I daresay we can lend you five quid between us," said Towers.

"What's the good of a loan to an honest man?" I asked. "Can't we work the joke without such a lot of capital? The first thing is to get out of these rooms, and into that cosy little crib near you. I can say I yearn for your society."

"But have you the courage to look Jones in the face and tell him that?" queried Towers dubiously.

I hesitated. I felt instinctively that Jones would be dreadfully shocked if I changed my palatial apartments for a cheap bedroom; that it would be better if some one else broke the news.

"Oh, the Infant'll explain," I said lightly.

"Nothing of the sort," said the Infant; "it won't wash now. Besides, they'd make you shell out in any case. They'd pretend they turned lots of applicants away this morning, because the rooms were let. No, keep the bedroom, and we'll go shares in this sitting-room. It's jollier to have a proper private room."

"Good!" I said. "Then it only remains to escape from these special meals and the champagne."

"You leave that to me," said the Infant. "I'll tell Jones that you hunger for our company at meals, but that we can't consent to come up here, because you, with that reckless prodigality which is wearing the dowager-duchess to a shadow, insist on paying for everything consumed on your premises, so that you must e'en come to the general table. Jones will be glad enough to trot you round."

"And I'll tell him," added Towers, "that, with that determined dipsomania which is making the money-lenders daily friendlier to your little brother, you swill champagne till you fly at waiters' throats like a mad dog, and that it is our sacred duty to diet you on table-beer or Tintara."

"Wouldn't it be simpler to tell him the truth?" I asked feebly.

"What!" gasped the Infant, "chuck up the sponge? Don't spoil the loveliest holiday I ever had, old man. Just think how you will go up in his estimation, when we tell him you are a spendthrift and a drunkard! For pity's sake, don't throw a gloom over Jones's life."

"Very well," I said, relenting. "Only the exes must be cut down. The motto must be, 'Extravaganza without extravagance, or farces economically conducted.'"

"Right you are!" they said; and then we smoked on in halcyon voluptuousness, now and then passing the matches or a droll remark about Jones. In the middle of one of the latter there was a knock at the door, and Jones entered.

"The carriage will be round in five minutes, my lord," he announced.

"The carriage!" I faltered, growing pale.

"Yes, my lord. I took the liberty of thinking your lordship wouldn't waste such a fine afternoon indoors."

"No; I'm going out at once," I said resolutely. "But I shan't drive."

"Very well, my lord; I will countermand the carriage, and order a horse. I presume your lordship would like a spirited one? Jayes, up the street, has a beautiful bay steed."

"Thank you; I don't care for riding—er—other people's horses."

"No; of course not, my lord. I'll see that the *May blossom* is reserved for your lordship's use this afternoon. Your lordship will have time for a glorious sail before dinner."

He hastened from the room.

"You'd better have the carriage," said the Infant drily; "it's cheaper than the yacht. You'll have to have it once, and you may as well get it over. After one trial, you can say it's too springless and the cushions are too crustaceous for your delicate anatomy."

"I'll see him at Jericho first!" I cried, and wrenched at the bell-pull with angry determination.

"Yes, my lord!"

He stood bent and insinuative before me.

"I won't have the yacht."

"Very well, my lord; then I won't countermand the carriage."

He turned to go.

"Jones!" I shrieked.

He looked back at me. His eyes, full of a trusting reverence, met mine. My resolution began oozing out at every pore.

"Is—is—are *you* going with the carriage?" I stammered, for want of something to say.

"No, my lord," he answered wistfully.

That settled it. I let him depart without another word.

It was certainly a pleasant drive through the delightful scenery of the Isle, and I determined, since I had to pay the piper, to enjoy the dance. The Infant and Towers were hilarious to the point of vulgarity: I let myself go at the will of Jones. When we got back, we realised with a start that it was half-past six. The dressing-gong was sounding. Jones met me in the passage.

"Dinner at seven, my lord, in your room."

I made frantic motions to the Infant.

"Tell him!" I breathed.

"It's too late now," he whispered back. "To-morrow!"

I telegraphed desperately to Towers. He shook his thick head helplessly.

"Have you invited my friends to dinner?" I asked Jones bitingly.

"No, my lord," he said simply. "I thought your lordship 'ad seen enough of them to-day."

There was a suggestion of reproach in the apology. Jones was more careful of my dignity than I was.

When I got to my room, I found, to my horror, my dress-clothes laid out on the bed—I had brought them on the off-chance of going to a local dance. Jones had opened my portmanteau. For a moment a cold chill traversed my spine, as I thought he must have seen the monogram on my linen, and discovered the imposture. Then I remembered with joy that it was an "E," which is the more formal initial of Ted, and would do for Everett. In my relief, I felt I must submit to the nuisance of dressing—in honour of Jones. While changing my trousers, a sudden curiosity took me. I peeped through the keyhole of my sitting-room, and saw Jones just arriving with another bottle of Heidsieck. I groaned. I knew I should have to drink it, to keep up the fiction Towers was going to palm off on Jones to-morrow. I felt like bolting on the spot, but I was in my Jaegers. Presently Jones sidled mysteriously towards my door and knelt down before it. It flashed upon me he wanted the keyhole I was occupying. I jumped up in alarm, and dressed with the decorum of a god with a worshipper's eye on him.

I swallowed what Jones gave me, fuming. With the roast, a blessed thought came to soothe me. Thenceforward I chuckled continuously. I refused the *parfait aux frais* and the savoury in my eagerness for the end of the meal. Revenge was sufficient sweets.

"Haw, hum!" I murmured, caressing my moustache. "Bring me a Damtidam."

I knew his little phial must be exhausted long since. I intended to give him a bottle.

"Did your lordship say Damtidam?"

"Damtidam!" I roared, while my heart beat voluptuous music. "You don't mean to say you don't keep it?"

"Oh no, my lord! We laid in a big stock of it; but Lord Porchester was that fond of it (used to drink it like your lordship does champagne), I doubt if I could lay my hand on a bottle."

"What an awful bo-ah!" I yawned. "I suppose I'll have to get a bottle of my own out of that little black box under my bed. I couldn't possibly go without it after dinner. Hang it all, the key is in my other trousers!"

"Oh, don't trouble, my lord," said Jones anxiously. "I'll run and see if I can find any."

I waited, gloating.

Jones returned gleefully.

"I've found plenty, my lord," he said, setting down a brimming liqueur-glass.

He lingered about, clearing the table. His eye was upon me. I drank the Damtidam. Then Jones departed, and I went about kicking the furniture, and striding about in my desolate grandeur, like Napoleon at St. Helena.

Presently the Infant and Towers came rushing in, choking with laughter.

"Your arrival has fired afresh all Jones's aristocratic ambitions," gurgled Towers. "Ha! ha! ha!"

"Ho! ho! ho!" panted the Infant. "He's coaxed us out of all our remaining Damtidam."

I grinned a sickly response.

"Great Scot!" the Infant bellowed. "What's this howling wilderness of shirt-front?"

"It's cooler," I explained.

III

THE QUEEN COMES INTO PLAY

I had to breakfast in my room, but by lunch the next day my friends had found an opportunity to explain me to Jones. They had on several occasions strongly exhorted Jones to secrecy as to my rank, so that the eyes of the whole table were on me when I entered. I ate with the ease of one conscious of giving involuntary lessons in etiquette to a furtive-glancing bourgeoisie. The Infant gave me Tintara, to break me gradually of champagne and reduce me to malt. After lunch Towers remonstrated with Jones on having obviously given me away.

"Sir," protested Jones, in righteous indignation, "I promised to tell no one in the hotel, and I have kept my word!"

"Well, how do they know then?" enquired Towers.

"I shouldn't be surprised if they read it in the *Visitors' List*," Jones answered.

Being now half-emancipated, I fell into the usual routine of a seaside holiday. I swam, I rowed, I walked, I lounged, whenever Jones would let me. One wet morning we even congratulated ourselves on our luxurious sitting-room, as we sat and smoked before the rain-whipt sea, till, unexpected, Jones brought up lunch for three. That evening, as we were entering the dining-room, Jones observed humbly to the Infant and Towers:

"Excuse me, gentlemen; I 'ave 'ad to separate you from his lordship. We've 'ad such a influx of visitors for the Review, I've been 'ard put to it to squeeze them all in."

Those wretched cowards marched feebly to a new extremity of the table, while I walked to my usual seat near the window, with anger flaming duskily on my brow. This time I was determined. I would stick to table-beer all the same.

But before I dropped into my chair every trace of anger vanished. My heart throbbed violently, my dazzled eyes surveyed my *serviette*. At my side was one of the most charming girls I had ever met. When the Heidsieck came, I raised my glass as in a dream, and silently drank to the glorious creature nearest my heart—on the left hand.

We medicos are not easily upset by woman's beauty; we know too well what it is made of. But there was something so exquisite about this girl's face as to make a hardened materialist hesitate to resolve her into a physiological formula. It was not long before I offered to pass her the pepper. She declined with thanks and brevity. Her accent grated unexpectedly on my ear: I was puzzled to know why. I spoke of the rain that still tapped at the window, as if anxious to come in.

"It was raining when I left Paris," she said; "but up till then I had a lovely time."

Now I saw what was the matter. She suffered from twang and was American. I have always had a prejudice against Americans—chiefly, I believe, because they always seem to be having "a lovely time." It was with a sense of partial disenchantment that I continued the conversation:

"So you have been in Paris?" I said, thinking of the old joke about good Americans going there when they die. "I must admit you look as if you had come from Heaven!"

"So wretched as all that!" she retorted, laughing merrily. There was no twang in the laugh; it was a ripple of music.

"I don't mean an exile from Heaven," I answered: "an excursionist, with a return-ticket."

"Oh! but I'm not going back," she said, shaking her lovely head.

"Not even when you die?" I asked, smiling.

"I guess I shall need a warmer climate then!" she flashed back audaciously.

"You're too good for that," I answered, without hesitation.

I caught a mischievous twinkle in her blue eyes, as she answered:

"Gracious! you're very spry at giving strange folks certificates."

"It's my business to give certificates," I answered, smiling.

"Marriage certificates, my lord?" she asked roguishly.

I was about to answer "Doctors' certificates," but her last two syllables froze the words on my lips.

"You—you—know me?" I stammered.

"Yes, your lordship," with a mock bow.

"Why—how—?" I faltered. "You've only just come."

"Jones," she answered.

"Jones!" I repeated, vexed.

"Yes, my lord."

He glided up and re-filled my glass.

"Jones is a nuisance," I said, when he was out of earshot again.

"Jones is a Britisher!" she said enigmatically. "Surely you don't mind people knowing who you are?"

"I'm afraid I do," I replied uneasily.

"I guess your reputation must be real shady," she said, with her American candour. "You English lords, we have just about sized you up in the States."

"I—I—" I stammered.

"No! don't tell me," she interrupted quickly; "I'd rather not know. My aunt here, that lady on my left,—she's a widow and half a Britisher, and respectable, don't you know,—will want me to cut you."

"And you don't want to?" I exclaimed eagerly.

"Well, one must talk to somebody," she said, arching her eyebrows. "It's all very well for my aunt. She's left her children at home. That's happiness enough for her. But that don't make things equally lively for me."

"Your language is frank," I said laughingly.

"Yes, that's one of the languages you've forgotten how to speak in this old country."

Again that musical ripple of mirth. Her fascination was fast enswathing me like another Jones, only a thousandfold more sweetly. Already I found her twang delightful, lending the last touch of charm to her original utterances. I looked up suddenly, and saw the Infant and Towers glaring enviously at me from the other end of the table. Then I was quite happy. True, they had the sprightly O'Rafferty between them, but he did not seem to console them—rather to chaff them.

"Ho! ho!" I roared, when we reached our sitting-room that night. "There's virtue in the peerage after all."

"Shut up!" the Infant snarled. "If you think you're going to annex that ripping creature, I warn you that bloated aristocracy will have to settle up for its marble halls. We're running this thing by syndicate, remember."

"Yes, but this isn't part of the profits," I urged defiantly.

"Oh, isn't it?" put in Towers. "Why do you suppose Jones sat her next to you, if not as a prerogative of nobility?"

"Well, but if I can get her to go out with me alone, that's a private transaction."

"No go, Teddy," said the Infant. "We don't allow you to play for your own hand."

"Or hers," added Towers. "While you were spooning, Jones was telling us all about her. Her name's Harper—Ethelberta Harper, and her old man is a Railway King, or something."

"She's a queen—I don't care of what!" I said fervently. "We got very chummy, and I'm going to take her for a row to-morrow morning. It's not my fault if she doesn't pal on to you."

"Stow that cant!" cried the Infant. "Either you surrender her to the syndicate or pay your own exes. Choose!"

"Well, I'll compromise!" I said desperately.

"No, you don't! It's to prevent your compromising her we want to stand in. We'll all go for that row."

"No, listen to my suggestion. I'll invite her to lunch after the row, and I'll invite you fellows to meet her."

"But how do you know she'll come?" said Towers.

"She will if I ask her aunt too."

"Scoundrel, you've asked them both already!" cried the Infant. "Where's the compromise?"

"I hadn't asked *you* already," I reminded him.

"No, but now you propose to use the capital of the syndicate!" he rejoined sharply.

"Nothing of the kind," I retorted rashly.

So it was settled. I had four guests to lunch, and Jones expanded visibly. The Infant and Towers kept Miss Harper pretty well to themselves, while I was left to entertain Mrs. Windpeg, a comely but tedious lady, who gave me details of her life in England since she left New York, a newly married wife, twenty years before. She seemed greatly interested in these details. Ethelberta paid no attention to her aunt, but a great deal to my friends. Several times I found myself gnawing my lip instead of my wing. But I had my revenge at the *table d'hôte*. Jones kept my friends remorselessly at bay, and religiously guarded my proximity to the lovely American. Strange mental revolution! The idea of tipping Jones actually commenced to germinate in my mind.

It was on Review-day that I realised I was hopelessly in love. Of course my quartet of friends was at the windows of my sitting-room. Jones also selected this room to see the Review from, and I fancy he regaled my visitors with delicate refreshments throughout the day, and I remember being vaguely glad that he made amends for the general neglect of Mrs. Windpeg by offering her the choicest titbits; but I have no clear recollection of anything but Ethelberta. Her face was my Review, though there was no powder on it. The play of light on her cheeks and hair was all the manoeuvres I cared for—the pearls of her mouth were my ranged rows of ships; and when everybody else was peering hopelessly into the thick smoke, my eyes were feasting on the sunshine of her face. I did not hear the cannon, nor the long, endless clamour of the packed streets, only the soft words she spoke from time to time.

"To-morrow morning I must go away," I murmured to her at dinner. I fancied she grew paler, but I could not be sure, for Jones at that moment changed my plate.

"I am sorry," she said simply. "Must you go?"

"Yes," I answered sadly. "My beautiful holiday is over. To-morrow, to work."

"I thought, for you lords, life was one long holiday," she said, surprised.

I was glad of the reminder. My love was hopeless. A struggling doctor could not ask for the hand of an heiress. Even if he could, it would be a poor recommendation to start with a confession of imposture. To ask, without confessing, were to become a scoundrel and a fortune-hunter of the lowest type. No; better to pass from her ken, leaving her memory of me untainted by suspicion—leaving my memory of her an idyllic, unfinished dream. And yet I could not help reflecting, with agony, that if I had not begun under false colours, if I had come to her only as what I was, I might have dared to ask for her love—yea, and perhaps have won it. Oh, how weak I had been not to tell her from the first! As if she would not have appreciated the joke! As if she would not have enrolled herself joyously in the campaign against Jones!

"Ah! my life will be anything but a long holiday, I fear," I sighed.

"Say, you're not an hereditary legislator?" she asked.

"Legislation is not the hereditary disease I complain of," I said evasively.

"What then?"

"Love!" I replied desperately.

She laughed gaily.

"I guess that's an original view of love."

"Why? My parents suffered from it: at least, I hope they did."

"Doubtful! Your Upper Ten is usually supposed to have cured marriage of it."

She bent her head over her plate, so that I strove in vain to read her eyes.

"Well, it's a beastly shame," I said. "Don't you think so, Miss Harper—Ethelberta? May I call you Ethelberta?"

"If it gives you any comfort," she said plumply.

"It gives me more than comfort," I rejoined.

A wild hope flamed in my breast. What if she loved me after all! I would speak the word. But no! If she did, I had won her love under a false glamour of nobility. Better, far better, to keep both my secrets in my own breast. Besides, had I not seen she was a flirt? I continued to call her Ethelberta, but that was all. When we rose from table I had not spoken; knowing that my friends would claim my society for the rest of the evening, I held out my hand in final farewell. She took it. Her own hand was hot. I clasped it for a moment, gazing into the wonderful blue eyes; then I let it go, and all was over.

"I do believe Teddy is hit!" Towers said when I came into our room, whither they had preceded me.

"Rot!" I said, turning my face away. "A seasoned bachelor like me. Heigho! I shall be awfully glad to get to work again to-morrow."

"Yes," said the Infant. "I see from the statistics that the mortality of your district has declined frightfully. That Robins must be a regular duffer."

"I'll soon set that right!" I exclaimed, with a forced grin.

"She certainly is a stunner," Towers mused.

"Hullo! I'm afraid it's Merton that's damaged," I laughed boisterously.

"Well, if she wasn't an heiress—" began Towers slowly.

"She might have you," finished the Infant. "But I say, boys, we'd better ask for our bills; we've got to be off in the morning by the 8.5. Jones mightn't be up when we leave."

The room echoed with sardonic laughter at the idea. There was no need to ring for Jones; he found two pretexts an hour to come and gaze upon me. When my bill came, I went to the window for air and to hide my face from Jones.

"All right, Jones!" cried the Infant, guessing what was up. "We'll leave it on the table before we go to bed."

"Well?" my friends enquired eagerly, when Jones had crawled off.

"Twenty-seven pounds two and tenpence!" I groaned, letting the accursed paper drift helplessly to the floor.

"D——d reasonable!" said the Infant.

"You would go it!" Towers added soothingly.

"Reasonable or not," I said, "I've only got six pounds in my pockets."

"You said you brought ten," said Towers.

"Yes! but what of carriage-sails and yacht-drives?" I cried agitatedly.

"You're drunk," said the Infant brutally. "However, I suppose, before going into dividing exes we must get together the gross sum."

It was easier said than done. When every farthing had been scraped together, we were thirteen pounds short on the three bills. We held a long council of war, discussing the possibilities of surreptitious pledging—the unspeakable Jones, playing his blindfold game, had reduced us to pawn—but even these were impracticable.

"Confound you!" cried Merton Towers. "Why didn't you think of the bill before?"

As if I had not better things to think of!

The horror of facing Jones in the morning drove us to the most desperate devices; but none seemed workable.

"There's only one way left of getting the coin, Teddy," said the Infant at last.

"What's that?" I cried eagerly.

"Ask the heiress."

It was an ambiguous phrase, but in whatever sense he meant it, it was a cruel and unmanly thrust; in my indignation I saw light.

"What fools we have been!" I shouted. "It's as easy as A B C. I'm not in an office like you, bound to be back to the day—I stay on over to-morrow, and you send me on the money from town."

"Where are we to get it from?" growled Towers.

"Anywhere! anybody!" I cried excitedly; "I'll write to Robins at once for it."

"Why not wire?" said the Infant.

"I don't see the necessity for wasting sixpence," I said; "we must be economical. Besides, Jones would read the wire."

IV

The Winning Move

Time slipped on; but I could not tear myself away from this enchanted hotel. The departure of my friends allowed me to be nearly all day with Ethelberta.

I had drowned reason and conscience: day followed day in a golden languor and the longer I stopped, the harder it was to go. At last Robins's telegrams became too imperative to be disregarded, and even my second supply of money would not suffice for another day.

The bitter experience of parting had to be faced again; the miserable evening, when I had first called her Ethelberta, had to be repeated. We spoke little at dinner; afterwards, as I had not my friends to go to this time, we left Mrs. Windpeg sitting over her dessert, and paced up and down in the little cultivated enclosure which separated the hotel from the parade. It was a balmy evening; the moon was up, silvering the greenery, stretching a rippling band across the sea, and touching Ethelberta's face to a more marvellous fairness. The air was heavy with perfume; everything combined to soften my mood. Tears came into my eyes as I thought that this was the very last respite. Those tears seemed to purge my vision: I saw the beauty of truth and sincerity, and felt that I could not go away without telling her who I really was; then, in future years, whatever she thought of me, I, at least, could think of her sacredly, with no cloud of falseness between me and her.

"Ethelberta!" I said, in low trembling tones.

"Lord Everett!" she murmured responsively.

"I have a confession to make."

She flushed and lowered her eyes.

"No, no!" she said agitatedly; "spare me that confession. I have heard it so often; it is so conventional. Let us part friends."

She looked up into my face with that frank, heavenly glance of hers. It shook my resolution, but I recovered myself and went on:

"It is not a conventional confession. I was not going to say I love you."

"No?" she murmured.

Was it the tricksy play of the moon among the clouds, or did a shade of disappointment flit across her face? Were her words genuine, or was she only a coquette? I stopped not to analyse; I paused not to enquire; I forgot everything but the loveliness that intoxicated me.

"I—I—mean I was!" I stammered awkwardly; "I have loved you from the first moment I saw you."

I strove to take her hand; but she drew it away haughtily.

"Lord Everett, it is impossible! Say no more."

The twang dropped from her speech in her dignity; her accents rang pure and sweet.

"Why not?" I cried passionately. "Why is it impossible? You seemed to care for me."

She was silent; at last she answered slowly:

"You are a lord! I cannot marry a lord."

My heart gave a great leap, then I felt cold as ice.

"Because I am a lord?" I murmured wonderingly.

"Yes! I—I—flirted with you at first out of pure fun—believe me, that was the truth. If I loved you now," her words were tremulous and almost inaudible, "it would be right that I should be punished. We must never meet again. Good-bye!"

She stood still and extended her hand.

I touched it with my icy fingers.

"Oh! if you had only let me confess just now what I wanted to!" I cried in agony.

"Confess what?" she said. "Have you not confessed?"

"No! You may disbelieve me now; but I wanted to tell you that I am not a lord at all, that I only became one through Jones."

Her lovely eyes dilated with surprise. I explained briefly, confusedly.

She laughed, but there was a catch in her voice.

"Listen!" she said hurriedly, starting pacing again; "I, too, have a confession to make. Jones has corrupted me too. I'm not an heiress at all, nor even an American—just a moderately successful London actress, resting a few weeks, and Mrs. Windpeg is only my companion and general factotum, the widow of a drunken stage-carpenter, who left her without resources, poor thing. But we had hardly crossed the steps of the hotel, before Jones mentioned Lord Everett was in the place, and buzzed the name so in our ears that the idea of a wild frolic flashed into my head. I am a great flirt, you know, and I thought that while I had the chance I would test the belief that English lords always fall in love with American heiresses."

"It was no test," I interrupted. "A Chinese Mandarin would fall in love with you equally."

"I let Mrs. Windpeg tell Jones all about me—imaginatively," she went on with a sad smile; "I told her to call me Harper, because *Harper's Magazine* came into my mind. But it was Jones who seated us together. I will believe that you took a genuine liking to me; still, it was a foolish freak on both sides, and we must both forget it as soon as possible."

"I can never forget it!" I said passionately; "I love you; and I dare to think you care for me, though while you fancied I was a peer you stifled the feeling that had grown up despite you. Believe me, I understand the purity of your motives, and love you the more for them."

She shook her head.

"Good-bye!" she faltered.

"I will not say 'good-bye'! I have little to offer you, but it includes a heart that is aching for you. There is no reason now why we should part."

Her lips were white in the moonlight.

"I never said I loved you," she murmured.

"Not in so many words," I admitted; "but why did you let me call you Ethelberta?" I asked passionately.

"Because it is not my name," she answered; and a ghost of the old gay smile lit up the lovely features.

I stood for a moment dumbfounded. Unconsciously we had come to a standstill under the window of the dining-room.

She took advantage of my consternation to say more lightly:

"Come, let us part friends."

I dimly understood that, in some subtle way I was too coarse to comprehend, she was ashamed of the part she had played throughout, that she would punish herself by renunciation. I knew not what to say; I saw the happiness of my life fading before my eyes. She held out her hand for the last time and I clasped it mechanically. So we stood, silent.

"What does that matter, Mrs. Windpeg? You're a real lady, that's enough for me. It wasn't because I thought you had money that I ventured to raise my eyes to you."

We started. It was the voice of Jones. Mrs. Windpeg had evidently lingered too long over her dessert.

"But I tell you I have nothing at all—nothing!" came the voice of Mrs. Windpeg.

"I don't want it. You see, I'm like you—not what I seem. This place belongs to me, only I was born and bred a waiter in this very hotel, and

I don't see why the 'ouse shouldn't profit by the tips instead of a stranger. My son does the show part; but he ain't fit for anything but reading Dickens and other low-class writers, and I feel the want of a real lady, knowing the ways of the aristocrats. What with Lord Porchester and Lord Everett, it looks as if this hotel is going to be fashionable and I know there's lots of 'igh-class wrinkles I ain't picked up yet. Only lately I was flummoxed by a gent asking for a liqueur I'd never 'eard of. You're mixed up with tip-top swells; I loved you from the moment I saw you fold your first *serviette*. I'm a widower, you're a widow. Let bygones be bygones. Why shouldn't we make a match of it?"

We looked at each other and laughed; false subtleties were swept away by a wave of mutual merriment.

"'Let bygones be bygones. Why shouldn't we make a match of it?'" I echoed. "Jones is right." I tightened my grasp of her hand and drew her towards me, almost without resistance. "You're going to lose your companion, you'll want another."

Her lovely face came nearer and nearer.

"Besides," I said gaily, "I understand you're out of an engagement."

"Thanks," she said; "I don't care for an engagement in the Provinces, and I have sworn never to marry in the profession: they're a bad lot."

"Call me an actor?"

My lips were almost on hers.

"You played Lord Dundreary—not unforgivably."

Our lips met!

"Oh, Augustus," came the voice of Mrs. Windpeg, "I feel so faint with happiness!"

"Loose your arms a moment, my popsy. I'll fetch you a drop of Damtidam!" answered the voice of Jones.

THE PRINCIPAL BOY

I

To sit out a play is a bore; to sit out a dance demands less patience. Even when you do it merely to prevent your partner dancing with you, it is the less disagreeable alternative. But it sometimes makes you giddier than galoping. Frank Redhill lost his head—a well-built head—completely through indulging in it; and without the head to look after it, the heart soon goes. He held Lucy's little hand in his hot clasp. She wished he would get himself gloves large enough not to split at the thumbs, and felt quite affectionate towards the dear, untidy boy. As a woman almost out of her teens, she could permit herself a motherly feeling for a lad who had but just attained his majority. The little thing looked very sweet in a demure dress of nun's veiling, which Frank would have described as "white robes." For he was only an undergraduate. Some undergraduates are past masters in the science and art of woman; but Frank was not in that set. Nor did he herd with the athletic, who drift mainly into the unpaid magistracy, nor with the worldly, who usually go in for the church. He was a reading man. Only he did not stick to the curriculum, but fed himself on the conceits of the poets, and thirsted to redeem mankind. So he got a second-class. But this is anticipating. Perhaps Lucy had been anticipating, too. At any rate she went through the scene as admirably as if she had rehearsed for it. And yet it was presumably the first time she had been asked to say: "I love you"—that wonderful little phrase, so easy to say and so hard to believe. Still, Lucy said and Frank believed it.

Not that Lucy did not share his belief. It must be for love that she was conceding Frank her hand—since her mother objected to the match. As the nephew of a peer, Frank could give her rather better society than she now enjoyed, even if he could not give her that of the peer, who had an hereditary feud with him. Of course she could not marry him yet, he was quite too poor for that, but he was a young man of considerable talents—which are after all gold pieces. When fame and fortune came to him, Lucy would come and join the party. *En attendant*, their souls would be wed. They kissed each other passionately, sealing the contract of souls with the red sealing-wax of burning lips. To them in Paradise entered the Guardian Angel with flaming countenance, and drove them into the outer darkness of the brilliant ball-room.

"My dear," said the Guardian Angel, who was Lucy Grayling's mother, "there is going to be an interval, and Mrs. Bayswater is so anxious for you to give that sweet recitation from Racine."

So Lucy declaimed one of Athalie's terrible speeches in a way that enthralled those who understood it, and made those who didn't, enthusiastic.

The applause did not seem to gratify the Guardian Angel as much as usual. Lucy wondered how much she had seen, and, disliking useless domestic discussion, extorted a promise of secrecy from her lover before they parted. He did not care about keeping anything from his father— especially something of which his approval was dubious. Still, all's fair and honourable in love—or love makes it seem so.

Frank took a solemn view of engagement, and embraced Lucy in his general scheme for the redemption of mankind. He felt she was a sacred as well as a precious charge, and he promised himself to attend to her spiritual salvation in so far as her pure instincts needed guidance. He directed her reading in bulky letters bearing the Oxford post-mark. Meantime, Lucy disapproved of his neckties. She thought he would be even nicer with a loving wife to look after his wardrobe.

II

When Frank achieved the indistinction of a second-class, as prematurely revealed, he went to Canada, and became a farm-pupil. It was not that his physique warranted the work, but there seemed no way in the old country of making enough money to marry Lucy (much less to redeem mankind) on. He was suffering, too, at the moment from a disgust with the schools, and a sentimental yearning to "return to nature."

The parting with Lucy was bitter, but he carried her bright image in his heart, and wrote to her by every mail. In Canada he did not look at a woman, as the saying goes; true, the opportunities were scant on the lonely log-farm. Absence, distance, lent the last touch of idealisation and enchantment to his conception of Lucy. She stood to him not only for Womanhood and Purity, but for England, Home, and Beauty. Nay, the thought of her was even Culture, when the evening found him too worn with physical toil to read a page of the small library he had brought with him. He saw his way to profitable farming on his own account in a few years' time. Then Lucy would come out to him, if they should be too impatient to wait till he had made money enough to go to her.

Lucy's letters did nothing to disabuse him of his ideals or his aims. They were charming, affectionate, and intellectual. Midway, in the batch he treasured more than eastern jewels, the sheets began to wear mourning for Lucy's mother. The Guardian Angel was gone—whether to continue the rôle none could say. Frank comforted the orphaned girl as best he could with epistolary kisses and condolences, and hoped she would get along pleasantly with her aunt till the necessity for that good relative vanished. And so the correspondence went on, Lucy's mind improving visibly under her lover's solicitous guidance. Then one day Redhill the elder cabled that by the death of his brother and nephew within a few days of each other, he had become Lord Redhill, and Frank consequently heir to a fine old peerage, and with an heir's income. Whereupon Frank returned forthwith from nature to civilisation. Now he could marry Lucy (and redeem mankind) immediately. Only he did not tell Lucy he was coming. He could not deny himself (or her) the pleasure of so pleasurable a surprise.

III

I t was a cold evening in early November when Frank's hansom drove up to the little house near Bond Street, where Lucy's aunt resided. He had not been to see his father yet; Lucy's angel-face hovered before him, warming the wintry air, and drawing him onwards towards the roof that sheltered her. The house was new to him; and as he paused outside for a moment, striving to still his emotion, his eye caught sight of a little placard in the window of the ground floor, inscribed "Apartments." He shuddered, a pang akin to self-reproach shot through him. Lucy's aunt was poor, was reduced to letting lodgings. Lucy herself had, perhaps, been left penniless. Delicacy had restrained her from alluding to her poverty in her letter. He had taken everything too much for granted— surely, straitened as were his means, he should have proffered her some assistance. A suspicion that he lacked worldly wisdom dawned upon him for the first time, as he rang the bell. Poor little Lucy! Well, whatever she had gone through, the bright days were come at last. The ocean which had severed them for so many weary moons no longer rolled between them—thank God, only the panels of the street-door divided them now. In another instant that darling head—no more the haunting elusive phantom of dream—would be upon his breast. Then as the door opened, the thought flashed upon him that she might not be in—the idea of waiting a single moment longer for her turned him sick. But his fears vanished at the encouraging expression on the face of the maid servant who opened the door.

"Miss Gray's upstairs," she mumbled, without waiting for him to speak. And, all intelligent reflection swamped by a great wave of joy, he followed her up one narrow flight of stairs, and passed eagerly into a room to which she pointed. It was a bright, cosy room, prettily furnished, and a cheerful fire crackled on the hearth. There were books and flowers about, and engravings on the walls. The little round table was laid for tea. Everything smiled "welcome." But these details only gradually penetrated Frank's consciousness—for the moment all he saw was that *She* was not there. Then he became aware of the fire, and moved involuntarily towards it, and held his hands over it, for they were almost numbed with the cold. Straightening himself again, he was startled by his own white face in the glass.

He gazed at it dreamily, and beyond it towards the folding-doors,

ISRAEL ZANGWILL

which led into an adjoining room. His eyes fixed themselves fascinated upon these reflected doors, and strayed no more. It was through them that she would come.

Suddenly a dreadful thought occurred to him. When she came through those doors, what would be the effect of his presence upon her? Would not the sudden shock, joyful though it was, upset the fragile little beauty? Had he not even heard of people dying from joy? Why had he not prepared her for his return, if only to the tiniest extent? The suspicion that he lacked worldly wisdom gained in force. Tumultuous suggestions of retreat crossed his mind—but before he could move, the folding-doors in the mirror flew apart, and a radiant image dashed lightly through them. It was a vision of dazzling splendour that made his eyes blink—a beautiful glittering figure in tights and tinsel, the prancing prince of pantomime. For an infinitesimal fraction of a second, Frank had the horror of the thought that he had come into the wrong house.

"Good evening, George," the Prince cried: "I had almost given you up."

Great God! Was the voice, indeed, Lucy's? Frank grasped at the mantel, sick and blind, the world tumbling about his ears. The suspicion that he lacked worldly wisdom became a certainty. Slowly he turned his head to face the waves of dazzling colour that tossed before his dizzy eyes.

The Prince's outstretched hand dropped suddenly. A startled shriek broke from the painted lips. The re-united lovers stood staring half blindly at each other. More than the Atlantic rolled between them.

Lucy broke the terrible silence.

"Brute!"

It was his welcome home.

"Brute?" he echoed interrogatively, in a low, hoarse whisper.

"Brute and cad!" said the Prince vehemently, the musical tones strident with anger. "Is this your faith, your loyalty—to sneak back home like a thief—to peep through the keyhole to see if I was a good little girl—?"

"Lucy! Don't!" he interrupted in anguished tones. "As there is a heaven above us, I had no suspicion—"

"But you have now," the Prince interrupted with a bitter laugh. Neither made any attempt to touch the other, though they were but a few inches apart. "Out with it!"

"Lucy, I have nothing to say against you. How should I? I know nothing. It is for you to speak. For pity's sake tell me all. What is this masquerade?"

"This masquerade?" She touched her pink tights—he shuddered at the touch. "These are—" She paused. Why not tell the easy lie and be done with the whole business, and marry the dear, devoted boy? But the mad instinct of revolt and resentment swept over her in a flood that dragged the truth from her heart and hurled it at him. "These are the legs of Prince Prettypet. If I am lucky, I shall stand on them in the pantomime of *The Enchanted Princess; or, Harlequin Dick Turpin*, at the Oriental Theatre. The man who has the casting of the part is coming to see how I look."

"You have gone on the stage?"

"Yes; I couldn't live on your lectures," Prince Prettypet said, still in the same resentful tone. "I couldn't fritter away the little capital I had when mamma died, and then wait for starvation. I had no useful accomplishments. I could only recite—*Athalie*."

"But surely your aunt—"

"Is a fiction. Had she been a fact it would have been all the same. I had had enough of mamma. No more leading-strings!"

"Lucy! And you wept over her so in your letters?"

"Crocodile's tears. Heavens, are women to have no lives of their own?"

"Oh, why did you not write to me of your difficulties?" he groaned. "I would have come over and fetched you—we would have borne poverty together."

"Yes," the Prince said mockingly. "''E was werry good to me, 'e was.' Do you think I could submit to government by a prig?"

He started as if stung. The little tinselled figure, looking taller in its swashbuckling habits, stared at him defiantly.

"Tell me," he said brokenly, "have you made a living?"

"No. If truth must be told, Lucy Gray—docked at the tail, sir—hasn't made enough to keep Lucy Grayling in theatrical costumes. I got plenty of kudos in the Provinces, but two of my managers were bogus."

"Yes?" he said vaguely.

"No treasury, don't you know? Ghost didn't walk. No oof, rhino, shiners, coin, cash, salary!"

"Do I understand you have travelled about the country by yourself?"

"By myself! What, in a company? You've picked up Irish in America. Ha! ha! ha!"

"You know what I mean, Lucy." It seemed strange to call this new person Lucy, but "Miss Grayling" would have sounded just as strange.

"Oh, there was sure to be a married lady—with her husband—in the troupe, poor thing!" The Prince had a roguish twinkle in the eye. "And surely I am old enough to take care of myself. Still, I felt you wouldn't like it. That's why I was anxious to get a London appearance—if only in East-end pantomime. The money's safe, and your notices are more valuable. I only want a show to take the town. I do hope George won't disappoint me. I thought you were he."

"Who is George?" he said slowly, as if in pain.

The shrill clamour of the bell answered him.

"There he is!" said the Prince joyfully. "George is only Georgie Spanner, stage-manager of the Oriental. I have been besieging him for two days. Bella Bright, who had to play Prince Prettypet, has gone and eloped with the property-man, and as soon as I heard of it, I got a letter of introduction to Georgie Spanner, and he said I was too little, and I said that was nonsense—that I had played in burlesque at Eastbourne—Come in!"

"Are you at home, miss?" said the maid, putting her head inside the door.

"Certainly, Fanny. That's Mr. Spanner I told you of—" The girl's head looked puzzled as it removed itself. "And so he said if I would put my things on, he would try and run down for an hour this evening, and see if I looked the part."

"And couldn't all that be done at the theatre?"

"Of course it could. But it's ten times more convenient for me here. And it's very considerate of Georgie to come all this way—he's a very busy man, I can tell you."

The street-door slammed loudly.

A sudden paroxysm shook Frank's frame. "Lucy, send this man away—for God's sake." In his excitement he came nearer, he laid his hand pleadingly upon the glittering shoulder. The Prince trembled a little under his touch, and stood as in silent hesitancy. The stairs creaked under heavy footsteps.

"Go to your room," he said more imperatively. Even in the wreck of his ideal, it was an added bitterness to think that limbs whose shapeliness had never even occurred to him, should be made a public spectacle. "Put on decent clothes."

It was the wrong chord to touch. The Prince burst into a boisterous laugh. "Silly old MacDougall!"

The footsteps were painfully near.

"You are mad," Frank whispered hoarsely. "You are killing me—you whom I throned as an angel of light; you who were the first woman in the world—"

"And now I'm going to be the Principal Boy," she laughed quietly back. "Is that you, dear old chap? Come in, George."

The door opened—Frank, disgusted, heart-broken, moved back towards the window-curtains. A corpulent, beef-faced, double-chinned man, with a fat cigar and a fur overcoat, came in.

"How do, Lucy? Cold, eh? What, in your togs? That's right."

"There, you bad man! Don't I look ripping?"

"Stunning, Lucy," he said, approaching her.

"Well, then, down on your knees, George, and apologise for saying I was too little."

"Well, I see more of you now, he! he! he! Yes, you'll do. What swell diggings!"

"Come to the fire. Take that easy-chair. There, that's right, old man. Now, what is it to be? There's tea laid—you've let it get cold, unpunctual ruffian. Perhaps you'd like a brandy and soda better?"

"M' yes."

She rang the bell. "So glad—because there's only tea for two, and I know my friend would prefer tea," with a sneering intonation. "Let me introduce you—Mr. Redhill, Mr. Spanner, you have heard of Mr. Spanner, the celebrated author and stage-manager?"

The celebrated author and stage-manager half rose in his easy-chair, startled, and not over-pleased. The pale-faced rival visitor, half hidden in the curtains, inclined his head stiffly, then moved towards the door.

"Oh, no, don't run away like that, without a cup of tea, in this bitter weather. Mr. Spanner won't mind talking business before you, will you, George? Such a dear old friend, you know."

It was a merry tea-party. Lucy rattled away bewitchingly, overpowering Mr. Spanner like an embodied brandy and soda. The slang of the green room and the sporting papers rolled musically off her tongue, grating on Frank's ear like the scraping of slate pencils. He had not insight enough to divine that she was accentuating her vulgar acquirements to torture him. Spanner went at last—for the Oriental boards claimed him—leaving behind him as nearly definite a promise of the part as a stage-manager can ever bring himself to utter. Lucy accompanied him downstairs. When she returned, Frank was still sitting as she had left him—one hand playing with the spoon in his cup, the rest of the body lethargic, immobile. She bent over him tenderly.

"Frank!" she whispered.

He shivered and looked up at the lovely face, daubed with rouge and pencilled at the eyebrows with black—as for the edification of the distant "gods." He lowered his eyes again, and said slowly: "Lucy, I have come back to marry you. What date will be most convenient to you?"

"You want to marry me," she echoed in low tones. "All the same!" A strange wonderful light came into her eyes. The big lashes were threaded with glistening tears. She put her little hand caressingly upon his hair, and was silent.

"Yes! it is an old promise. It shall be kept."

"Ah!" She drew her hand away with an inarticulate cry. "Like a duty dance, but you do not love me?"

He ignored the point. "I am rich now—my father has unexpectedly become Lord Redhill—you probably heard it!"

"You don't love me! You can't love me!" It sounded like the cry of a soul in despair.

"So there's no need for either of us to earn a living."

"But you don't love me! You only want to save me."

"Well, of course Lord Redhill wouldn't like his daughter-in-law to be—"

"The Principal Boy—ha! ha! ha! But what—ho! ho! ho! I must laugh, Frank, old man, it *is* so funny—what about the Principal Boy? Do you think he'd cotton to the idea of marrying a peer in embryo! Not if Lucy Gray knows it; no, by Jove! Why, when your coronet came along, I should have to leave the stage, or else people 'ud be saying I couldn't act worth a cent. They'd class me with Lady London and Lady Hansard—oh, Lord! Fancy me on the Drury Lane bills—Prince Prettypet, Lady Redhill. And then, great Scot, think whom they'd class you with. Ha! ha! ha! No, my boy, I'm not going to marry a microcephalous idiot. Ho! ho! ho! I wish somebody would put all this in a farce."

"Do I understand that you wish to break off the engagement?" Frank said slowly, a note of surprise in his voice.

"You've hit it—now that I hear about this peerage business—why didn't you tell me before? I'm out of all the gossip of court circles, and it wasn't in the *Era*. No, I might have redeemed my promise to a commoner, but a lord, ugh! I never had your sense of duty, Frank, and must really cry 'quits.' Now you see the value of secret engagements—ours is off, and nobody will be the wiser—or the worse. Now get thee to his lordship—concealment, like a worm i' the bud, no longer preying upon thy damask cheek. I was alway sorry you had to keep it from the old buffer. But it was for the best, wasn't it?—ha! ha!—it was for the best! Ha! ha! ha! ha! ha!"

Frank fled down the staircase followed by long peals of musical laughter. They followed him into the bleak night, which had no frost for him; but they became less musical as they rang on, and as the terrified maid and the landlady strove in vain to allay the hysterical tempest.

IV

The Oriental, on Boxing Night, was like a baker's oven for temperature, and an unopened sardine-barrel for populousness. The East-end had poured its rollicking multitudes into the vast theatre, which seethed over with noisy vitality. There was much traffic in ginger beer, oranges, Banbury cakes, and "bitter." The great audience roared itself hoarse over old choruses with new words. Lucy Gray, as Prince Prettypet, made an instant success. The mashers of the Oriental ogled her in silent flattery. Her clear elocution, her charming singing voice, her sprightly dancing, her *chic*, her frank vulgarity, when she "let herself go," took every heart captive. Every heart, that is, save one, which was filled with sickness and anguish, and covered with a veil of fine linen. The heir of the house of Redhill cowered at the back of the O.P. stage-box—the only place in the house disengaged when he drove up in a mistaken dress-suit. It was the first time he had seen Prince Prettypet since the merry tea-party, and he did not know why he was seeing her now. He hoped she did not see him. She pirouetted up to the front of his box pretty often during the evening, and several times hurled ancient wheezes at the riotous funnymen from that coign of vantage. Spoken so near his ear, the vulgar jokes tingled through him like lashes from a whip. Once she sang a chorus, winking in his direction. But that was the business of the song, and impersonal. He saw no sure signs of recognition, and was glad.

When, during the gradual but gorgeous evolution of the Transformation Scene, he received a note from her, he remained glad. It ran, "The bearer will take you behind. I have no one to see me home. Always your friend—Lucy." He went "behind," following his guide through a confusion of coatless carpenters waving torches of blue and green fire from the wings, and gauzy, highly coloured Whitechapel girls ensconcing themselves in uncomfortable attitudes on wooden pedestals, which were mounting and descending.

Georgie Spanner was bustling about, half crazed, amid a hubbub perfectly inaudible from the front; but he found time to scowl at Frank, as that gentleman stumbled over the pantaloon and fell against a little iron lever, whose turning might have plunged the stage in darkness. Frank found Lucy in a tiny cellar with whitewashed walls and a rough counter, on which stood a tin basin and a litter of "make up" materials.

She had "changed" before he came. It was the first time for years he had seen her in her true womanly envelope. Assuredly she had grown far lovelier, and her face was flushed with triumph; otherwise it was the old Lucy. The Prince was washed off with the paint.

Frank's eyes filled with tears. How hard he had been on her! Nay, had he not misjudged her? She looked so frail, so little, so childish, what guile could she know? It was all mere surface-froth on her lips! How narrow to set up his life, his ideals, as models, patterns! The poor little thing had her own tastes, her own individuality! How hard she worked to earn her own living! He bent down and kissed her forehead, remorsefully, as one might kiss an overscolded child. She drew his head down lower and kissed him—passionately—on the lips. "Let us wait a little," she said, as he spoke of sending for a hansom. "Sloman, the lessee, gives a little supper on the stage after the show—he'll be annoyed if I don't stay. He'll be delighted to have you."

The pantomime had gone better than anyone had expected. It had been insufficiently rehearsed, and though everybody had said "it'll be all right at night"—in the immemorial phrase of the profession— they had said it more automatically than confidently. Consequently everyone was in high feather, and agreeably surprised at the accuracy of the prophesying. Even Georgie Spanner ceased to scowl under the genial influences of success and Sloman's very decent champagne. The air was full of laughter and gaiety, and everybody (except the clown) cracked jokes. The leading ladies made themselves pleasant, and did not swear. Everybody seemed to have acquired a new respect for Lucy, seeing her with such a real Belgravian swell. Probably she would soon have a theatre of her own.

It was the Prig's first excursion into Bohemia, and he thought the natives very civil-spoken, naïve, and cordial. Frank had no doubt now that Lucy was right, that he was a Prig to want to redeem mankind. And the conviction that he lacked worldly wisdom was sealed for aye.

V

S o he married her.

AN ODD LIFE

It was the most curious case of croup I had ever attended. Not that there was anything unusual about the symptoms—they were so correct as to be devoid of the slightest interest. Certainly they were not worth while being called up for in the middle of the night. The patient it was that attracted my attention. He was a handsome baby of one year and nine months—by name Willy Streetside—with such an expression of candour and intelligence that I was moved to see him suffer. I sat down by his bedside, took his poor little feverish hand, and felt the weak quick pulse, and knew it had not much longer to beat. I put the glass of barley and water to his lips, and he drank eagerly. He seemed to be an orphan, in charge of a strange, silent serving-man, apparently the only other occupant of the luxurious and artistically furnished flat. I judged Downton to be a man of some culture, from the latest magazines strewn about the bedroom; but I could not help thinking that a female, more familiar with infantile ailments, might have been more useful. Apathetic and torpid though I was, from eighteen hours' continuous activity in a hundred sickrooms, my eyes filled with tears, and I sat for an instant, holding the little hand, listening to the poor child's painful breathing, and speculating on the mystery of that existence so early recalled. All his organs were sound. But for this accidental croup, I told myself, he might have lived till eighty. "Poor Willy Streetside!" I murmured, for his curious name clung to my memory.

Suddenly the baby turned his blue eyes full on me, and said:

"I suppose it's all up, doctor?"

I started violently, and let go his hand. The words were perhaps not altogether beyond the capacity of an infant; but the air of manly resignation with which they were uttered was astonishing. For more reasons than one, I hesitated.

"You need not be afraid to tell me the truth," said the baby, with a wistful smile; "I'm not afraid to hear it."

"Well—well, you're pretty bad," I stammered.

"Ah! thank you," the child replied gratefully. "How many hours do you give me?"

The baby's gravity took my breath away. He spoke with an old-world courtesy and the ingenuous stateliness of an infant prince.

"It may not be quite hopeless," I murmured.

Willy shook his head, the pretty, wan features distorted by a quaint grimace.

"I suppose I'm too young to rally," he said quietly, and closed his eyes.

Presently he re-opened them, and added:

"But I should have liked to live to see the Irish question settled."

"You would?" I exclaimed, overwhelmed.

"Yes," he said, adding with a whimsical expression in the wee blue eyes: "You mustn't think I crave for earthly immortality. I use 'settled' in a merely rough sense. My mother was an Irish poetess, over whose songs impetuous Celts still break their hearts and their heads."

I gazed speechless at this wonder-child, pushing the golden locks back from his feverish baby-brow, as if to assure myself by touching him that he was not a phantom.

"Ah, well!" he finished, "it doesn't matter. I have had my day, and mustn't grumble. I scarcely thought, when I witnessed the dissolution of the third Gladstone Government, that I should have lived to see him Premier a fourth time. Three doctors told me I was breaking up fast."

I began to be frightened of this extraordinary infant, divining some wizardry behind the candid little face—some latter-day mystery of re-incarnation, esoteric Buddhism, what-not. The child perceived my perturbation.

"You are thinking I have packed a good deal into my short life," he said, with an amused smile. "And yet some men will make a Gladstone bag hold as much as a portmanteau. Gladstone has done so; and why not I, in my humble degree?"

"True," I answered; "but you cannot begin to pack before you are born."

"You are entirely mistaken," replied the baby, "if you think I have done anything so precocious as that."

"Then you must have lived an odd life," I said, puzzled.

"You have hit it!" exclaimed the child, with a suspicion of eagerness, not unmingled with surprise. "I did not mean to tell anyone; but since you are a man of science and I am on the point of death, you may as well know you have guessed the truth."

"Have I?" I said, more bewildered than ever.

"Yes. In all these years no one has suspected it. It has been carefully kept from outsiders. But now it would, perhaps, be childish folly to be reticent about it. It is the truth—the plain, literal truth—I have lived an odd life."

"How did it begin?" I asked, scarce knowing what I said or what I meant.

"You shall know all," said Willy. "I must begin before I was born—before I could begin packing, as you put it."

His breath came and went painfully. Overwrought with curiosity as I was, I experienced a pang of compunction.

"No, no; never mind," I said; "you have not the strength to speak much—you must not waste what you have."

"It can only cost me a few minutes of life—I can spare the time," he answered, almost peevishly.

Now that he had been strung up to speaking point, he seemed to resent my diminished interest.

I put the glass of barley and water to his lips, and forced him to moisten his throat.

"I can spare the time," he repeated, while an air of grim satisfaction came over the tiny features. "I have stolen plenty—I have outwitted the arch-thief himself. I have survived my own death."

"What!" I gasped. "Have you already died?"

"No, no," he replied fretfully; "I am only just going to die. That is how I have survived my death. How dull you are!"

"You were going to begin at the beginning," I murmured feebly.

"No! What is the use of beginning at the beginning?" this *enfant terrible* enquired, in the same peevish tones. "I was going to begin before the beginning."

"Yes, yes," I said soothingly, patting his golden curls; "you were going to begin before you were born."

"With my mother," he said more gently. "She did not lead a very happy life—it enabled her to hymn the wrongs of her country. Her childhood was a succession of sorrows, her girlhood a mass of misfortunes; and when she married the man she loved, she found herself deserted by him a few months later. It was then that she first conceived the thought that has changed my life. It came to her in a moment of tears, as she sat over the ashes of her happiness. From that moment the thought never left her."

There was a wild look in the baby's eyes. I began to suspect him of premature insanity.

"What was this thought?" I murmured.

"I am coming to it. There came into her head suddenly the refrain of a song she had learnt at school: 'Life like a river with constant motion.' 'The river of life! The stream of life! How true it is!' she mused. 'How much more than mere metaphors these phrases are! Verily, one's life flows on towards the dark ocean of death, irresistibly, unrestingly, willy-nilly—whether swift or slow, whether long or short—whether it flows through pleasant champaigns or dreary marshes, past romantic castled crags, or by bleak quarries. What is the use of experience, of knowledge of past bits of the route, when no two bits are ever really alike, when the future course is hidden and is always a panorama of surprises, when no life-stream knows what awaits it round the corner every time it turns, when the scenery of the source avails one nothing in one's resistless progress towards the scenery of the mouth? What is life but a series of mistakes, whose fruit is wisdom, maybe, but wisdom overripe? We do not pluck the fruit till it will no longer serve our appetites. Nothing repeats itself on the stage of existence—always new situations and new follies. *Experientia docet.* Experience teaches, indeed; but her lesson is that nothing can be learnt.'"

The baby paused, and reached out his wasted hand for the glass. His pinafore and his tiny shoes on the chest of drawers caught my eye, and moistened it with the thought he would never don them again.

"As my mother brooded upon this bitter truth," he resumed, when he had refreshed himself, "and saw how sad an illustration of it was her own life—with its sufferings and its mistakes—she could not help wishing existence had been ordered otherwise. If we had had at least two lives, we might profit in the second by the first. But, she told herself, with a sigh, this was vain day-dreaming. Then suddenly *the* thought flashed upon her. Granting that more than one life was impossible upon this planet, why should it not be differently distributed? Suppose, instead of flowing on like a stream, one's life progressed like a London street—the odd numbers on the one side and the even on the other, so that after doing the numbers 1, 3, 5, 7, 9, 11, &c., &c., one could return and do the numbers 2, 4, 6, 8, 10, 12, &c., &c. Without craving from Providence more than man's allotted span, what if, by a slight re-arrangement of the years, it were possible to extort an infinitely greater degree of happiness from one's lifetime! What if it were possible to live the odd years, gleaning experience as well as joys, and then to return to the even years, armed with all the wisdom of one's age! What if *her* child could enjoy this inestimable privilege! The thought haunted her, she brooded on it day and night; and when I was born, she drew me eagerly towards her, as if to see some mark of promise written on my forehead. But a year passed before she dared to think her wish had found fulfilment. On the eve of my first birthday she measured and weighed me with intense anxiety, though pretending to herself she only wished to keep a register of my growth. In the morning I was more by a year's inches and pounds. I had shot up at a bound into my third year, and manifested sudden symptoms of walking and talking. She almost fainted with joy when my unexpected teeth bit her finger. She could not get my shoes on me, nor my frock. But, although my mother had made no preparations for my changed condition, she welcomed the trouble I put her to, and carefully laid aside my useless garments, knowing I should want them again. The neighbours noticed nothing; they thought me a big boy for my age, and extremely precocious. When I was in my fifth year I went on the stage as an 'infant phenomenon,' my age being attested by my certificate of birth, though you will of course see that I was really in my ninth. In the next few years I made enough money to gild my mother's few declining years; and when I retired temporarily from the boards at the advice of my critics, it was of course with the intention of studying and returning to the stage when I was younger. And so I advanced to manhood, skipping the alternate years. I rejoice to say that my mother, though she died when I was seventy-three, had the satisfaction of knowing what felicity her unselfish aspiration had brought into my life. She told me of my strange exemption from the common burden of continuous existence, as soon as I had skipped into years of discretion. Not for me did Time pass with that tragic footstep which never returns on itself; for me he was not the irrevocable, the relentless. I regretted my lost youth—but it was not with hopeless, passionate tears, with mutinous yearnings after the impossible; it was as one who waves a regretful adieu to a charming girl he will meet again."

"Ah! but you will not meet her again," I said softly.

"No; but the feeling was the same. Of course, when I was thirty I did not know I should die before I was two. I had no more privilege of prescience than the ordinary mortal. But in everything else how enviable was my lot compared to his whom every day is sweeping towards Death, for whom no vision of renewed youth gleams behind the black hangings! Oh! the glory of growing old without dread, with the assurance that age, which is ripening you, is not ripening you for the Gleaner, that the years will add wisdom without eternally subtracting the capacity for joy, and that every tottering step is bringing you nearer, not the Grave, but the joyous resurrection of your youth!"

"And you have experienced that?" I cried, with envious incredulity.

"Yes," answered the baby solemnly. "Of course I prepared for the Great Change. Not that Nature did not herself smooth the metamorphosis. The loss of teeth, the gradual baldness, the feeble limbs, everything pointed to the proximity of my Second Childhood. I knew that my odd life had not much longer to run, that at any moment the transformation might take place and the even numbers begin. Giving out that I was going to explore the African deserts, and accompanied only by my faithful body-servant, Downton, I retired to Egypt to await the great event, having previously ordered baby-linen and the various requisites of infantile toilette. I had at one time meditated providing myself with parents, but ultimately concluded that they would prove too troublesome to manage, and that it would be better to trust myself entirely to the management of Downton, since I had already placed myself in his power by leaving him all my money."

"But what necessity was there for that?" I enquired.

"Every necessity," he replied gravely. "Do you not see that I had to arrange all my affairs and make my will before being born again, because afterwards I should not be of legal age for ten years. At first I thought of leaving all my money to myself and passing as my own child, but there would have been difficulties. I was unmarried and seventy-seven. Downton could easily pretend his septuagenarian master had died in the African deserts, but he could not so easily patch up a marriage there. I had no option, therefore, but to make Downton my heir, and I have never had occasion to regret it from the day of my rebirth to this, the day of my death. As soon as I was born we returned to England, and I wrote my obituary and drove to the Press Association with it. Downton took it into the office while I waited in Fleet Street in the hansom. I can scarcely hope to convey to you an idea of the intensity and agreeableness of my sensations at this unprecedented epoch. The variegated life of Fleet Street gave me the keenest joy: every sight and every sound—beautiful or sordid—thrilled my nerves to rapture. I was interested in everything. Imagine the delicious freshness of one's second year supervening upon the jaded sensibilities of seventy-seven. All my wide and varied knowledge of life lay in my soul as before, but transfigured. Over my large experience of men and things was shed a stream of sunshine which irradiated everything with divine light; every streak of cynicism faded. I had the wisdom of an old man and the heart of a little child. I believed in man again, and even in woman. I shed tears of pure ecstasy; and when I heard a female of the lower classes say: 'Poor little thing! What a shame to leave it crying in a cab!' I laughed aloud in glee. She exclaimed: 'Ah! now it's laughing, my petsy-wootsy!' Her conversation saddened me again, and I was glad I had not burdened myself with a mother, and that I took my milk from a bottle instead of a doting nurse. And how exquisite was this same apparently monotonous menu of milk to an epicurean who had ruined his digestion! I felt I was recuperating on a vegetarian diet, and I rejoiced to think some years must elapse before I would care for champagne or re-acquire a taste for full-flavoured Manillas. Perhaps somewhat unreasonably, I was proud of my strength of will, which had enabled me in one day to abandon tobacco without a pang, and seven-course dinners without repining. I slept a good deal, too, at this period, whereas I had previously been greatly exercised by insomnia. But these joys of the senses were as nothing to the joys of the intellect. An exquisite curiosity played like a sea-breeze about my long-stagnant soul. All my early interests revived; worldly propositions I had thought settled showed themselves unstable and volant; everything was shaken by the moving spirit of youth. Theology, poetry, and even metaphysics became alive; all sorts of unpractical questions became suddenly burning. I saw in myself the seeds of a great thinker: a felicitous congruity of opposite capacities that had never before met in a single man—the sobriety of age tempered by the audacity of youth, fire and water, judgment and inspiration. I was revolutionist and reactionary in one. I read all the new books, and agreed with all the old."

"All you tell me only makes the pathos of your premature death more intolerable," I said in moved accents. "You are, like Keats and Chatterton,—only an earlier edition,—an inheritor of unfulfilled renown."

The little blue eyes smiled wistfully at me.

"Not at all," said the wee rose-lips, with a quiver. "Don't you see, I have already dodged Death? Evidently, if I had taken my second year in its natural order, I should have been cut short by croup at the outset. Apparently I had enough vital energy in me to have lasted till seventy-seven, if I could only get over the croup. I think one ought to be satisfied with having survived himself by thirty odd years."

"Yes, if you put it like that, the pathos lightens," I admitted. "Of course I saw from the first that you were considerably in advance of your age. Did you assure your life?" I asked, with a sudden thought.

"I did; but by an oversight I let the policy be invalidated by my imaginary expedition to the African deserts. Downton has, however, taken out a fresh policy for my new life."

"What a baffling complex of probabilities would be added to Life Assurances if your way of living were to become general!" I observed.

"Downton will probably more than recoup himself for his first loss. Have you always been a bachelor, by the way?" I asked.

"Yes," said the baby, with a sigh. "I missed marriage; it probably fell in an even year."

"Poor child!" I cried, my eyes growing humid again. To think, too, of that beautiful young girl, that fond wife, waiting for him who would never come; that innocent maiden cheated of love and happiness because her appointed husband had not lived in the other alternate series of years,—to think of this tangled tragedy moved me to fresh tears, not a few of which were for the husband who never was.

"Nay, do not pity me," said the baby, and his tones were hushed and low, and in his heavenly blue eyes I seemed to read the high sorrowful wisdom of the ages; "for, since I have lain here on this bed of sickness with no spectacular whirl to claim my thoughts, with four walls for my horizon, and the agony of death in my throat, the darker side of my dual existence has been borne in upon me. I see the shadow cast by the sunshine of my privilege of double birth; I see the curse which is the obverse of the blessing my mother's prayers brought me; I see myself dissipating a youth which I knew would recur, throwing away a manhood which I knew would come again, and sinking into a sensual senility which I knew would pass into an innocent infancy. I see myself rejecting the best gifts and the highest duties of To-Day for the illusory felicities and the far-away virtues of the Day-After-To-Morrow. I see myself passing by Love with the reflection that I should be passing again; putting off Purity with the thought that I should be round that way presently; and waving to Duty an amicable salute of 'Expect me soon.' And in this moment of clear vision I see not only my past, I realise what my future would be if I lived. I see the influx of fresh feeling gradually exhausted, overcome, ousted, and finally replaced by a satiety more horrible than that of the septuagenarian, as I came to realise that life for me held no surprises, no lures to curiosity, that the future was no enchanted realm of mysterious possibilities, that the white clouds revealed no seraph shapes on the horizon, that Hope did not stand like a veiled bride with beckoning finger, that fairies were not lurking round every corner nor magic palaces waiting to start up at every turn. I see life stretching before me like old ground I had been over—in my mother's image like a street one side of which I had walked down. What could the other offer of fresh, of delightful? It is so rarely one side differs from the other: a church for a public-house, a grocer's instead of a bookshop. Conceive the horror of foreknowledge: of having no sensations to learn and few new emotions to feel; to have, moreover, the enthusiasm of youth sicklied over with the prescience of senile cynicism, and the healthy vigour of manhood made flaccid by anticipations of the dodderings of age! I foresee the ever-growing dismay at the leaps and bounds with which my youth was fleeting. I see myself, instead of profiting by my experience, feverishly clutching at every pleasure on my path, as a drowning man, borne along by a torrent, snatches at every scrap of flotsam and jetsam. I see manhood arrive only to pass away, as an express passes through a petty station, full speed for the terminus. I see a panic terror close upon me with every hurrying year at the knowledge that my hours were thirty minutes and my months virtually fortnights, and that I was leading the fastest life on record. Add to this the anguish of feeling myself torn from the bosom of the wife I loved and hurried away from the embraces of the children whose careers it would be my solicitude to watch over. Imagine the agony if I had been cruelly spared to my seventy-eighth year—the agony of a condemned criminal who does not know on what day he is to be execu—"

His voice failed suddenly. He had slightly raised himself on his pillow in his excitement, but now his head fell back, revealing the fatal white patches on the baby throat. I seized his hand quickly to feel his pulse. The little palm lay cold in mine. I started violently and sat up rigidly in my chair.

The child was dead. Downton was sobbing at my side.

As I was writing out the certificate, an odd thought came into my head. I scribbled what I thought an appropriate epitaph and showed it to Downton, but he glared at me furiously. I hastened home to bed.

My epitaph ran:

HERE LIES
WILLIAM ("WILLY") STREETSIDE,
WHO LED A DOUBLE LIFE,
AND DIED IN BLAMELESS REPUTE,
AT THE AVERAGE AGE
OF 39 YEARS.

"And in their death they were not divided."

CHEATING THE GALLOWS

I

A Curious Couple

They say that a union of opposites makes the happiest marriage, and perhaps it is on the same principle that men who chum together are always so oddly assorted. You shall find a man of letters sharing diggings with an auctioneer, and a medical student pigging with a stockbroker's clerk. Perhaps each thus escapes the temptation to talk "shop" in his hours of leisure, while he supplements his own experiences of life by his companion's.

There could not be an odder couple than Tom Peters and Everard G. Roxdal—the contrast began with their names, and ran through the entire chapter. They had a bedroom and a sitting-room in common, but it would not be easy to find what else. To his landlady, worthy Mrs. Seacon, Tom Peters's profession was a little vague, but everybody knew that Roxdal was the manager of the City and Suburban Bank, and it puzzled her to think why a bank manager should live with such a seedy-looking person, who smoked clay pipes and sipped whisky-and-water all the evening when he was at home. For Roxdal was as spruce and erect as his fellow-lodger was round-shouldered and shabby; he never smoked, and he confined himself to a small glass of claret at dinner.

It is possible to live with a man and see very little of him. Where each of the partners lives his own life in his own way, with his own circle of friends and external amusements, days may go by without the men having five minutes together. Perhaps this explains why these partnerships jog along so much more peaceably than marriages, where the chain is drawn so much tighter, and galls the partners rather than links them. Diverse, however, as were the hours and habits of the chums, they often breakfasted together, and they agreed in one thing—they never stayed out at night. For the rest Peters sought his diversions in the company of journalists, and frequented debating rooms, where he propounded the most iconoclastic views; while Roxdal had highly respectable houses open to him in the suburbs, and was, in fact, engaged to be married to Clara Newell, the charming daughter of a retired corn factor, a widower with no other child.

Clara naturally took up a good deal of Roxdal's time, and he often dressed to go to the play with her, while Peters stayed at home in a faded dressing-gown and loose slippers. Mrs. Seacon liked to see gentlemen about the house in evening dress, and made comparisons not favourable to Peters. And this in spite of the fact that he gave her infinitely less trouble than the younger man. It was Peters who first took the apartments, and it was characteristic of his easy-going temperament that he was so openly and naïvely delighted with the view of the Thames obtainable from the bedroom window, that Mrs. Seacon was emboldened to ask twenty-five per cent more than she had intended. She soon returned to her normal terms, however, when his friend Roxdal called the next day to inspect the rooms, and overwhelmed her with a demonstration of their numerous shortcomings. He pointed out that their being on the ground floor was not an advantage, but a disadvantage, since they were nearer the noises of the street—in fact, the house being a corner one, the noises of two streets. Roxdal continued to exhibit the same finicking temperament in the petty details of the *ménage*. His shirt fronts were never sufficiently starched, nor his boots sufficiently polished. Tom Peters, having no regard for rigid linen, was always good-tempered and satisfied, and never acquired the respect of his landlady. He wore blue check shirts and loose ties even on Sundays. It is true he did not go to church, but slept on till Roxdal returned from morning service, and even then it was difficult to get him out of bed, or to make him hurry up his toilette operations. Often the mid-day meal would be smoking on the table while Peters would be still reading in bed, and Roxdal, with his head thrust through the folding-doors that separated the bedroom from the sitting-room, would be adjuring the sluggard to arise and shake off his slumbers, and threatening to sit down without him, lest the dinner be spoilt. In revenge, Tom was usually up first on week-days, sometimes at such unearthly hours that Polly had not yet removed the boots from outside the bedroom door, and would bawl down to the kitchen for his shaving-water. For Tom, lazy and indolent as he was, shaved with the unfailing regularity of a man to whom shaving has become an instinct. If he had not kept fairly regular hours, Mrs. Seacon would have set him down as an actor, so clean shaven was he. Roxdal did not shave. He wore a full beard, and, being a fine figure of a man to boot, no uneasy investor could look upon him without being reassured as to the stability of the bank he managed so successfully. And thus the two men lived in an economical comradeship, all the firmer, perhaps, for their mutual incongruities.

II

A Woman's Instinct

It was on a Sunday afternoon in the middle of October, ten days after Roxdal had settled in his new rooms, that Clara Newell paid her first visit to him there. She enjoyed a good deal of liberty, and did not mind accepting his invitation to tea. The corn factor, himself indifferently educated, had an exaggerated sense of the value of culture, and so Clara, who had artistic tastes without much actual talent, had gone in for painting, and might be seen, in pretty toilettes, copying pictures in the Museum. At one time it looked as if she might be reduced to working seriously at her art, for Satan, who finds mischief still for idle hands to do, had persuaded her father to embark the fruits of years of toil in bubble companies. However, things turned out not so bad as they might have been, a little was saved from the wreck, and the appearance of a suitor, in the person of Everard G. Roxdal, ensured her a future of competence, if not of the luxury she had been entitled to expect. She had a good deal of affection for Everard, who was unmistakably a clever man, as well as a good-looking one. The prospect seemed fair and cloudless. Nothing presaged the terrible storm that was about to break over these two lives. Nothing had ever for a moment come to vex their mutual contentment, till this Sunday afternoon. The October sky, blue and sunny, with an Indian summer sultriness, seemed an exact image of her life, with its aftermath of a happiness that had once seemed blighted.

Everard had always been so attentive, so solicitous, that she was as much surprised as chagrined to find that he had apparently forgotten the appointment. Hearing her astonished interrogation of Polly in the passage, Tom shambled from the sitting-room in his loose slippers and his blue check shirt, with his eternal clay pipe in his mouth, and informed her that Roxdal had gone out suddenly earlier in the afternoon.

"G-g-one out?" stammered poor Clara, all confused. "But he asked me to come to tea."

"Oh, you're Miss Newell, I suppose," said Tom.

"Yes, I am Miss Newell."

"He has told me a great deal about you, but I wasn't able honestly to congratulate him on his choice till now."

Clara blushed uneasily under the compliment, and under the ardour of his admiring gaze. Instinctively she distrusted the man. The very first tones of his deep bass voice gave her a peculiar shudder. And then his impoliteness in smoking that vile clay was so gratuitous.

"Oh, then you must be Mr. Peters," she said in return. "He has often spoken to me of you."

"Ah!" said Tom laughingly, "I suppose he's told you all my vices. That accounts for your not being surprised at my Sunday attire."

She smiled a little, showing a row of pearly teeth. "Everard ascribes to you all the virtues," she said.

"Now that's what I call a friend!" he cried ecstatically. "But won't you come in? He must be back in a moment. He surely would not break an appointment with *you*." The admiration latent in the accentuation of the last pronoun was almost offensive.

She shook her head. She had a just grievance against Everard, and would punish him by going away indignantly.

"Do let *me* give you a cup of tea," Tom pleaded. "You must be awfully thirsty this sultry weather. There! I will make a bargain with you! If you will come in now, I promise to clear out the moment Everard returns, and not spoil your *tête-à-tête*." But Clara was obstinate; she did not at all relish this man's society, and besides, she was not going to throw away her grievance against Everard. "I know Everard will slang me dreadfully when he comes in if I let you go," Tom urged. "Tell me at least where he can find you."

"I am going to take the 'bus at Charing Cross, and I'm going straight home," Clara announced determinedly. She put up her parasol in a pet, and went up the street into the Strand. A cold shadow seemed to have fallen over all things. But just as she was getting into the 'bus, a hansom dashed down Trafalgar Square, and a well-known voice hailed her. The hansom stopped, and Everard got out and held out his hand.

"I'm so glad you're a bit late," he said. "I was called out unexpectedly, and have been trying to rush back in time. You wouldn't have found me if you had been punctual. But I thought," he added, laughing, "I could rely on you as a woman."

"I *was* punctual," Clara said angrily. "I was not getting out of this 'bus, as you seem to imagine, but into it, and was going home."

"My darling!" he cried remorsefully. "A thousand apologies." The regret on his handsome face soothed her. He took the rose he was wearing in the buttonhole of his fashionably cut coat and gave it to her.

"Why were you so cruel?" he murmured, as she nestled against him in the hansom. "Think of my despair if I had come home to hear you had come and gone. Why didn't you wait a moment?"

A shudder traversed her frame. "Not with that man, Peters!" she murmured.

"Not with that man, Peters!" he echoed sharply. "What is the matter with Peters?"

"I don't know," she said. "I don't like him."

"Clara," he said, half sternly, half cajolingly, "I thought you were above these feminine weaknesses; you are punctual, strive also to be reasonable. Tom is my best friend. From boyhood we have been always together. There is nothing Tom would not do for me, or I for Tom. You must like him, Clara; you must, if only for my sake."

"I'll try," Clara promised, and then he kissed her in gratitude and broad daylight.

"You'll be very nice to him at tea, won't you?" he said anxiously. "I shouldn't like you two to be bad friends."

"I don't want to be bad friends," Clara protested; "only the moment I saw him a strange repulsion and mistrust came over me."

"You are quite wrong about him—quite wrong," he assured her earnestly. "When you know him better, you'll find him the best of fellows. Oh, I know," he said suddenly, "I suppose he was very untidy, and you women go so much by appearances!"

"Not at all," Clara retorted. "'Tis you men who go by appearances."

"Yes, you do. That's why you care for me," he said, smiling.

She assured him it wasn't, and she didn't care for him so much as he plumed himself, but he smiled on. His smile died away, however, when he entered his rooms and found Tom nowhere.

"I daresay you've made him run about hunting for me," he grumbled.

"Perhaps he knew I'd come back, and went away to leave us together," she answered. "He said he would when you came."

"And yet you say you don't like him!"

She smiled reassuringly. Inwardly, however, she felt pleased at the man's absence.

III

POLLY RECEIVES A PROPOSAL

If Clara Newell could have seen Tom Peters carrying on with Polly in the passage, she might have felt justified in her prejudice against him. It must be confessed, though, that Everard also carried on with Polly. Alas! it is to be feared that men are much of a muchness where women are concerned; shabby men and smart men, bank managers and journalists, bachelors and semi-detached bachelors. Perhaps it was a mistake after all to say the chums had nothing patently in common. Everard, I am afraid, kissed Polly rather more often than Clara, and although it was because he respected her less, the reason would perhaps not have been sufficiently consoling to his affianced wife. For Polly was pretty, especially on alternate Sunday afternoons, and she liked to receive the homage of real gentlemen, setting her white cap at all indifferently. Thus, just before Clara knocked on that memorable Sunday afternoon, Polly, being confined to the house by the unwritten code regulating the lives of servants, was amusing herself by flirting with Peters.

"You *are* fond of me a little bit," the graceless Tom whispered, "aren't you?"

"You know I am, sir," Polly replied.

"You don't care for anyone else in the house?"

"Oh no, sir. I wonder how it is, sir?" Polly replied ingenuously.

And that very evening, when Clara was gone and Tom still out, Polly turned without the faintest atom of scrupulosity, or even jealousy, to the more fascinating Roxdal. If it would seem at first sight that Everard had less excuse for such frivolity than his friend, perhaps the seriousness he showed in this interview may throw a different light upon the complex character of the man.

"You're quite sure you don't care for anyone but me?" he asked earnestly.

"Of course not, sir!" Polly replied indignantly. "How could I?"

"But you care for that soldier I saw you out with last Sunday?"

"Oh no, sir, he's only my young man," she said apologetically.

"Would you give him up?" he hissed suddenly.

Polly's pretty face took a look of terror. "I couldn't, sir! He'd kill me! He's such a jealous brute, you've no idea."

"Yes, but suppose I took you away from here?" he whispered eagerly. "Somewhere where he couldn't find you—South America, Africa, somewhere thousands of miles across the seas."

"Oh, sir, you frighten me!" whispered Polly, cowering before his ardent eyes, which shone in the dimly lit passage.

"Would you come with me?" he hissed. She did not answer; she shook herself free and ran into the kitchen, trembling with a vague fear.

IV

The Crash

One morning, earlier than his earliest hour of demanding his shaving-water, Tom rang the bell violently and asked the alarmed Polly what had become of Mr. Roxdal.

"How should I know, sir?" she gasped. "Ain't he been in, sir?"

"Apparently not," Tom answered anxiously. "He never remains out. We have been here three weeks now, and I can't recall a single night he hasn't been home before twelve. I can't make it out." All enquiries proved futile. Mrs. Seacon reminded him of the thick fog that had come on suddenly the night before.

"What fog?" asked Tom.

"Lord! didn't you notice it, sir?"

"No, I came in early, smoked, read, and went to bed about eleven. I never thought of looking out of the window."

"It began about ten," said Mrs. Seacon, "and got thicker and thicker. I couldn't see the lights of the river from my bedroom. The poor gentleman has been and gone and walked into the water." She began to whimper.

"Nonsense, nonsense," said Tom, though his expression belied his words. "At the worst I should think he couldn't find his way home, and couldn't get a cab, so put up for the night at some hotel. I daresay it will be all right." He began to whistle as if in restored cheerfulness. At eight o'clock there came a letter for Roxdal, marked "immediate," but as he did not turn up for breakfast, Tom went round personally to the City and Suburban Bank. He waited half-an-hour there, but the manager did not make his appearance. Then he left the letter with the cashier and went away with anxious countenance.

That afternoon it was all over London that the manager of the City and Suburban had disappeared, and that many thousand pounds of gold and notes had disappeared with him.

Scotland Yard opened the letter marked "immediate," and noted that there had been a delay in its delivery, for the address had been obscure, and an official alteration had been made. It was written in a feminine hand and said: "On second thoughts I cannot accompany you. Do not try to see me again. Forget me. I shall never forget you."

There was no signature.

Clara Newell, distracted, disclaimed all knowledge of this letter. Polly deposed that the fugitive had proposed flight to her, and the routes to Africa and South America were especially watched. Some months passed without result. Tom Peters went about overwhelmed with grief and astonishment. The police took possession of all the missing man's effects. Gradually the hue and cry dwindled, died.

V

Faith and Unfaith

At last we meet!" cried Tom Peters, while his face lit up in joy. "How *are* you, dear Miss Newell?" Clara greeted him coldly. Her face had an abiding pallor now. Her lover's flight and shame had prostrated her for weeks. Her soul was the arena of contending instincts. Alone of all the world she still believed in Everard's innocence, felt that there was something more than met the eye, divined some devilish mystery behind it all. And yet that damning letter from the anonymous lady shook her sadly. Then, too, there was the deposition of Polly. When she heard Peters's voice accosting her all her old repugnance resurged. It flashed upon her that this man—Roxdal's boon companion—must know far more than he had told to the police. She remembered how Everard had spoken of him, with what affection and confidence! Was it likely he was utterly ignorant of Everard's movements? Mastering her repugnance, she held out her hand. It might be well to keep in touch with him; he was possibly the clue to the mystery. She noticed he was dressed a shade more trimly, and was smoking a meerschaum. He walked along at her side, making no offer to put his pipe out.

"You have not heard from Everard?" he asked. She flushed. "Do you think I'm an accessory after the fact?" she cried.

"No, no," he said soothingly. "Pardon me, I was thinking he might have written—giving no exact address, of course. Men do sometimes dare to write thus to women. But, of course, he knows you too well—you would have put the police on his track."

"Certainly," she exclaimed indignantly. "Even if he is innocent he must face the charge."

"Do you still entertain the possibility of his innocence?"

"I do," she said boldly, and looked him full in the face. His eyelids drooped with a quiver. "Don't you?"

"I have hoped against hope," he replied, in a voice faltering with emotion. "Poor old Everard! But I am afraid there is no room for doubt. Oh, this wicked curse of money—tempting the noblest and the best of us."

The weeks rolled on. Gradually she found herself seeing more and more of Tom Peters, and gradually, strange to say, he grew less repulsive.

From the talks they had together, she began to see that there was really no reason to put faith in Everard; his criminality, his faithlessness, were too flagrant. Gradually she grew ashamed of her early mistrust of Peters; remorse bred esteem, and esteem ultimately ripened into feelings so warm, that when Tom gave freer vent to the love that had been visible to Clara from the first, she did not repulse him.

It is only in books that love lives for ever. Clara, so her father thought, showed herself a sensible girl in plucking out an unworthy affection and casting it from her heart. He invited the new lover to his house, and took to him at once. Roxdal's somewhat supercilious manner had always jarred upon the unsophisticated corn factor. With Tom the old man got on much better. While evidently quite as well informed and cultured as his whilom friend, Tom knew how to impart his superior knowledge with the accent on the knowledge rather than on the superiority, while he had the air of gaining much information in return. Those who are most conscious of defects of early education are most resentful of other people sharing their consciousness. Moreover, Tom's *bonhomie* was far more to the old fellow's liking than the studied politeness of his predecessor, so that on the whole Tom made more of a conquest of the father than of the daughter. Nevertheless, Clara was by no means unresponsive to Tom's affection, and when, after one of his visits to the house, the old man kissed her fondly and spoke of the happy turn things had taken, and how, for the second time in their lives, things had mended when they seemed at their blackest, her heart swelled with a gush of gratitude and joy and tenderness, and she fell sobbing into her father's arms.

Tom calculated that he made a clear five hundred a year by occasional journalism, besides possessing some profitable investments which he had inherited from his mother, so that there was no reason for delaying the marriage. It was fixed for May-day, and the honeymoon was to be spent in Italy.

VI

The Dream and the Awakening

B ut Clara was not destined to happiness. From the moment she had
promised herself to her first love's friend, old memories began to
rise up and reproach her. Strange thoughts stirred in the depths of her
soul, and in the silent watches of the night she seemed to hear Everard's
accents, charged with grief and upbraiding. Her uneasiness increased
as her wedding-day drew near. One night, after a pleasant afternoon
spent in being rowed by Tom among the upper reaches of the Thames,
she retired to rest full of vague forebodings. And she dreamt a terrible
dream. The dripping form of Everard stood by her bedside, staring at
her with ghastly eyes. Had he been drowned on the passage to his land
of exile? Frozen with horror, she put the question.

"I have never left England!" the vision answered.

Her tongue clove to the roof of her mouth.

"Never left England?" she repeated, in tones which did not seem to
be hers.

The wraith's stony eyes stared on, but there was silence.

"Where have you been then?" she asked in her dream.

"Very near you," came the answer.

"There has been foul play then!" she shrieked.

The phantom shook its head in doleful assent.

"I knew it!" she shrieked. "Tom Peters—Tom Peters has done away
with you. Is it not he? Speak!"

"Yes, it is he—Tom Peters—whom I loved more than all the world."

Even in the terrible oppression of the dream she could not resist
saying, woman-like:

"Did I not warn you against him?"

The phantom stared on silently and made no reply.

"But what was his motive?" she asked at length.

"Love of gold—and you. And you are giving yourself to him," it said
sternly.

"No, no, Everard! I will not! I will not! I swear it! Forgive me!"

The spirit shook its head sceptically.

"You love him. Women are false—as false as men."

ISRAEL ZANGWILL

She strove to protest again, but her tongue refused its office.

"If you marry him, I shall always be with you! Beware!"

The dripping figure vanished as suddenly as it came, and Clara awoke in a cold perspiration. Oh, it was horrible! The man she had learnt to love, the murderer of the man she had learnt to forget! How her original prejudice had been justified! Distracted, shaken to her depths, she would not take counsel even of her father, but informed the police of her suspicions. A raid was made on Tom's rooms, and lo! the stolen notes were discovered in a huge bundle. It was found that he had several banking accounts, with a large, recently deposited amount in each bank. Tom was arrested. Attention was now concentrated on the corpses washed up by the river. It was not long before the body of Roxdal came to shore, the face distorted almost beyond recognition by long immersion, but the clothes patently his, and a pocket-book in the breast-pocket removing the last doubt. Mrs. Seacon and Polly and Clara Newell all identified the body. Both juries returned a verdict of murder against Tom Peters, the recital of Clara's dream producing a unique impression in the court and throughout the country, especially in theological and theosophical circles. The theory of the prosecution was that Roxdal had brought home the money, whether to fly alone or to divide it, or whether, even for some innocent purpose, as Clara believed, was immaterial; that Peters determined to have it all, that he had gone out for a walk with the deceased, and, taking advantage of the fog, had pushed him into the river, and that he was further impelled to the crime by love for Clara Newell, as was evident from his subsequent relations with her. The judge put on the black cap. Tom Peters was duly hung by the neck till he was dead.

VII

Brief Résumé of the Culprit's Confession

When you all read this I shall be dead and laughing at you. I have been hung for my own murder. I am Everard G. Roxdal. I am also Tom Peters. We two were one. When I was a young man my moustache and beard wouldn't come. I bought false ones to improve my appearance. One day, after I had become manager of the City and Suburban Bank, I took off my beard and moustache at home, and then the thought crossed my mind that nobody would know me without them. I was another man. Instantly it flashed upon me that if I ran away from the Bank, that other man could be left in London, while the police were scouring the world for a non-existent fugitive. But this was only the crude germ of the idea. Slowly I matured my plan. The man who was going to be left in London must be known to a circle of acquaintance beforehand. It would be easy enough to masquerade in the evenings in my beardless condition, with other disguises of dress and voice. But this was not brilliant enough. I conceived the idea of living with him. It was Box and Cox reversed. We shared rooms at Mrs. Seacon's. It was a great strain, but it was only for a few weeks. I had trick clothes in my bedroom like those of quick-change artistes; in a moment I could pass from Roxdal to Peters and from Peters to Roxdal. Polly had to clean two pairs of boots a morning, cook two dinners, &c., &c. She and Mrs. Seacon saw one or the other of us every moment; it never dawned upon them they never saw us *both together*. At meals I would not be interrupted, ate off two plates, and conversed with my friend in loud tones. A slight ventriloquial gift enabled me to hold audible conversations with him when he was supposed to be in the bedroom. At other times we dined at different hours. On Sundays he was supposed to be asleep when I was in church. There is no landlady in the world to whom the idea would have occurred that one man was troubling himself to be two (and to pay for two, including washing). I worked up the idea of Roxdal's flight, asked Polly to go with me, manufactured that feminine letter that arrived on the morning of my disappearance. As Tom Peters I mixed with a journalistic set. I had

ISRAEL ZANGWILL

another room where I kept the gold and notes till I mistakenly thought the thing had blown over. Unfortunately, returning from here on the night of my disappearance, with Roxdal's clothes in a bundle I intended to drop into the river, it was stolen from me in the fog, and the man into whose possession it ultimately came appears to have committed suicide, so that his body dressed in my clothes was taken for mine. What, perhaps, ruined me was my desire to keep Clara's love, and to transfer it to the survivor. Everard told her I was the best of fellows. Once married to her, I would not have had much fear. Even if she had discovered the trick, a wife cannot give evidence against her husband, and often does not want to. I made none of the usual slips, but no man can guard against a girl's nightmare after a day up the river and a supper at the Star and Garter. I might have told the judge he was an ass, but then I should have had penal servitude for bank robbery, and that is worse than death. The only thing that puzzles me, though, is whether the law has committed murder or I suicide. What is certain is that I have cheated the gallows.

SANTA CLAUS

A Story for the Nursery

A lthough Bob was asleep on the doorstep the children in the passage talked so loudly that they woke him up. They did not mean to do it, for they were nice, clean, handsome children. Bob was always pretty dirty, so nobody knew if he was pretty clean. He was not a dog, though you might think so from his name and the way he was treated. Nobody cared for Bob except Tommy whom he could fight one-hand. The lucky nice clean children had jam to lick, but Bob had only Tommy. Poor Tommy!

Bob sat up on his stony doorstep, drawing his rags around him. His toes were freezing. When you have no boots it is awkward to stamp your feet. That is why they are so cold. Bob's idea of heaven was a place with a fire in it. He lived before Free Education and his ideas were mixed.

Bob heard the children inside talking about Santa Claus and the presents they expected. Bob gathered that he was a kind-hearted old gentleman, and he thought to himself: "If I could find out Santa Claus's address, I'd go and arx 'im for some presents too." So he waited outside, shivering, till a pretty little girl and boy came out, when he said to them: "Please, can you tell me where Santa Claus lives?"

The little girl and boy drew back when he spoke to them, because they had strict orders to keep their pinafores clean. But when they heard his strange question, they looked at each other with large eyes. Then their pretty faces filled with smiling sunshine, and they said: "He lives in the sky. He is a spirit."

Bob's face fell. "Oh, then I carn't call upon 'im," he said. "But 'ow is it *I* never gets no presents like I 'ears yer say *you* does?"

"Perhaps you are not a good child," said the little girl gravely.

"Yes, look how you've torn your clothes," said the little boy reprovingly.

"Well, but 'ow is *you* goin' to get presents from the sky?"

"We hang up our stockings to-night, just before Christmas, and in the night Santa Claus fills them," they explained, and just then the maid came out and led them away.

Now Bob understood. He had never had any stockings in his life. He felt mad to think how much else he had missed through the want of a pair. If he could only get a pair of stockings to hang up, he might be a rich boy and dine off bread and treacle. He wandered through the courts and alleys looking for stockings in the gutters and dustbins. They were not there. Old boots were to be found in abundance though not in couples (which was odd); but Bob soon discovered that people never throw away their stockings. At last he plucked up courage and begged from house to house, but nobody had a pair to spare. What becomes of all the old stockings? Not everybody hoards treasure in them. Bob met plenty of kind hearts; they offered him bread when he asked for a stocking.

At last, weary and footsore, he returned to his doorstep and pondered. He wondered if he could cheat Santa Claus by making a pair out of a piece of newspaper he had picked up. But perhaps Mr. Claus was particular about the material and admitted nothing under cotton. He thought of stepping deeply into the mud and caking a pair, but then he could only remove them at night by brushing them off in little pieces; he feared they would stick too tight to come off whole. He also thought of painting his calves with stripes from "wet paint," on the off chance that Mr. Claus would drop the presents carelessly down along his legs. But he concluded that if Mr. Claus lived in the sky he could look down and see all he was doing. So he began to cry instead.

"What are you crying about?" said a quavering voice, and Bob, startled, became aware of a wretched old creature dining on the doorstep at his side.

"I ain't got no stockings," he sobbed in answer.

"Well, I'll give you mine," said his neighbour.

Bob hesitated. The poor old woman looked so brokendown herself, it seemed mean to accept her offer.

"Won't you be cold?" he asked timidly.

"I shan't be warmer," mumbled the old woman. "But then you will."

"No, I won't have them, thank you kindly, mum," said Bob stoutly.

"Then I'll tell you what to do," said the old woman, who was really a fairy, though she had lost both wings—they had been amputated in a surgical operation. "It's easy enough to get stockings if you only know how. Run away now and pick out any person you meet and say, 'I wish that person's stockings were on my feet.' You can only wish once, so be careful, especially, not to wish for a pair of blue stockings, as they won't suit you."

She grinned and vanished. Bob jumped up and was about to wish off the stockings of the first man he met, when a horrible thought struck him. The man had nice clothes and looked rich, but what proof was there he had stockings on? Bob really could not afford to risk wasting his wish. He walked about and looked at all the people—the men with their long trousers, the women with their trailing skirts; and the more he walked, the more grew his doubt and his agony. A terrible scepticism of humanity seized him. They looked very prim and demure without, these men and women, with their varnished boots and their satin gowns, but what if they were all hypocrites, walking about without stockings! Night came on. Half distracted by distrust of his kind, he wandered on to the docks, and there to his joy he saw people coming off a steamer by a narrow plank. As they walked the ladies lifted up their skirts so as not to tumble over them, and he caught several glimpses of dainty stockings. At last he selected a lady with very broad stockings, that looked as if they would hold lots of Mr. Claus's presents, and wished. Instantly he felt very funny about the feet, and the lady wobbled about so in her big boots that she overbalanced herself and fell into the water and was drowned.

Bob ran back to his doorstep, and when it was dark slipped off his stockings carefully and hung them up on the knocker. And—sure enough!—in the morning they were fall of fine cigars and Spanish lace. Bob sold the lace for a penny, but he kept the cigars and smoked the first with his penn'uth of Christmas plum-duff.

Moral:—England expects every man to pay his duty.

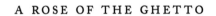

A ROSE OF THE GHETTO

One day it occurred to Leibel that he ought to get married. He went to Sugarman the Shadchan forthwith.

"I have the very thing for you," said the great marriage-broker.

"Is she pretty?" asked Leibel.

"Her father has a boot and shoe warehouse," replied Sugarman enthusiastically.

"Then there ought to be a dowry with her," said Leibel eagerly.

"Certainly a dowry! A fine man like you!"

"How much do you think it would be?"

"Of course it is not a large warehouse; but then you could get your boots at trade price, and your wife's, perhaps, for the cost of the leather."

"When could I see her?"

"I will arrange for you to call next Sabbath afternoon."

"You won't charge me more than a sovereign?"

"Not a *groschen* more! Such a pious maiden! I'm sure you will be happy. She has so much way-of-the-country (breeding). And, of course, five per cent on the dowry?"

"H'm! Well, I don't mind!" "Perhaps they won't give a dowry," he thought, with a consolatory sense of outwitting the Shadchan.

On the Saturday Leibel went to see the damsel, and on the Sunday he went to see Sugarman the Shadchan.

"But your maiden squints!" he cried resentfully.

"An excellent thing!" said Sugarman. "A wife who squints can never look her husband straight in the face and overwhelm him. Who would quail before a woman with a squint?"

"I could endure the squint," went on Leibel dubiously, "but she also stammers."

"Well, what is better, in the event of a quarrel? The difficulty she has in talking will keep her far more silent than most wives. You had best secure her while you have the chance."

"But she halts on the left leg," cried Leibel, exasperated.

"*Gott in Himmel!* Do you mean to say you do not see what an advantage it is to have a wife unable to accompany you in all your goings?"

Leibel lost patience.

"Why, the girl is a hunchback!" he protested furiously.

"My dear Leibel," said the marriage-broker, deprecatingly shrugging his shoulders and spreading out his palms. "You can't expect perfection!"

Nevertheless, Leibel persisted in his unreasonable attitude. He accused Sugarman of wasting his time, of making a fool of him.

"A fool of you!" echoed the Shadchan indignantly, "when I give you a chance of a boot and shoe manufacturer's daughter. You will make a fool of yourself if you refuse. I daresay her dowry would be enough to set you up as a master-tailor. At present you are compelled to slave away as a cutter for thirty shillings a week. It is most unjust. If you only had a few machines you would be able to employ your own cutters. And they can be got so cheap nowadays."

This gave Leibel pause, and he departed without having definitely broken the negotiations. His whole week was befogged by doubt, his work became uncertain, his chalk-marks lacked their usual decision, and he did not always cut his coat according to his cloth. His aberrations became so marked that pretty Rose Green, the sweater's eldest daughter, who managed a machine in the same room, divined, with all a woman's intuition, that he was in love.

"What is the matter?" she said in rallying Yiddish, when they were taking their lunch of bread and cheese and ginger-beer, amid the clatter of machines, whose serfs had not yet knocked off work.

"They are proposing me a match," he answered sullenly.

"A match!" exclaimed Rose. "Thou!" She had worked by his side for years, and familiarity bred the second person singular. Leibel nodded his head, and put a mouthful of Dutch cheese into it.

"With whom?" asked Rose. Somehow he felt ashamed. He gurgled the answer into the stone ginger-beer bottle, which he put to his thirsty lips.

"With Leah Volcovitch!"

"Leah Volcovitch!" gasped Rose. "Leah, the boot and shoe manufacturer's daughter?"

Leibel hung his head—he scarce knew why. He did not dare meet her gaze. His droop said "Yes." There was a long pause.

"And why dost thou not have her?" said Rose. It was more than an enquiry. There was contempt in it, and perhaps even pique.

Leibel did not reply. The embarrassing silence reigned again, and reigned long. Rose broke it at last.

"Is it that thou likest me better?" she asked.

Leibel seemed to see a ball of lightning in the air; it burst, and he felt the electric current strike right through his heart. The shock threw his head up with a jerk, so that his eyes gazed into a face whose beauty and tenderness were revealed to him for the first time. The face of his old acquaintance had vanished—this was a cajoling, coquettish, smiling face, suggesting undreamed-of things.

"*Nu*, yes," he replied, without perceptible pause.

"*Nu*, good!" she rejoined as quickly.

And in the ecstasy of that moment of mutual understanding Leibel forgot to wonder why he had never thought of Rose before. Afterwards he remembered that she had always been his social superior.

The situation seemed too dreamlike for explanation to the room just yet. Leibel lovingly passed the bottle of ginger-beer and Rose took a sip, with a beautiful air of plighting troth, understood only of those two. When Leibel quaffed the remnant it intoxicated him. The relics of the bread and cheese were the ambrosia to this nectar. They did not dare kiss—the suddenness of it all left them bashful, and the smack of lips would have been like a cannon-peal announcing their engagement. There was a subtler sweetness in this sense of a secret, apart from the fact that neither cared to break the news to the master-tailor—a stern little old man. Leibel's chalk-marks continued indecisive that afternoon; which shows how correctly Rose had connected them with love.

Before he left that night Rose said to him: "Art thou sure thou wouldst not rather have Leah Volcovitch?"

"Not for all the boots and shoes in the world," replied Leibel vehemently.

"And I," protested Rose, "would rather go without my own than without thee."

The landing outside the workshop was so badly lighted that their lips came together in the darkness.

"Nay, nay, thou must not yet," said Rose. "Thou art still courting Leah Volcovitch. For aught thou knowest, Sugarman the Shadchan may have entangled thee beyond redemption."

"Not so," asserted Leibel. "I have only seen the maiden once."

"Yes. But Sugarman has seen her father several times," persisted Rose. "For so misshapen a maiden his commission would be large. Thou must go to Sugarman to-night, and tell him that thou canst not find it in thy heart to go on with the match."

"Kiss me, and I will go," pleaded Leibel.

"Go, and I will kiss thee," said Rose resolutely.

"And when shall we tell thy father?" he asked, pressing her hand, as the next best thing to her lips.

"As soon as thou art free from Leah."

"But will he consent?"

"He will not be glad," said Rose frankly. "But after mother's death—peace be upon her—the rule passed from her hands into mine."

"Ah, that is well," said Leibel. He was a superficial thinker.

Leibel found Sugarman at supper. The great Shadchan offered him a chair, but nothing else. Hospitality was associated in his mind with special occasions only, and involved lemonade and "stuffed monkeys."

He was very put out—almost to the point of indigestion—to hear of Leibel's final determination, and plied him with reproachful enquiries.

"You don't mean to say that you give up a boot and shoe manufacturer merely because his daughter has round shoulders!" he exclaimed incredulously.

"It is more than round shoulders—it is a hump!" cried Leibel.

"And suppose? See how much better off you will be when you get your own machines! We do not refuse to let camels carry our burdens because they have humps."

"Ah, but a wife is not a camel," said Leibel, with a sage air.

"And a cutter is not a master-tailor," retorted Sugarman.

"Enough, enough!" cried Leibel. "I tell you I would not have her if she were a machine warehouse."

"There sticks something behind," persisted Sugarman, unconvinced.

Leibel shook his head. "Only her hump," he said, with a flash of humour.

"Moses Mendelssohn had a hump," expostulated Sugarman reproachfully.

"Yes, but he was a heretic," rejoined Leibel, who was not without reading. "And then he was a man! A man with two humps could find a wife for each. But a woman with a hump cannot expect a husband in addition."

"Guard your tongue from evil," quoth the Shadchan angrily. "If everybody were to talk like you, Leah Volcovitch would never be married at all."

Leibel shrugged his shoulders, and reminded him that hunchbacked girls who stammered and squinted and halted on left legs were not usually led under the canopy.

"Nonsense! Stuff!" cried Sugarman angrily. "That is because they do not come to me."

"Leah Volcovitch *has* come to you," said Leibel, "but she shall not come to me." And he rose, anxious to escape.

Instantly Sugarman gave a sigh of resignation. "Be it so! Then I shall have to look out for another, that's all."

"No, I don't want any," replied Leibel quickly.

Sugarman stopped eating. "You don't want any?" he cried. "But you came to me for one?"

"I—I—know," stammered Leibel. "But I've—I've altered my mind."

"One needs Hillel's patience to deal with you!" cried Sugarman. "But I shall charge you all the same for my trouble. You cannot cancel an order like this in the middle! No, no! You can play fast and loose with Leah Volcovitch. But you shall not make a fool of me."

"But if I don't want one?" said Leibel sullenly.

Sugarman gazed at him with a cunning look of suspicion. "Didn't I say there was something sticking behind?"

Leibel felt guilty. "But whom have you got in your eye?" he enquired desperately.

"Perhaps you may have some one in yours!" naïvely answered Sugarman.

Leibel gave a hypocritic long-drawn, "U-m-m-m. I wonder if Rose Green—where I work—" he said, and stopped.

"I fear not," said Sugarman. "She is on my list. Her father gave her to me some months ago, but he is hard to please. Even the maiden herself is not easy, being pretty."

"Perhaps she has waited for some one," suggested Leibel.

Sugarman's keen ear caught the note of complacent triumph.

"You have been asking her yourself!" he exclaimed in horror-stricken accents.

"And if I have?" said Leibel defiantly.

"You have cheated me! And so has Eliphaz Green—I always knew he was tricky! You have both defrauded me!"

"I did not mean to," said Leibel mildly.

"You *did* mean to. You had no business to take the matter out of my hands. What right had you to propose to Rose Green?"

"I did not," cried Leibel excitedly.

"Then you asked her father!"

"No; I have not asked her father yet."

"Then how do you know she will have you?"

"I—I know," stammered Leibel, feeling himself somehow a liar as well as a thief. His brain was in a whirl; he could not remember how the thing had come about. Certainly he had not proposed; nor could he say that she had.

"You know she will have you," repeated Sugarman, reflectively. "And does *she* know?"

"Yes. In fact," he blurted out, "we arranged it together."

"Ah! You both know. And does her father know?"

"Not yet."

"Ah! then I must get his consent," said Sugarman decisively.

"I—I thought of speaking to him myself."

"Yourself!" echoed Sugarman, in horror. "Are you unsound in the head? Why, that would be worse than the mistake you have already made!"

"What mistake?" asked Leibel, firing up.

"The mistake of asking the maiden herself. When you quarrel with her after your marriage, she will always throw it in your teeth that you wished to marry her. Moreover, if you tell a maiden you love her, her father will think you ought to marry her as she stands. Still, what is done is done." And he sighed regretfully.

"And what more do I want? I love her."

"You piece of clay!" cried Sugarman contemptuously. "Love will not turn machines, much less buy them. You must have a dowry. Her father has a big stocking—he can well afford it."

Leibel's eyes lit up. There was really no reason why he should not have bread-and-cheese with his kisses.

"Now, if *you* went to her father," pursued the Shadchan, "the odds are that he would not even give you his daughter—to say nothing of the dowry. After all, it is a cheek of you to aspire so high. As you told me from the first, you haven't saved a penny. Even my commission you won't be able to pay till you get the dowry. But if *I* go, I do not despair of getting a substantial sum—to say nothing of the daughter."

"Yes, I think you had better go," said Leibel eagerly.

"But if I do this thing for you I shall want a pound more," rejoined Sugarman.

"A pound more!" echoed Leibel, in dismay. "Why?"

"Because Rose Green's hump is of gold," replied Sugarman oracularly. "Also, she is fair to see, and many men desire her."

"But you have always your five per cent on the dowry."

"It will be less than Volcovitch's," explained Sugarman. "You see, Green has other and less beautiful daughters."

"Yes; but then it settles itself more easily. Say five shillings."

"Eliphaz Green is a hard man," said the Shadchan instead.

"Ten shillings is the most I will give!"

"Twelve and sixpence is the least I will take. Eliphaz Green haggles so terribly."

They split the difference, and so eleven and threepence represented the predominance of Eliphaz Green's stinginess over Volcovitch's.

The very next day Sugarman invaded the Green work-room. Rose bent over her seams, her heart fluttering. Leibel had duly apprised her of the roundabout manner in which she would have to be won, and she had acquiesced in the comedy. At the least it would save her the trouble of father-taming.

Sugarman's entry was brusque and breathless. He was overwhelmed with joyous emotion. His blue bandanna trailed agitatedly from his coat-tail.

"At last!" he cried, addressing the little white-haired master-tailor, "I have the very man for you."

"Yes?" grunted Eliphaz, unimpressed. The monosyllable was packed with emotion. It said: "Have you really the face to come to me again with an ideal man?"

"He has all the qualities that you desire," began the Shadchan, in a tone that repudiated the implications of the monosyllable. "He is young, strong, God-fearing—"

"Has he any money?" grumpily interrupted Eliphaz.

"He *will* have money," replied Sugarman unhesitatingly, "when he marries."

"Ah!" The father's voice relaxed, and his foot lay limp on the treadle. He worked one of his machines himself, and paid himself the wages so as to enjoy the profit. "How much will he have?"

"I think he will have fifty pounds; and the least you can do is to let him have fifty pounds," replied Sugarman, with the same happy ambiguity.

Eliphaz shook his head on principle.

"Yes, you will," said Sugarman, "when you learn how fine a man he is."

The flush of confusion and trepidation already on Leibel's countenance became a rosy glow of modesty, for he could not help overhearing what was being said, owing to the lull of the master-tailor's machine.

"Tell me, then," rejoined Eliphaz.

"Tell me, first, if you will give fifty to a young, healthy, hard-working, God-fearing man, whose idea it is to start as a master-tailor on his own account? And you know how profitable that is!"

"To a man like that," said Eliphaz, in a burst of enthusiasm, "I would give as much as twenty-seven pounds ten!"

Sugarman groaned inwardly, but Leibel's heart leaped with joy. To get four months' wages at a stroke! With twenty-seven pounds ten he could certainly procure several machines, especially on the instalment system. Out of the corners of his eyes he shot a glance at Rose, who was beyond earshot.

"Unless you can promise thirty it is waste of time mentioning his name," said Sugarman.

"Well, well—who is he?"

Sugarman bent down, lowering his voice into the father's ear.

"What! Leibel!" cried Eliphaz, outraged.

"Sh!" said Sugarman, "or he will overhear your delight, and ask more. He has his nose high enough as it is."

"B—b—b—ut," sputtered the bewildered parent, "I know Leibel myself. I see him every day. I don't want a Shadchan to find me a man I know—a mere hand in my own workshop!"

"Your talk has neither face nor figure," answered Sugarman sternly. "It is just the people one sees every day that one knows least. I warrant that if I had not put it into your head you would never have dreamt of Leibel as a son-in-law. Come now, confess."

Eliphaz grunted vaguely, and the Shadchan went on triumphantly. "I thought as much. And yet where could you find a better man to keep your daughter?"

"He ought to be content with her alone," grumbled her father.

Sugarman saw the signs of weakening, and dashed in, full strength. "It's a question whether he will have her at all. I have not been to him about her yet. I awaited your approval of the idea." Leibel admired the verbal accuracy of these statements, which he just caught.

"But I didn't know he would be having money," murmured Eliphaz.

"Of course you didn't know. That's what the Shadchan is for—to point out the things that are under your nose."

"But where will he be getting this money from?"

"From you," said Sugarman frankly.

"From me?"

"From whom else? Are you not his employer? It has been put by for his marriage-day."

"He has saved it?"

"He has not *spent* it," said Sugarman, impatiently.

"But do you mean to say he has saved fifty pounds?"

"If he could manage to save fifty pounds out of your wages he would be indeed a treasure," said Sugarman. "Perhaps it might be thirty."

"But you said fifty."

"Well, *you* came down to thirty," retorted the Shadchan. "You cannot expect him to have more than your daughter brings."

"I never said thirty," Eliphaz reminded him. "Twenty-seven ten was my last bid."

"Very well; that will do as a basis of negotiations," said Sugarman resignedly. "I will call upon him this evening. If I were to go over and speak to him now he would perceive you were anxious and raise his terms, and that will never do. Of course, you will not mind allowing me a pound more for finding you so economical a son-in-law?"

"Not a penny more."

"You need not fear," said Sugarman resentfully. "It is not likely I shall be able to persuade him to take so economical a father-in-law. So you will be none the worse for promising."

"Be it so," said Eliphaz, with a gesture of weariness, and he started his machine again.

"Twenty-seven pounds ten, remember," said Sugarman, above the whirr.

Eliphaz nodded his head, whirring his wheelwork louder.

"And paid before the wedding, mind?"

The machine took no notice.

"Before the wedding, mind," repeated Sugarman. "Before we go under the canopy."

"Go now, go now!" grunted Eliphaz, with a gesture of impatience. "It shall be all well." And the white-haired head bowed immovably over its work.

In the evening Rose extracted from her father the motive of Sugarman's visit, and confessed that the idea was to her liking.

"But dost thou think he will have me, little father?" she asked, with cajoling eyes.

"Anyone would have my Rose."

"Ah, but Leibel is different. So many years he has sat at my side and said nothing."

"He had his work to think of; he is a good, saving youth."

"At this very moment Sugarman is trying to persuade him—not so? I suppose he will want much money."

"Be easy, my child." And he passed his discoloured hand over her hair.

Sugarman turned up the next day, and reported that Leibel was unobtainable under thirty pounds, and Eliphaz, weary of the contest, called over Leibel, till that moment carefully absorbed in his scientific chalk-marks, and mentioned the thing to him for the first time. "I am not a man to bargain," Eliphaz said, and so he gave the young man his tawny hand, and a bottle of rum sprang from somewhere, and work was suspended for five minutes, and the "hands" all drank amid surprised excitement. Sugarman's visits had prepared them to congratulate Rose. But Leibel was a shock.

The formal engagement was marked by even greater junketing, and at last the marriage-day came. Leibel was resplendent in a diagonal frock-coat, cut by his own hand, and Rose stepped from the cab a medley of flowers, fairness, and white silk, and behind her came two bridesmaids—her sisters—a trio that glorified the spectator-strewn pavement outside the Synagogue. Eliphaz looked almost tall in his shiny high hat and frilled shirt-front. Sugarman arrived on foot, carrying red-socked little Ebenezer tucked under his arm.

Leibel and Rose were not the only couple to be disposed of, for it was the thirty-third day of the Omer—a day fruitful in marriages.

But at last their turn came. They did not, however, come in their turn, and their special friends among the audience wondered why they had lost their precedence. After several later marriages had taken place, a whisper began to circulate. The rumour of a hitch gained ground steadily, and the sensation was proportionate. And, indeed, the rose was not to be picked without a touch of the thorn.

Gradually the facts leaked out, and a buzz of talk and comment ran through the waiting Synagogue. Eliphaz had not paid up!

At first he declared he would put down the money immediately after the ceremony. But the wary Sugarman, schooled by experience, demanded its instant delivery on behalf of his other client. Hard-pressed, Eliphaz produced ten sovereigns from his trousers' pocket, and tendered them on account. These Sugarman disdainfully refused, and the negotiations were suspended. The bridegroom's party was encamped in one room, the bride's in another, and after a painful delay Eliphaz sent an emissary to say that half the amount should be forthcoming, the extra five pounds in a bright new Bank of England note. Leibel, instructed and encouraged by Sugarman, stood firm.

And then arose a hubbub of voices, a chaos of suggestions; friends rushed to and fro between the camps, some emerging from their seats in the Synagogue to add to the confusion. But Eliphaz had taken his stand upon a rock—he had no more ready money. To-morrow, the next day, he would have some. And Leibel, pale and dogged, clutched tighter at those machines that were slipping away momently from him. He had not yet seen his bride that morning, and so her face was shadowy compared with the tangibility of those machines. Most of the other maidens were married women by now, and the situation was growing desperate. From the female camp came terrible rumours of bridesmaids in hysterics, and a bride that tore her wreath in a passion of shame and humiliation. Eliphaz sent word that he would give an I O U for the balance, but that he really could not muster any more current coin. Sugarman instructed the ambassador to suggest that Eliphaz should raise the money among his friends.

And the short spring day slipped away. In vain the minister, apprised of the block, lengthened out the formulæ for the other pairs, and blessed them with more reposeful unction. It was impossible to stave off the Leibel-Green item indefinitely, and at last Rose remained the only orange-wreathed spinster in the Synagogue. And then there was a hush of solemn suspense, that swelled gradually into a steady rumble of babbling tongues as minute succeeded minute and the final bridal party still failed to appear. The latest bulletin pictured the bride in a dead faint. The afternoon was waning fast. The minister left his post near the canopy, under which so many lives had been united, and came to add his white tie to the forces for compromise. But he fared no better than the others. Incensed at the obstinacy of the antagonists, he declared he would close the Synagogue. He gave the couple ten minutes to marry in or quit. Then chaos came, and pandemonium—a frantic babel of suggestion and exhortation from the crowd. When five minutes had passed, a legate from Eliphaz announced that his side had scraped together twenty pounds, and that this was their final bid.

Leibel wavered; the long day's combat had told upon him; the reports of the bride's distress had weakened him. Even Sugarman had lost his cocksureness of victory. A few minutes more and both commissions might slip through his fingers. Once the parties left the Synagogue it would not be easy to drive them there another day. But he cheered on his man still—one could always surrender at the tenth minute.

At the eighth the buzz of tongues faltered suddenly, to be transposed into a new key, so to speak. Through the gesticulating assembly swept that murmur of expectation which crowds know when the procession is coming at last. By some mysterious magnetism all were aware that the BRIDE herself—the poor hysteric bride—had left the paternal camp, was coming in person to plead with her mercenary lover.

And as the glory of her and the flowers and the white draperies loomed upon Leibel's vision his heart melted in worship, and he knew his citadel would crumble in ruins at her first glance, at her first touch. Was it fair fighting? As his troubled vision cleared and as she came nigh unto him, he saw to his amazement that she was speckless and composed—no trace of tears dimmed the fairness of her face, there was no disarray in her bridal wreath.

The clock showed the ninth minute.

She put her hand appealingly on his arm, while a heavenly light came into her face—the expression of a Joan of Arc animating her country.

"Do not give in, Leibel," she said. "Do not have me! Do not let them persuade thee. By my life thou must not! Go home!"

("'BY MY LIFE THOU MUST NOT!'")

So at the eleventh minute the vanquished Eliphaz produced the balance, and they all lived happily ever afterwards.

A DOUBLE-BARRELLED GHOST

I was ruined. The bank in which I had been a sleeping-partner from my cradle smashed suddenly, and I was exempted from income tax at one fell blow. It became necessary to dispose even of the family mansion and the hereditary furniture. The shame of not contributing to my country's exchequer spurred me to earnest reflection upon how to earn an income, and, having mixed myself another lemon-squash, I threw myself back on the canvas garden-chair, and watched the white, scented wreaths of my cigar-smoke hanging in the drowsy air, and provoking inexperienced bees to settle upon them. It was the sort of summer afternoon on which to eat lotus, and to sip the dew from the lips of Amaryllises; but although I had an affianced Amaryllis (whose Christian name was Jenny Grant), I had not the heart to dally with her in view of my sunk fortunes. She loved me for myself, no doubt, but then I was not myself since the catastrophe; and although she had hastened to assure me of her unchanged regard, I was not at all certain whether *I* should be able to support a wife in addition to all my other misfortunes. So that I was not so comfortable that afternoon as I appeared to my perspiring valet: no rose in the garden had a pricklier thorn than I. The thought of my poverty weighed me down; and when the setting sun began flinging bars of gold among the clouds, the reminder of my past extravagance made my heart heavier still, and I broke down utterly.

Swearing at the manufacturers of such collapsible garden-chairs, I was struggling to rise when I perceived my rings of smoke comporting themselves strangely. They were widening and curving and flowing into definite outlines, as though the finger of the wind were shaping them into a rough sketch of the human figure. Sprawling amid the ruins of my chair, I watched the nebulous contours grow clearer and clearer, till at last the agitation subsided, and a misty old gentleman, clad in vapour of an eighteenth-century cut, stood plainly revealed upon the sun-flecked grass.

"Good afternoon, John," said the old gentleman, courteously removing his cocked hat.

"Good afternoon!" I gasped. "How do you know my name?"

"Because I have not forgotten my own," he replied. "I am John Halliwell, your great-grandfather. Don't you remember me?"

A flood of light burst upon my brain. Of course! I ought to have recognised him at once from the portrait by Sir Joshua Reynolds, just about to be sold by auction. The artist had gone to full length in painting him, and here he was complete, from his white wig, beautifully frizzled by the smoke, to his buckled shoes, from his knee-breeches to the frills at his wrists.

"Oh! pray pardon my not having recognised you," I cried remorsefully; "I have such a bad memory for faces. Won't you take a chair?"

"Sir, I have not sat down for a century and a half," he said simply. "Pray be seated yourself."

Thus reminded of my undignified position, I gathered myself up, and readjusting the complex apparatus, confided myself again to its canvas caresses. Then, grown conscious of my shirt-sleeves, I murmured,—

"Excuse my deshabille. I did not expect to see you."

"I am aware the season is inopportune," he said apologetically. "But I did not care to put off my visit till Christmas. You see, with us Christmas is a kind of Bank Holiday; and when there is a general excursion, a refined spirit prefers its own fireside. Moreover, I am not, as you may see, very robust, and I scarce like to risk exposing myself to such an extreme change of temperature. Your English Christmas is so cold. With the pyrometer at three hundred and fifty, it is hardly prudent to pass to thirty. On a sultry day like this the contrast is less marked."

"I understand," I said sympathetically.

"But I should hardly have ventured," he went on, "to trespass upon you at this untimely season merely out of deference to my own valetudinarian instincts. The fact is, I am a *littérateur*."

"Oh, indeed," I said vaguely; "I was not aware of it."

"Nobody was aware of it," he replied sadly; "but my calling at this professional hour will, perhaps, go to substantiate my statement."

I looked at him blankly. Was he quite sane? All the apparitions I had ever heard of spoke with some approach to coherence, however imbecile their behaviour. The statistics of insanity in the spiritual world have never been published, but I suspect the percentage of madness is high. Mere harmless idiocy is doubtless the prevalent form of dementia, judging by the way the poor unhappy spirits set about compassing their ends; but some of their actions can only be explained by the more violent species of mania. My great-grandfather seemed to read the suspicion in my eye, for he hastily continued:—

"Of course it is only the outside public who imagine that the spirits of literature really appear at Christmas. It is the annuals that appear at Christmas. The real season at which we are active on earth is summer, as every journalist knows. By Christmas the authors of our being have completely forgotten our existence. As a writer myself, and calling in connection with a literary matter, I thought it more professional to pay my visit during the dog days, especially as your being in trouble supplied me with an excuse for asking permission to go beyond bounds."

"You knew I was in trouble?" I murmured, touched by this sympathy from an unexpected quarter.

"Certainly. And from a selfish point of view I am not sorry. You have always been so inconsiderately happy that I could never find a seemly pretext to get out to see you."

"Is it only when your descendants are in trouble that you are allowed to visit them?" I enquired.

"Even so," he answered. "Of course spirits whose births were tragic, who were murdered into existence, are allowed to supplement the inefficient police departments of the upper globe, and a similar charter is usually extended to those who have hidden treasures on their conscience; but it is obvious that if all spirits were accorded what furloughs they pleased, eschatology would become a farce. Sir, you have no idea of the number of bogus criminal romances tendered daily by those wishing to enjoy the roving license of avenging spirits, for the ex-assassinated are the most enviable of immortals, and cases of personation are of frequent occurrence. Our actresses, too, are always pretending to have lost jewels; there is no end to the excuses. The Christmas Bank Holiday is naturally inadequate to our needs. Sir, I should have been far happier if my descendants had gone wrong; but in spite of the large fortune I had accumulated, both your father and your grandfather were of exemplary respectability and unruffled cheerfulness. The solitary outing I had was when your father attended a séance, and I was knocked up in the middle of the night. But I did not enjoy my holiday in the least; the indignity of having to move the furniture made the blood boil in my veins as in a spirit-lamp, and exposed me to the malicious badinage of my circle on my return. I protested that I did not care a rap; but I was mightily rejoiced when I learnt that your father had denounced the proceedings as a swindle, and was resolved never to invite me to his table again. When you were born I thought you were born to trouble, as the sparks fly upwards from our dwelling-place; but I was mistaken. Up till now your life has been a long summer afternoon."

"Yes, but now the shades are falling," I said grimly. "It looks as if my life henceforwards will be a long holiday—for you."

He shook his wig mournfully.

"No, I am only out on parole. I have had to give my word of honour to try to set you on your legs again as soon as possible."

"You couldn't have come at a more opportune moment," I cried, remembering how he had found me. "You are a good as well as a great-grandfather, and I am proud of my descent. Won't you have a cigar?"

"Thank you, I never smoke—on earth," said the spirit hurriedly, with a flavour of bitter in his accents. "Let us to the point. You have been reduced to the painful necessity of earning your living."

I nodded silently, and took a sip of lemon-squash. A strange sense of salvation lulled my soul.

"How do you propose to do it?" asked my great-grandfather.

"Oh, I leave that to you," I said confidingly.

"Well, what do you say to a literary career?"

"Eh? What?" I gasped.

"A literary career," he repeated. "What makes you so astonished?"

"Well, for one thing it's exactly what Tom Addlestone, the leader-writer of the *Hurrygraph*, was recommending to me this morning. He said: 'John, my boy, if I had had your advantages ten years ago, I should have been spared many a headache and supplied with many a dinner. It may turn out a lucky thing yet that you gravitated so to literary society, and that so many press men had free passes to your suppers. Consider the number of men of letters you have mixed drinks with! Why, man, you can succeed in any branch of literature you please.'"

My great-grandfather's face was radiant. Perhaps it was only the setting sun that touched it.

"A chip of the old block," he murmured. "That was I in my young days. Johnson, Goldsmith, Sheridan, Burke, Hume, I knew them all—gay dogs, gay dogs! Except that great hulking brute of a Johnson," he added, with a sudden savage snarl that showed his white teeth.

"I told Addlestone that I had no literary ability whatever, and he scoffed at me for my simplicity. All the same, I think he was only poking fun at me. My friends might puff me out to bull-size; but I am only a frog, and I should very soon burst. The public might be cajoled into buying one book; they could not be duped a second time. Don't you think I was right? I haven't any literary ability, have I?"

"Certainly not, certainly not," replied my great-grandfather with an alacrity and emphasis that would have seemed suspicious in a mere mortal. "But it does seem a shame to waste so great an opportunity. The ball that Addlestone waited years for is at your foot, and it is grievous to think that there it must remain merely because you do not know how to kick it."

"Well, but what's a man to do?"

"What's a man to do?" repeated my great-grandfather contemptuously. "Get a ghost, of course."

"By Jove!" I cried with a whistle. "That's a good idea! Addlestone has a ghost to do his leaders for him when he's lazy. I've seen the young fellow myself. Tom pays him six guineas a dozen, and gets three guineas apiece himself. But of course Tom has to live in much better style, and that makes it fair all round. You mean that I am to take advantage of my influence to get some other fellow work, and take a commission for the use of my name? That seems feasible enough. But where am I to find a ghost with the requisite talents?"

"Here," said my great-grandfather.

"What! You?"

"Yes, I," he replied calmly.

"But you couldn't write—"

"Not now, certainly not. All I wrote now would be burnt."

"Then how the devil—?" I began.

"Hush!" he interrupted nervously. "Listen, and I will a tale unfold. It is called *The Learned Pig*. I wrote it in my forty-fifth year, and it is full of sketches from the life of all the more notable personages of my time, from Lord Chesterfield to Mrs. Thrale, from Peg Woffington to Adam Smith and the ingenious Mr. Dibdin. I have painted the portrait of Sir Joshua quite as faithfully as he has painted mine. Of course much of the dialogue is real, taken from conversations preserved in my note-book. It is, I believe, a complete picture of the period, and being the only book I ever wrote or intended to write, I put my whole self into it, as well as all my friends."

"It must be, indeed, your masterpiece," I cried enthusiastically. "But why is it called *The Learned Pig*, and how has it escaped publication?"

"You shall hear. The learned pig is Dr. Johnson. He refused to take wine with me. I afterwards learnt that he had given up strong liqueurs altogether, and I went to see him again, but he received me with epigrams. He is the pivot of my book, all the other characters revolving about him. Naturally, I did not care to publish during his lifetime; not entirely, I admit, out of consideration to his feelings, but because foolish admirers had placed him on such a pedestal that he could damn any book he did not relish. I made sure of surviving him, so many and diverse were his distempers; whereas my manuscript survived me. In the moment of death I strove to tell your grandfather of the hiding-place in which I had bestowed it; but I could only make signs to which he had not the clue. You can imagine how it has embittered my spirit to have missed the aim of my life and my due niche in the pantheon of letters. In vain I strove to be registered among the 'hidden treasure' spirits, with the perambulatory privileges pertaining to the class. I was told that to recognise manuscripts under the head of 'treasures' would be to open a fresh door to abuse, there being few but had scribbled in their time and had a good conceit of their compositions to boot. I could offer no proofs of the value of my work, not even printers' proofs, and even the fact that the manuscript was concealed behind a sliding panel availed not to bring it into the coveted category. Moreover, not only did I have no other pretext to call on my descendants, but both my son and grandson were too respectable to be willingly connected with letters and too flourishing to be enticed by the prospects of profit. To you, however, this book will prove the avenue to fresh fortune."

"Do you mean I am to publish it under your name?"

"No, under yours."

"But, then, where does the satisfaction come in?"

"Your name is the same as mine."

"I see; but still, why not tell the truth about it? In a preface, for instance."

"Who would believe it? In my own day I could not credit that Macpherson spoke truly about the way Ossian came into his possession, nor to judge from gossip I have had with the younger ghosts did anyone attach credence to Sir Walter Scott's introductions."

"True," I said musingly. "It is a played-out dodge. But I am not certain whether an attack on Dr. Johnson would go down nowadays. We are aware that the man had porcine traits, but we have almost canonised him."

"The very reason why the book will be a success," he replied eagerly. "I understand that in these days of yours the best way of attracting attention is to fly in the face of all received opinion, and so in the realm of history to whitewash the villains and tar and feather the saints. The sliding panel of which I spoke is just behind the picture of me. Lose no time. Go at once, even as I must."

The shadowy contours of his form waved agitatedly in the wind.

"But how do you know anyone will bring it out?" I said doubtfully. "Am I to haunt the publishers' offices till—"

"No, no, I will do that," he interrupted in excitement. "Promise me you will help me."

"But I don't feel at all sure it stands a ghost of a chance," I said, growing colder in proportion as he grew more enthusiastic.

"It is the only chance of a ghost," he pleaded. "Come, give me your word. Any of your literary friends will get you a publisher, and where could you get a more promising ghost?"

"Oh, nonsense!" I said quietly, unconsciously quoting Ibsen. "There must be ghosts all the country over, as thick as the sand of the sea."

I was determined to put the matter on its proper footing, for I saw that under pretence of restoring my fortunes he was really trying to get me to pull his chestnuts out of the fire, and I resented the deceptive spirit that could put forward such tasks as favours. It was evident that he cherished a post-mortem grudge against the great lexicographer, as well as a posthumous craving for fame, and wished to use me as the instrument of his reputation and his revenge. But I was a man of the world, and I was not going to be rushed by a mere phantom.

"I don't deny there are plenty of ghosts about," he answered with insinuative deference. "Only will any of the others work for nothing?"

He saw he had scored a point, and his eyes twinkled.

"Yes, but I don't know that I approve of black-legs," I answered sternly. "You are taking the bread and butter out of some honest ghost's mouth."

The corners of his own mouth drooped; his eyes grew misty; he looked fading away. "Most true," he faltered; "but be pitiful. Have you no great-grand-filial feelings?"

"No, I lost everything in the crash," I answered coldly. "Suppose the book's a frost?"

"I shan't mind," he said eagerly.

"No, I don't suppose you *would* mind a frost," I retorted witheringly. "But look at the chaff you'd be letting me in for. Hadn't you better put off publication for a century or two?"

"No, no," he cried wildly; "our mansion will pass into strange hands. I shall not have the right of calling on the new proprietors."

"Phew!" I whistled; "perhaps that's why you timed your visit now, you artful old codger. I have always heard appearances are deceptive. However, I have ever been a patron of letters; and although I cannot approve of post-mundane malice, and think the dead past should be let bury its dead, still, if you are set upon it, I will try and use my influence to get your book published."

"Bless you!" he cried tremulously, with all the effusiveness natural to an author about to see himself in print, and trembled so violently that he dissipated himself away.

I stood staring a moment at the spot where he had stood, pleased at having out-manoeuvred him; then my chair gave way with another crash, and I picked myself up painfully, together with the dead stump of my cigar, and brushed the ash off my trousers, and rubbed my eyes and wondered if I had been dreaming. But no! when I ran into the cheerless dining-room, with its pervading sense of imminent auction, I found the sliding panel behind the portrait by Reynolds, which seemed to beam kindly encouragement upon me, and, lo! *The Learned Pig* was there in a mass of musty manuscript.

As everybody knows, the book made a hit. The *Acadæum* was unusually generous in its praise: "A lively picture of the century of farthingales and stomachers, marred only by numerous anachronisms and that stilted air of faked-up archæological knowledge which is, we suppose, inevitable in historical novels. The conversations are particularly artificial. Still, we can forgive Mr. Halliwell a good deal of inaccuracy and inacquaintance with the period, in view of the graphic picture of the literary dictator from the novel point of view of a contemporary who was not among the worshippers. It is curious how the honest, sterling character of the man is brought out all the more clearly from the incapacity of the narrator to comprehend its greatness—to show this was a task that called for no little skill and subtlety. If it were only for this one ingenious idea, Mr. Halliwell's book would stand out from the mass of abortive attempts to resuscitate the past. He has failed to picture the times, but he has done what is better—he has given us human beings who are alive, instead of the futile shadows that flit through the Walhalla of the average historical novel."

All the leading critics were at one as to the cleverness with which the great soul of Dr. Johnson was made to stand out on the background of detraction, and the public was universally agreed that this was the only readable historical novel published for many years, and that the anachronisms didn't matter a pin. I don't know what I had done to Tom Addlestone; but when everybody was talking about me, he went about saying that I kept a ghost. I was annoyed, for I did not keep one in any sense, and I openly defied the world to produce him. Why, I never saw him again myself—I believe he was too disgusted with the fillip he had given Dr. Johnson's reputation, and did not even take advantage of the Christmas Bank Holiday. But Addlestone's libel got to Jenny Grant's ears, and she came to me indignantly, and said: "I won't have it. You must either give up me or the ghost."

"To give up you would be to give up the ghost, darling," I answered soothingly. "But you, and you alone, have a right to the truth. It is not my ghost at all, it is my great-grandfather's."

"Do you mean to say he bequeathed him to you?"

"It came to that."

I then told her the truth, and showed how in any case the profits of my ancestor's book rightfully reverted backwards to me. So we were married on them, and Jenny, fired by my success, tried *her* hand on a novel, and published it, truthfully enough, under the name of J. Halliwell. She has written all my stories ever since, including this one; which, if it be necessarily false in the letter, is true in the spirit.

VAGARIES OF A VISCOUNT

That every man has a romance in his life has always been a pet theory of mine, so I was not surprised to find the immaculate Dorking smoking a clay pipe in Cable Street (late Ratcliff Highway) at half-past eight of a winter's morning. Nor was I surprised to find myself there, because, as a romancer, I have a poetic license to go anywhere and see everything. Viscount Dorking had just come out of an old clo' shop, and was got up like a sailor. Under his arm was a bundle. He lurched against me without recognising me, for I, too, was masquerading in my shabbiest and roughest attire, and the morning was bleak and foggy, the round red sun flaming in the forehead of the morning sky like the eye of a cyclop. But there could be no doubt it was Dorking—even if I had not been acquainted with the sedate Viscount (that paradox of the peerage, whose treatises on pure mathematics were the joy of Senior Wranglers) I should have suspected something shady from the whiteness of my sailor's hands.

Dorking was a dapper little man, almost dissociable from gloves and a chimneypot. The sight of him shambling along like one of the crew of H. M. S. *Pinafore* gave me a pleasant thrill of excitement. I turned, and followed him along the narrow yellow street. He made towards the Docks, turning down King David Lane. He was apparently without any instrument of protection, though I, for my part, was glad to feel the grasp of the old umbrella that walks always with me, hand in knob. Hard by the Shadwell Basin he came to a halt before a frowsy coffee-house, reflectively removed his pipe from his mouth, and whistled a bar of a once popular air in a peculiar manner. Then he pushed open the bleared glass door, and was lost to view.

After an instant's hesitation I pulled my sombrero over my eyes and strode in after him, plunging into a wave of musty warmth not entirely disagreeable after the frigid street. The boxes were full of queer waterside characters, among whom flitted a young woman robustly beautiful. The Viscount was already smiling at her when I entered. "Bring us the usual," he said, in a rough accent.

"Come along, Jenny, pint and one," impatiently growled a weather-beaten old ruffian in a pilot's cap.

"Pawn your face!" murmured Jenny, turning to me with an enquiring air.

"Pint and one," I said boldly, in as husky a tone as I could squeeze out.

Several battered visages, evidently belonging to *habitués* of the place, were bent suspiciously in my direction; perhaps because my rig-out, though rough, had no flavour of sea-salt or river-mud, for no one took the least notice of Dorking, except the comely attendant. I waited with some curiosity for my fare, which turned out to be nothing more mysterious than a pint of coffee and one thick slice of bread and butter. Not to appear ignorant of the prices ruling, I tendered Jenny a sixpence, whereupon she returned me fourpence-halfpenny. This appeared to me so ridiculously cheap that I had not the courage to offer her the change as I had intended, nor did she seem to expect it. The pint of coffee was served in one great hulking cup such as Gargantua might have quaffed. I took a sip, and found it of the flavour of chalybeate springs. But it was hot, and I made shift to drink a little, casting furtive glances at Dorking, three boxes off across the gangway.

My gentleman sailor seemed quite at home, swallowing stolidly as though at his own breakfast-table. I grew impatient for him to have done, and beguiled the time by studying a placard on the wall offering a reward for information as to the whereabouts of a certain ship's cook who was wanted for knifing human flesh. And presently, curiously enough, in comes a police-sergeant on this very matter, and out goes Dorking (rather hastily, I thought), with me at his heels.

No sooner had he got round a corner than he started running at a rate that gave me a stitch in the side. He did not stop till he reached a cab-rank. There was only one vehicle on it, and the coughing, red-nosed driver, unpleasantly suggesting a mixture of grog and fog, was climbing to his seat when I came cautiously and breathlessly up, and Dorking was returning to his trousers' pocket a jingling mass of gold and silver coins, which he had evidently been exhibiting to the sceptical cabman. He seemed to walk these regions with the fearlessness of Una in the enchanted forest. I had no resource but to hang on to the rear, despite the alarums of "whip behind," raised by envious and inconsiderate urchins.

And in this manner, defiantly dodging the cabman, who several times struck me unfairly behind his back, I drove through a labyrinth of sordid streets to the Bethnal Green Museum. Here we alighted, and the Viscount strolled about outside the iron railings, from time to time anxiously scrutinising the church clock and looking towards the fountain which only performs in the summer, and was then wearing its winter night-cap. At last, as if weary of waiting, he walked with sudden precipitation towards the turnstile, and was lost to view within. After a moment I followed him, but was stopped by the janitor, who, with an air of astonishment, informed me there was sixpence to pay, it being a Wednesday. I understood at once why the Viscount had selected this day, for there was no one to be seen inside, and it was five minutes ere I discovered him. He was in the National Portrait Gallery, before one of Sir Peter Lely's insipid beauties, which to my surprise he was copying in pencil. Evidently he was trying to while away the time. At eleven o'clock to the second he scribbled something underneath the sketch, folded it up carefully, picked up his bundle and walked unhesitatingly downstairs into the second gallery, where, after glancing about to assure himself that the policeman's head was turned away, he deposited the paper between two bottles of tape-worms, and stole out through the back door. Feverishly seizing the sketch, I followed him, but the policeman's eye was now upon me, and I had to walk with dignified slowness, though I was in agonies lest I should lose my man. My anxiety was justified; when I reached the grounds, the Viscount was nowhere to be seen. I ran hither and thither like a madman, along the back street and about the grounds, hacking my shins against a perambulator, and at last sank upon a frigid garden seat, breathless and exhausted. I now bethought me of the paper clenched in my fist, and, smoothing it out, deciphered these words faintly pencilled beneath a caricature of the Court beauty:—

"Not my fault you missed me. If you are still set on your folly, you will find me lunching at the Chingford Hotel."

I sprang up exultant, new fire in my veins. True, the mystery was darkening, but it was the darkness that precedes the dawn.

"*Cherchez la femme!*" I muttered, and darting down Three Colts Lane I reached the Junction, only to find the barrier dashed in my face. But half-a-crown drove it back, and I sprang into the guard's van on his very heels. A shilling stifled the oath on his lips, and transferred it to mine when I discovered I had jumped into the Enfield Fast. Before I really got to Chingford it was long past noon. But I found him.

The Viscount was toying with a Chartreuse in the dining-room. The waiters eyed me suspiciously, for I was shabby and dusty and haggard-looking. To my surprise Dorking had doffed the sailor, and wore a loud checked suit! He looked up as I entered, but did not appear to recognise me. There was no one with him. Still I had found him. That was the prime thing.

Becoming conscious I was faint with hunger, I took up the menu, when to my vexation I saw the Viscount pay his bill, and don an overcoat and a billy-cock, and ere I could snatch bite or sup I was striding along the slimy forest paths, among the gaunt, fog-wrapped trees, following the Viscount by his footprints whenever I lost him for a moment among the avenues. Dorking marched with quick, decisive steps. In the heart of the forest, by a great oak, whose roots sprawled in every direction, he came to a standstill. Hidden behind some brushwood, I awaited the sequel with beating heart.

The Viscount took out a great coloured handkerchief, and spread it carefully over the roots of the oak; then he sat down on the handkerchief, and whistled the same bar of the same once popular air he had whistled outside the coffee-house. Immediately a broken-nosed man emerged from behind a bush, and addressed the Viscount. I strained my ears, but could not catch their conversation, but I heard Dorking laugh heartily, as he sprang up and clapped the man on the shoulder. They walked off together.

I was now excited to the wildest degree; I forgot the pangs of baffled appetite; my whole being was strung to find a key to the strange proceedings of the mathematical Viscount. Tracking their double footsteps through the mist, I found them hobnobbing in a public-house on the forest border. After peeping in, I ran round to another door, and stood in an adjoining bar, where, without being seen, I could have a snack of bread and cheese, and hear all.

"Could you bring her round to my house to-night?" said Dorking, in a hoarse whisper. "You shall have the money down."

"Right, sir!" said the man. And then their pewters clinked.

To my chagrin this was all the conversation. The Viscount strode out alone—except for my company. The fog had grown deeper, and I was glad to be conducted to the station. This time we went to Liverpool Street. Dorking lingered at the book-stall, and at last enquired if they had yesterday's *Times*. Receiving a reply in the negative, he clucked his tongue impatiently. Then, as with a sudden thought, he ran up to the North London Railway book-stall, only to be again disappointed. He took out the great coloured handkerchief, and wiped his forehead. Then he entered into confidential conversation with an undistinguished stranger, fat and foreign, who had been looking eagerly up and down at the extreme end of the platform. Re-descending into the street, he jumped into a Charing Cross 'bus. As he went inside I had no option but to go outside, though the air was yellow and I felt chilled to the bone.

Alighting at Charing Cross, he went into the telegraph office, and wrote a telegram. The composition seemed to cause him great difficulty. Standing outside the door, I saw him discard two half-begun forms. When he came out I made a swift calculation of the chances, and determined to secure the two forms, even at the risk of losing him. Neither had an address. One read: "If you are still set on your fol—"; the other: "Come to-night if you are still—" Bolting out with these precious scraps of evidence, that only added fuel to the flame of curiosity that was consuming me, I turned cold to find the Viscount swallowed up in the crowd. After an instant's agonised hesitation, I hailed a hansom, and drove to his flat in Victoria Street. The valet told me the Viscount was ill in bed, and could not see me. I read in his face that it was a lie. I resolved to loiter outside the building till Dorking's return.

I had not long to wait. In less than ten minutes a hansom discharged him at my feet. Had I not been prepared for anything, I should not have recognised him again in his red whiskers, white hat, and blue spectacles. He rang the bell, and enquired of his own valet if Viscount Dorking was at home. The man said he was ill in bed.

"Oh, we'll soon put him on his legs again," interrupted Dorking, with a professional air, and pushed his valet aside. In that moment the solution dawned upon me. *Dorking was mad!* Nothing but insanity would account for his day's vagaries. I felt it was my duty, as a fellow-creature, to look to him. I followed him, to the open-eyed consternation of the valet. Suddenly he turned upon me, and seized me savagely by the throat. I felt choking. My worst fear was confirmed.

"No further, my man," he cried, flinging me back. "Now go, and tell her ladyship how you have earned your fee!"

"Dorking! are you mad?" I gasped. "Don't you remember me—Mr. Pry—from the Bachelor's Club?"

"Great heavens, Paul!" he cried. Then he fell back on an ottoman, and laughed till the whiskers ran down his sides. He always had a sense of humour, I remembered.

We explained the situation to each other. Dorking had an eccentric aunt who wished to leave her money to him. Suddenly Dorking learnt from his valet, who was betrothed to her ladyship's maid, that she had taken it into her head he could not be so virtuous and so devoted to pure mathematics as he appeared, and so she had commissioned a private detective agency to watch her nephew, and discover how deep the still waters ran. Incensed at the suspicion, he had that day started a course of action calculated to bamboozle the agency, and having no other meaning whatever.

When he caught sight of me gazing at him so curiously he mistook me for one of its minions, and determined to lead me a dance; the mistake was confirmed by my patient obedience to his piping.

The broken-nosed man was an accident. Anticipating his value as a beautiful false clue, Dorking laughed uproariously at the sight of him, and readily agreed to buy a French poodle.

THE QUEEN'S TRIPLETS, A NURSERY TALE
FOR THE OLD

O nce upon a time there was a Queen who unexpectedly gave birth to three Princes. They were all so exactly alike that after a moment or two it was impossible to remember which was the eldest or which was the youngest. Any two of them, sort them how you pleased, were always twins. They all cried in the same key and with the same comic grimaces. In short, there was not a hair's-breadth of difference between them—not that they had a hair's-breadth between them, for, like most babies, they were prematurely bald.

The King was very much put out. He did not mind the expense of keeping three Heir Apparents, for that fell on the country, and was defrayed by an impost called "The Queen's Tax." But it was the consecrated custom of the kingdom that the crown should pass over to the eldest son, and the absence of accurate knowledge upon this point was perplexing. A triumvirate was out of the question; the multiplication of monarchs would be vexation to the people, and the rule of three would drive them mad.

The Queen was just as annoyed, though on different grounds. She felt it hard enough to be the one mother in the realm who could not get the Queen's bounty, without having to suffer the King's reproaches. Her heart was broken, and she died soon after of laryngitis.

To distinguish the triplets (when it was too late) they were always dressed one in green, one in blue, and one in black, the colours of the national standard, and naturally got to be popularly known by the sobriquets of the Green Prince, the Blue Prince, and the Black Prince. Every year they got older and older till at last they became young men. And every year the King got older and older till at last he became an old man, and the fear crept into his heart that he might be restored to his wife and leave the kingdom embroiled in civil feud unless he settled straightway who should be the heir. But, being human, notwithstanding his court laureates, he put off the disagreeable duty from day to day, and might have died without an heir, if the envoys from Paphlagonia had not aroused him to the necessity of a decision. For they announced that the Princess of Paphlagonia, being suddenly orphaned, would be sent to him in the twelfth moon that she might marry his eldest son as covenanted by ancient treaty. This was the last straw. "But I don't know who is my eldest son!" yelled the King, who had a vast respect for covenants and the Constitution.

In great perturbation he repaired to a famous Oracle, at that time worked by a priestess with her hair let down her back. The King asked her a plain question: "Which is my eldest son?"

After foaming at the mouth like an open champagne bottle, she replied:—

"The eldest is he that the Princess shall wed."

The King said he knew that already, and was curtly told that if the replies did not give satisfaction he could go elsewhere. So he went to the wise men and the magicians, and held a levée of them, and they gave him such goodly counsel that the Chief Magician was henceforth honoured with the privilege of holding the Green, Black, and Blue Tricolour over the King's head at mealtimes. Soon after, it being the twelfth moon, the King set forward with a little retinue to meet the Princess of Paphlagonia, whose coming had got abroad; but returned two days later with the news that the Princess was confined to her room, and would not arrive in the city till next year.

On the last day of the year the King summoned the three Princes to the Presence Chamber. And they came, the Green Prince, and the Blue Prince, and the Black Prince, and made obeisance to the Monarch, who sat in moiré antique robes, on the old gold throne, with his courtiers all around him.

"My sons," he said, "ye are aware that, according to the immemorial laws of the realm, one of you is to be my heir, only I know not which of you he is; the difficulty is complicated by the fact that I have covenanted to espouse him to the Princess of Paphlagonia, of whose imminent arrival ye have heard. In this dilemma there are those who would set the sovereignty of the State upon the hazard of a die. But not by such undignified methods do I deem it prudent to extort the designs of the gods. There are ways alike more honourable to you and to me of ascertaining the intentions of the fates. And first, the wise men and the magicians recommend that ye be all three sent forth upon an arduous emprise. As all men know, somewhere in the great seas that engirdle our dominion, somewhere beyond the Ultimate Thule, there rangeth a vast monster, intolerable, not to be borne. Every ninth moon this creature approacheth our coasts, deluging the land with an inky vomit. This plaguy Serpent cannot be slain, for the soothsayers aver it beareth a charmed life, but it were a mighty achievement, if for only one year, the realm could be relieved of its oppression. Are ye willing to set forth separately upon this knightly quest?"

Then the three Princes made enthusiastic answer, entreating to be sped on the journey forthwith, and a great gladness ran through the Presence Chamber, for all had suffered much from the annual incursions of the monster. And the King's heart was fain of the gallant spirit of the Princes.

"'Tis well," said he. "To-morrow, at the first dawn of the new year, shall ye fare forth together; when ye reach the river ye shall part, and for eight moons shall ye wander whither ye will; only, when the ninth moon rises, shall ye return and tell me how ye have fared. Hasten now, therefore, and equip yourselves as ye desire, and if there be aught that will help you in the task, ye have but to ask for it."

Then, answering quickly before his brothers could speak, the Black Prince cried: "Sire, I would crave the magic boat which saileth under the sea and destroyeth mighty armaments."

"It is thine," replied the King.

Then the Green Prince said: "Sire, grant me the magic car which saileth through the air over the great seas."

The Black Prince started and frowned, but the King answered, "It is granted." Then, turning to the Blue Prince, who seemed lost in meditation, the King said: "Why art thou silent, my son? Is there nothing I can give thee?"

"Thanks, I will take a little pigeon," answered the Blue Prince abstractedly.

The courtiers stared and giggled, and the Black Prince chuckled, but the Blue Prince was seemingly too proud to back out of his request.

So at sunrise on the morrow the three Princes set forth, journeying together till they came to the river where they had agreed to part company. Here the magic boat was floating at anchor, while the magic car was tied to the trunk of a plane-tree upon the bank, and the little pigeon, fastened by a thread, was fluttering among the branches.

Now, when the Green Prince saw the puny pigeon, he was like to die of laughing.

"Dost thou think to feed the Serpent with thy pigeon?" he sneered. "I fear me thou wilt not choke him off thus."

"And what hast thou to laugh at?" retorted the Black Prince, interposing. "Dost thou think to find the Serpent of the Sea in the air?"

"He is always in the air," murmured the Blue Prince, inaudibly.

"Nay," said the Green Prince, scratching his head dubiously. "But thou didst so hastily annex the magic boat, I had to take the next best thing."

"Dost thou accuse me of unfairness?" cried the Black Prince in a pained voice. "Sooner than thou shouldst say that, I would change with thee."

"Wouldst thou, indeed?" enquired the Green Prince eagerly.

"Ay, that would I," said the Black Prince indignantly. "Take the magic boat, and may the gods speed thee." So saying he jumped briskly into the magic car, cut the rope, and sailed aloft. Then, looking down contemptuously upon the Blue Prince, he shouted: "Come, mount thy pigeon, and be off in search of the monster."

But the Blue Prince replied, "I will await you here."

Then the Green Prince pushed off his boat, chuckling louder than ever. "Dost thou expect to keep the creature off our coasts by guarding the head of the river?" he scoffed.

But the Blue Prince replied, "I will await you both here till the ninth moon."

No sooner were his brothers gone than the Blue Prince set about building a hut. Here he lived happily, fishing his meals out of the river or snaring them out of the sky. The pigeon was never for a moment in danger of being eaten. It was employed more agreeably to itself and its master in operations which will appear anon. Most of the time the Blue Prince lay on his back among the wild flowers, watching the river rippling to the sea or counting the passing of the eight moons, that alternately swelled and dwindled, now showing like the orb of the Black Prince's car, now like the Green Prince's boat. Sometimes he read scraps of papyrus, and his face shone.

One lovely starry night, as the Blue Prince was watching the heavens, it seemed to him as if the eighth moon in dying had dropped out of the firmament and was falling upon him. But it was only the Black Prince come back. His garments were powdered with snow, his brows were knitted gloomily, he had a dejected, despondent aspect.

"Thou here!" he snapped.

"Of course," said the Blue Prince cheerfully, though he seemed a little embarrassed all the same. "Haven't I been here all the time? But go into my hut, I've kept supper hot for thee."

"Has the Green Prince had his?"

"No, I haven't seen anything of him. Hast thou scotched the Serpent?"

"No, I haven't seen anything of him," growled the Black Prince. "I've passed backwards and forwards over the entire face of the ocean, but nowhere have I caught the slightest glimpse of him. What a fool I was to give up the magic boat! He never seems to come to the surface."

All this while the Blue Prince was dragging his brother with suspicious solicitude towards the hut, where he sat him down to his own supper of ortolans and oysters. But the host had no sooner run outside again, on the pretext of seeing if the Green Prince was coming, than there was a disturbance and eddying in the stream as of a rally of water-rats, and the magic boat shot up like a catapult, and the Green Prince stepped on deck all dry and dusty, and with the air of a draggled dragon-fly.

"Good evening, hast thou er—scotched the Serpent?" stammered the Blue Prince, taken aback.

"No, I haven't even seen anything of him," growled the Green Prince. "I have skimmed along the entire surface of the ocean, and sailed every inch beneath it, but nowhere have I caught the slightest glimpse of him. What a fool I was to give up the magic car! From a height I could have commanded an ampler area of ocean. Perhaps he was up the river."

"No, I haven't seen anything of him," replied the Blue Prince hastily. "But go into my hut, thy supper must be getting quite cold." He hurried his verdant brother into the hut, and gave him some chestnuts out of the oven (it was the best he could do for him), and then rushed outside again, on the plea of seeing if the Serpent was coming. But he seemed to expect him to come from the sky, for, leaning against the trunk of the plane-tree by the river, he resumed his anxious scrutiny of the constellations. Presently there was a gentle whirring in the air, and a white bird became visible, flying rapidly downwards in his direction. Almost at the same instant he felt himself pinioned by a rope to the tree-trunk, and saw the legs of the alighting pigeon neatly prisoned in the Black Prince's fist.

"Aha!" croaked the Black Prince triumphantly. "Now we shall see through thy little schemes."

He detached the slip of papyrus which dangled from the pigeon's neck.

"How darest thou read my letters?" gasped the Blue Prince.

"If I dare to rob the mail, I shall certainly not hesitate to read the letters," answered the Black Prince coolly, and went on to enunciate slowly (for the light was bad) the following lines:—

> *"Heart-sick I watch the old moon's ling'ring death,*
> *And long upon my face to feel thy breath;*
> *I burn to see its final flicker die,*
> *And greet our moon of honey in the sky."*

"What is all this moonshine?" he concluded in bewilderment.

Now the Blue Prince was the soul of candour, and seeing that nothing could now be lost by telling the truth, he answered:—

"This is a letter from a damsel who resideth in the Tower of Telifonia, on the outskirts of the capital; we are engaged. No doubt the language seemeth to thee a little overdone, but wait till thy turn cometh."

"And so thou hast employed this pigeon as a carrier between thee and this suburban young person?" cried the Black Prince, feeling vaguely boiling over with rage.

"Even so," answered his brother, "but guard thy tongue. The lady of whom thou speakest so disrespectfully is none other than the Princess of Paphlagonia."

"Eh? What?" gasped the Black Prince.

"She hath resided there since the twelfth moon of last year. The King received her the first time he set out to meet her."

"Dost thou dare say the King hath spoken untruth?"

"Nay, nay. The King is a wise man. Wise men never mean what they say. The King said she was confined to her room. It is true, for he had confined her in the Tower with her maidens for fear she should fall in love with the wrong Prince, or the reverse, before the rightful heir was discovered. The King said she would not arrive in the city till next year. This also is true. As thou didst rightly observe, the Tower of Telifonia is situated in the suburbs. The King did not bargain for my discovering that a beautiful woman lived in its topmost turret."

"Nay, how couldst thou discover that? The King did not lend thee the magic car, and thou certainly couldst not see her at that height without the magic glass!"

"I have not seen her. But through the embrasure I often saw the sunlight flashing and leaping like a thing of life, and I knew it was what the children call a 'Johnny Noddy.' Now a 'Johnny Noddy' argueth a mirror, and a mirror argueth a woman, and frequent use thereof argueth a beautiful woman. So, when in the Presence Chamber the King told us of his dilemma as to the hand of the Princess of Paphlagonia, it instantly dawned upon me who the beautiful woman was, and why the King was keeping her hidden away, and why he had hidden away his meaning also. Wherefore straightway I asked for a pigeon, knowing that the pigeons of the town roost on the Tower of Telifonia, so that I had but to fly my bird at the end of a long string like a kite to establish communication between me and the fair captive. In time my little messenger grew so used to the journey to and fro that I could dispense with the string. Our courtship has been most satisfactory. We love each other ardently, and—"

"But you have never seen each other!" interrupted the Black Prince.

"Thou forgettest we are both royal personages," said the Blue Prince in astonished reproof.

"But this is gross treachery—what right hadst thou to make these underhand advances in our absence?"

"Thou forgettest I had to scotch the Serpent," said the Blue Prince in astonished reproof. "Thou forgettest also that she can only marry the heir to the throne."

"Ah, true!" said the Black Prince, considerably relieved. "And as thou hast chosen to fritter away the time in making love to her, thou hast taken the best way to lose her."

"Thou forgettest I shall have to marry her," said the Blue Prince in astonished reproof. "Not only because I have given my word to a lady, but because I have promised the King to do my best to scotch the Serpent of the Sea. Really thou seemest terribly dull to-day. Let me put the matter in a nutshell. If he who scotches the Sea Serpent is to marry the Princess, then would I scotch the Sea Serpent by marrying the Princess, and marry the Princess to scotch the Sea Serpent. Thou hast searched the face of the sea, and our brother has dragged its depths, and nowhere have ye seen the Sea Serpent. Yet in the ninth moon he will surely come, and the land will be covered with an inky vomit as in former years. But if I marry the Princess of Paphlagonia in the ninth moon, the Royal Wedding will ward off the Sea Serpent, and not a scribe will shed ink to tell of his advent. Therefore, instead of ranging through the earth, I stayed at home and paid my addresses to the—"

"Yes, yes, what a fool I was!" interrupted the Black Prince, smiting his brow with his palm, so that the pigeon escaped from between his fingers, and winged its way back to the Tower of Telifonia as if to carry his words to the Princess.

"Thou forgettest thou art a fool still," said the Blue Prince in astonished reproof. "Prithee, unbind me forthwith."

"Nay, I am a fool no longer, for it is I that shall wed the Princess of Paphlagonia and scotch the Sea Serpent, it is I that have sent the pigeon to and fro, and unless thou makest me thine oath to be silent on the matter I will slay thee and cast thy body into the river."

"Thou forgettest our brother, the Green Prince," said the Blue Prince in astonished reproof.

"Bah! he hath eyes for naught but the odd ortolans and oysters I sacrificed that he might gorge himself withal, while I spied out thy secret. He shall be told that I returned to exchange my car for thy pigeon even as I exchanged my boat for his car. Come, thine oath or thou diest." And a jewelled scimitar shimmered in the starlight.

The Blue Prince reflected that though life without love was hardly worth living, death was quite useless. So he swore and went in to supper. When he found that the Green Prince had not spared even a baked chestnut before he fell asleep, he swore again. And on the morrow when the Princes approached the Tower of Telifonia, with its flashing "Johnny Noddy," they met a courier from the King, who, having informed himself of the Black Prince's success, ran ahead with the rumour thereof. And lo! when the Princes passed through the city gate they found the whole population abroad clad in all their bravery, and flags flying and bells ringing and roses showering from the balconies, and merry music swelling in all the streets for joy of the prospect of the Sea Serpent's absence. And when the new moon rose, the three Princes, escorted by flute-players, hied them to the Presence Chamber, and the King embraced his sons, and the Black Prince stood forward and explained that if a Prince were married in the ninth moon it would prevent the monster's annual visit. Then the King fell upon the Black Prince's neck and wept and said, "My son! my son! my pet! my baby! my tootsicums! my popsy-wopsy!"

And then, recovering himself, and addressing the courtiers, he said: "The gods have enabled me to discover my youngest son. If they will only now continue as propitious, so that I may discover the elder of the other two, I shall die not all unhappy."

But the Black Prince could repress his astonishment no longer. "Am I dreaming, sire?" he cried. "Surely I have proved myself the eldest, not the youngest!"

"Thou forgettest that thou hast come off successful," replied the King in astonished reproof. "Or art thou so ignorant of history or of the sacred narratives handed down to us by our ancestors that thou art unaware that when three brothers set out on the same quest, it is always the youngest brother that emerges triumphant? Such is the will of the gods. Cease, therefore, thy blasphemous talk, lest they overhear thee and be put out."

A low, ominous murmur from the courtiers emphasised the King's warning.

"But the Princess—she at least is mine," protested the unhappy Prince. "We love each other—we are engaged."

"Thou forgettest she can only marry the heir," replied the King in astonished reproof. "Wouldst thou have us repudiate our solemn treaty?"

"But I wasn't really the first to hit on the idea at all!" cried the Black Prince desperately. "Ask the Blue Prince! he never telleth untruth."

"Thou forgettest I have taken an oath of silence on the matter," replied the Blue Prince in astonished reproof. "The Black Prince it was that first hit on the idea," volunteered the Green Prince. "He exchanged his boat for the car and the car for the pigeon."

So the three Princes were dismissed, while the King took counsel with the magicians and the wise men who never mean what they say. And the Court Chamberlain, wearing the orchid of office in his buttonhole, was sent to interview the Princess, and returned saying that she refused to marry any one but the proprietor of the pigeon, and that she still had his letters as evidence in case of his marrying anyone else.

"Bah!" said the King, "she shall obey the treaty. Six feet of parchment are not to be put aside for the whim of a girl five foot eight. The only real difficulty remaining is to decide whether the Blue Prince or the Green Prince is the elder. Let me see—what was it the Oracle said? Perhaps it will be clearer now:—

> "'The eldest is he that the Princess shall wed.'

"No, it still seems merely to avoid stating anything new."

"Pardon me, sire," replied the Chief Magician; "it seems perfectly plain now. Obviously, thou art to let the Princess choose her husband, and the Oracle guarantees that, other things being equal, she shall select the eldest. If thou hadst let her have the pick from among the three, she would have selected the one with whom she was in love—the Black Prince to wit, and that would have interfered with the Oracle's arrangements. But now that we know with whom she is in love, we can remove that one, and then, there being no reason why she should choose the Green Prince rather than the Blue Prince, the deities of the realm undertake to inspire her to go by age only."

"Thou hast spoken well," said the King. "Let the Princess of Paphlagonia be brought, and let the two Princes return."

So after a space the beautiful Princess, preceded by trumpeters, was conducted to the Palace, blinking her eyes at the unaccustomed splendour of the lights. And the King and all the courtiers blinked their eyes, dazzled by her loveliness. She was clad in white samite, and on her shoulder was perched a pet pigeon. The King sat in his moiré robes on the old gold throne, and the Blue Prince stood on his right hand, and the Green Prince on his left, the Black Prince as the youngest having been sent to bed early. The Princess courtesied three times, the third time so low that the pigeon was flustered, and flew off her shoulder, and, after circling about, alighted on the head of the Blue Prince.

"It is the Crown," said the Chief Magician, in an awestruck voice. Then the Princess's eyes looked around in search of the pigeon, and when they lighted on the Prince's head they kindled as the grey sea kindles at sunrise.

An answering radiance shone in the Blue Prince's eyes, as, taking the pigeon that nestled in his hair, he let it fly towards the Princess. But the Princess, her bosom heaving as if another pigeon fluttered beneath the white samite, caught it and set it free again, and again it made for the Blue Prince.

Three times the bird sped to and fro. Then the Princess raised her humid eyes heavenward, and from her sweet lips rippled like music the verse:—

"Last night I watched its final flicker die."

And the Blue Prince answered:—

"Now *greet our moon of honey in the sky.*"

Half fainting with rapture the Princess fell into his arms, and from all sides of the great hall arose the cries, "The Heir! The Heir! Long live our future King! The eldest-born! The Oracle's fulfilled!"

Such was the origin of lawn tennis, which began with people tossing pigeons to each other in imitation of the Prince and Princess in the Palace Hall. And this is why love plays so great a part in the game, and that is how the match was arranged between the Blue Prince and the Princess of Paphlagonia.

A SUCCESSFUL OPERATION

R obert came home, anxious and perturbed. For the first time since his return from their honeymoon he crossed the threshold of the tiny house without a grateful sense of blessedness.

"What is it, Robert?" panted Mary, her sweet lips cold from his perfunctory kiss.

"He is going blind," he said in low tones.

"Not your father!" she murmured, dazed.

"Yes, my father! I thought it was nothing, or rather I scarcely thought about it at all. The doctor at the Eye Hospital merely asked him to bring some one with him next time; naturally he came to me." There was a touch of bitterness about the final phrase.

"Oh, how terrible!" said Mary. Her pretty face looked almost wan.

"I don't see that you're called upon to distress yourself so much, dear," said Robert, a little resentfully. "He hasn't even been a friend to you."

"Oh, Robert! how can you think of all that now? If he did try to keep you from marrying a penniless, friendless girl, if he did force you to work long years for me, was it not all for the best? Now that his fortune has been swept away, where would you be without money or occupation?"

"Where would Providence be without its women-defenders?" murmured Robert. "You don't understand finance, dear. He might easily have provided for me long before the crash came."

"Never mind, Robert. Are we not all the happier for having waited for each other?" And in the spiritual ecstasy of her glance he forgot for a while his latest trouble.

Robert's father lived in a little room on a small allowance made him by his outcast son. Broken by age and misfortune, he pottered about chess-rooms and debating forums, garrulous and dogmatic, and given to tippling. But now the consciousness of his coming infirmity crushed him, and he sat for days on his bed brooding, waiting in terror for the darkness, and glad when day after day ended only in the shadows of eve. Sometimes, instead of the dreaded darkness, sunlight came. That was when Mary dropped in to cheer him up, and to repeat to him that the hospital took a most hopeful view of his case, was only waiting for the darkness to be thickest to bring back the dawn. It took four months before the light faded utterly, and then another month before the film was opaque enough to allow the cataract to be couched. The old man was to go into the hospital for the operation. Robert hired a lad to be with him during the month of waiting, and sometimes sat with him in the evenings, after business, and now and then the landlady looked in and told him her troubles, and the attendant was faithful and went out frequently to buy him gin. But it was only Mary who could really soothe him now, for the poor old creature's soul groped blindly amid new apprehensions—a nervous dread of the chloroforming, the puncturing, the strange sounds of voices of the great blank hospital, where he felt confusedly he would be lost in an ocean of unfathomable night, incapable even of divining, from past experience, the walls about him or the ceiling over his head, and withal a paralysing foreboding that the operation would be a failure, that he would live out the rest of his days with the earth prematurely over his eyes.

"I am very glad to see you, my dear," he would say when Mary came, and then he fell a-maundering self-pitifully.

Mary went home one day and said, "Robert, dear, I have been thinking."

"Yes, my pet," he said encouragingly, for she looked timid and hesitant.

"Couldn't we have the operation performed here?"

He was startled; protested, pointed out the impossibility. But she had answers for all his objections. They could give up their own bedroom for a fortnight—it would only be a fortnight or three weeks at most—turn their sitting-room into a bedroom for themselves. What if infinite care would be necessary in regulating the "dark room," surely they could be as careful as the indifferent hospital nurses if they were only told what to do, and as for the trouble, that wasn't worth considering.

"But you forget, my foolish little girl," he said at last, "if he comes here we shall have to pay the expenses of the operation ourselves."

"Well, would that be much?" she asked innocently.

"Only fifty guineas or so, I should think," he replied crushingly. "What with the operating fee, and the nurse, and the subsequent medical attendance."

But Mary was not altogether crushed. "It wouldn't be all our savings," she murmured.

"Are you forgetting what we shall be needing our savings for?" he said with gentle reproach, as he stroked her soft hair.

She blushed angelically. "No, but surely there will be enough left and—and I shall be making all his things myself—and by that time we shall have put by a little more."

In the end she conquered. The old man, to whom no faintest glimmer now penetrated, was installed in the best bedroom, which was darkened by double blinds and strips of cloth over every chink and a screen before the door; and a nurse sat on guard lest any ray or twinkle should find its way into the pitchy gloom. The great specialist came with two assistants, and departed in an odour of chloroform, conscious of another dexterous deed, to return only when the critical moment of raising the bandage should have arrived. During the fortnight of suspense an assistant replaced him, and the old man lay quiet and hopeful, rousing himself to talk dogmatically to his visitors. Mary gave him such time as she could spare from household duties, and he always kissed her on the forehead (so that his bandage just grazed her hair), remarking he was very glad to see her. It was a strange experience, these conversations carried on in absolute darkness, and they gave her a feeling of kinship with the blind. She discovered that smiles were futile, and that laughter alone availed in this uncanny intercourse. For compensation, her face could wear an anxious expression without alarming the patient. But it rarely did, for her spirits mounted with his. Before the operation she had been terribly anxious, wondering at the last moment if it would not have been performed more safely at the hospital, and ready to take upon her shoulders the responsibility for a failure. But as day after day went by, and all seemed going well, her thoughts veered round. She felt sure they would not have been so careful at the hospital. It was owing to this new confidence that one fatal night, carrying her candle, she walked mechanically into her bedroom, forgetting it was not hers. The nurse sprang up instantly, rushed forward, and blew out the light. Mary screamed, the screen fell with a clatter, the blind old man awoke and shrieked nervously—it was a terrible moment.

After that Mary went through agonies of apprehension and remorse. Fortunately the end of the operation was very near now. In a day or two the great specialist came to remove the bandage, while the nurse carefully admitted a feeble illumination. If the patient could see now, the rest was a mere matter of time, of cautious gradation of light in the sick chamber, so that there might be no relapse. Mary dared not remain in the room at the instant of supreme crisis; she lingered outside, overwrought. Slowly, with infinite solicitude, the bandage was raised.

"Can you see anything?" burst from Robert's lips.

"Yes, but what makes the window look red?" grumbled the old man.

"I congratulate you," said the great specialist in loud, hearty accents.

"Thank God!" sobbed Mary's voice outside.

When her child was born it was blind.

FLUTTER-DUCK

A Ghetto Grotesque

I

Flutter-Duck in Feather

"So sitting, served by man and maid,
She felt her heart grow prouder."

—Tennyson: *The Goose*

Although everybody calls her "Flutter-Duck" now, there was a time when the inventor had exclusive rights in the nickname, and used it only in the privacy of his own apartment. That time did not last long, for the inventor was Flutter-Duck's husband, and his apartment was a public work-room among other things. He gave her the name in Yiddish—*Flatterkatchki*—a descriptive music in syllables, full of the flutter and quack of the farm-yard. It expressed his dissatisfaction with her airy, flighty propensities, her love of gaiety and gadding. She was a butterfly, irresponsible, off to balls and parties almost once a month, and he, a self-conscious ant, resented her. From the point of view of piety she was also sadly to seek, rejecting wigs in favour of the fringe. In the weak moments of early love her husband had acquiesced in the profanity, but later all the gain to her soft prettiness did not compensate for the twinges of his conscience.

Flutter-Duck's husband was a furrier—a master-furrier, for did he not run a workshop? This workshop was also his living-room, and this living-room was also his bedroom. It was a large front room on the first floor, over a chandler's shop in an old-fashioned house in Montague Street, Whitechapel. Its shape was peculiar—an oblong stretching streetwards, interrupted in one of the longer walls by a square projection that might have been accounted a room in itself (by the landlord), and was, indeed, used as a kitchen. That the fireplace had been built in this corner was thus an advantage. Entering through the door on the grand staircase, you found yourself nearest the window with the bulk of the room on your left, and the square recess at the other end of your wall, so that you could not see it at first. At the window, which, of course, gave on Montague Street, was the bare wooden table at which the "hands"—man, woman, and boy—sat and stitched. The finished work—a confusion of fur caps, boas, tippets, and trimmings—hung over the dirty wainscot between the door and the recess. The middle of the room was quite bare, to give the workers freedom of movement, but the wall facing you was a background for luxurious furniture. First—nearest the window—came a sofa, on which even in the first years of marriage Flutter-Duck's husband sometimes lay prone, too unwell to do more than superintend the operations, for he was of a consumptive habit. Over the sofa hung a large gilt-framed mirror, the gilt protected by muslin drapings, in the corners of which flyblown paper flowers grew. Next to the sofa was a high chest of drawers crowned with dusty decanters, and after an interval filled up with the Sabbath clothes hanging on pegs and covered by a white sheet; the bed used up the rest of the space, its head and one side touching the walls, and its foot stretching towards the kitchen fire. On the wall above this fire hung another mirror,—small and narrow, and full of wavering, watery reflections,—also framed in muslin, though this time the muslin served to conceal dirt, not to protect gilt. The kitchen-dresser, decorated with pink needle-work paper, was at right angles to the fireplace, and it faced the kitchen table, at which Flutter-Duck cleaned fish, peeled potatoes, and made meat *kosher* by salting and soaking it, as Rabbinic law demanded.

By the foot of the bed, in the narrow wall opposite the window, was a door leading to a tiny inner room. For years this door remained locked; another family lived on the other side, and the furrier had neither the means nor the need for an extra bedroom. It was a room made for escapades and romances, connected with the back-yard by a steep ladder, up and down which the family might be seen going, and from which you could tumble into a broken-headed water-butt, or, by a dexterous back-fall, arrive in a dustbin. Jacob's ladder the neighbours called it, though the family name was Isaacs.

And over everything was the trail of the fur. The air was full of a fine fluff—a million little hairs floated about the room covering everything, insinuating themselves everywhere, getting down the backs of the workers and tickling them, getting into their lungs and making them cough, getting into their food and drink and sickening them till they learnt callousness. They awoke with "furred" tongues, and they went to bed with them. The irritating filaments gathered on their clothes, on their faces, on the crockery, on the sofa, on the mirrors (big and little), on the bed, on the decanters, on the sheet that hid the Sabbath clothes—an impalpable down overlaying everything, penetrating even to the drinking-water in the board-covered zinc bucket, and covering "Rebbitzin," the household cat, with foreign fur. And in this room, drawing such breath of life, they sat—man, woman, boy—bending over boas bewitching young ladies would skate in; stitch, stitch, from eight till two and from three to eight, with occasional overtime that ran on now and again far into the next day; till their eyelids would not keep open any longer, and they couched on the floor on a heap of finished work; stitch, stitch, winter and summer, all day long, swallowing hirsute bread and butter at nine in the morning, and pausing at tea-time for five o'clock fur. And when twilight fell the gas was lit in the crowded room, thickening still further the clogged atmosphere, charged with human breaths and street odours, and wafts from the kitchen corner and the leathery smell of the dyed skins; and at times the yellow fog would steal in to contribute its clammy vapours. And often of a winter's morning the fog arrived early, and the gas that had lighted the first hours of work would burn on all day in the thick air, flaring on the Oriental figures with that strange glamour of gas-light in fog, and throwing heavy shadows on the bare boards; glazing with satin sheen the pendent snakes of fur, illuming the bowed heads of the workers and the master's sickly face under the tasselled smoking-cap, and touching up the faded fineries of Flutter-Duck, as she flitted about, chattering and cooking.

Into such an atmosphere Flutter-Duck one day introduced a daughter, the "hands" getting an afternoon off, in honour not of the occasion but of decency. After that the crying of an infant became a feature of existence in the furrier's workshop; gradually it got rarer, as little Rachel grew up and reconciled herself to life. But the fountain of tears never quite ran dry. Rachel was a passionate child, and did not enjoy the best of parents.

Every morning Flutter-Duck, who felt very grateful to Heaven for this crowning boon,—at one time bitterly dubious,—made the child say her prayers. Flutter-Duck said them word by word, and Rachel repeated them. They were in Hebrew, and neither Flutter-Duck nor Rachel had the least idea what they meant. For years these prayers preluded stormy scenes.

"*Médiâni!*" Flutter-Duck would begin.

"*Médiâni!*" little Rachel would lisp in her piping voice. It was two words, but Flutter-Duck imagined it was one. She gave the syllables in recitative, the *âni* just two notes higher than the *médi*, and she accented them quite wrongly. When Rachel first grew articulate, Flutter-Duck was so overjoyed to hear the little girl echoing her, that she would often turn to her husband with an exclamation of "Thou hearest, Lewis, love?"

And he, impatiently: "Nee, nee, I hear."

Flutter-Duck, thus recalled from the pleasures of maternity to its duties, would recommence the prayer. "*Médiâni!*"

Which little Rachel would silently ignore.

"*Médiâni!*" Flutter-Duck's tone would now be imperative and ill-tempered.

Then little Rachel would turn to her father querulously. "She thayth it again, *Médiâni*, father!"

And Flutter-Duck, outraged by this childish insolence, would exclaim, "Thou hearest, Lewis, love?" and incontinently fall to clouting the child. And the father, annoyed by the shrill ululation consequent upon the clouting: "Nee, nee, I hear too much." Rachel's refusal to be coerced into giving devotional over-measure was not merely due to her sense of equity. Her appetite counted for more. Prayers were the avenue to breakfast, and to pamper her featherheaded mother in repetitions was to put back the meal. Flutter-Duck was quite capable of breaking down, even in the middle, if her attention was distracted for a moment, and of trying back from the very beginning. She would, for example, get as far as "Hear—my daughter—the instruction—of thy mother," giving out the words one by one in the sacred language which was to her abracadabra.

And little Rachel, equally in the dark, would repeat obediently, "Hear—my daughter—the instruction of—thy mother." Then the kettle would boil, or Flutter-Duck would overhear a remark made by one of the "hands," and interject: "Yes, I'd *give* him!" or, "A fat lot *she* knows about it," or some phrase of that sort; after which she would grope for the lost thread of prayer, and end by ejaculating desperately:—

"*Médiâni!*"

And the child sternly setting her face against this flippancy, there would be slapping and screaming, and if the father protested, Flutter-Duck would toss her head, and rejoin in her most dignified English: "If I bin a mother, I bin a mother!"

To the logical adult it will be obvious that the little girl's obstinacy put the breakfast still further back; but then, obstinate little girls are not logical, and when Rachel had been beaten she would eat no breakfast at all. She sat sullenly in the corner, her pretty face swollen by weeping, and her great black eyes suffused with tears. Only her father could coax her then. He would go so far as to allow her to nurse "Rebbitzin," without reminding her that the creature's touch would make her forget all she knew, and convert her into a "cat's-head." And certainly Rachel always forgot not to touch the cat. Possibly the basis of her father's psychological superstition was the fact that the cat is an unclean animal, not to be handled, for he would not touch puss himself, though her pious title of "Rebbitzin," or Rabbi's wife, was the invention of this master of nicknames. But for such flashes no one would have suspected the stern little man of humour. But he had it—dry. He called the cat "Rebbitzin" ever since the day she refused to drink milk after meat. Perhaps she was gorged with the meat. But he insisted that the cat had caught religion through living in a Jewish family, and he developed a theory that she would not eat meat till it was *kosher*, so that in its earlier stages it might be exposed without risk of feline larceny.

Cats are soothing to infants, but they ceased to satisfy Rachel when she grew up. Her education, while it gratified Her Majesty's Inspectors, was not calculated to eradicate the domestic rebel in her. At school she learnt of the existence of two Hebrew words, called *Moudeh anî*, but it was not till some time after that it flashed upon her that they were closely related to *Médiâni*, and the discovery did not improve her opinion of her mother. She was a bonny child, who promised to be a beautiful girl, and her teachers petted her. They dressed well, these teachers, and Rachel ceased to consider Flutter-Duck's Sabbath shawl the standard of taste and splendour. Ere she was in her teens she grumbled at her home surroundings, and even fell foul of the all-pervading fur, thereby quarrelling with her bread and butter in more senses than one. She would open the window—strangely fastidious—to eat her bread and butter off the broad ledge outside the room, but often the fur only came flying the faster to the spot, as if in search of air; and in the winter her pretentious queasiness set everybody remonstrating and shivering in the sudden draught.

Her objection to fur did not, however, embrace the preparation of it, for after school hours the little girl sat patiently stitching till late at night, by way of apprenticeship to her future, buoyed up by her earnings, and adding strip to strip, with the hair going all the same way, till she had made a great black snake. Of course she did not get anything near three-halfpence for twelve yards, like the real "hands," but whatever she earnt went towards her Festival frocks, which she would have got in any case. Not knowing this, she was happy to deserve the pretty dresses she loved, and was least impatient of her mother's chatter when Flutter-Duck dinned into her ears how pretty she looked in them. Alas! it is to be feared Lewis was right, that Flutter-Duck was a rattle-brain indeed. And the years which brought Flutter-Duck prosperity, which emancipated her from personal participation in the sewing, and gave Rachel the little bedroom to herself, did not bring wisdom. When Flutter-Duck's felicity culminated in a maid-servant (if only one who slept out), she was like a child with a monkey-on-a-stick. She gave the servant orders merely to see her arms and legs moving. She also lay late in bed to enjoy the spectacle of the factotum making the nine o'clock coffee it had been for so many years her own duty to prepare for the "hands." How sweetly the waft of chicory came to her nostrils! At first her husband remonstrated.

"It is not beautiful," he said. "You ought to get up before the 'hands' come."

Flutter-Duck flushed resentfully. "If I bin a missis, I bin a missis," she said with dignity. It became one of her formulæ. When the servant developed insolence, as under Flutter-Duck's fostering familiarity she did, Flutter-Duck would resume her dignity with a jerk.

"If I bin a missis," she would say, tossing her flighty head haughtily, "I bin a missis."

II

A Migratory Bird

"There strode a stranger to the door,
And it was windy weather."

—Tennyson: *The Goose*

O ne day, when Rachel was nineteen, there came to the workshop a handsome young man. He had been brought by a placard in the window of the chandler's shop, and was found to answer perfectly to its wants. He took his place at the work-table, and soon came to the front as a wage-earner, wielding a dexterous needle that rarely snapped, even in white fur. His name was Emanuel Lefkovitch, and his seat was next to Rachel's. For Rachel had long since entered into her career, and the beauty of her early-blossoming womanhood was bent day after day over strips of rabbit-skin, which she made into sealskin jackets. For compensation to her youth Rachel walked out on the Sabbath elegantly attired in the latest fashion. She ordered her own frocks now, having a banking account of her own, in a tin box that was hidden away in her little bedroom. Her father honourably paid her a wage as large as she would have got elsewhere—otherwise she would have gone there. Her Sabbath walks extended as far as Hyde Park, and she loved to watch the fine ladies cantering in the Row, or lolling in luxurious carriages. Sometimes she even peeped into fashionable restaurants. She became the admiring disciple of a girl who worked at a Jewish furrier's in Regent Street, and whose occidental habitat gave her a halo of aristocracy. Even on Friday nights Rachel would disappear from the sacred domesticity of the Sabbath hearth, and Flutter-Duck suspected that she went to the Cambridge Music Hall in Spitalfields. This led to dramatic scenes, for Rachel's frowardness had not decreased with age. If she had only gone out with some accredited young man, Flutter-Duck could have borne the scandal in view of the joyous prospect of becoming a grandmother. But no! Rachel tolerated no matrimonial advances, not even from the most seductive of *Shadchanim*, though her voluptuous figure and rosy lips marked her out for the marriage-broker's eye. Her father had grown sterner with the growth of his malady, and though at the bottom of his heart he loved and was proud of his beautiful Rachel, the words that rose to his lips were often as harsh and bitter as Flutter-Duck's own, so that the girl would withdraw sullenly into herself and hold no converse with her parents for days.

Nevertheless, there were plenty of halcyon intervals, especially in the busy season, when the extra shillings made the whole work-room brisk and happy, and the furriers gossiped of this and that, and told stories more droll than decorous. And then, too, every day was a delightfully inevitable sweep towards the Sabbath, and every Sabbath was a spoke in the great revolving wheel that brought round to them picturesque Festivals, or solemn Fasts, scarcely less enjoyable. And so there was an undercurrent of poetry below the sordid prose of daily life, and rifts in the grey fog, through which they caught glimpses of the azure vastness overarching the world. And the advent of Emanuel Lefkovitch distinctly lightened the atmosphere. His handsome face, his gay spirits, were like an influx of ozone. Rachel was perceptibly the brighter for his presence. She was gentler to everybody, even to her parents, and chatted vivaciously, and walked with an airier step! The sickly master-furrier's face lit up with pleasure as from his sofa he watched Emanuel's assiduous attentions to his girl in the way of picking up scissors and threading needles, and he frowned when Flutter-Duck hovered about the young man, chattering and monopolising his conversation.

But one fine morning, some months after Emanuel's arrival, a change came over the spirit of the scene. There was a knock at the door, and an ugly, shabby woman, in a green tartan shawl, entered. She scrutinised the room sharply, then uttered a joyful cry of "Emanuel, my love!" and threw herself upon the handsome young man with an affectionate embrace. Emanuel, flushed and paralysed, was a ludicrous figure, and the workers tittered, not unfamiliar with marital *contretemps*.

"Let me be," he said sullenly at last, as he untwined her dogged arms. "I tell you I won't have anything to do with you. It's no use."

"Oh no, Emanuel, love, don't say that; not after all these months?"

"Go away!" cried Emanuel hoarsely.

"Be not so obstinate," she persisted, in wheedling accents, stroking his flaming cheeks. "Kiss little Joshua and little Miriam."

Here the spectators became aware of two woebegone infants dragging at her skirts.

"Go away!" repeated Emanuel passionately, and pushed her from him with violence.

The ugly, shabby woman burst into hysterical tears.

"My own husband, dear people," she sobbed, addressing the room. "My own husband—married to me in Poland five years ago. See, I have the *Cesubah*!" She half drew the marriage parchment from her bosom. "And he won't live with me! Every time he runs away from me. Last time I saw him was in Liverpool, on the eve of Tabernacles. And before that I had to go and find him in Newcastle, and he promised me never to go away again—yes, you did, you know you did, Emanuel, love. And here have I been looking weeks for you at all the furriers and tailors, without bread and salt for the children, and the Board of Guardians won't believe me, and blame me for coming to London. Oh, Emanuel, love, God shall forgive you."

Her dress was dishevelled, her wig awry; big tears streamed down her cheeks.

"How can I live with an old witch like that?" asked Emanuel, in brutal self-defence.

"There are worse than me in the world," rejoined the woman meekly.

"Nee, nee," roughly interposed the master-furrier, who had risen from his sofa in the excitement of the scene. "It is not beautiful not to live with one's wife." He paused to cough. "You must not put her to shame."

"It's she who puts me to shame." Emanuel turned to Rachel, who had let her work slip to the floor, and whose face had grown white and stern, and continued deprecatingly, "I never wanted her. They caught me by a trick."

"Don't talk to me," snapped Rachel, turning her back on him.

The woman looked at her suspiciously—the girl's beauty seemed to burst upon her for the first time. "He is my husband," she repeated, and made as if she would draw out the *Cesubah* again.

"Nee, nee, enough!" said the master-furrier curtly. "You are wasting our time. Your husband shall live with you, or he shall not work with me."

"You have deceived us, you rogue!" put in Flutter-Duck shrilly.

"Did I ever say I was a single man?" retorted Emanuel, shrugging his shoulders.

"There! He confesses it!" cried his wife in glee. "Come, Emanuel, love," and she threw her arms round his neck, and kissed him passionately. "Do not be obstinate."

"I can't come now," he said, with sulky facetiousness. "Where are you living?"

She told him, and he said he would come when work was over.

"On your faith?" she asked, with another uneasy glance at Rachel.

"On my faith," he answered.

She moved towards the door, with her draggle-tail of infants. As she was vanishing, he called shame-facedly to the departing children,—

"Well, Joshua! Well, Miriam! Is this the way one treats a father? A nice way your mother has brought you up!"

They came back to him dubiously, with unwashed, pathetic faces, and he kissed them. Rachel bent down to pick up her rabbit-skin. Work was resumed in dead silence.

FLIGHT

"The goose flew this way and flew that,
And filled the house with clamour."

—TENNYSON: *The Goose*

Flutter-Duck could not resist rushing in to show the gorgeous goose she had bought from a man in the street—a most wonderful bargain. Although it was only a Wednesday, why should they not have a goose? They were at the thick of the busy season, and the winter promised to be bitter, so they could afford it.

"Nee, nee; there are enough Festivals in our religion already," grumbled her husband, who, despite his hacking cough, had been driven to the work-table by the plentifulness of work and the scarcity of "hands."

"Almost as big a goose as herself!" whispered Emanuel Lefkovitch to his circle. He had made his peace with his wife, and was again become the centre of the work-room's gaiety. "What a bargain!" he said aloud, clucking his tongue with admiration. And Flutter-Duck, consoled for her husband's criticism, scurried out again to have her bargain killed by the official slaughterer.

When she returned, doleful and indignant, with the goose still in her basket, and the news that the functionary had refused it Jewish execution, and pronounced it *tripha* (unclean) for some minute ritual reason, she broke off her denunciation of the vendor from a sudden perception that some graver misfortune had happened in her absence.

"Nee, nee," said Lewis, when she stopped her chatter. "Decidedly God will not have us make Festival to-day. Even you must work."

"Me?" gasped Flutter-Duck.

Then she learnt that Emanuel Lefkovitch, whom she had left so gay, had been taken with acute pains—and had had to go home. And work pressed, and Flutter-Duck must under-study him in all her spare moments. She was terribly vexed—she had arranged to go and see an old crony's daughter married in the Synagogue that afternoon, and she would have to give that up, if indeed her husband did not even expect her to give up the ball in the evening. She temporarily tethered the goose's leg to a bed-post by a long string, so that for the rest of the day the big bird waddled pompously about the floor and under the bed, unconscious to what or whom it owed its life, and blissfully unaware that it was *tripha*.

"Nee, nee," sniggered Lewis, as Flutter-Duck savagely kicked the cat out of her way. "Don't be alarmed, Rebbitzin won't attack it. Rebbitzin is a better judge of *triphas* than you."

It was another cat, but it was the same joke.

Flutter-Duck began to clean the fish with intensified viciousness. She had bought them as a substitute for the goose, and they were a constant reminder of her complex illhap. Very soon she cut her finger, and scoured the walls vainly in search of cobweb ligature. Bitter was her plaint of the servant's mismanagement; when she herself had looked after the house there had been no lack of cobwebs in the corners. Nor was this the end of Flutter-Duck's misfortunes. When, in the course of the afternoon, she sent up to Mrs. Levy on the second floor to remind her that she would be wanting her embroidered petticoat for the evening, answer came back that it was the anniversary of Mrs. Levy's mother's death, and she could not permit even her petticoat to go to a wedding. Finally, the gloves that Flutter-Duck borrowed from the chandler's wife were split at the thumbs. And so the servant was kept running to and fro, spoiling the neighbours for the greater glory of Flutter-Duck. It was only at the eleventh hour that an embroidered petticoat was obtained.

Altogether there was electricity in the air, and Emanuel was not present to divert it down the road of jocularity. The furriers stitched sullenly, with a presentiment of storm. But it held over all day, and there was hope the currents would pass harmlessly away.

With the rising of Flutter-Duck from the work-table, however, the first rumblings began. Lewis did not attempt to restrain her from her society dissipation, but he fumed inwardly throughout her toilette. More than ever he realised, as he sat coughing and bending over the ermine he was tufting with black spots, the incompatibility of this union between ant and butterfly, and occasionally his thought would shoot out in dry sarcasm. But Flutter-Duck had passed beyond the plane in which Lewis existed as her husband. All day she had talked freely, if a whit condescendingly, to her fellow-furriers, lamenting the mischances of the day; but in proportion as she began to get clean and beautiful, as the muslins of the great mirror became a frame for a gorgeous picture of a lady, Flutter-Duck grew more and more aloof from workaday interests, felt herself borne into a higher world of radiance and elegance, into a rarefied atmosphere of gentility, that froze her to statue-like frigidity.

She was not Flutter-Duck then.

And when she was quite dressed for the wedding, and had put on the earrings with the coloured stones and the crowning glory of the chignon of false plaits, stuck over with little artificial white flowers, the female neighbours came crowding into the work-room boudoir to see how she looked, and she revolved silently for their inspection like a dressmaker's figure, at most acknowledging their compliments with monosyllables. She had invited them to come and admire her appearance, but by the time they came she had grown too proud to speak to them. Even the women of whose finery she wore fragments, and who had contributed to her splendour, seemed to her poor dingy creatures, whose contact would sully her embroidered petticoat. In grotesque contrast with her peacock-like stateliness, the big *tripha* goose began to get lively, cackling and flapping about within its radius, as if the soul of Flutter-Duck had passed into its body.

The moment of departure had come. The cab stood at the street-door, and a composite crowd stood round the cab. In the Ghetto a cab has special significance, and Flutter-Duck would have to pass to hers through an avenue of polyglot commentators. At the last moment, adjusting her fleecy wrap over her head like any *grande dame* (from whom she differed only in the modesty of her high bodice and her full sleeves), Flutter-Duck discovered that there was a great rent in one part of the wrap and a great stain in another. She uttered an exclamation of dismay—this seemed to her the climax of the day's misfortunes.

"What shall I do? What shall I do?" she cried, her dignity almost melting in tears.

The by-standers made sympathetic but profitless noises.

"Oh, double it another way," jerked Rachel from the work-table. "Come here, I'll do it for you."

"Are you too lazy to come here?" replied Flutter-Duck irritably. Rachel rose and went towards her, and rearranged the wrap.

"Oh no, that won't do," complained Flutter-Duck, attitudinising before the glass. "It shows as bad as ever. Oh, what shall I do?"

"Do you know what I'll tell you?" said her husband meditatively: "Don't go!"

Flutter-Duck threw him a fiery look.

"Oh well," said Rachel, shrugging her shoulders and thrusting forward her lip contemptuously, "it'll have to do."

"No, it won't—lend me your pink one."

"I'm not going to have my pink one dirtied, too," grumbled Rachel.

"Do you hear what I say?" exclaimed Flutter-Duck, with increasing wrath. "Give me the pink wrap! When the mother says is said!" And she looked around the group of spectators, in search of sympathy with her trials and admiration for her maternal dignity.

"I can never keep anything for myself," said Rachel sullenly. "You never take care of anything."

"I took care of you," screamed Flutter-Duck, goaded beyond endurance by the thought that her neighbours were witnessing this filial disrespect. "And a fat lot of good it's done me."

"Yes, much care you take of me. You only think of enjoying yourself. It's young girls who ought to go out, not old women."

"You impudent face!" And with an irresistible impulse of savagery, a reversion to the days of *Médiâni*, Flutter-Duck swung round her arm, and struck Rachel violently on the cheek with her white-gloved hand.

The sound of the slap rang hollow and awful through the room.

The workers looked up and paused, the neighbours held their breath; there was a dread silence, broken only by the hissings of the excited goose, and the half involuntary apologetic murmurings of Flutter-Duck's lips: "If I bin a mother, I bin a mother."

For an instant Rachel's face was a white mask, on which five fingers stood out in fire; the next it was one burning mass of angry blood. She clenched her fist, as if about to strike her mother, then let the fingers relax; half from a relic of filial awe, half from respect for the finery. There was a peculiar light in her eyes. Without a word she turned slowly on her heel and walked into her little room, emerging, after an instant of general suspense, with the pink wrap in her hand. She gave it to her mother, without looking at her, and walked back to her work, and poor foolish Flutter-Duck, relieved, triumphant, and with an irreproachable head-wrap, passed majestically from the room, amid the buzz of the neighbours (who accompanied her downstairs with valedictory brushings of fur-fluff from her shoulders), through the avenue of polyglot commentators, into the waiting cab.

All this time Flutter-Duck's husband had sat petrified, but now a great burst of coughing shook him. He did not know what to say or do, and prolonged the cough artificially to cover his embarrassment. Then he opened his mouth several times, but shut it indecisively. At last he said soothingly, with kindly clumsiness: "Nee, nee; you shouldn't irritate the mother, Rachel. You know what she is."

Rachel's needle plodded on, and the uneasy silence resumed its sway.

Presently Rachel rose, put down her piece of work finished, and without a word passed back to her bedroom, her beautiful figure erect and haughty. Lewis heard her key turn in the lock. The hours passed, and she did not return. Her father did not like to appear anxious before the "hands," but he had a discomforting vision of her lying on her bed, in a dumb agony of shame and rage. At last eight o'clock struck, and, backward as the work was, Lewis did not suggest overtime. He even dismissed the servant an hour before her time. He was in a fever of impatience, but delicacy had kept him from intruding on his daughter's grief before strangers. Now he hastened to her door, and knocked timidly, then loudly.

"Nee, nee, Rachel," he cried, with sympathetic sternness, "Enough!"

But a chill silence alone answered him.

He burst open the rickety door, and saw a dark mass huddled up in the shadow on the bed. A nearer glance showed him it was only clothes. He opened the door that led on to Jacob's ladder, and called her name. Then by the light streaming in from the other apartment he hastily examined the room. It was obvious that she had put on her best clothes, and gone out.

Half relieved, he returned to the sitting-room, leaving the door ajar, and recited his evening prayer. Then he began to prepare a little meal for himself, telling himself that she had gone for a walk, after her manner; perhaps was shaking off her depression at the Cambridge Music Hall. Supper over and grace said, he started doing the overwork, and then, when sheer weariness forced him to stop, he drew his comfortless wooden chair to the kitchen fire, and studied Rabbinical lore from a minutely printed folio.

The Whitechapel Church clock, suddenly booming midnight, awoke him from these sacred subtleties with a start of alarm. Rachel had not returned.

The fire burnt low. He shivered, and threw on some coal. Half an hour more he waited, listening for her footstep. Surely the music-hall must be closed by now. He crept down the stairs, and wandered vaguely into the cold, starless night, jostled by leering females, and returned forlorn and coughing. Then the thought flashed upon him that his girl had gone to her mother, had gone to fetch her from the wedding ball, and to make it up with her. Yes; that would be it. Hence the best clothes. It could be nothing else. He must not let any other thought get a hold on his mind. He would have run round to the festive scene, only he did not know precisely where it was, and it was too late to ask the neighbours.

One o'clock!

A mournful monotone, stern in its absoluteness, like the clang of a gate shutting out a lost soul.

One more hour of aching suspense, scarcely dulled by the task of making hot coffee, and cutting bread and butter for his returning womankind; then Flutter-Duck came back. Alone!

Came back in her cab, her fading features flushed with the joy of life, with the artificial flowers in her false chignon, and the pink wrap over her head.

"Where is Rachel?" gasped poor Lewis, meeting her at the street-door.

"Rachel! isn't she here? I left her with you," answered Flutter-Duck, half sobered.

"Merciful God!" exclaimed her husband, and put his hand to his breast, pierced by a shooting pain.

"I left her with you," repeated Flutter-Duck with white lips. "Why did you let her go out? Why didn't you look after her?"

"Silence, you sinful mother!" cried Lewis. "You shamed her before strangers, and she has gone out—to drown herself—what do I know?"

Flutter-Duck burst into hysterical sobbing.

"Yes, take her part against me! You always make me out wrong."

"Restrain yourself!" he whispered imperiously. "Do you wish to have the neighbours hear you again?"

"I daresay she's only hiding somewhere, sulking, as she did when a child," said Flutter-Duck. "Have you looked under the bed?"

Foolish as he knew her words were, they gave him a gleam of hope. He led the way upstairs without answering, and taking a candle, examined her bedroom again with ludicrous minuteness. This time the sight of her old clothes was comforting; if she had wanted to drown herself, she would not—he reasoned with perhaps too masculine a logic—have taken her best clothes to spoil. With a sudden thought he displaced the hearthstone. He had early discovered where she kept her savings, though he had neither tampered with them nor betrayed his knowledge. The tin box was broken open, empty! In the drawers there was not a single article of her jewellery. Rachel had evidently left home! She had gone by way of Jacob's ladder—secretly.

Prostrated by the discovery, the parents sat down in helpless silence. Then Flutter-Duck began to wring her white-gloved hands, and to babble incoherent suggestions and reproaches, and protestations that she was not to blame. The hot coffee cooled untasted, the pink wrap lay crumpled on the floor.

Lewis revolved the situation rapidly. What could be done? Evidently nothing—for that night at least. Even the police could do nothing till the morning, and to call them in at all would be to publish the scandal to the whole world. Rachel had gone to some lodging—there could be no doubt about that. And yet he could not go to bed, his heart still expected her, though his brain had given up hope. He walked about restlessly, racked by fits of coughing, then he dropped back into his seat before the decaying fire. And Flutter-Duck, frightened into silence at last, sat on the sofa, dazed, in her trappings and gewgaws, with the white flowers glistening in her false hair, and her pallid cheeks stained with tears.

And so they waited in the uncouth room in the solemn watches of the night, pricking up their ears at a rare footstep in the street, and hastening to peep out of the window; waiting for the knock that came not, and the dawn that was distant. The silence lay upon them like a pall.

Suddenly, in the weird stillness, they heard a fluttering and a skurrying, and, looking up, they saw a great white thing floating through the room. Flutter-Duck uttered a terrible cry. "Hear, O Israel!" she shrieked.

"Nee, nee," said Lewis reassuringly, though scarcely less startled. "It is only the *tripha* goose got loose."

"Nay, nay, it is the Devil!" hoarsely whispered Flutter-Duck, who had covered her face with her hands, and was shaking as with palsy.

Her terror communicated itself to her husband. "Hush, hush! Talk not so," he said, shivering with indefinable awe.

"Say psalms, say psalms!" panted Flutter-Duck. "Drive him out."

Lewis opened the window, but the unclean bird showed no desire to flit. It was evidently the Not-Good-One himself.

"Hear, O Israel!" wailed Flutter-Duck. "Since he came in this morning everything has been upside down."

The goose chuckled.

Lewis was seized with a fell terror that gave him a mad courage. Murmuring a holy phrase, he grabbed at the goose, which eluded him, and fluttered flappingly hither and thither. Lewis gave chase, his lips praying mechanically. At last he caught it by a wing, haled it, hissing and struggling and uttering rasping cries, to the window, flung it without, and closed the sash with a bang. Then he fell impotent against the work-table, and spat out a mouthful of blood.

"God be praised!" said Flutter-Duck, slowly uncovering her eyes. "Now Rachel will come back."

And with renewed hope they waited on, and the deathly silence again possessed the room.

All at once they heard a light step under the window; the father threw it open and saw a female form outlined in the darkness. There was a rat-tat-tat at the door.

"Ah, there she is!" hysterically exclaimed Flutter-Duck, starting up.

"The Holy One be blessed!" cried Lewis, rushing down the stairs.

A strange figure, the head covered by a green tartan shawl, greeted him. A cold ague passed over his limbs.

"Thank God, it's all right," said Mrs. Lefkovitch. "I see from your light you are still working; but isn't it time my Emanuel left off?"

"Your Emanuel?" gasped Lewis, with a terrible suspicion. "He went home early in the day; he was taken ill."

Flutter-Duck, who had crept at his heels bearing a candle, cried out, "God in Israel! She has flown away with Emanuel."

"Hush, you piece of folly!" whispered Lewis furiously.

"Yes, it was already arranged, and you blamed me!" gasped Flutter-Duck, with a last instinct of self-defence ere consciousness left her, and she fell forward.

"Silence," Lewis began, but there was an awful desolation at his heart and the salt of blood was in his mouth as he caught the falling form. The candlestick rolled to the ground, and the group was left in the heavy shadows of the staircase and the cold blast from the open door.

"God have mercy on me and the poor children! I knew all along it would come to that!" wailed Emanuel's wife.

"And I advanced him his week's money on Monday," Lewis remembered in the agony of the moment.

IV

Poor Flutter-Duck

"Her cap blew off, her gown blew up,
And a whirlwind cleared the larder."

—Tennyson: *The Goose*

It was New Year's Eve.

In the Ghetto, where "the evening and the morning are one day," New Year's Eve is at its height at noon. The muddy market-places roar, and the joyous medley of squeezing humanity moves slowly through the crush of mongers, pickpockets, and beggars. It is one of those festival occasions on which even those who have migrated from the Ghetto gravitate back to purchase those dainties whereof the heathen have not the secret, and to look again upon the old familiar scene. There is a stir of goodwill and gaiety, a reconciliation of old feuds in view of the solemn season of repentance, and a washing-down of enmities in rum.

At the point where the two main market-streets met, a grey-haired elderly woman stood and begged.

Poor Flutter-Duck!

Her husband dead, after a protracted illness that frittered away his savings; her daughter lost; her home a mattress in the corner of a strange family's garret; her faded prettiness turned to ugliness: her figure thin and wasted; her yellow-wrinkled face framed in a frowsy shawl; her clothes tattered and flimsy; Flutter-Duck stood and *schnorred*.

But Flutter-Duck did not do well. Her feather-head was not equal to the demands of her profession. She had selected what was ostensibly the coign of most vantage, forgetting that though everybody in the market must pass her station, they would already have been mulcted in the one street or the other.

But she held out her hand pertinaciously, appealing to every passer-by of importance, and throwing audible curses after those that ignored her. The cold of the bleak autumn day and the apathy of the public chilled her to the bone; the tears came into her eyes as she thought of all her misery and of the happy time—only a couple of years ago—when

New Year meant new dresses. Only a grey fringe—the last vanity of pauperdom—remained of all her fashionableness. No more the plaited chignon, the silk gown, the triple necklace,—the dazzling exterior that made her too proud to speak to admiring neighbours,—only hunger and cold and mockery and loneliness. No plumes could she borrow, now that she really needed them to cover her nakedness. She who had reigned over a work-room, who had owned a husband and a marriageable daughter, who had commanded a maid-servant, who had driven in shilling cabs!

Oh, if she could only find her daughter—that lost creature by whose wedding-canopy she should have stood, radiant, the envy of Montague Street! But this was not a thought of to-day. It was at the bottom of all her thoughts always, ever since that fatal night. During the first year she was always on the lookout, peering into every woman's face, running after every young couple that looked like Emanuel and Rachel. But repeated disappointment dulled her. She had no energy for anything except begging. Yet the hope of finding Rachel was the gleam of idealism that kept her soul alive.

The hours went by, but the streams of motley pedestrians and the babel of vociferous vendors and chattering buyers did not slacken. Females were in the great majority, housewives from far and near foraging for Festival supplies. In vain Flutter-Duck wished them "A Good Sealing." It seemed as if her own Festival would be black and bitter as the Feast of Ab.

But she continued to hold out her bloodless hand. Towards three o'clock a fine English lady, in a bonnet, passed by, carrying a leather bag.

"Grant me a halfpenny, lady, dear! May you be written down for a good year!"

The beautiful lady paused, startled. Then Flutter-Duck's heart gave a great leap of joy. The impossible had happened at last. Behind the veil shone the face of Rachel—a face of astonishment and horror.

"Rachel!" she shrieked, tottering.

"Mother!" cried Rachel, catching her by the arm. "What are you doing here? What has happened?"

"Do not touch me, sinful girl!" answered Flutter-Duck, shaking her off with a tragic passion that gave dignity to the grotesque figure. Now that Rachel was there in the flesh, the remembrance of her shame surged up, drowning everything. "You have disgraced the mother who bore you and the father who gave you life."

The fine English lady—her whole soul full of sudden remorse at the sight of her mother's incredible poverty, shrank before the blazing eyes. The passers-by imagined Rachel had refused the beggar-woman alms.

"What have I done?" she faltered.

"Where is Emanuel?"

"Emanuel!" repeated Rachel, puzzled.

"Emanuel Lefkovitch that you ran away with."

"Mother, are you mad? I have never seen him. I am married."

"Married!" gasped Flutter-Duck ecstatically. Then a new dread rose to her mind. "To a Christian?"

"Me marry a Christian! The idea!"

Flutter-Duck fell a-sobbing on the fine lady's fur jacket. "And you never ran away with Lefkovitch?"

"Me take another woman's leavings? Well, upon my word!"

"Oh," sobbed Flutter-Duck. "Oh, if your father could only have lived to know the truth!"

Rachel's remorse became heartrending. "Is father dead?" she murmured with white lips. After awhile she drew her mother out of the babel, and giving her the bag to carry to save appearances, she walked slowly towards Liverpool Street, and took train with her for her pretty little cottage near Epping Forest.

Rachel's story was as simple as her mother's. After the showing up of Emanuel's duplicity, home had no longer the least attraction for her. Her nascent love for the migratory husband changed to a loathing that embraced the whole Ghetto in which such things were possible. Weary of Flutter-Duck's follies, indifferent to her father, she had long meditated joining her West-end girl-friend in the fur establishment in Regent Street, but the blow precipitated matters. She felt she could not remain a night more under her mother's roof, and her father's clumsy comment was but salt on her wound. Her heart was hard against both; month after month passed before her passionate, sullen nature would let her dwell on the thought of their trouble, and even then she felt that the motive of her flight was so plain that they would feel only remorse, not anxiety. They knew she could always earn her living, just as she knew they could always earn theirs. Living "in," and going out but rarely, and then in the fashionable districts, she never met any drift from the Ghetto, and the busy life of the populous establishment soon effaced the old, which faded to a forgotten dream. One day the chief provincial traveller of the house saw her, fell in love, married her, and took her about the country for six months. He was coming back to her that very evening for the New Year. She had gone back to the Ghetto that day to buy New Year honey, and, softened by time and happiness, rather hoped to stumble across her mother in the market-place, and so save the submission of a call. She never dreamed of death and poverty. She would not blame herself for her father's death—he had always been consumptive—but since death was come at last, it was lucky she could offer her mother a home. Her husband would be delighted to find a companion for his wife during his country rounds.

"So you see, mother, everything is for the best."

Flutter-Duck listened in a delicious daze.

What! Was everything then to end happily after all? Was she—the shabby old starveling—to be restored to comfort and fine clothes? Her brain seemed bursting with the thought of so much happiness; as the train flew along past green grass and autumn-tinted foliage, she strove to articulate a prayer of gratitude to Heaven, but she only mumbled "*Médiâni*," and lapsed into silence. And then, suddenly remembering she had started a prayer and must finish it, she murmured again "*Médiâni*."

When they came to the grand house with the front garden, and were admitted by a surprised maid-servant, infinitely nattier than any Flutter-Duck had ever ruled over, the poor creature was palsied with excess of bliss. The fire was blazing merrily in the luxurious parlour: could this haven of peace and pomp—these arm-chairs, those vases, that side-board—be really for her? Was she to spend her New Year's night surrounded by love and luxury, instead of huddling in the corner of a cold garret?

And as soon as Rachel had got her mother installed in a wonderful easy-chair, she hastened with all the eagerness of maternal pride, with all the enthusiasm of remorse, to throw open the folding-doors that led to her bedroom, so as to give Flutter-Duck the crowning surprise—the secret titbit she had reserved for the grand climax.

"There's a fine boy!" she cried.

And as Flutter-Duck caught sight of the little red face peeping out from the snowy draperies of the cradle, a rapture too great to bear seemed almost to snap something within her foolish, overwrought brain.

"I have already a grandchild!" she shrieked, with a great sob of ecstasy; and, running to the cradle-side, she fell on her knees, and covered the little red face with frantic kisses, repeating "Lewis love, Lewis love,

Lewis love," till the babe screamed, and Rachel had to tear the babbling creature away.

You may see her almost any day walking in the Ghetto market-place—a meagre, old figure, with a sharp-featured face and a plaited chignon. She dresses richly in silk, and her golden earrings are set with coloured stones, and her bonnet is of the latest fashion. She lives near Epping Forest, and almost always goes home to tea. Sometimes she stands still at the point where the two market streets meet, extending vacantly a gloved hand, but for the most part she wanders about the by-streets and alleys of Whitechapel with an anxious countenance, peering at every woman she meets, and following every young couple. "If I could only find her!" she thinks yearningly.

Nobody knows whom she is looking for, but everybody knows she is only "Flutter-Duck."

A Note About the Author

Israel Zangwill (1864–1926) was a British writer. Born in London, Zangwill was raised in a family of Jewish immigrants from the Russian Empire. Alongside his brother Louis, a novelist, Zangwill was educated at the Jews' Free School in Spitalfields, where he studied secular and religious subjects. He excelled early on and was made a teacher in his teens before studying for his BA at the University of London. After graduating in 1884, Zangwill began publishing under various pseudonyms, finding editing work with *Ariel* and *The London Puck* to support himself. His first novel, *Children of the Ghetto: A Study of Peculiar People* (1892), was published to popular and critical acclaim, earning praise from prominent Victorian novelist George Gissing. His play *The Melting Pot* (1908) was a resounding success in the United States and was regarded by Theodore Roosevelt as "among the very strong and real influences upon (his) thought and (his) life." He spent his life in dedication to various political and social causes. An early Zionist and follower of Theodor Herzl, he later withdrew his support in favor of territorialism after he discovered that "Palestine proper has already its inhabitants." Despite distancing himself from the Zionist community, he continued to advocate on behalf of the Jewish people and to promote the ideals of feminism alongside his wife Edith Ayrton, a prominent author and activist.

A Note from the Publisher

Spanning many genres, from non-fiction essays to literature classics to children's books and lyric poetry, Mint Edition books showcase the master works of our time in a modern new package. The text is freshly typeset, is clean and easy to read, and features a new note about the author in each volume. Many books also include exclusive new introductory material. Every book boasts a striking new cover, which makes it as appropriate for collecting as it is for gift giving. Mint Edition books are only printed when a reader orders them, so natural resources are not wasted. We're proud that our books are never manufactured in excess and exist only in the exact quantity they need to be read and enjoyed.

Discover more of your favorite classics with Bookfinity™.

- Track your reading with custom book lists.
- Get great book recommendations for your personalized Reader Type.
- Add reviews for your favorite books.
- AND MUCH MORE!

Visit **bookfinity.com** and take the fun Reader Type quiz to get started.

Enjoy our classic and modern companion pairings!

Printed in the USA
CPSIA information can be obtained
at www.ICGtesting.com
JSHW022211140824
68134JS00018B/984

9 781513 282749